"Come now. You ~~must~~ ~~~~ ~~~~ ~~~~ out with Jewish girls," Ruth said to the priest.

"Nice Jewish girls," Jim said with careful emphasis. "When you went out with a nice Jewish girl, I remember you always had to wait until the third date to kiss her good night. Was that true in your generation, too?"

"In my generation?" She looked at him. "Yes."

It was very quiet for a few seconds.

"Ruth," he said finally, breaking the silence; and hearing her name spoken for the first time that evening, she shivered. "Look, I'm no good at this. I haven't done it for ten years. I want to make love to you. You won't make me wait till I've seen you three times, will you?"

"No," she said, looking at the floor, answering affirmatively, "I want you, too."

A
Book
of
Ruth

Syrell Rogovin Leahy

A FAWCETT CREST BOOK

Fawcett Books, Greenwich, Connecticut

A BOOK OF RUTH

THIS BOOK CONTAINS THE COMPLETE TEXT OF THE
ORIGINAL HARDCOVER EDITION

Published by Fawcett Crest Books, CBS Publications,
CBS Consumer Publishing, a Division of CBS Inc.,
by arrangement with Simon and Schuster

The author wishes to thank The Macmillan Publishing Co., Inc.,
for permission to quote from "Lapis Lazuli" in *Collected Poems*
by William Butler Yeats. Copyright 1940 by Georgie Yeats,
renewed 1968 by Bertha Georgie Yeats, Michael Butler Yeats
and Anne Yeats.

Alternate Selection of Woman Today Book Club, February 1975
Selection of the Literary Guild, November 1974

Printed in the United States of America

3   4   5   6   7   8   9   10   11   12

To Renee from Elizabeth
Wherever she is ...

If you trap the moment before it's ripe,
The tears of repentance you'll certainly wipe;
But if once you let the ripe moment go
You can never wipe off the tears of woe.

WILLIAM BLAKE

I tell you,
There comes one moment, once—and God help those
Who pass that moment by!

EDMOND ROSTAND

A
Book
of
Ruth

1

~~~~~~

So how does it feel to wake up for the twenty-sixth consecutive New Year's Day of your life alone in bed?

Like hell. Ask me another one.

And to have the second day of your period besides?

Christ, if I don't get out of bed in sixty seconds, I'm going to regret it all day.

Somewhere, church bells were ringing. Noon on the first day of another election year. Well—dragging herself out—this one could hardly be as bad as the last one. The last election year, that is.

Dressing, making coffee, buttering toast, it came back to her, the scene last night in this apartment that had not—ah, fate—ended on the bed. His face when she told him. Jesus, she had been hinting at it all night.

"Ruth, stop playing games."

"I'm not playing games. I can't."

"You mean you don't want to."

"I've got my period, damn it."

"Come off it. Who do you think you're kidding?"

"I'm *not* kidding. I *hurt*."

"Christ." He turned away, walked to the closet where his coat hung.

"I'm sorry," she said. "I'm really sorry." She really was.

He put his coat on, came back to her. "Are you putting me on?" he asked.

"I'm not putting you on, putting you down, turning you off or any other separable verb. I have my period and I hurt like hell. And I'm sorry." The last, a little more softly.

"I'll call you."

Sure.

He kissed her as if she were his sister-in-law.

Well, there's another one down the drain.

She sipped her coffee, looking at the unopened letters still lying on the table. Christmas cards, a couple of bills, a bunch of ads—they never give up, do they? Not even on vacation. What the hell was that? A newspaper clipping. She picked it up. "Dr. Edelman Weds Miss Rothenberg." Ah, yes, the clipping Mother had sent in December. Thank you, Mother, for reminding me so subtly of all you have lost. Good luck, Miss Rothenberg. I hope you fare better than I did.

She crumpled the small bit of paper and added it to the pile of ads. The end of that.

New Year's Day. What was there to relieve the boredom of the first day of the year? Around five or six there would be Cassie's annual New Year's Day party. Well, since Al was out of the picture, she might as well put on a dress later on and see what she could find at Cassie's place. She always had a crew of attractive men on hand on New Year's Day. Some of them were even interesting. In the meantime, maybe she could scrounge up a *New York Times* somewhere. And after that— looking at her watch to reckon the time available— drop in on Teresa.

Funny, she thought, sitting on the big four-poster as she dialed Teresa's number, in September the whole point of going was Anthony; now when I go I'm visiting Teresa.

There were two rings, when an operator asked what

number she was calling. She repeated the number, silently cursing the equipment.

"I'm sorry, that number has been disconnected," the operator said coolly.

Sudden panic, chill creeping down the back of her neck, fear. The number had been working before Christmas. She hung up, grabbed her jacket, went downstairs to the car, drove fast, whipping around Harvard Square, parked where she could see the car from the living-room window, raced up the stairs, knocked loudly.

"Yeah?"

Relief accompanied by trembling of the hands. "Teresa, it's Ruth."

"Just a minute."

Anthony opened the door, eight years of joy. He hugged her.

"Hi, love," she said. "Where's your mom?"

"In the kitchen. You gonna take me somewhere?"

"Let me see your mom first." Her arm around Anthony, she went into the kitchen where Teresa was dropping potatoes into a stew pot. "How are you? Happy New Year."

"Thanks, the same to you. I'm fine. Sit down and I'll make you some coffee."

"OK. I could have a cup."

"You still single? I thought maybe someone would propose over the holiday."

"It wasn't exactly a proposal."

Teresa laughed. "Yeah, well, what do you care? You got it nice anyway."

"What's with the phone, Teresa? I had a heart attack when I called."

"I made them take it out. Today's the first day without it. You should see how quiet it is here now."

"Suppose you need a doctor."

"I got neighbors."

"Suppose they're not home."

"So Anthony'll go to the drugstore, right, Anthony?"

"Sure," he said. "I can call from the phone in the drugstore, Ruth. I did it once already with a dime."

"Teresa, if it's the four and a half dollars a month, I could—"

"No you couldn't. Anyway, it's not the money. I like it quiet."

She spent the rest of the afternoon with them, taking them for a ride about three, watching Teresa put on a coat now too big on her, Anthony in a jacket getting too small for him. At four-thirty she went home, changed her clothes, drove into Boston to Cassie's, where the party was in full swing.

She and Cassie had been friends for years. They had lived down the hall from each other their freshman year, had eyed each other with some curiosity once or twice but had never exchanged more than a greeting. Then, in their second semester, they had found themselves the only two girls at home on a Saturday night, each for a different reason, and they had struck up a conversation and, by early Sunday morning, a friendship. The friendship had endured, but for the most part, the two girls were the only intersection of the sets to which they belonged.

Cassie was enviably gorgeous today as always, and had a new man in tow, Hal Somebody. Looked like he owned a bank. All of Cassie's men owned banks. Except that one a year ago. Poor Cassie. Even she was not immune.

The party dragged. Lots of Hi's, What do you do's, and Where are you from's. Mostly the guys were a bore. She gave them her phone number and refused their invitations to leave and have dinner. She munched some hors d'oeuvres, said a few words to Cassie, and started for the door. A hand touched her shoulder. She turned to look.

"We haven't met. I'm Barry Peters."

There was something intriguing about him, the voice maybe, or the eyes. She gave it a try. "Hi, I'm Ruth Gold."

"You work in Cassie's office?"

"No, I teach. Cassie and I went to school together."

"You're not from Boston, are you?"

"Brooklyn," she said, hitting him with the acid test, "the heart of Brooklyn."

"Well, that's being honest." His eyes began to rove.

"I used to say 'New York' but it gave people the wrong idea. They thought I meant Sutton Place but the skeletons in my closet live on Ocean Parkway."

"Yeah. Well, nice meeting you."

Yeah.

She resumed her march to the door and went home, nice, safe, secure home, the backwards apartment with the kitchen under the baylike window overlooking the street and the dresser on the back wall between the bathroom door and the closet door. It was small but it had compensations—charm, nearness to school, the four-poster. And it was four hundred miles from Ocean Parkway.

She undressed and went to bed.

Sometime in the middle of the night, the phone rang. Three A.M., she thought without looking at the clock. Pete, you amaze me. How can a guy so organize his anguish that it all crystallizes, regularly and repeatedly, at three A.M.?

She glanced at the luminous dial next to the telephone. Two minutes after.

"Hello?"

"Hi."

"Hi, Pete."

"Uh—"

"Yes, you did. But it's OK. I can sleep tomorrow."

"Could I come over, Ruthie? Just for a little while?"

Something softened inside. "Sure, Pete. I'll make some coffee."

Drag yourself out, put on a robe—pretty pink-and-lavender robe; shame nobody ever sees it but Pete—turn on all the lights, grind the coffee, boil the water, drip it through the filter, yawn sleepily and think about Pete—Pete and Boston, one and the same—think how she had come to Boston three years ago last August, recovered finally from all the physical ailments (but none of the other ones) that had plagued her first year of teaching, bringing with her as the plane set down at Logan the knowledge, the sweet, secure, beautiful knowledge that she had arrived. All through that awful winter and spring of Sixty-eight, she had wondered if anything would ever touch her, move her, make her explode. But when she stepped off the plane at Logan a few months later—the promised land with a Mystic River—she was someone else, someone new with a great new gift to try out and a great new desire to try it.

Only nothing had happened.

She and Cassie had found the apartment and there had been Pete almost from the beginning, Pete teaching in her school a few days a week, Pete noticing her, talking to her, taking her out and—and nothing. She had fallen in love with him—or thought she had; what was the difference, anyway?—and lived with the love, but not with Pete, through the whole school year. After a while—everything looks different in the spring—the feeling had passed, leaving only a warmth, a friendship that seemed to satisfy them both. Then a year ago, he had reappeared after a long hiatus. But this time the tables had turned; he loved and she cared not at all. He had reasoned with her, argued, begged, pleaded with her to give it a try, one more time, come on, Ruthie, it could be so good, but her heart wasn't in it even though she saw him when she wasn't seeing anyone else, and last summer, of course, they had both been at camp and nothing had happened there either.

There were footsteps on the stairs, a knock.

"Hi, Pete. Come on in." She closed the door, yawning. "You look tired."

"So do you, Ruthie I shouldn't do this to you."

"Anything special tonight?" Pouring the coffee, finding a piece of pound cake.

"General malaise."

"You'll feel better in the spring."

"Sure. Ah, that tastes good. Sorry I'm unshaven." Rubbing the side of his face.

There's never a point, is there? He just wants to talk

to me, look at me if he can, maybe touch me if I don't move fast enough.

"Would you do something for me, Ruthie?"

Why not? "Sure, Pete."

"Monday after school. I want to visit Jim. Come with me."

"Jim who?"

"Kendall. From camp."

"Oh, Father Jim."

"Just Jim when you talk to him."

"Go yourself, Pete. I don't mix well with the clergy."

"Look, I really don't want to go alone and I haven't seen him since he came to my folks' place for dinner in September. Will you come with me?"

"Tell me one fact about him to prove it's not going to be the dullest day of a dull New Year."

"He understands dirty jokes."

"Come on. Does he tell any?"

"Christ, Ruthie, sometimes I wonder why I love you."

"OK, Pete, truce. I'll go with you. Monday after school. I'll leave my car home."

She had bought the car that first year in Boston with her savings and a small loan. She had thought briefly about using Abraham's money but rejected the idea. The inheritance from her grandfather was for something that would appreciate in value, not a car.

The car had taken her to and from Brooklyn more times than she cared to remember, back to Cornell two summers ago, and to a tutoring camp last summer, camp which, like so many other things in her life she had gone to for one reason and stuck with for quite another.

She had wanted to get away from the city, have the

afternoons free for swimming and the nights free to meet someone, get laid maybe, if she was lucky. Incidentally, she would teach the kids to read six mornings a week. But after two weeks she gave up on the nights —creepy college boys—and she fell in love with the kids instead—Anthony, Betsy, the whole bunch of them, who were really reading now and getting tanned and learning how to swim.

When, at the end of August, the camp director asked for someone to take Anthony home for a week or ten days while his mother went to the hospital for tests, he found an immediate volunteer. So she had come to know Teresa. And a whole lot of other things.

On Monday at lunch, Jeff, the faculty creep, asked her out for the ninetieth time. He was smoking a pipe today, to add, she assumed, to his image. Years before, she had wondered what happened to creeps when they grew up. Now she knew: when all else failed, they started smoking a pipe. No, thanks, Jeff, I'm all tied up.

Pete was at the curb after school. The day was almost balmy. The third of January and winter had forgotten to come.

When they reached the church, she recognized it. During her first weeks in Boston, she had driven her new car in and out of every one of these streets to get the feel of the neighborhood. Made of old stone, the church had caught her eye and found a place in her memory.

"Does he expect us?" she asked.

"No," he said uncomfortably. "I called yesterday but he was out. Guy said he'd be here this afternoon."

They got out of the car. To the left of the church

was an old school, old but with none of the charm or character of the church. On the other side was a playground in the back of which a football game of sorts was in progress.

"Let's try back there," Pete suggested.

They walked along the edge of the playground, passing a group of teen-age boys shooting baskets, loudly cheering each other on. A couple of them were good and she stopped to watch.

"Go on," she said to Pete. "I'll catch up in a minute."

As she stood watching, she became aware of someone behind her, something spoken, mumbled really. An obscenity? She turned around. A tall, gangly adolescent boy stood there, grinning, showing his crooked teeth.

"Hi," he said.

"Hi." She turned and went toward Pete. Pete was standing a few yards ahead, waiting for her. He really hadn't wanted to come alone.

They walked toward the football game. One side must have made a first down as they approached because a cheer went up from some of them and boys and men of all sizes started to untangle.

"Hiya, Jim," Pete said, stepping up his pace.

The taller of the two priests separated from the group, smiling as he saw Pete. They shook hands. Then Pete said something and the priest turned to look at her. It was an odd look, strangely unwelcome. What the hell had she done to deserve that?

"Nice to see you," he said then, offering his hand, shaking hers firmly. "I'd like you both to meet Father Reilly. Friends of mine from camp last summer, Ruth Gold and Pete Gruber."

They shook hands, and Father Reilly reached into his pocket and took out his glasses.

"Hey," Pete said, "don't let us interrupt your game. Can you use me somewhere?"

"Why don't you take my place?" Father Reilly offered, a little too eagerly. "I'll show Miss Gold around." He smiled at her and turned toward the church.

"I think some of your campers may be in the church basement now," the priest said.

"I'd like to see them." She reached out for a platitude, anything to keep the conversation from dying. "I didn't know football was one of your religious activities."

"Some things came as a surprise to me, too. Sometimes I think God sent Father Kendall to us because He knew we needed strength in the backfield." He was adept at platitudes too.

She smiled and went through the door he held open. Inside the church, he led her to an office or study and hung their coats on hooks.

She glanced around the room. It made her feel uncomfortable in a vaguely familiar way. The pictures on the wall brought back the memory of the surprise of that first visit to Teresa's apartment, the statue of Jesus, the one of Mary, the dollar ninety-eight picture of the Pope on the wall. Would Mother have hung a dollar ninety-eight picture of Ben-Gurion in the dining room? Jesus.

She turned to the priest, trying desperately to think of something to say besides how warm it was for January. He was a gentle, scholarly-looking man, relieved that she was rescuing him from football while in fact she was merely putting him in the hopelessly awkward position of having to talk to her. She sought for something that might link them. They were Americans and they both spoke English; surely there must be something more, something more binding.

"I've never been inside your church before," she began as they left the study, "but the outside is beautiful. I noticed it when I first moved up here. It has so much more character than a lot of the new churches."

"It does have character," he said, brightening, "and a kind of solidity that you don't find in some of the more modern churches. What I mean to say is, while I admire them architecturally, they seem rather fragile. I don't think a church should look fragile."

"I never thought of that," she said, "but I agree with you. Fragility would seem out of place here."

He smiled at her. "Every once in a while someone suggests modernizing the building, putting in new pews or something like that. I never quite understand it."

"What's wrong with the pews?"

He seemed apologetic. "They creak a little. Age and the climate, I suppose. But the wood is beautiful."

"May I see them?"

"Of course." He opened a door and they walked into the sanctuary alongside the altar.

"It *is* beautiful," she said, meaning it. She sat down at one end of a pew. No creak. "Don't sell out," she said, looking up at the priest. She had made him happy. She forgave Pete for dragging her here today.

"Shall we visit the children?" he asked and they went down to the basement.

The children spread out in the downstairs room were the half that didn't play football, mostly girls and some very small boys. The decor of the room was strikingly secular—worn play equipment on the floor and large portrait cartoons taped along the walls. Most were of the children; but one was identifiably the teacher, Mrs. McConnell, a woman who appeared to have a natural talent for mothering large groups of children. She also knew who Ruth was.

"Betsy's Ruth," she said after Father Reilly mentioned camp. "Somehow I expected you to be eight feet tall."

"Me? I don't even make the pews creak."

Betsy was there, too, little Betsy who had learned to read last July under her tutelage. It was a shy, giggly reunion. They sat on the floor and drew pictures for each other until the football team returned and she and Pete prepared to go.

"Since you have a friend here," Mrs. McConnell said at the door, "maybe you'd like to come down once in a while on a busman's holiday after school. I'm alone here and when it gets colder, the boys will add to the crowd."

The idea appealed to her and she promised to think about it. Something that afternoon had touched her— Betsy giggling, perhaps, or Mrs. McConnell among the children, or maybe Father Reilly moving through his unfragile church. One of these days she would come back.

Father Kendall walked them to the car. It had grown dark, and darkness brought the chill of winter more predictably and more effectively than the season. She approached the car almost hungrily, yearning for its shelter. At the curb, she said a few perfunctorily polite words of parting and, shivering, reached for the door.

"I'd like to take you two to dinner tomorrow evening, if you're free, that is," the priest said, stalling her effort.

She began to decline the invitation but Pete got there first with an encompassing acceptance. Annoyed, she got into the car. Dinner tomorrow meant dragging this out another thirty hours, sitting next to Pete while he touched her under the eyes of a dull clergyman.

Through the window she heard them discussing the time, the place, the car they would take. I'll drive. No, let me. Christ, the time grown men could waste on trivia.

In the end, the priest picked them up and took them somewhere she had never been, outside the city limits, and they sat three at a round table. For Pete it was sheer joy, his buddy on one side, she on the other, close enough to pat her shoulder, rub her neck, thoroughly infuriate her while she turned a placid mask to their host and benefactor.

On the way home, Pete asked to be dropped at her place and she snapped, "For Christ's sake let me be," and the priest let him off at his apartment.

She sat stonily the rest of the way home, regretting her outburst, reluctant to apologize and make it more of an issue. At her house, she thanked the priest.

"I'm sorry about tonight," he said. "It was an error in judgment."

"I'm sorry, too."

"I wonder—" He looked at his watch, held it briefly to his ear. "There was someone I wanted to talk to you about. It's kind of important. If you have the time one of these days."

One of the kids, she thought, another problem. Goddamn. "Of course," she said accommodatingly. "I get out of school at three."

"Afternoons are impossible, I'm afraid. I'm sorry." He sounded very apologetic. "I thought maybe one evening. I have some time on Friday. I could drop over about eight-thirty."

Friday. She had been thinking about Al most of the evening, toying with the idea of inviting him to dinner. There was something new she wanted to try.

"How would you like to be a guinea pig?" she asked.

"A laboratory experiment?"

"No, I had something culinary in mind. Dinner. Something still untried."

"It sounds poetic."

"You've got the wrong guy. It's not poetry he's interested in, it's more—Anyway, if it doesn't kill you, this meal may change my whole life."

"Friday, then. Eight-thirty."

What bothered her over the next three days was why she had invited the priest to dinner, why she was trying out the new recipe. She kept thinking about Al.

You really want to go to bed with him, don't you? she said to herself Tuesday night, lying on the four-poster, looking up at the canopy, remembering the day a month ago that he had first walked in and seen it, the center, the main attraction of the apartment, and he had said, "What an invitation," and she had said, "Not an open one." But she was opening it now, wasn't she? Give him a ring and ask him to come to dinner.

Ask him to bed.

Just to dinner. A nice quiet dinner tested in our exclusive kitchen.

The four-poster had been dropped in her lap by

Marilyn Klein almost a year ago. Marilyn was getting married soon and was anxious to divest herself of her past, including the four-poster she had inherited when her aunt turned in a house in Concord for an apartment in Brookline.

The bed completed the apartment. When she first moved in, the landlord had built shelves for her books and records to the left of the kitchen-under-the-windows and, not wanting to struggle with curtains, she had hung flowerpots between the windows over the curved counter and planted flowers and herbs in them. When the bed came, the room was perfect.

Friday came eventually (no word from Al), shopping done, pie made last night, street lights on, time to start cooking, showering, dressing, thinking of what you're going to talk about when the conversation starts lagging (i.e., after we've said hello and worked out the kid's problem). Well, there was always church architecture. It worked with Father Reilly; maybe it'll work with this one. But what about when those five sentences are over? What had Pete talked to him about all those weeks? The priest had come in August, for the second session, and had roomed with Pete. They had never stopped talking, those two, working side by side building the new lodge at camp, sweating in the hot sun. Politics? Religion? Music? What do you talk about to a priest?

She put the salad in the refrigerator, took the cheeses out to warm up to room temperature, set the table. Yawning, she straightened up the apartment, piling the week's accumulation of *New York Times*es in a corner, dusting the desk, and the top of the dresser, cleaning the bathroom sink. Which kid, what problem, why me?

Pick out something to wear, something dark, something all covered up—the black pants suit with the impossible zipper. Always easier to reach at the end of the day when you're all stretched out (and worn out) than in the morning when your muscles are tight and your body all rested.

The phone rang. She glanced at her watch—almost seven—and sat down on the bed next to the night table that had the phone.

"Hello?"

"Hi. This is Jim Kendall."

"Oh, hello, Father." Damn, he was backing out.

"Can I bring a bottle of wine?"

Ah, how pleasantly unexpected. "That would be very nice of you."

"Red or white?"

"White would be fine."

"Do you prefer French or German?"

Well! "To tell you the truth, I'm making something Swiss. Why don't you make the choice? Whatever you like will be fine."

"OK, then. See you later."

She assembled her clothes, went into the shower. The wine was a nice idea but somehow, it didn't fit. Didn't fit what? Didn't fit her image of the priest. She tried to imagine Father Reilly climbing up the stairs carrying a bottle of wine.

The shower woke her up a little. (Later, the wine would have the reverse effect. It would make her feel good, warm and sleepy.) Under the spray, she planned her strategy. What was needed was a schedule: fifteen minutes of polite conversation over drinks, cook the main course while discussing the kid's problem, eat, good night. Out by ten-thirty. A good night's sleep to prepare for a nothing week-end, nothing but correcting papers and maybe some shopping. Call Cassie and see what's at Lord and Taylor.

Oh, yes, something else was needed besides a schedule. An approach, an attitude. Reserve and politeness. It had worked with Father Reilly.

By seven-thirty she was dressed. She curled up in a chair with the *New York Times*. Contentment was sitting in an apartment that had your name on the mailbox and reading the *New York Times*.

At eight-thirty she heard footsteps on the stairs. When they passed the landing she stood up, smoothed her clothes, dropped the *Times* on top of the pile and assumed the decided-upon attitude. There were two short raps on the door. Strangely, she had the feeling of having been here before, an eerie kind of *déjà vu*, but it was absurd and she shook it off as she opened the door.

The priest was dressed in a dark suit, white shirt, dark tie and black coat and he was carrying a bottle in a brown paper bag.

"You're in mufti," she said with some relief. "Come on in."

"I'm off duty," he said, handing her the package. "I think you may want this chilled." It was a white Swiss wine.

"Very apropos," she said. "I'll be back for your coat."

"I hope it's good, besides being apropos." He took off his coat and turned to look at the apartment.

She put the wine in the refrigerator and returned for his coat.

"It kind of dominates," he said, hands in his pockets, looking at the four-poster.

"It's meant to," she said from the front closet, approving his comment. "This is the whole thing—" indicating the apartment with a sweep of her right hand, the two-second Cook's tour, the concession to politeness. "Won't you sit down? Can I get you a drink?" The schedule calls for fifteen minutes of polite talk. We can start now.

"Thank you," he said moving toward the sofa. "I wonder if I could have something to eat with my drink."

"Eat?" He had caught her unawares. The main part of dinner was still to be cooked. It was the crucial part, the new recipe, the part that required time, concentration, and practice.

"I missed lunch. Anything would—"

"Why did you miss lunch?" she demanded, being herself for a moment, forgetting her reserve, forgetting even the politeness. "I know you people take vows of poverty but I didn't think starvation was included."

He laughed, took his hands from his pockets, and sat down. "We don't take a vow of poverty, the church is not trying to starve us, and I will tell you about it if you'll be kind enough to feed me something."

"How's cheese and crackers?"

"Great."

She brought the tray over. "And to drink?"

"Some Scotch. On the rocks, please."

She went to the liquor cabinet and found a precious bottle that she saved for more serious drinkers. She looked back. He was really hungry. The cheese wouldn't last long. "Tell me the reason," she said, taking out a tray of ice.

"For what?"

"For missing lunch."

"Oh, lunch. I was in court all day."

"What kind of trouble are you in?"

"Do you always jump to conclusions like that?"

She was taken aback. "I'm sorry. I suppose I do."

He smiled. "Don't be. I do it myself. Very good cheese."

"Thank you." She was starting to be amused, interested. She hadn't expected a personality; she had expected a Father Reilly.

"It was a custody case, a child in my parish. The parents are separating and each one wanted custody."

"How were you involved?"

"I was trying to help the father gain custody."

"The father? Isn't that unusual?"

"He's the better parent. Shouldn't the better parent have custody?"

"I wasn't challenging you," she said gently. "I was just asking."

"Sorry. I've been challenged all day. I'm a little edgy."

She handed him his drink.

"Thanks," he said, taking a sip. "Good Scotch."

"How did it turn out? The case, I mean."

"We lost."

"I'm sorry." She brought a Bloody Mary with her as she sat down in the chair next to the sofa to help herself to what was left of the cheese. "You know, you're much easier to talk to than Father Reilly."

"Father Reilly is difficult to talk to, not because he's a priest—I assume that's what you're driving at—but because he's John Reilly. He's a very quiet, introverted guy. He was very impressed with you, by the way."

"Oh? I didn't know I'd been talked about."

"Relax," he said. "You were mentioned, not talked about. What part of New York are you from?"

"It still shows, doesn't it? Brooklyn."

"I'm from the Irish end," he said.

"Then we're neighbors."

"No." He shook his head. "We were never neighbors. I suppose you made the daily trip to Bronx Science."

"Naturally. Did you?"

"No. I went to a good school."

"A Catholic one."

"A Catholic one."

"Did you always intend to be a priest, then?"

"My mother intended it." He took another drink. "My mother had two shocks in her life. The first was when I decided not to be a priest. The second was when I did."

"My mother would gladly have settled for only two. Does she still live in Brooklyn?"

He shook his head. "She died last year."

"Oh." All other comments seemed inadequate or artificial. "Where in Brooklyn did you live?"

"Not where you did," he said.

"You don't know where I lived."

"It wasn't near us," he said distantly.

She got up, the last of the reserve slipping away, went to her desk and found a pad of plain white paper and a pencil and brought them back to where the priest was sitting. "Draw me a picture," she said.

"Of what?"

"Of where you lived. Of Brooklyn. I want to count how many blocks from me you lived."

"I'm not an artist."

"No one said you were. Don't make it a picture. Draw a map."

"Cartography wasn't one of my—"

"Of course it wasn't," she interrupted. "My goodness, I'm glad I don't have you in class."

"How do you know what I was going to say?"

"Draw," she ordered.

He started sketching. Sipping her drink, she watched. "It looks like Greenland," she said when the outline was completed. He looked at her with raised eyebrows and wrote BROOKLYN across one edge of the sheet. "Put in Coney Island," she said, "so I'll be able to locate my neighborhood." He turned the sheet around and wrote Coney I. where she had expected to see the Brooklyn Bridge.

"Greenland never looked like this," he said, drawing in Flatbush Avenue and the bridges to Manhattan.

"Put in Prospect Park," she said.

"Would you like me to draw the Brooklyn Museum and label all the exhibits?"

"Don't get angry. I think you're doing very well. When I go to Greenland, I'm taking it with me."

"Will you settle for Ebbets Field?" he asked.

"Ebbets Field. God, do you remember Ebbets Field?"

"Only vaguely," he said, "the way I remember Teddy Roosevelt and San Juan Hill."

She laughed. "It's a beautiful map. Now show me where you lived."

He sketched in a cartoon figure of a man with a serious face, a priest's collar, and a large cross on his chest.

"That's very good," she said with surprise. "You were right. You aren't a cartographer at all; you're a cartoonist. Here's where I lived." She pointed with her index finger to an area that seemed spaced appropriately from both Coney Island and Prospect Park. He drew a cartoon of a girl, smiling, and put a large Jewish star on her chest.

"OK?" he asked.

"Superb. Now, where did we meet?"

He looked out the window with a frown. "Maybe the Brooklyn Museum," he said.

"Did your mother take you there too?"

"I went myself," he said, tearing the sheet off the pad and starting to crumple it.

"Oh, don't do that," she said, taking it from him and smoothing out the wrinkles. "I want to keep it. It's very nice."

"You know—" he leaned back comfortably with his

glass— "when I was a kid in Brooklyn, in my teens, I guess—and we used to go out with nice Jewish girls—"

"You!" She was caught off guard again, amused in spite of herself, enjoying the conversation. "Come now. You never went out with Jewish girls."

"*Nice* Jewish girls," he said with careful emphasis, lifting an index finger and wagging it at her.

"All right, *nice* Jewish girls. What did your Irish mother say about that?"

"My Irish mother didn't know anything about it," he said, finishing his drink and putting the glass on the table. "And you've interrupted my story."

"Forgive me."

"When you went out with a nice Jewish girl, I remember you always had to wait until the third date to kiss her good night. Was that true in your generation?"

"In my generation?" She looked at him. Pete had said the priest was ten years older than he. "Yes, I suppose it was still true in my generation. I was a nice Jewish girl." Once.

She looked at her watch. It was almost nine o'clock. Whole schedule shot to hell. "I'd better get dinner started," she said, "or we won't eat tonight."

She stood up, realized the glass in her hand was empty, made a decision, announced it. "I'm having another drink. I've changed my mind about you."

He looked amused. "Tell me about it."

"I thought it would be much harder, talking to you, I mean. I've never entertained a member of the clergy before." She ran a hand down the front of her pants suit. "Like I'm wearing black." He was laughing now.

"You do know how to laugh, don't you?" she said. "Well, I've just decided to enjoy myself this evening."

He handed her his glass and stood up too. "Am I allowed to look at your books?"

"You're invited to," she said, pouring Scotch over his ice. "You can even play the records."

He pulled out a few. "It makes it comfortable here, all these books and records."

"They're the first things I ever owned, I mean paid for with my own money. In college we used to will them to whoever we were in love with. You know—and if I die, give him my books and records. Here, let me help you."

He had picked out some modern folk songs. She put them on and turned on the record player, pausing to listen to the first few bars. Then she went back to the kitchen. He followed her to the counter.

"Now I see where the herb garden came from," he said, inspecting the flowerpots. "That was a nice garden you had last summer. The kids all seemed to like it."

"I like herbs." She picked off a basil leaf and offered it to him. "They leave something behind them."

"Very nice," he said, dropping the leaf on the counter. He walked back to the bookcase, looked over the books, and took one down. "Your Yeats looks well-worn."

She felt a pang, the mother possessive of her child. Once, last year, some guy had taken that book down and she had leaped at him like a cat. Put it down, she had yelled, hating him for being an idiot and hating him even more for touching her Yeats.

"It was given to me," she said, watching him touch it. "It was someone else's before it was mine."

She took down her pans and started two burners. This was the part that had to be done all at once at the last minute. She glanced at the priest. The book rested on his open left hand. He was turning pages. He walked to a chair and sat down, book in hand.

It must be lonely, she thought, seeing people only when they need you. Who does a guy like that go to when he needs someone? I wonder if anyone comes to him just to be friendly, not out of necessity, but just because it's a nice day and it would be a nice thing to see Father Kendall when you don't need him. Funny, that's what Pete had done on Monday. She felt a wave of guilt at having resisted Pete's invitation. Pete was such a good guy. It was a shame she didn't love him.

The small pieces of veal were becoming tender. Working rapidly, she removed them, went on to the next step. She added the cooking wine, enjoying the aroma, flipped the potatoes in the other pan. Craig Claiborne would be proud of her. She turned again to the chair. The priest was still reading the Yeats. She relaxed. It was safe in his hands.

The summer before last, after two years in Boston, she had returned to Cornell for two days. Someone had told her that Professor Hillman, a favorite literature professor, was ill, and she had decided to see him. She remembered the scene in his garden, the professor sitting in a summer chair, books on a canopied round table, a German shepherd noisily guarding his master from the young intruder. When she was there, finally,

sitting near him, and his wife had left them with lemonade and cookies and the dog had quieted down and
she had answered his questions about New York and
Boston and why and how long and do you remember,
she had been unable to say what she had come all this
way to say to him: Look at me, I am someone because
of you. Instead, she had asked him about his work and
what he was writing and which book he was reading
and whether he could tell her something about a book
from his course that she had reread last month and did
he think Dylan Thomas would stand the test of time as
well as Yeats had and how she didn't care anyhow because he would for her even if she wasn't using the
most acceptable methods of criticism, if he would forgive her. And he smiled and drank half of his lemonade
and didn't eat a single cookie even though he looked
thinner than she remembered ever seeing him and they
talked about things she hadn't come to talk about until
finally she could see the sun going down and she said
perhaps she ought to be leaving and the professor stood
up for the first time that afternoon and tucked a book
under his left arm and said, "Let me show you the garden before you go," and he walked slowly around the
garden with her, naming the flowers and talking about
them, the green bells of Ireland, the yellow marigolds,
the deep red hibiscus, and at the end showing her a
long row of azaleas, hybrid azaleas he said they were,
and weren't they fine-looking even though they weren't
in bloom but of course, it was too late in the season
and maybe if she came next year in May she could see
the azaleas. And she said, yes, she would try to and

then he called his wife who came from the house with
an apron over her denim skirt and thanked her for
coming and was all good cheer and smiles and Ruth
wondered bitterly if wives understood anything at all or
if she had ever read a book. Then the professor said,
"It was good of you to come, Ruth," and she thought,
how did he know my name? He had never called her
anything but Miss Gold before and he handed her the
book he had been carrying as they made their rounds
of the garden and said, "Here, why don't you take this
back to Boston with you? It may answer some of your
questions," and she had been so close to tears that she
had hardly managed to say "Thank you" and "Goodbye." Later, in her small room at the Straight she had
cried uncontrollably because she had made this long
trip and in the end he had been the one to give her
something.

Well, it had been one step better than the year she
was twenty-two and her favorite aunt, a great-aunt really, who lived in a little house in New Jersey, had
died. Ruth had known for months she was dying and
had promised to make the trip—not a long trip, really,
a tunnel, a bridge, some highway—but she had never
made it, and the aunt had died and Ruth had vowed it
would never happen again that way. So she had made
the trip to see the professor and she had left everything
unsaid.

Then, last April after reading the editorial page in
the *New York Times,* she had turned the page and seen
the obituary, Professor Charles J. Hillman, English
Literature. How cruel, how terribly cruel, that he had
not seen the azaleas bloom again. She had written a

short note to his wife—how much he meant to me, how good it was to see him last summer, the loss to all of us, how sad he missed the azaleas—all the things everybody else would write.

But two weeks later a letter arrived from Mrs. Charles J. Hillman—how thoughtful of Ruth to have written a note, how much her husband had appreciated her traveling that great distance last summer just to see him, how many times he had mentioned it in the fall as his health was failing. Yes, he had missed the azaleas. Only today, the first bud opened, cheeriest thing around the house now. Would Ruth be passing this way again some time? Charles had left a wonderful collection of books. Perhaps she would like to take some for herself.

It had been hard to imagine she could have misjudged the professor's wife so badly.

The book had become her treasure. At one time or another, she had turned every page, read every annotation, glanced at every one of the *Collected Poems*. Now the priest who people came to when they needed him and who had come to dinner tonight to talk about somebody's problem sat reading the Yeats given to her by the man she had gone to say goodbye to, the man with the wonderful wife and the beautiful garden. How sad for the priest that in his life he would have neither. She brushed away an unexpected tear.

Turning away from the stove, she asked, "Were you an English major?"

"I? No." He seemed amused at the thought. "I was a chemistry major."

"Chemistry!"

"What's so strange about that? I once had a wild notion I wanted to be a doctor."

"But?"

"Things changed. I started reading." He held up the Yeats. "It's a little hard to explain."

"So you became a priest."

"Something like that, I suppose."

"You're much nicer than I thought you were," she said, feeling the alcohol start to work. "Read me your favorite poem and let's see how good my memory is."

"I don't think I have a favorite."

"Then one you like. Any one." She studied her recipe while he leafed through the book.

> *"One asks for mournful melodies;*
> *Accomplished fingers begin to play.*
> *Their eyes mid many wrinkles, their eyes,*
> *Their ancient, glittering eyes are gay."*

"That's not fair."

"Why isn't it fair?"

"I had a marker at that one."

"There's no marker." He held the book up. "I take it you know that one."

"It's my favorite."

"Well, that's a good beginning, then," he said.

She turned back to the stove. On the counter next to the range was her glass, empty except for the melting ice cubes and a piece of lime. In the last few moments she had become aware of a vague physical discomfort, familiar but unidentifiable. "We'll eat soon," she said, dismissing the feeling. "It's almost ready now."

"Whose music is that on the record?" he asked.

She listened for a moment. "Bob Dylan's. But that's Judy Collins singing." He shrugged. "How are you at opening wine?"

"Respectable," he said, joining her near the sink.

He was better than that. The cork come out smoothly, neatly, and intact. When he sniffed it and set it down on the counter, she noticed the back of his hand. It was covered with scar tissue.

"What happened?" she asked, running the tip of her index finger over the uneven surface. And then, "Oh, I'm sorry," as if he were untouchable. "I didn't mean to do that."

He put his hand in his pocket. "It's an old war wound," he said easily.

"You were in the service?"

"The navy."

"Were you a priest then?"

He shook his head. "It was a long time ago." He picked up a small snapshot at the back of the counter. "Is that Anthony?" he asked.

"Yes. I took it in September, when he stayed with me."

"He stayed with you?" He sounded surprised.

"After camp. I thought you knew. Teresa had to go back to the hospital for tests the beginning of September. Shall we sit down?" They moved to the table and he poured the wine. "He needed a place to stay so I took him. I really love that kid," she said, tasting the wine which was just barely cool and very delicious. "Do you know them?"

"They lived in my parish until last spring. That was very nice of you to take him."

"How sick is Teresa?" she asked, wanting to know and afraid to hear.

"Very sick, I'm afraid. Do you still see them?"

"Every couple of weeks. I went over on New Year's Day." To redeem the year, remember? "Where is her husband? Do you know anything about him?" The wine was good. It made talking even easier.

"He comes and goes," the priest said. "Things are better for them when he's away. He sends checks and he doesn't hurt anybody."

"Who would he hurt?" she asked, reacting soberly to panic. "Anthony?"

"Don't worry," he said kindly. "A friend of mine is a curate in that parish. He looks in on them from time to time."

"What's a curate?"

He smiled at her. "What I am."

"Oh. As Anthony says, 'I don't know nothin'.'"

"That sounds like Anthony."

She offered him another helping.

"It's very good," he said, accepting. "I've been talking too much to tell you. I don't eat this well very often."

"Do you do your own cooking?" she asked, watching him fill her glass again, wanting to drink it and wondering how she would manage.

"There's a housekeeper in the rectory," he said.

"Oh. A housekeeper." She yawned. "You do interesting things, don't you? Anthony, the day in court. I never thought a priest would do interesting things." The wine was a beautiful color in the glass. "You play football too. That's what I would do if I were a priest. I'd play football with the kids."

"It's not the sort of thing you can do twelve hours a day."

"Do you put in twelve hours a day?"

"When I'm lucky."

"Do you get paid?"

"Anthony was right about you, wasn't he?"

"Anthony?" she asked, trying—without much effort —to see the connection.

"I get paid," he said.

They talked and they ate and the food was good and he refilled their glasses again. The wine was good, too, good going down, good up in her head. After a while, he asked her who he was trying the meal out for.

"I'm not sure," she said, feeling very lazy now. "I'm re—reevaluating." The verb came out with the wrong number of syllables. You had to be so careful with syllables when you drank wine.

She wondered why she was reevaluating. The thing to do was to call him up, ask him to dinner, get herself laid. That was the thing to do.

What was the alternative? Calling up Pete some day: OK, Pete, let's get married. I'm so goddamn tired of living alone and not having a man when I want one.

She got up from the table, sleepy now, put the water on to boil and went for the coffee beans. "How many cups will you drink?" she asked, opening the coffee mill, waiting for his answer.

"I beg your pardon?"

"Coffee," she said, stifling a yawn. "A cup? Two cups?"

"Make a pot," he said. "There are things you can't always decide in advance."

"Brandy?" she asked, fulfilling her final culinary obligation.

"That would be very nice."

She put the bottle on the table and two snifters. "Are you going back to camp?" he asked.

"It depends what Pete does."

"If he goes, you'll go?"

She tried to sort it out. After alcohol, there was always trouble with premises and conclusions, positives and negatives. "If he doesn't go," she said carefully, "I'll go."

"I like Pete very much," he said.

"I like him too. I don't love him. I don't want to marry him. I don't want to sit in restaurants and have him touch me all night." She paused, regretting the involuntary flow of words. "I think the coffee's ready." She poured it, spilling a little in his saucer, and put the pot on the warmer. She sat down, cut the pie, and drank some coffee. Come on, coffee, she thought, start working. She looked across the table. He had blue eyes. She hadn't noticed his blue eyes before. "Look," she said, "could we be friends?"

He smiled. When he smiled, his blue eyes smiled too. "I didn't know we were enemies."

"We weren't enemies." He seemed determined to confound her. She touched her cheek. It was very warm. She sipped some of the brandy. It was scorching. "I would like to tell you about Pete. Pete spent last summer telling you about me."

"He didn't."

"Of course he did. After this much to drink, I know

what happened last summer." She looked at him. "Are we friends?"

"We're friends."

"He thinks he's in love with me. Maybe he is. I'm not too sure if that counts—you know, one-sided. He calls me up all the time. I stopped going out with him but he still calls to talk to me. He tells me his troubles. Even when he has no troubles, he tells them to me. Sometimes he comes over and just sits here and we talk. In the middle of the night. I should stop that too, shouldn't I? Just put an end to it—" she snapped her fingers but there was no sound— "just like that."

"I think he's very lucky," the priest said, "to have someone he can call in the middle of the night and talk to. I'm sure he knows how you feel. Why don't you just let it ride awhile? More brandy?"

"I don't think I should."

He poured her another glass. "What happens when you've had too much?"

"I fall asleep," she said. "What happens to you?"

"I become morose."

"I knew it," she said drunkenly. "We do different things but they're triggered by the same phenomenon." Syllables again.

"Which is?"

"Thinking about the past. Mine is a bore so I fall asleep. Yours gets to you so you become morose."

"The brandy seems to have made you very perceptive. Maybe you shouldn't have any more."

"Maybe I should."

"I would be very disappointed if you fell asleep."

"I would be even more disappointed if you became morose."

"I won't become morose," he said.

"I like you," she said, feeling the warmth within her surround her, reach out and surround him too. "I didn't think I'd like you. I thought I would have to talk to you about church architecture."

"I'm glad it worked out. I don't know much about church architecture."

"In fact, I don't even think you're a priest. I think you're an English professor in disguise."

"No way," he said. "Not in this man's lifetime."

"I would like some more coffee but I don't think I can get up to get it."

He went for the coffee, poured it with a steady hand, put it back on the warmer.

"Pete told me something about you," she said when he had sat down.

He looked at her, a hint of a smile, a twinkle of the blue eyes.

She nodded seriously. "He said you understood dirty jokes."

"I understand dirty jokes. What would make Pete tell you that?"

"I asked him to give me one reason for visiting you on Monday. That was the reason. You weren't very happy to see me, were you?"

"That was before we were friends."

"Right," she said. "That makes sense." It would all work out if she could hang on a little longer. "Pete said you weren't always a priest. What were you before you were a priest?"

"A rake," he said.

"Were you really?"

"I really was."

"I see it all now," she said, sipping the coffee. "You're atoning for your sins. That makes sense too. Was she beautiful?"

"I beg your pardon?"

"The girl. The woman. Was she beautiful?"

He seemed uncomfortable. "I don't know," he said. "I never stopped to look."

"Ah. Then you have a lot to atone for. Good luck," she said magnanimously. "How about getting some more coffee?"

She watched him walk to the counter where the pot sat on the warmer and heard him switch the warmer off. Very thoughtful. Now we won't have a fire tonight. He walked back with the coffee. His hips were slim. He was big and good-looking in an attractive Irish way.

"Are you going back to camp?" she asked.

"I don't know," he said. "I haven't worked it out yet."

The last record had ended while they were eating and the record player had turned itself off. They had finished their coffee and even the sounds of the cups and saucers had stopped.

"Do you feel all right?" he asked.

"Yes, I'm pulling out of it now."

"Can I suggest something to you?"

"Of course."

"I think you should go back to camp next summer. Regardless of Pete. Go because you're good for the kids. Go because someone cared for you enough to give you the Yeats."

She looked down at the table with the remains of dinner for two. "You remind me of the shuttle," she said, sadness welling up in her as she spoke. "Do you ever fly the shuttle?"

"I never go to New York."

"I take it every couple of months. Someone always sits next to me, some stranger, a man usually, for an hour from Logan to LaGuardia. They always say one great important thing as we're about to land. I never forget what they say and I never see them again."

"Because you don't want to?"

"Because it wouldn't work out."

"Do you spend the hour interrogating them?" he asked, surprising her.

She looked across the table at him and she was angry. He was riding her now, accusing her, pushing it too far. "No," she said, "I don't interrogate them. They just talk. I never ask a question," she lied, exaggerating her case. "They tell me everything without a question. I just listen."

"What do they tell you? What they majored in and what kind of poetry they like? Do you have them read you their favorite poem?"

"No," she said. "We never talk about poetry. You know what they tell me? They tell me they're not making it with their wives."

"And you feel sorry for them."

"No," she said. "I never feel sorry for them. I feel sorry for their wives."

He got up from the table and walked to the record player. "May I turn them over?" he asked, not looking at her.

"Go ahead," she said, standing up and collecting the dessert dishes and taking them to the sink. Do whatever you want. She turned the water on and rinsed the dishes that had accumulated during dinner.

She was angry now, angry and hurt. She hadn't deserved that. It had been gratuitous, unkind. She looked for a little dart, something small and sharp, that she could toss back.

"You really like those kids in the church basement, don't you?" she asked, finding it.

He turned and looked at her.

"Don't you ever feel sad," she went on, "that you'll never have any of your own?"

She saw it land, one tiny movement of a face muscle, gone almost before it happened.

"Do you feel sad that you don't have any?"

"No," she said. "I'll have them some day. When I'm ready."

"How can you be so sure?"

"I am sure."

"Why? Because you think that if nothing works out you can always call Pete and tell him you've changed your mind?"

She could feel her eyes opening wider. She turned to the dishwasher, trying to steady her breathing, control her fury, keep the tears back. She shoved the top rack in, slammed the door of the dishwasher, started to clean the sink as if scrubbing it would somehow ease the pain. The discomfort was there again, more acute now, more familiar. She knew what it was now. It was the same thing that had been gnawing at her for months, for a year even, for half her goddamn life.

The song on the record finished. There was a pause, that moment of silence that gave you time to prepare for what was coming next: hold your breath a second; something else is coming. The sink was clean, the enamel shiny. She squeezed out the sponge and turned off the water. The voices returned, the beautiful female voices singing "Bring Me a Rose." She dried her hands on the damp dish towel hanging on her left shoulder. In front of her, out the window, it was dark except for the street lights. She started to take the dish towel from her shoulder, but the priest was there and he took it from her and laid it on the counter.

"Dance with me," he said, turning her around, the parish priest who had come to dinner, putting his arms around her, holding her, touching her, dancing with her, the man on the shuttle reaching her finally as the plane dipped through the fog and skimmed Flushing Bay, ready for touchdown, the only stop, the end of the line.

"No," she said, her arms around him, wanting him.

She heard him draw a breath, felt his hands tighten on her back, felt the hardness against her stomach.

"Oh no," she said, understanding everything now and afraid because she understood. "I can't."

She pushed him and turned away, pivoting halfway round, steadying herself on the kitchen counter. She felt him touch the back of her head, gently, down along her neck, and she fought the tears again.

She waited a moment, then turned back, half afraid he would still be standing there, but he had walked to the bookcase and was looking at the titles again, his hands in his pockets.

"I'm sorry," she said, in one word apologizing for the lost reserve, the unmet schedule, the ache inside her that she had never really felt for Al, only wanted to feel.

"Would you let me borrow the Yeats?" he asked. "I know what it means to you. I'll be very careful with it."

The book was still on the shelf. He was waiting for her permission to touch it, her gesture of conciliation. When Miss Gold tells you, you may take the book, but not until then.

It was more than an ache now; it was almost pounding. She had done everything wrong this evening, right from the start. He was a priest from a local parish and she had treated him like a man. She should go to the phone, call Al and say, OK, Al, I'm ready for you now. But it was too late, too late for Al, too late for all of them. She ran her hand along the kitchen counter and her fingers touched a piece of paper. It was the map of Brooklyn with the two cartoon figures on it. She laid her palm on it, feeling the wrinkles. Everything became clear. I want him. I want to go to bed with him.

"Yes," she said and her voice sounded hoarse. She cleared her throat. "You can have the Yeats."

"Thank you," he said, reaching for the book. "I'll take good care of it."

"I know you will," she said, and she waited. Something would happen now. He would take the book, ask for his coat and leave. Tomorrow morning, when she had slept off the alcohol, her body would be more reasonable.

She waited for the move that would end the evening.

"May I turn this off?" he asked, nodding toward the record player.

"Sure."

The remaining records clicked down, one after the other, and the turntable turned itself off. He bent down and shut off the power.

It was very quiet for a few seconds. Outside, a car went down the street too fast. Then there was nothing.

"Ruth," he said finally, breaking the silence, and hearing her name spoken for the first time that evening, she shivered. "Look, I'm no good at this. I haven't done it for ten years. I want to make love to you. You won't make me wait till I've seen you three times, will you?"

Oh, Jesus Christ, they had done nothing right this evening. Didn't he even know that making love was a ballet, a man and a woman entering from opposite ends of the stage, moving by degrees to the center, the point of contact, that they touched there, first fingertips, then hands, lips, bodies, first clothed, then without thinking or planning or caring, unclothed, standing face to face. Why had he done it this way, making her love him and hate him first, want him without touching him, hurt him without knowing him, and now, finally, on the point of leaving, the very moment of departure, ask her —Christ, *ask* her—getting the positives and negatives all mixed up as if he were the intoxicated one, forcing her to say it, to commit herself, in the hearing of all present? (And reminding her, even as Mother would want her to be reminded, that she was a Jewish girl, that it was he who would wake up tomorrow and re-think, reconsider, do what was best?)

"No," she said, looking at the floor, answering affirmatively, "I want you too."

He didn't move. He was making her do that too, the foreshortened ballet across ten feet of stage. He was still holding the Yeats, his knuckles white. She took it from him, ran her hand over the worn cover as in a caress, laid it on a table, touched his cheek with the same hand, gave herself to him.

He took her in his arms and held her, not kissing her, just held her, rubbing her back, as if holding her were the only thing he wanted from her.

"I want you," he said, and she could feel his heart beating, racing, running away. "Since last August. I've wanted you since August."

"Oh, Jesus Christ," she said, trembling against him. "Kiss me, will you? Will you please kiss me?"

He kissed her. He knew how to do that, and how to find the zipper and take the top off and keep her trembling and then the pants came off and she winced because her pantyhose had a run up the side because those are the ones you save to wear under pants where no one will see them. Then he was undressing and she touched him while he moved and watched him put a hand in a pocket and pull out his keys and change and put them on the table and then the other hand pulled out a wallet and she thought of the other times she had watched a guy reach into a pocket and pull out keys and coins, a little knife, a wallet, a condom once. . . .

When he was undressed he put his arm around her shoulder—two lovers going for a walk in the woods— and he said, "I didn't come prepared for this, I'm sorry. I should have told you before."

"It's OK," she said, everything falling into place now. "I'll take care of it."

She got her robe—the robe only she and Pete had
seen—and found the little white kit and went into the
bathroom, trying to remember how to use the diaphragm, which side was up, how much you squeeze on
it, hating herself for using a diaphragm, for having to
leave him for three precious minutes without her.

There was an instruction book with it, telling you in
antiseptic language how to prepare for love—"a teaspoonful of jelly"—leaving out all the good parts because nobody could ever tell you that, not the girls at
home who had dropped out of Brooklyn College to
marry their Bernies and Arnies and Ronnies or even
the boy a long time ago who had loved you and made it
so good. So she read the instructions and she used too
much jelly and she thought about physiology as she
pushed it inside her and then she put on the robe—
what did she need a robe for anyway?—and she
stopped and looked at herself in the mirror, briefly,
awkwardly, Ruth Gold confronting Ruth Gold, and
then she went out to where he was waiting for her, all
the lights off now except one next to the bed, and she
stood in front of him and knew why she had put the
robe on, so he could untie the belt and push it with his
fingertips over her shoulders so it slithered down to the
floor in a heap and they could stand there, face to face
and body to body and she could be scared.

The first time is being scared. Even the second first
time and the thousandth first time. The last one knew
you, knew your body, knew how to get you there, knew
what to do with you. But this was the first time and the
first time is being scared. It's wanting to explain a couple of little things about yourself—there's this list, you

see, just a few points, maybe we could talk about it, it won't take long, I've had a copy Xeroxed for you, perhaps I could use the blackboard. . . . Ah, fantasy. Resort rather to prayer: Let it be good. Let it not be the last time.

She stood against him, feeling the silky robe at her ankles, feeling him hard against her the way a man ought to feel against you. Then he put his arm around her shoulder again and they started toward the bed.

Take it slow, she thought as he reached for her in the dark, under the blanket, just take it slow, please. But she knew he wouldn't, couldn't this time even if he wanted to. And then, after a minute, it didn't matter. It was all happening so fast that it didn't matter. She suddenly understood the meaning of the word "respond." All these years out of school and she had learned a new word. She felt her love rising inside her, responding, surging, the love, the passion, the feeling, the desire. He came inside her, easily, smoothly, all the way. He spoke to her.

"Ruth," he said, calling her by name, "come now. I want you to come with me."

Anywhere she thought, the wave inside her rising, cresting now. I will go anywhere with you. Cresting—oh—cresting, getting there together—ah. Subsiding. Lapping the beach. A little more. Anywhere, anywhere, I love you.

She hung on to him, not letting him go, holding him there, heavy on top of her, still hard inside her, feeling the sweat on his face where it touched her shoulder.

He turned over finally and lay next to her. "Give me your hand," he said.

She gave him her right hand and he took it in his right hand. Friends, she thought. Jesus, we're friends.

"Tell me something," he said.

"What?"

"If it was good."

She felt the tears again. All evening they'd been there, waiting. "Great," she said, turning to him. "You were great. You're fantastic."

"Hey," he said, "do you know that my name is Jim?"

And that's when she started to cry.

Weep, she thought, weep for the end as you begin the beginning, aware that when the end comes, the time for tears will be long past. The end, always the end. Why do you think of the end at the beginning?

When it was over, they started to talk, softly, intimately, the pressure off now, talk about things lovers never talk about.

"Tell me something," her voice still unsteady.

"What?"

"Your middle name. I want to know your middle name."

"Michael. You're beautiful. Do you know you're beautiful?"

"Michael. I like that."

Usually they had gone to sleep afterwards, both of them too tired to do anything else. Sometimes there was a cab ride home or a walk; once or twice a subway ride. Sitting in a subway, a stranger on one side of you, and feeling it pour out of you.

Next week we'll go to my cousin's place. They're going to the Catskills.

"Tell me how old you are."

"Almost twenty-six."

"You're a baby, aren't you?"

"Am I?"

She wanted him again. Half an hour and she wanted him again. That was new too. Usually it had been once and finished. Goodbye, see you, don't forget your cigarettes.

"Jim?"

"What darling?" Darling. Jesus. Darling.

"What's wrong with Teresa?"

"It's a malignancy. There isn't very much they can do any more. Don't think about it. Just keep seeing her."

Why couldn't she tell him she wanted him? Such an easy thing to say, I want you. Hey, Jim, I want you. But she knew she would never say it.

"I want you again," he was saying. "Do you think I'm crazy?"

"You're not crazy. Will you take it slow this time?"

"Will you make it if I take it slow?"

"I'll make it. Just go slow."

Afterwards he brought her her robe and he got dressed. That's something to watch, a man getting dressed. The way he stands up and stretches a little when he zips the zipper, leaves the top button on his shirt open, rolls his sleeves, puts the keys back and the change, the black wallet fraying at the edges, the folded tie that it's too late to put on. The way he touches you when his hand is free, relaxed now, something that wasn't there at eight o'clock.

"What are you so sad about?"

"Not sad, just tired."

"You think I can't tell the difference between sorrow and fatigue?" He put his hand on her knee. "I'll call you," he said.

She looked at the back of his hand resting on the pink robe, the hand, the wrist with the small bone protruding at one side, the back of his arm bare halfway to the elbow, the scar partly covered by hair. She ran her hand gently over the back of his, up to where the shirt was rolled. He owed her that from before.

She was sad, sad and tired. "Jim?" she said, looking at his hand on her leg.

"What, darling?"

"Are you scared?"

A momentary pause, almost imperceptible in its duration. "No, I'm not scared."

"Because if you wake up tomorrow morning and you have second thoughts—"

"I'll call you," he said.

He took the Yeats—he really wanted the Yeats—and said good night. There was a gentle kiss, the car starting up downstairs and then the agony, listening to the record again, taking a warm shower, getting into bed so tired that sleep should have been instantaneous, only it wouldn't come, remembering, her body reacting to the remembering.

She got up, eventually, found an anthology of English poems and looked for the one by Yeats. Not there. There were half a dozen others but not the one she wanted. She poured a little brandy and sipped it. It was hot going down, good for what ailed her. She got back into bed and turned off the light. It was almost three o'clock.

The phone rang.

Oh, Pete, she pleaded telepathically, please. Your friend Ruth doesn't exist tonight. Go away. Just this once, leave me alone. It rang again.

"Hello?" She was wide awake, ready for a week's worth of malaise.

"I couldn't sleep either." Jesus.

"Look," she said, raising herself up in bed, "I have to tell you something. About the shuttle. I want to tell you the truth about the shuttle."

"I want to see you tonight."

"I interrogate hell out of them. I never stop asking them questions the whole hour."

"Nine o'clock," he said. "Can I see you at nine?"

"And it isn't just their wives—"

"Save the pie for me, will you? You didn't give me a second piece tonight. Are you listening to me?"

"Nine o'clock," she said soberly. "I'll save the pie."

"I knew you couldn't keep quiet for an hour on an airplane."

When she hung up, she found she had made a decision.

Next week she would go to a doctor and get the pill.

2

Waking up was one thing; turning over was quite another. There was no reason to be surprised but the emptiness of the other half of the bed came as a shock.

She got out of bed feeling alone, made coffee for one, juice for one, and toast for one, and ate them alone. It was Saturday, the day for taking care of the dull odds and ends of life. She was on her way out with the laundry when the phone rang. Overly optimistic, she turned back and ran for it. It was the long arm of Brooklyn.

"We haven't heard a word from you all week," her mother complained. "Are you all right?"

"I'm fine, Mom."

"So how was New Year's Eve?"

"It was very nice, Mom. The party was beautiful. They had decorations there you would have—"

"Did he ask you anything interesting?"

"Plenty of things but nothing you would care about."

"Give him time," her mother advised from her reservoir of inexperience. "Be nice to him."

Yes, Mother. No, Mother. She would let them dangle another week, then drop them a note. Maybe put it on a postcard so that Joe, the mailman, could commiserate with Mother.

It had grown cold overnight and she wound the long knitted scarf around her neck as she stepped outside with the laundry. Her first stop was the hardware store where she had an extra key made for the apartment. From there she walked to the laundromat and dropped off the clothes. Then, shivering, she turned in the direction of the drugstore. The wind blew thoughts of pneumonia, election-year pneumonia. There was no obvious reason for the association. The first attack had been in sixty-seven, not sixty-eight, and had been utterly unrelated to the weather. It had come at the end of one of the most disappointing times of her life, more a response to it than a result of it. She had returned from Europe to her first job, which she loved, and to her ancestral home, which she did not. What had made her think that four years away, a college degree, a trip to Europe, a job teaching, and a monthly paycheck would have altered her parents' perception of her as their baby, their daughter, their strayed little angel, who would confide, abide, and obey till death did them part?

And then there had been the loss, the unheralded, unreported death of Abraham, her father's father. Even today, riding on the Belt Parkway could bring it back.

So she had had pneumonia, her first and only attempt at suicide.

The reaction of her parents—predictably—had been wildly verbal. They vied with each other over decibels.

Europe, her mother had screamed, you had to go to Europe. A month in the mountains, you'd have your health *and* a husband.

Teaching is too much for you (Father). You need a job that takes less out of you.

(Cop-out, her brother had said.)

Get a nurse, her father had yelled one night to her mother. You're killing yourself. Call the doctor. She should go to a hospital. (A nice Jewish hospital.)

It was all over in a couple of weeks and she went

back to being exactly what she had been before—or perhaps a little worse. On her first Saturday night out after the pneumonia, she met Sandy at a party and she knew right away that this was it, the right thing, the way out.

Besides being Jewish, he was a medical student. Sandy was a find and a prize. And he loved her, loved her with a delicate, undemanding passion, so delicate and so undemanding that he took her out twelve times before going to bed with her in the bed she had slept in since she was three years old. It would be so easy. Just say yes when he asked you, give him your hand, wear his ring, tell Mother to send out the invitations, hire one of those places in Manhattan Beach, walk down the aisle in a white dress. It was what they wanted and you owed them something, after all, for the four years of college, the month at Grossinger's that you traded for a summer in Europe, for taking care of you when you had pneumonia. Marry him, Ruthie. Be a doctor's wife and live on Long Island. With luck, you may even make Westchester.

As for the small, inconsistent detail—that she didn't love him—well, why should that stand in the way? Her mother loved him—wasn't that enough?—her father respected him, her brother even talked to him. There would be harmony in the family; the nagging would stop. And he was nice; God, he was a nice guy. Shouldn't she do it? Wasn't this really the right thing to do?

She left the matter to fate. She had been unsuccessful coping with anything that had happened that fall and there had been the death in the family besides. It didn't matter very much any more what she decided. So she left it to fate. It was their twelfth date—she went back later to check it in her engagement book. Her parents had gone away to the Concord for the weekend and her brother had gone to Washington to visit his girlfriend—Washington? their mother had said. A million nice girls in Brooklyn and he has to find one in Washington!—and when Sandy brought her home to the apartment, dark for the first time because she had forgotten to leave a light on the way Mother always did, she knew as she walked through the door that it was out of her hands now. Relax, Ruthie. This is it. Take it as it comes.

Except that now, at the moment of truth, she knew she didn't want to be Mrs. Sanford Edelman and live in a house in Hastings-on-Hudson (or any other hyphenated town) with this very nice, very bright, very promising young man who had probably had an erection before they walked in the door to the dark apartment and who had waited all these weeks for somebody's parents, for Christ's sake, to go to the Concord.

But on the other hand, she was bored with her virginity and tired of it. People talked poetically of losing it but it was third-rate poetry. Most of them gave it away, clawed their way through armies to find one soul kind enough to take it. She had shied away from that her first two years at Cornell; after that, they had all been so young, so—unappetizing. Better to give it to Sandy.

In the bedroom, dark except for the light that came down the hall from the living room, he undressed her—carefully, lovingly—laying her clothes on the delicate white furniture Mother had ordered for her seventh birthday, and she shivered, not from passion or antici-

pation or love but because it was late, damn it, and she
was tired and cold and not yet completely recovered
from the pneumonia which had left her so thin he was
able to touch and count her ribs when her dress was
off.

He began in earnest, then, working over her body
carefully, methodically, thoroughly, as once he must
have turned the pages of his anatomy textbook, and she
lay on her bed in the dark room wishing he would
reach the final chapter and get it over with because
something was missing, something he hadn't found in
the textbook. She lay there tensely, an observer in a
stranger's bedroom, feeling his hands, his lips, his teeth
and his tongue—feeling all of that and feeling nothing,
absolutely nothing. She was cold and she was unmoved
and she knew with a sudden flash of insight that nothing would ever happen to her, not tonight or any other
night of her life, and then, finally—God, it *must* have
been hours later—breathing hard—what a sweat he
had worked himself into—he tried to put it inside her
and if it had been bad up to that point, well, it was
much worse now and she thought, My God, it was better up at school when we did it the other way. It ended
eventually. With a great commotion, a fanfare of trum-
pets, he came, and it was all over; he was lying next to
her, telling her he loved her and it would be better next
time, and how beautiful it had been for him.

After he left, she changed the sheets and took a very
warm shower and went to sleep. She slept till noon on
Sunday and woke up feeling numb, absolutely blank.
She wanted to call someone, anyone, and just talk, just
hear the sound of her voice—maybe she would call her
friend Renee in New Jersey. But she couldn't do that;

Mother would see the phone bill and wonder what had happened that Saturday night for Ruth to call New Jersey on Sunday. So she called no one and she talked to no one, just bought the *New York Times* and read it all afternoon till her parents came home at suppertime and she finally heard her voice for the first time that day. Yes, she had had a good time. No, they hadn't come home late. No, he hadn't asked her out for next weekend or for dinner tonight, but don't worry, he would call and she would go.

He asked her to get the pill but she said, no, a diaphragm would be better. She knew a diaphragm wouldn't be better but the pill seemed like such a commitment—what did people do between men? Stop taking it and look or keep taking it and hope?—so she went to a doctor her family didn't know and told him she was getting married. He must have known when he examined her, a girl off the street asking for a diaphragm, but he didn't say anything, just gave her the prescription, and so her first affair had begun.

That was December of 1967. Through the winter months of 1968 she saw Sandy regularly and he schemed and planned and devised to arrange for them to be alone together, first in his apartment when his parents were in Florida, then making the round of friends' apartments, once even traveling to the Bronx— Christ, the Bronx on a subway so you could get laid in somebody's vacant apartment. But it was never any good. While he worked over her—arousing himself, depressing her even further—she tried to pass the time profitably, using her mind while he used her body. She made a stab at composing light verse—unsuccessfully —and progressed to planning lessons and working out her finances. As she lay on the strange bed in the strange apartment, she would figure out her expenses for the following week, add them up, and subtract the total from her paycheck, holding all five digits of her check and the decimal point in her head, and proving the remainder around the time he came.

Once she felt something move, ever so slightly, within her, and she thought, Now, tonight it will happen and I will be able to love him, but nothing happened; it was a false alarm, and after that, she even stopped hoping.

She started setting limits to their relationship: if he takes me to a Holiday Inn, that'll be the end. But he never took her to a Holiday Inn. If he makes me do something in bed I don't want to, I'll never see him again. But he never made her do anything. Just be there. Just accept.

Through it all, Mother was hoping for a June wedding, or August if June couldn't be arranged, or, at the very latest, next December.

But by April, she knew she would never be Mrs. Sanford Edelman in Hastings or anywhere else but she didn't know how to break it off with so many people now to be hurt. Of all of them, only her brother had retained his equilibrium, but he always retained his equilibrium.

That weekend Sandy took her to a cousin's apartment in Manhattan, past a doorman and an elevator operator to have his Saturday night orgasm. Even nature had refused to accommodate her, she thought as they walked down the carpeted hallway with the geometric wallpaper. She always got her period on a Monday and by the weekend she was ready for his passion again. They hadn't missed a Saturday since December.

That night he spent more time than usual working her over and as she lay there in the dark, alone (except for Sandy), she wondered suddenly if he remembered who she was. If she asked him her name, would he know? Would he have to stop and think? She was so consumed with this thought that she abandoned her lesson plans, neglected her weekly finances, and finally, just at the wrong moment, she said, "Sandy, do you know who I am?"

"What?" he said, pulling away from her—she had never spoken before during their lovemaking—and then, with a groan, he came, all over her stomach and his cousin's sheets.

It was a disaster. She laughed, almost hysterically, relieved that there was finally something funny in this long, sad affair, and he became angry—well, thank God, he *knew* how to be angry—and they cleaned up and went home and she finally told him what she had wanted to say that first night in December. Go back to your cadaver, Sandy. I'm finished.

The uproar could have been heard across the river, but she was determined. By morning, she knew what she would do. She worked for days making lesson plans for the rest of the semester, with tests and assignments, everything careful and meticulous, and then she went to the principal, who was one of those great people you're lucky enough to meet once in a while, and she told him what she wanted to do and gave him her lesson plans up to the end of June and asked him to forgive her—there was no reason for him to, but he did—and then she went home and packed a bag and took all

her money out of the bank (except Grandpa's) and she
flew to Oregon to help get McCarthy elected in the primary.

The wails of her mother and the shouts of her father
accompanied her to the airport, into the plane, and
right through takeoff. But once aloft, even the air was
different, and she looked out the window, straight
ahead over the engines, to where they were flying into
the setting sun. In Oregon she worked twenty hours a
day, mostly in rain, it seemed then, and while they
were winning the primary she fell in love, which made
it even better, but when the time came to go to California the inevitable had happened; she was sick. She
had never really recovered from the pneumonia last fall
and Oregon had been rain and long hours, hard work
and little sleep, so she got on a plane and flew to New
York and that was the end of the adventure.

She recovered again but she knew she had come
home for the last time. On Sunday, less than a week
after her return, she called Cassie in Boston and told
her her plan. Cassie's father was a judge outside of
Boston. The job she wanted was hers. In August, she
packed her possessions and got on the shuttle for the
flight to the promised land.

Just across the street was the drugstore. I have come
of age, she thought, stepping off the curb and walking
into the wind. It was an exhilarating thought, an exhilarating feeling. Coming of age. She had always asso-
ciated the phrase with the first vote, a certain birthday,
the first full-time job. She had been wrong. Coming of
age was loving Jim.

She walked into the drugstore, found the necessary

tube of jelly and brought it to the counter. The clerk put it in a bag as she found the money in her purse. Waiting for her change, she heard someone call her name. She turned around, dreading the encounter. It was Pete.

"I'm in luck today," he said. "How about lunch?"

She took her change, put it away, keeping her back to the counter where the package was. "Gee, Pete, I have so much—"

"You'll do it later. How about corned beef on rye?"

The thought turned her stomach. "I don't think so."

"For God's sake, Ruthie, lunch, just lunch."

"OK, Pete," she said relenting. "Sure I'd like some lunch." She started for the door.

"Hey," he said, "don't forget your toothpaste."

Lunch was corned beef on rye and strained conversation, and by the time she got home with her clean laundry she was starting to feel uncomfortable. She went through the motions of housecleaning, took a nap, read the paper, did some work, waited for the phone to ring. It didn't ring. She felt worse. Everything was empty today, the bed, the apartment, some huge cavity inside her. Why wouldn't he call? What would keep him so busy on a Saturday that there would be no time for a phone call?

He should have stayed last night, she thought, lonely in the empty apartment. She should have awakened next to him, blending the first night with the first morning. But the gap was here, the room was empty, the telephone quiet.

Supper was tomato juice and two saltines. Later, the pie would add milk, eggs, and calories. The well-balanced diet: tomato juice and chocolate cream pie.

The hours passed and there was no phone call. She dug herself a little grave in the corner of the sofa, crawled into it, and mourned the passing of what was about to be born. When he arrived, a little after nine, she was still immersed in grief.

"You look unhappy," he said.

"It was this morning. Waking up was a letdown."

"I felt it when I went to sleep last night."

"Is that why you called?"

"Partly."

"Is the phone next to your bed?" She craved an image, a picture of him in a physical context.

"The upstairs extension is in the hall. I got dressed and went out to make the call."

"Then you don't live alone."

"There are four of us, Costello, Reilly, Romero and I." He spoke patiently, explaining. "We live in that big house next to the playground. My room is on the second floor. It's a very comfortable room. I have everything there that I need—a desk, a bed, the usual things. I built in some bookcases when I got there. When I feel like being alone, it's a nice place to go."

"And when you want company?"

"There's television in the living room. I can always find company there. I also have friends, real live people who aren't priests."

She smiled. "And you're happy."

"Content," he said. "I get to do a lot of things I always wanted to do. I've been quite content for a long time. At least, I was until recently."

"I thought you would call today," she said, airing a grievance, feeling the pressure of his last sentence.

"I did, about twelve-thirty. There was no answer."

"I ran into Pete at the drugstore. He insisted I have lunch with him." She patted her stomach. "I've been paying for it ever since. You could have called later, you know. I was home all afternoon."

"I'm very busy on Saturday. In the afternoon, I listen to confessions."

"People telling you their sins?"

"It's not usually as horrifying as it sounds."

"Do you forgive them?"

He smiled. "Wouldn't you?"

She was standing with her back to the sink, holding herself intentionally aloof. He had made himself comfortable on the sofa, comfortable and inviting.

"Tell me about yourself," she said.

"Well—" he smiled and stretched out his hands as if to inspect his fingernails—"I was born with ten fingers and ten toes."

"And that's it?"

"That's all that's relevant. Everything else is past history, past and gone. I try to do most of my thinking in the present tense."

She sat down near him and touched the scar tissue on the back of his hands, conspicuous evidence of past history.

"Why the navy?" she asked irrelevantly.

"Why does an eighteen-year-old do anything?"

"You talk about yourself as if you were a different person."

"I think of myself that way."

"I see myself as being continuous."

"Maybe you are."

"Maybe you are too."

"It's a possibility I've learned to live with."

It was a cover, then, the irrelevance of the past. She felt almost sick with sadness. A thousand questions would go unanswered—unasked now. He had drawn a boundary beyond which neither could inquire. She made an effort to adjust herself, at least temporarily, at least superficially, to what he thought he wanted.

"Is it forgiving people that makes you content?" she asked in the present tense.

"That's part of it." He was holding both her hands. "The group you saw downstairs with Mrs. McConnell is my special project. Some of the mothers in the parish work. We take care of the children there between school and when they come home. What do you think of her?"

"She's very good with them. I think she likes being there."

"She's a great woman. She's there mostly as a favor to me." He opened his hands as if afraid of restricting her. "She could use help, even one or two afternoons a week." It was an invitation, a request.

"Maybe Monday," she said tentatively, "maybe Tuesday."

"Not Tuesday, darling. Tuesday's my day off."

"Then I'll see you here on Tuesday."

"I was sort of counting on it." He was touching her very gently, as if he knew her, as if he knew all about her, as if nothing were irrelevant.

He reached into his pocket and put his keys on the coffee table, big keys, small keys, dozens of keys. "I want to make love to you now," he said.

They undressed in the dark beside the bed, her fourposter that she had never shared with anyone else, would never sleep on with anyone but Jim, the bed that

would make it all continuous, last night, tonight, another night, every night. She had lived through it now,
the first day, the breakfast alone, the lunch with Pete,
the mistimed phone call, the confessions. What did they
confess, these people who talked to him on Saturday
when she wanted him and couldn't have him?

He went for brandy afterwards and they sat drinking
it in the light of the lamp next to his side of the bed,
the establishment of a ritual, rituals bringing continuity
to discontinuous lives.

"You said you were twenty-six," he said, holding
the brandy glass.

"Almost twenty-six."

"You look younger than that but I thought you were
older, nearer thirty."

"Why?"

"Maybe I was hoping. I'm so much older than you."
He sipped his brandy. "When is your birthday?"

"Later this month, on the twentieth."

"January twentieth. That's the Eve of Saint Agnes."

"Yes. It's the only poetic thing Mother ever did."

He smiled, a gesture of sympathy for poor, unpoetic
Mother. "I'll try to get free early that night. Maybe we
can have a party." He went to the table where his
things lay and made a note in a small book. "Can I tell
Mrs. McConnell to expect you Monday?"

"I'll be there."

He made another note and came back to bed.

Mrs. McConnell was expecting her. Father Kendall
had alerted her and she was ready to welcome Ruth
into the family. It was an expanded family now, the
cold weather forcing the boys inside. There were names

to learn and biographical tidbits about almost every child. There were also three new additions today—new ones, old ones, they all looked the same the first day— their mother having begun a new job. Something about a law office. Father Kendall knew one of the lawyers.

She made herself useful, waiting edgily for the door to open and Jim to come in. When it happened, she was sitting on the floor, reading to a small group from a coverless story book. She held her voice steady and read on until he stopped next to her, the fabric of his clothing brushing her bare arm. Stopping momentarily, she looked up, murmured, "Good afternoon" (the way teachers had done when she was the listener), and went back to the story, flubbing an easy line, convinced now that it would never work, someone would find out, re- alize what was happening, Mrs. McConnell perhaps, or Father Reilly, and that would be the end for him, the end of the contentment, the end of everything.

When she left the building at five-thirty, she ran into the tall dark-haired boy who had been shooting bas- kets the week before, and he grinned at her lewdly as if he already knew.

On the way home, she considered the choice of a doctor. She had been directed to one the year before when a case of flu gave her pneumonia jitters. The flu had been cured and she had kept his number, but grudgingly. As a pill dispenser he seemed perfectly ad- equate, but beyond that he had struck her as unima- ginative, uninteresting, and uncommunicative.

Her friend Marilyn had fared better, medically speaking. (Have fun, Miss Klein—at six minutes after midnight when she called to check on the efficacy of the pill she was about to test for the first time.) But calling Marilyn presented so many problems, required so many explanations.

When she got home, she dialed poor old unimaginative Dr. Fischer. It took a little pleading but she finally got the last appointment on Friday.

She had promised to make a steak for him on Tuesday, pink, juicy and thick. He would meet her at the apartment at four. That gave her exactly an hour from the end of school.

Moving rapidly after the last child left, she assembled her coat, boots, and bag. She sat down on her chair in the empty room and pulled on the first boot. Once, in Brooklyn, a mother had come into her room after school and asked if she was Alexander's teacher. No, she had wanted to say, I'm Ruth Gold, wondering how long it had taken the woman in the doorway to become accustomed to being Alexander's mother. Here we are, she had thought that day, two strangers, united by Alexander.

Today she had a different visitor. Standing in the doorway was Frank Giraldi, the assistant principal, just what she needed on Tuesday at three o'clock. She gave him a nod reflecting only the commonest courtesy, more, probably, than he deserved. His visits were never short, never casual, never impromptu, but they were planned to appear that way.

"How are you, Ruth?" he said, coming in, giving her the warm, friendly treatment he reserved for days when he felt neither warm nor friendly.

"Fine, Mr. Giraldi. Nice to see you." You son of a bitch. His visits were strategically timed. He had a propensity for dropping in on people when they were late for dentist appointments, second jobs, trysts.

They played verbal volleyball for a few minutes. She was almost sure he glanced at his watch to see how much time had elapsed before he moved on to the topic.

"How are your reading sessions with Ellen Pascal coming along, Ruth?"

"Just fine," she said, getting her first clue.

"I understand you've switched her from after school to before school."

It took her by surprise. "Yes. I wrote a note to her mother asking if she would mind."

"Mrs. Pascal phoned this afternoon, Ruth." He had the unnerving habit of addressing people by name at almost every comma. "She seems to feel the other arrangement was more convenient."

Screw her. "Oh?"

"Yes. You know, it's hard to get these youngsters out so early in the morning and sometimes a mother appreciates that little bit of extra time in the afternoon."

"My schedule has changed," she said flatly, immovably.

"Ah."

Don't "ah" me, you son of a bitch. I have somewhere to go. Let me out of here.

The pause lengthened. She started pulling on the second boot.

"It's nice to accommodate the parents whenever possible, Ruth," he said, smiling.

"It's not possible." She zipped the boot. "I'm sorry."

"You know," he said, frowning, "the school budget

comes up for a vote soon. When the parents have a friendly feeling toward the school, it tends to make them think positively at the polls."

That's right, Frank. When the budget goes down, you can always blame the defeat on Ruth Gold.

"I'm doing some volunteer work after school. Church volunteer work."

"Ah, the church."

"Yes."

"Every day?"

"Several days a week."

"Ah."

She put her coat on. He started to walk along the side of the classroom, slowly, looking at the displays— the two-line poems her second-graders had written, their attempts at art, the arithmetic papers, the winter mural they had finished before Christmas.

He turned to her from the back of the room. "Very creative," he said. "I like to see creative work." His vocabulary reflected current trends in education. She tried to remember whether "creative" was an in word this year or if he was putting her down.

"Thank you," she said, to be on the safe side.

"I'm not keeping you, am I, Ruth?"

"I have an appointment," she said, glancing at the big round clock on the wall.

"I see," he said sympathetically. "Tell me, what church are you working at?"

Son of a bitch. He didn't believe her. "It's across town," she said vaguely. "You wouldn't know it."

She drove to the butcher's in a quiet fury, thoughts of assassination mingling with possibilities of transferring to another school, even another school system—

cleaner air, maybe even more money. Except that there was something else to consider now. There was Jim.

She got to the butcher's in record time but couldn't park. The afternoon had become an obstacle course. She drove around the block, missed a spot by a fraction of a minute, and swore. She double-parked and ran in.

"I'm in a rush, Tony," she said. "I need a steak, two inches thick, and no questions."

"Aha!" The butcher wielded a cleaver triumphantly. "You're in love. Who is he?"

"I said no questions. Just cut."

"One question," he said, "and I give you half an inch on the house. Why Tuesday?"

"It's his—it's convenient, that's all."

"You don't think—" the butcher put the cleaver down and came nearer the counter, conspiratorially—"you don't think there's someone else on the weekend, do you?"

She laughed. "You're worse than my mother, Tony, but you're a doll for worrying. No, he doesn't have a wife and six children. Tuesday is just a good day of the week."

He was sitting at the wheel of his car, reading from a black book that looked like a worn old Bible. When he saw her, he closed it, left it on the seat of the car, and they went upstairs. She put the key in the lock and he shut the door behind them, firmly, shutting out Giraldi and his pointless conversations. Their coats lay on chairs and the steak, two inches thick, came slowly to room temperature as they lay on the bed, under the canopy, set apart.

He brought brandy to her and they drank it, digestif

and aperitif all in one. She would learn to live backwards, drink her brandy, take a shower, begin to make dinner with her hair still wet.

"There was a boy at Church," she said. "I saw him last Monday and again yesterday. He plays basketball and has black hair and gives me a creepy feeling."

"Very tall, very thin, chews gum?"

"Yes."

"Did he say anything to you?"

"Nothing worth remembering."

"His name is Angelo," Jim said. He went to the table where his things lay and made a note in his small book. "Sometimes I dream about Angelo. They're not very happy dreams."

"What do you do with the little book when it's all used up?"

"I tear the pages out one by one as I use them. What's left gets tossed out. I suppose you would keep yours forever."

"I suppose I would."

He had brought a record with him, Gregorian chant, and he played it after dinner. They shared the *Times* and listened to the music.

Are you Alexander's teacher?

No, I'm Ruth Gold.

"What would you be doing if you weren't a priest?"

He looked up from the paper. "I don't know. What would you be doing if you weren't teaching?"

"I'd be studying something. Maybe I'd be in Europe. Maybe I'd sit in a library and just read every day until it got dark." She thought about it with a touch of wistfulness. "You didn't answer my question."

"I'd live in a small town somewhere, maybe in Maine, and I'd be a volunteer fireman."

"Why a fireman?"

"They're the only people in the world that never disappoint you."

Who are you?

I'm the wife of a volunteer fireman.

Don't kid yourself, Ruthie.

"Why Maine?"

"My brother lives there, my oldest brother. I like it and I'd like to live near him."

Who are you?

I'm Alexander's teacher, damn it.

How about the rest of the day?

The record had ended. He took it off, slipped it into its jacket, and put it among her records.

"I don't see your Bible here," he said.

"How do you know I have one?"

"Something I heard you say, a long time back."

"We've only known each other a few days."

"I suppose you're right. Have you read the Book of Ruth?"

"A long time ago. I don't remember the story any more, just the famous quotation, 'Whither' something."

"Read it again. It has other good lines."

"I'll look for it," she said. "It's put away somewhere."

When he was ready to go, she reminded him about the record.

"Do you mind if I leave it?"

"No. I was afraid you'd forgotten it."

"It sounds good here. I like this place." He looked around the apartment. "Everything sounds good here."

"Do you say a mass on Sunday?" she asked.

"I say a mass every day."

"I'd like to come to one."

"Don't," he said. It sounded like an order.

"Why not?"

"Because——" He pressed his lips together. "Very simply, you don't belong there."

You know who you are. Tell me.

I am Abraham Gold's granddaughter.

Tell him.

Wednesday was the night she came home very late and very tired but she never doubted whether it was worth it. On this Wednesday, the phone rang before she had her coat off.

"Where were you?" he asked. "I was worried about you."

"I was teaching. I teach on Wednesday nights."

"Not second grade?"

"No, older people, elderly. It's a special program. We're supposed to be making them better citizens, but most of them could teach the course themselves."

"You amaze me. What don't you do?"

"Oh, God," she said, shrugging out of her coat. "It would take me all night."

"Well, talk until my dime is finished."

They talked and they talked. She went to school happy, avoided Frank Giraldi, spent Thursday afternoon at the church with Mrs. McConnell and went home happy. She played his record and fiddled with the extra key she had had made on Saturday.

Friday after school, somewhat reluctantly, she went to visit Teresa before her doctor's appointment. Driving along the now familiar route across Cambridge, she remembered the day she and Pete had first made the trip, taking Anthony home after his week with her following camp.

The woman who had opened the door that Labor Day was young, slight, pretty (if pale and tired-looking), and she hated Ruth Gold. She had nodded to her adult guests and hugged her son.

"Were you a good boy?" was the first thing she said to him, as if challenging him to account for two months of behavior in two minutes.

"Yes, I was good. I had a milkshake for lunch."

"I hope you had something with vitamins too." She stood back and looked at him. "Where did you get those clothes? Those aren't your clothes, Anthony."

"Yes, they are. Ruth got them for me. We took a train."

The woman looked up at her company who were still standing, unwelcomed and unwelcome, near the door. "He didn't need new clothes," she said, more hurt than angry. "I would've bought him clothes. I was going to take him Saturday for new things."

"His summer things were a little worn from camp," Ruth said gently, cautiously accepting the unexpected challenge. "We happened to be in a store."

"Anthony's reading very well now," Pete put in quickly, trying a safer topic. "I think he'll be at the top of his class this year."

The woman remained sullen. "Did you take him to church?" she asked.

"Yes, we went to the ten o'clock mass." The statement had an authentic ring.

"I gave a dollar," Anthony said.

"A dollar? Where'd you get a dollar?"

"Ruth gave it to me."

"Is there anything we can do?" Ruth asked. "I understand you just got home from the hospital this morning."

The woman sat down. "My neighbor got me some things. Thanks. It's nice of you to ask."

"Shall we go?" Pete said.

She dug into her bag and found an old envelope and a pen. "Here's my name and phone number," she said, handing the woman the envelope. "I don't live far from here." There was no way of evoking a smile. "Goodbye, Anthony. I'll see you again soon." But it was only a wish. They had turned and left.

She had agonized most of the way home.

"Calm down," Pete said finally. "Let's talk about something neutral."

"Tell me something about your clergyman friend."

"What do you want to know?"

She raised her eyebrows and turned to look at him. "Is he circumcised?"

"Oh, Christ, Ruthie, sometimes I—"

"Is he?"

"Yes, damn it. What difference does it make?"

"What does it look like when you're not?"

"Where do you get these questions from?"

"I was just curious. I never saw anyone who wasn't. Pete, that was a red light. Tell me what it looks like, will you?"

"I'll give you a key to the men's faculty room and you can find out for yourself."

"It's no good," she said sadly. "I'm afraid they're all too young."

The following Sunday, over brunch, she had told Cassie about the fiasco at Anthony's house.

"Call her again," Cassie said. "She hadn't seen her son for two months, she'd been in the hospital. Maybe it was a little too much for her."

It confirmed her own feelings. At two o'clock she dialed the number. The woman answered.

"This is Ruth Gold—Anthony stayed with me last week. I wondered—how are you feeling?"

"I'm much better now."

"That's good. How's Anthony?"

"He's fine."

"I'm glad to hear it. I—uh—I thought, if you were free this afternoon, I might drop by for a few minutes and say hello."

"Yeah, that would be OK." The woman paused. "That's real nice of you. Anthony's been talking about you all week."

She went empty-handed, feeling it would be better that way. The woman had made coffee and they walked into the kitchen together. The table and chairs were at one end of the kitchen which had been arranged to look like a small dining room. Against the wall was a cupboard where the dishes were kept. On top of the cupboard were religious statues—the Virgin Mary, Jesus, assorted saints. On the wall was a framed color picture of the Pope, flanked by two smaller pictures of Anthony that had probably been taken by a school photographer.

"It's nice of you to come, Miss Gold," Anthony's mother had said formally, pouring the coffee. There was a plate of cookies on the table and she pushed them toward her guest.

"Ruth. My name is Ruth."

The woman relaxed a little. "Mine's Teresa."

"Hi, Teresa."

Teresa smiled. "I'm sorry I yelled about the clothes," she said, looking down at the table.

"It was my fault. I really didn't think."

"No, you were right. The things in that suitcase were awful. I guess I didn't figure right for two months. It was the first time he was ever away from me. I was in the hospital, you know, or I wouldn't've sent him for so long."

"How are you feeling now?"

"Much better. I guess they got it in time."

There was a pounding up the stairs and Anthony ran in. "Hey, Ruth. I didn't know you were coming."

"If you'd stay home a little more," Teresa said.

"Can I have a milkshake?"

"Ask your mother." It was probably the sentence that endeared her to Teresa more than anything else she ever said.

"Well," Teresa said, looking into pleading brown eyes, "I guess it's almost a week since his last one. A milkshake a week won't spoil him too much."

She took them for a milkshake and on subsequent weekends she took them other places, always calling first, never bringing anything, watching Teresa's health improve, listening to her talk, reticently at first, then with greater candor as the weeks went by. Perhaps she had been looking for someone to trust, another woman, a kindred spirit.

Once she had invited Ruth into her bedroom to show her her wedding gown. It was a flashy white satin dress scattered with sequins. Teresa's face was a mixture of pride and pleasure as she held it up in its heavy plastic covering.

"It's beautiful, Teresa." The lie came smoothly and glibly. She sounded like one of the girls in Brooklyn, but it was what Teresa wanted to hear.

"You can wear it if you want. I know a lot of girls who wore borrowed dresses."

"That's very nice of you. If I find the right man, I'll let you know."

"You'll find him. You go out all the time. One of these days, it'll be the right one."

"You sound like my mother, Teresa, an incurable optimist."

Through September and October she had gone to visit Teresa and Anthony almost every Sunday. Teresa's health improved slowly; she put on a little weight, she talked more about herself. She had been raised by foster parents, a couple already in middle age when she had come to them. They had died in the last few years and she had no family—except for Anthony, of course, and her husband.

By the beginning of November, something had changed. She had gone to see Teresa, prepared to take them for a drive. (Anthony loved riding in the car. The destination was of no consequence; all he wanted was to move.)

"Let's stay home today," Teresa had said a little petulantly. "I don't feel like going anywhere." The statement and the mood were out of place. Teresa was almost always agreeable, accepting with a quiet placidity what was offered.

"Why not? I thought we decided—"

"Well I changed my mind. I don't feel good enough to go out."

She felt a chill at the back of her neck. "What do you mean?"

"I'm a little tired."

"Do you see a doctor, Teresa?" She asked the question quietly.

"Yeah, I see a doctor. I go to church too."

"When do you see the doctor?" she asked impatiently. "When was the last time you went?"

"A couple of weeks ago. Maybe three."

"Do you have medicine to take?"

"Yeah. It's in the bathroom."

"Do you take it?"

"Sure I take it. What's going on? I didn't commit no crime. I just said I was tired."

But when they look at each other, it was clear that they both knew.

The visits had become more painful after that but she had kept them up through the remainder of the year and into January, despite the apprehension, despite the momentary flutter of dread each time she knocked on the door. But today, even that was diminished. After today's visit, she was going to see Dr. Fischer about the pill.

She sat in the kitchen with Teresa, drinking coffee and trying to sound very casual. "I saw Father Kendall last week."

"Oh yeah?" Teresa perked up. "I knew him when we lived in the old apartment. He's nice, isn't he?"

"Yes. Pete and I knew him from camp."

"I used to see him all the time," Teresa said. "I used

to watch the kids a couple of times a week in that group he runs after school—before I got sick, I mean. He always needed somebody, you know? And I could keep Anthony with me."

"I didn't know you did that, Teresa."

"Yeah, a few months last year when I was still feeling good. I used to like going there and he needed the help. I don't think they wanted him to do it."

"Who's 'they'?"

"I don't know—the church, the people at the church," Teresa said vaguely.

"Why didn't they want him to do it?"

"Well, Father Kendall wanted to pay someone to come in every day but they said there wasn't any money for it. That's what I heard, anyway. But you know, when they need it, they find the money."

"It's the same everywhere, Teresa."

"I guess so. But you'd think they'd let him have it when it's for something like that. He got a job for a friend of mine once when her husband got sick, you know that?"

"That's very nice of him."

"Yeah. They need more like him. Nowadays, the priests, they find themselves a woman, they leave the church. It's terrible what they do now."

"Yes, I've read about it." She looked at the Pope, who had probably also read about it, but he kept his opinions of the matter to himself.

"You know, Father Kendall was the one who got me to send Anthony to camp."

"What do you mean, 'got you'? Didn't you want to?"

"Well, to tell the truth—" Teresa seemed uncertain, even embarrassed—"I was against it at the beginning. I thought if he went anyplace he should go to a Catholic camp. You know me," she said apologetically. "I never knew anybody except my own."

"I'm glad you changed your mind, Teresa. He had a wonderful time at camp."

"Yeah. It was Father Kendall changed my mind. He said they'd get Anthony to church every Sunday—"

"They did."

"I know. Anthony told me. And he thought it would be good for Anthony to meet the other kids and play and everything. He even wrote the letter for Anthony to go. I never went to camp myself, you know. I never even knew anybody that went." She said it without sadness; it was a fact of her life.

"Teresa, I've never asked you . . ." She paused, changing the topic. "About your husband."

"There's not much to tell."

"Do you hear from him?"

"Oh, yeah, I hear from him. He sent me a check before Christmas."

"Where is he?"

"In New York somewhere. He says the work is better there. I don't know." She began to look tired. "Maybe he's living with some girl. I don't think I care any more. I did a couple of years ago, but I kinda got used to it. Living without him, I mean."

"When did you see him last?" she asked gently.

"In July, after my operation. He came up and stayed a couple of weeks." Her voice had grown softer with the remembering. "It was a good time to come. Anthony was in camp and I was in the hospital. No chance for trouble, you know?"

"Does he make trouble?"

"Oh, no," Teresa said hastily. "You want some more coffee? I got more in the pot."

"Sure. I'll get it."

"Sit down. You're my guest." She got the coffee, divided what was left between them, put the pot in the sink and sat down again, heavily for her weight and slender frame, on the wooden chair. "Yeah," she said, nodding her head, "he makes trouble. It's not really his fault, see? We were young when we got married. He didn't know how to be a father. He thought, if he said 'Shut up,' that was it. Anthony would shut up. You can't do that, you know?"

"I know."

"So Joe, he—Joe, that's my husband—he gets a little excited when Anthony doesn't do like he tells him. You know what I mean, he—"

"You don't have to tell me if you don't want to," she interrupted. "It's not my business, you know."

"Listen, Ruth, I think maybe I should tell you. Because if I get sick again, if I have to go back again—you know, I got no family—I couldn't leave Joe alone with Anthony. You know what I mean? I would be afraid of what he might do."

"Teresa, why don't you put your phone back in?"

"I don't need a phone," she said with annoyance. "My neighbor's got your number. But you could watch him for me, couldn't you? Like you did in September?"

"Of course I could. Don't worry about it."

"You're lucky you didn't marry young. There's a lot of misery when you marry young."

"I avoided it just by growing older."

"Yeah. It sounds easy when you say it like that. I had no family, you know. It's different when you got no family. If I'd of waited—but, you know, I got Anthony out of it, so you can't say it was all bad." She picked up the coffee cups and rinsed them in the sink, talking over the sound of the water. "If I'd of waited," she continued, raising her voice slightly, "it would've been one guy after another. This way, it was only Joe, the first and the last." She shut off the water and came back to the table. "You know," she said with a smile, "I was thinking about you over Christmas. I was hoping maybe that guy Pete you brought here once would ask you to marry him."

"I'm afraid I'm not interested."

"I'll never understand it. A good-looking guy who really goes for you. Education. Everything. And you're not interested."

"It's a funny world, Teresa."

Teresa shook her head. "I wish it was," she said, looking across the table. "But it isn't. It's a sad world."

On the way to the doctor's office, she prepared herself for the unpleasantness to come. She was full of recriminations. She should have sought out a more sympathetic doctor. She should have gotten the pill four years ago.

Dr. Fischer greeted her with a professional smile and a "Well, it's Miss Gold, isn't it?" as if he really remembered her, but she knew he had cribbed from the folder on his desk. "And how are you today?" he asked with the voice and manner he had learned in Doctor-Patient Relationships I thirty years before in medical school.

"Just fine," she said, responding in the same style.

"Well, then." He had come to the end of his script.

She stated her case simply. "I want the pill."

He pursed his lips, nodded, and made a notation on her chart. Ruth Gold, she thought, age almost twenty-six wants the pill. Well, what had she expected, to be clapped on the back and welcomed to the crowd?

He opened the door and spoke to the nurse. She caught the word "pelvic." Oh, Christ, he wasn't going to give her an internal, was he? Look, Dr. Fischer, you don't understand. I said *pill*. For the *mouth*.

The doctor walked out of the room and the nurse walked in, gray-haired, with fingernails cut to the quick, and she followed the instructions she had followed on other occasions and finally she was lying down, a sheet covering the front of her so that she could see nothing and he could see everything—such strange ideas of modesty the medical profession had—and the doctor returned and put on a single plastic glove and squeezed a tube of K-Y Jelly and she felt herself tense up from her neck to her toes.

"Come on, now. Just relax," the doctor said mechanically and she closed her eyes—there wasn't anything to see anyway except her sheet-covered knees—and insanely, she thought of the doctor's wife, his poor wife who must have suffered through a hundred tubes of K-Y Jelly and, thinking of it, she giggled and relaxed and the doctor went to work.

But that wasn't enough. No, this time he was going to shove pieces of metal inside her, expandable structural steel, to enlarge that small opening—well, it had been small before today—and spotlight what was inside.

And all this to make love, all so that she and Jim

could make love when they wanted to, without excusing herself to squeeze out a teaspoonful of jelly with trembling fingers in the bathroom while he lost his desire in the living room. What an ignominious experience to have to go through to enjoy one's lovemaking.

The doctor was finished now, the light off, the metal removed. With a curt "Get dressed," he walked out of the examining room. She struggled to a sitting position; the nurse helped her down from the table, and she dressed herself and walked stiffly to the outer office where the doctor was completing the latest grim chapter in Ruth Gold's Medical History. She sat down in the chair reserved for patients and listened while he explained when and how and in what circumstances and be on the lookout for and don't hesitate to call. Then he stopped and she waited and he stood up and she knew she was being dismissed. She took the prescription, looked at him, and said, finally, as acidly as she knew how, "Didn't you forget something?"

The doctor frowned and looked at her without understanding. Doctor-Patient Relationships I had been given before Ruth Gold and the pill had been born.

"Forget it," she said. "It was just my imagination."

Stiffly she walked to her car and drove home. Dr. Fischer had forgotten to say, "Have fun."

She filled the prescription and put it away. They fell into a pattern. Tuesday was Jim's day. Steak for dinner. During the week some phone calls, maybe a late visit. Never on Saturday, never on Sunday. He was on call those evenings; someone in the parish might need a priest and Jim would have to go, her Jim.

But I need Jim all the time,
Too damn bad. He belongs to the church.
He belongs to me.
Who the hell are you?
I am Abraham Gold's granddaughter and he belongs to me.

Her birthday was the Eve of St. Agnes, immortalized in verse by Keats. On this particular birthday, Jim was coming to dinner, bringing with him a poetic feast of sandwiches at nine in the evening and she spent the day being happy (i.e., avoiding Frank Giraldi).

Pete called around six to wish her a happy one and ask her out to celebrate on Saturday. She had never been good at lying so she accepted. There were cards from her parents, her friends and, believe it or not, from Frank Giraldi. Son of a bitch.

Jim came with the sandwiches, which she expected, and with a present, which she did not. It was a volume of Keats (with the ribbon marking "The Eve of St. Agnes") and he had written in it: "For Ruth, on the Eve of St. Agnes, 1972. Jim." It had been written in black with a narrow felt-tipped pen.

"I have something for you, too," she said, going to her dresser, still holding the inscribed book.

"Please don't give me anything. It's your birthday, not mine."

"When you come to a birthday party, you always leave with a favor. Mother said never to spend more than ten cents apiece for the favors but I never listen to Mother. I spent a quarter." She held up the key.

He looked at it so long that she was afraid he might not take it. Then he pulled his keys out of his pocket, the great bunch of keys that meant he would make love to her, make her live again, make her die a little. He opened the chain and put her key on it, next to a small gold cross that hung among the keys. The cross gave her a slight shock. She had accepted the priest; it was harder, somehow, to accept the Catholic.

"That was very nice of you," he said finally, softly, looking at the keys in his hand. He laid them on the table and she felt something move inside her, responding. I am Pavlov's dog, she thought irreverently. I respond to his keys.

He walked away from her, hands in his pockets, and stood looking out the window. "This can't go on forever, you know," he said, and she felt her throat tighten.

"I know."

"I wish I could move in here, just stay with you for a while. Maybe then I could . . ."

"Could what?"

"Nothing. I couldn't anyway," he said cryptically, leaving it forever in doubt—the moving in or the other thing. He walked back slowly and put his arm around her. "I want to make love to you," he said, almost apologetically. "You must think sometimes that that's all I want from you. I didn't mean to make you sad tonight."

They undressed each other by the side of the bed, the sensuous ritual that had become half the pleasure, half the excitement. It was always this way, like the first time, the urgency, the immediacy of going through it all again, this insane thing that they did in the bed, under the canopy where no one could see them—even God couldn't see them under the canopy—over and over, this link they had with eternity. Some day, she thought, some day we will both explode right here, feet on the ground, outside the canopy where God can see us.

"Get in bed," he said, not letting her move.

They lay down and he threw the covers off.

"Talk to me," he said, the urgency carrying them both along now. "Tell me how you want it. Tell me when you want to come. Talk to me this time."

"Now," she said. "Now. Don't fool around tonight. Make it now."

"Talk to me," he said urgently. "Say something, say my name." His sweat was touching her, covering her, drenching her.

Jimmy, she thought for the first time, Jimmy, but she said something else, a brief syllable lost in the roar, echoed afterwards in the silence. A few minutes later, he was asleep, his head on her, his arms flung out. It was a new twist to an old legend. It was she who should be dreaming now, dreaming of her intended. He had never slept before, never relaxed so completely.

He awoke with a start, half an hour later, his body suddenly stiff with panic, his voice tight. "The time," he said, sitting up. "What time is it?"

"It's all right, darling. It's only ten. I was awake."

He was breathing rapidly as in the aftermath of a shock. Rubbing his cheek nervously, he stood up. "I need a drink." He brought brandy back and drank his quickly.

"We'll set the alarm next time, Jim."

"I should think of things like that myself." He walked away from the bed, without direction. "What did you dream?" he asked, trying for a casual tone.

The legend came back, the prophetic dream on the Eve of St. Agnes. "I didn't sleep. Did you dream?"

"Yes, I still dream," he said, as if she thought he would have stopped by now, having outgrown dreams.

"What did you dream?"

"The same. A variation on the usual theme."

"Pete called," she said, moving away from the realm of dreams. "He wants to take me to dinner Saturday for my birthday."

"That's nice. At least you'll have a chance to see the outside world. I'm afraid you won't see much of it with me."

She said nothing.

He turned toward her. "You didn't expect a jealous rage, did you? You won't get one from me, you know. Enjoy yourself."

"Yes, I'll try." She was disappointed, disappointed she was going out with Pete, disappointed in his reaction. "Tell me something," she said, stretching out. "Do priests confess?"

"Priests are Catholics. They confess the way other Catholics confess."

"Who do they confess to?"

"Other priests."

"Do you confess?"

He watched her from the window for a long moment. "Yes."

"Have you confessed—" she paused, searching—"this?"

"Confessions are private matters. That's one very important feature of the confession." There was an edge to his voice.

"I see."

He went to where he had dropped his clothes and started dressing, as if covering his physical nakedness would somehow cover the other. She watched him as he moved, saying nothing. He walked over to the table, picked up the keys, and put them down again.

"I haven't confessed this," he said, turning to look at her. "I haven't confessed anything for a long time."

"Are you going to? Can you be forgiven, Jim? Can you find a priest who'll forgive you?"

"It depends more on me than on my confessor. It depends largely on how I feel about what's happened."

"Meaning?"

"Meaning that if I say—that is, if I'm truly sorry, I can be forgiven."

Unexplainably, something stung her eyes. "I won't be sorry," she said from the bed. "I'll never be sorry."

He came around to her side of the bed and sat down. "I know you won't. Maybe we could stop talking about it tonight. Maybe we don't have to talk about it at all."

The stinging had not gone away. "I don't close doors behind me and forget."

He walked away. "Do you think I do?"

"I don't know. I don't know enough about you. I think you could."

He walked over to the bookcase and looked across the shelves.

"I don't see your Bible here," he said. "I thought you would have found it by now."

"I haven't even looked."

"I see."

"Why are you a priest?" she asked.

He looked at her across the room. "Do you mean why I am one or why I became one?" he said evenly.

"Oh, damn, you know what I mean, why you became one."

"It doesn't matter.'"

"Do you mean it's not relevant?"

"I mean it doesn't matter. It doesn't affect you. You ask because you're curious. I wouldn't tell you just to satisfy your curiosity. I'll answer the other half of the question."

"You don't have to," she said. "I already know that answer."

"I suppose you do."

"I want to go to a mass, Jim." Pile it on all at once, Ruthie.

He shook his head. "I told you how I felt about that."

"I feel old tonight, Jim," she said mournfully.

He came back, the tension finally gone from his face. "Are there any other raw nerves we can irritate before we eat?" he asked.

"Oh, Christ, we haven't eaten yet." She got out of bed and took her robe out of the closet.

"Thanks for the key, darling," he said.

When she came home on Tuesday, he was waiting for her in the apartment. He had come early, let himself in with the key, and napped on the bed. She was pleased at the gesture. In giving him the key, she had offered up a piece of her privacy and he had accepted the offer. He had brought another record with him and when he left, he left the record.

Wednesday at six he telephoned. He would come over for a little while later tonight. When she came home from teaching her evening class, he would be waiting for her.

She tried to finish the class on time but failed as usual. Her students were full of questions again, about law, insurance, taxes, and medicine, all the things they believed she was expert in.

From the street, she looked up to her third-floor windows. The apartment was dark. Disappointed, she went up, turned on the lights, and waited. By eleven-fifteen she was starting to worry. A guy from the New Year's Day party at Cassie's place called. He had been calling all evening. She got rid of him. By twelve she was near panic. She sat at the phone, close to tears. How do you call the police and report that Father James Kendall has not shown up at your apartment? Are you kidding, lady? Father Kendall?

She tried to tell herself that nothing had happened. It was ridiculous to think he had been in an accident merely because he was late. She was, after all, only a small part of his life. He had other responsibilities, twenty-four hours of them. Someone had just called him at the church and he had gone to see a parishioner somewhere, to a home, perhaps, or to the hospital.

Her argument was reasonable enough, but the sick feeling inside her persisted. She knew something had happened, something terrible.

At twelve-thirty she showered, leaving the bathroom

door open, turning off the water at intervals to see if the phone was ringing. She went to bed finally, leaving one light on, just in case he drove by. It was two before she fell asleep.

When the phone rang, she was so disoriented, she reached toward Jim's side of the bed to answer it. She finally got it on the third ring. She might have known; it was Pete. How are you? How are things? What's doing with Frank Giraldi? Has he given you any more trouble?

It was hours before she fell asleep again, and almost immediately the alarm went off. She got up, sick with fear and exhaustion. Her mouth tasted terrible. The toast ended up in the garbage. There was no way to find out before three-fifteen. She could ask Mrs. McConnell where he was, tell her there was a message for him. During the day she would dream up the details.

While she was smoothing out the bed, the telephone rang.

"Hi," he said. "I'm glad I caught you. I'm sorry about last night. Something came up."

"Sorry?" she said, sitting down to ease the trembling. "You're sorry?"

There was a short silence. "It didn't occur to me you would be so upset."

"It didn't occur to you?" She was crying now, relief and anger mixed together, sitting like an idiot, alone in her apartment, her tears falling on the receiver. "I was worried sick."

"I'm really sorry," he said. "Please. I had no idea. Look, I'll see you later. I'll call you tonight."

They had a fire drill before the end of school so she

got to the church early. She went inside the empty
sanctuary and walked around, touching the worn pews,
seeing everything in a new way. This was Jim's church.
Scattered along the walls were the confessionals. She
walked over to the one nearest her. A brass plate next
to the door said: Rev. John F. Reilly. She walked to
the next one: Rev. James M. Kendall. She touched the
plate, left a fingerprint. She took out a Kleenex and
wiped it, put the Kleenex in her pocket with the other
junk.

"Hi. What are you doing here?" The voice hushed.

She turned around, startled, embarrassed at being
found out. It was the Rev. James M. Kendall.

"I was a little early. I just came in to—to be by myself." She matched his tone.

"I'm sorry about last night," he said, keeping a respectable distance between them. It was his church and
he would never touch her here, not if she died wanting
him. "It never occurred to me that anyone would worry
about me."

"I worried."

"I know." He reached into an inside pocket in his
coat, took out the little book and a pen, and wrote
something in it. "If you ever need me," he said, tearing
out the page, "you can get me at this number. I won't
let that happen again. I'll call you even if it's the middle of the night." He handed her the paper. She took it,
taking care to touch his fingers.

She left him standing there and went down to the
basement.

She pushed herself through the next two hours, left
at five-thirty, had a light supper and fell into an exhausted sleep. In the morning, she had her period. She

took a piece of plain paper and a marking pen and lettered the words: TAKE A PILL TODAY and taped it to the lower left-hand corner of the bathroom mirror. Then she took the diaphragm out of its neat little kit, and dropped it in this morning's garbage. An era had ended.

Tuesday was the first of February, and when she got home, Jim was there. He had seen the note in the bathroom.

"Explain it," he said.

"I started the pill this morning."

"Just like that? On your own initiative?"

"Just like that."

He shook his head. "Tell me something." He picked up a pack of small papers on the coffee table. "What in the name of all that is good and holy are these?"

God, what a slob she was. She had emptied her coat pockets finally last night (for the first time since before Christmas) and put the junk on the coffee table to be thrown out—dirty Kleenexes (breeding God knew what), receipts for small purchases, green stamps and receipts from every toll booth between Brooklyn and Cambridge.

"They're toll booth receipts. I ask for them as an excuse for stopping."

"What do you need an excuse for? Why do you stop?"

"To talk to them. It's such a lonely job now that they have exact change booths. They have no one to talk to except a few salesmen padding their expense accounts."

He shook his head again. "You're too much. Toll collectors and the pill."

She was happy. That morning she had made a tentative, shaky peace with Frank Giraldi.

And she and Jim had made it to February.

3 ∿∿∿∿∿∿∿∿∿∿∿∿∿∿∿∿∿

In a weak or charitable moment she had told Frank
Giraldi that she would compromise. Ellen could stay
after school on Wednesdays and could come on any
other morning or mornings her mother chose. It
seemed like a fair arrangement but Giraldi was disappointed. He read half a success as half a failure but he
had the sense to know when to accept a bargain. He
said he would call Mrs. Pascal and try to get things
going again. Since the second week in January, she had
seen Ellen only once a week, on Wednesday afternoons, Mrs. Pascal refusing to send her child early in
the morning and almost insisting, through Giraldi, that
Miss Gold remain after school, indefinitely if need be,
to bring Ellen up to par.

Saturday night Jim got a reprieve. Someone covered
for him and he was free. They talked about Angelo.
There had been a car-stealing incident last fall, he told
her (making light of it in a way he had when he talked
about other people's failings), and an arrangement with
the court. Angelo would work out, he was basically a
nice kid, he said. All he needed was some attention and
a little encouragement.

He preferred to talk about the kids in the basement.
The trick there had been to get it going. Once in motion, it was a hard project to kill.

Who would want to kill it? she asked.

He shrugged off the question. He would place no

blame. Anyway, it was something that need not concern her.

She expected to sleep until noon on Sunday but some demon got in the way and she found herself hopelessly awake at eight. She knew almost immediately that this was the day she would go to a mass. There was no reason for him ever to know she had been there. She would get there just at nine, sit in the back, and slip out quickly at the end. During the hour she was there, she would discover that part of him he kept to himself.

She parked a few blocks away and arrived at the church a couple of minutes late together with a handful of other latecomers. She walked in with them, glanced around rapidly, picked a seat in the second-last row. As she sat down, a man approached and stood in the aisle next to her, waiting for her to slide farther down the row. There was no choice. She moved over, hemmed in for as long as he sat in the seat beside her.

They were singing a hymn as she came in, a hymn with a catchy tune and an accompaniment of guitars. It was the folk mass she had seen posted outside the entrance to the church. She settled back to listen to the music. She had expected to hear an organ, heavy and overpowering. The lightness of the guitars was an unexpectedly welcome pleasure.

The boy who opened the service looked familiar. She had seen him around once or twice in the afternoon when she came to the church. Jim was sitting behind him on a bench with another teen-aged boy. Looking at him down the length of the entire church, she began to feel uneasy. He had a long green robe on, making him look heavier, less like himself. She had not expected a color; she had expected black. Maybe, she thought uneasily, maybe she shouldn't have come. The music was nice but maybe she shouldn't have come.

Next to her, the man on the aisle held in his hands a worn prayer book he had brought with him and he turned the pages without looking at them, as Jim spoke. (Abraham had read the Bible that way, looking off into the distance and reciting in Hebrew, turning a page from time to time but never looking down at the text.)

She had only been to one Sunday mass before, last September when Anthony was with her. The priest had been a white-haired, ruddy-faced Irishman with a thick New England accent, Boston's answer to the Southern drawl. He spoke with a kind of clerical boredom, a professional fatigue born of saying the same words in one language or another for almost forty years. Surely they had lost all meaning for him by now. Only the cadence was left, the rhythm of monotony.

But Jim spoke easily, conversationally, a familiar voice in an unfamiliar setting. It was the voice that had told her about Angelo last night. Look, Angelo is a special case, darling. Today he was saying a mass and the mass was a special case too.

It was impossible to leave now. She turned her head left and right, then settled in to accept her fate. She closed her eyes and listened to Jim's voice.

A gold goblet stood on the table in front of him. Someone at school had explained communion to her a long time ago but she had only half listened. Most of it was a mystery—the goblet, the words, the meaning.

He knelt quickly, touching one knee to the floor. Watching, she winced. Jim kneeling. Jesus Christ. There was no one Jim should kneel to.

Something about being free from sin when you took communion. She wondered if the man next to her was free from sin. Had he told a little lie this morning and was he truly sorry now? How forgiving would he be if he heard Jim's confession, if Jim were truly sorry?

A bell rang at the other end of the church and with it came a sharp image of the meaning of sin. She had never believed in sin, rarely even thought about it. But she saw it now, understood it with an ache and a sadness; sin was willfully invading someone else's privacy. And she had known it for years, since a day almost three years ago when she had sat on a plane from LaGuardia to Logan. He was in his early or mid-forties and had had a couple of drinks somewhere before boarding. She could never remember how the conversation had started but it had begun on the ground, waiting on the runway to be cleared for takeoff. His wife had died a year before, leaving him with two boys and half a life left to live without her. He had shaken his head, remembering.

And then one night he had returned a day early from a business trip to find his nineteen-year-old son in bed with some girl (some girl; they always think of it that way, don't they?) "and I looked at them for a minute lying there in my bed in a clinch and I had this tremendous feeling that now I understood the meaning of invasion of privacy. It was crazy, it was almost funny, looking at my son and this girl copulating on my bed and all I could think of was the meaning of some words. What a crazy thing to happen. Only, there was one thing I couldn't figure out; I didn't know whose privacy had been invaded." He paused and ran a hand through his hair. "I slept on that bed twenty-one years with my wife."

His voice had gone funny at that point and he had nervously reached into his pocket, pulled out a pack of cigarettes, lit one, and drawn deeply while she sat next to him wishing there were a right thing to say to make it all better, to erase the scene permanently.

"I think," he said, holding the cigarette—and his hand shook slightly—"I think I hated my son at that moment."

She turned to him, then, and touched him, the only man on the shuttle she had ever touched. "I'm sorry," she said.

"Will you have dinner with me when we land?" he asked and she said, yes, she would have dinner with him.

They ate in a restaurant outside the city and he was careful not to drink anything. Over coffee, he asked if she would come to his home; he had a house in Lexington. It was empty; the boys were away at school.

She smiled at his frankness and declined the invitation.

"I talked you out of it on the plane, didn't I?" he asked.

"No," she said honestly. "I talked myself out of it over dinner."

He took her home and never saw her again but the next day a florist brought her a dozen carnations and a note that said, "Thank you."

Two men were coming up the aisle now with baskets

at the end of rods. People were dropping money in, mostly bills. These people collected money at a service —how could she have forgotten? She opened her bag and looked inside. Her smallest bill was a five. In the change purse there was a dime and a nickel. She took out the five and dropped it in the basket when it slid past her, wishing she could run, wishing it were over. She would tell him some day that she had been here, ask him to forgive her, hope that he would understand. She hadn't meant to enter a private part of his life; she had only wanted to know him a little better, understand who he was because she loved him so damn much, because everything that affected him affected her too— everything, even this.

People were getting up now and walking to the front. The man on the aisle got up; perhaps this was the time to slip out. She looked around. No one was moving toward the doors; it would be too obvious. She would have to live out the rest of it.

Jim blessing them. The voice that had said her name last night, and the sound that had followed. She waited for him to leave, to walk to the little room at the side where the priests changed their clothes as the priest in the church last September had done. But he didn't. One of the boys took a large cross and he, the other boy, and Jim started up the aisle.

There was no exit, no escape. She knew before he had taken ten steps that he would see her. It was her punishment for having invaded his private world, or not having honored his one request.

Their eyes met and he fell momentarily out of step. She tried to interpret the look in his eyes. It had been surprise at first but something had replaced it. Anger?

Resignation? Annoyance? No, the look had been clear. It was sadness.

She ran out of the church, found her car, and drove home. Upstairs, she took the Keats down and looked at the inscription for a long time, his handwriting, his identity, his private world.

She had forgotten to get the Sunday paper but she knew she had to stay here now and wait for the inevitable.

It was eleven-fifteen when the phone rang. She let it ring five times before picking it up.

"Why did you do that?" he said.

"I'm sorry. Please, Jim, I'm sorry."

"I'll see you this afternoon."

She had wanted to go somewhere in the afternoon, get out and see somebody, do something, but she stayed home, waiting, feeling sick. He came at two, still angry, not quite in control. He stood near the door, his coat on, hands in his coat pockets. It had begun to snow and tiny melted snowflakes rested on his shoulders and in his hair, glistening as he stood at the entrance to her apartment. He looked so vulnerable there in front of the door, angry and vulnerable.

"What were you doing there?"

"I said I was sorry. I went on impulse. It was a mistake. I just made a mistake."

"I *told* you not to come." She had never really seen him angry before.

"Stop talking to me as if I were your child." She had never raised her voice to him before.

Such an incongruous situation, standing in this room where they had done nothing for a month but try to understand each other, and now they were looking at each other, this chasm between them. Surely he would take a step toward her in a moment and touch her; if he would only touch her, everything would be all right again.

"Look," he said, his voice softening, "there's no place for you in that part of my life."

How simple it sounded when he put it that way. Just compartmentalize your life, Jim. Solve all your problems. "Maybe there's no place for me in any part of your life." Her voice down to its normal register.

He was still looking at her, but oddly now, as if the notion had just struck him for the first time. He took his hands out of his pockets, pulled back the left cuff, looked at his watch. "I'll call you," he said, and left. But why? What had made him say that? Because it was the only way he knew to say goodbye?

On Monday afternoon she went to the church as usual after school. Tense, she waited for the door to open, waited to see him, to hear his voice talking to someone else across the room, to see the black shoes suddenly beside her where she sat on the floor.

Finally, at a quarter to five, she asked Mrs. McConnell.

"Oh, he's here somewhere," she said. "He's so busy, you know. I saw him about three, I think. He doesn't look very well at all today. I hope he's not coming down with flu. Two of mine had it last week. You don't look awfully well yourself, dear. Maybe you should go home and get some rest."

Sure, Mrs. McConnell. A couple of aspirins and a good night's sleep and life will be beautiful again.

She waited for his call that night, the Monday night call confirming the Tuesday afternoon date. It never came. On Tuesday, with growing apprehension, she stopped at the butcher's for steak.

"Two inches?" he asked.

"Make it two and a half, Tony."

"Aha! You're expecting a proposal."

"Quite the opposite. I'm apologizing."

"Apologizing? What'd you do? Look at another man?"

"No. I looked at him at the wrong time."

He shrugged. "When you're thirty," he said, "come back and explain it to me."

She took the steak and went home. The apartment was empty. She put the steak in the refrigerator and sat down with the *Times*. Four-thirty. She turned the lights on, put some records on. Six o'clock. She turned on the news. Six-thirty. Radio off. She picked up the telephone. Dial tone. Nothing wrong there. What the hell have I done? Why did I do it? How can he do this to me?

When do you give up? When do you put the steak in the freezer and just give up? Son of a bitch. I hate him.

You love him.

What the hell is the difference?

At eight o'clock the steak went into the freezer. She drank some tomato juice, took a shower, picked up a book, threw it on the floor, tried in vain to keep the tears away. When they came, it was a torrent, a downpour, a thunderstorm. It was neither love nor hate; it was loss, bereavement, absolute finality.

The prophecy of those first few moments after their lovemaking that first night in January had certainly been fulfilled. Where was he tonight? In the book-lined room, reading the black book at his desk? Out for din-

ner, perhaps, with a friend. Looking at a girl at another
table . . .

She dragged herself through the week, almost overcome by the necessity, the desire to call Pete. Take me
somewhere, anywhere, out of this apartment, into a
public place for a cup of coffee. You can even hold my
hand. How's that for generosity? You want to make
love to me, Pete? Come on, give it a try, I'm great in
bed. I have a list of references.

But she called no one. Thursday she went to the
church again, stayed till five-fifteen, excused herself.
No Jim. Nothing. I won't go back again, she told herself. Let him find someone else. He's had practice now.

What was worst, what hit her the hardest, was the
realization that he was the same as all the others. Not a
word, not a call, not a note—I've thought it over. A
mistake. Fun while it lasted.

She had thought he was different, thrived on the be-
lief that he was different. So she had gone to a goddamn mass. Did that disintegrate a relationship, nullify
an understanding, destroy an intimacy? Did he lack the
ability—oh, say it, Ruthie, say it, the *guts*—did he lack
the goddamn guts to see her once more and tell her
face to face in his own words that it had been a mistake, that it wouldn't work, that she was right after all
to have seen that if there was no place for her in that
part of his life then there was no place for her in any
part of his life?

Friday she went to see Anthony and Teresa. Teresa
looked worse. Anthony was hungry and his shoes were
worn down. She took him to the shoemaker, sat in the
little booth with him, watched him eat a candy bar,
picked up some groceries for Teresa, took him home.

She told Teresa she wasn't feeling well—that takes gall, telling a woman dying of cancer you don't feel well—and went home. Saturday she met Cassie for lunch. Over coffee, Cassie asked about Al. It took her thirty seconds to remember who Al was. Sunday she woke up early and almost succumbed to the idea of going to mass again. What would it prove? What the hell would it prove? Monday afternoon found her back at the church after school. If this keeps up, she thought, he'll have to go into hiding on Mondays and Thursdays. Maybe he'll write me a polite letter asking me not to come here any more.

The next day was Tuesday. You get through this one, it's all downhill. After school she had coffee with one of the other teachers. She had a second cup and they lingered. A notice had just been posted that the camp had definitely been re-funded. Positions were available. The other teacher had heard that Ruth had been there. Could she tell her anything about it? And then, sort of confidentially, could you meet anyone interesting there?

On the way home, she stopped and did the shopping she hadn't done last Friday or Saturday. Everything she bought was heavy, the Cokes, the sugar, the flour. She got the checkout clerk to put everything but the Cokes into one large bag. Two trips up those stairs was too much even to contemplate. You couldn't even leave the Cokes in the car overnight in this weather; they'd freeze solid.

She parked across the street from her house, turned off the lights and motor, got out on the street side, looked up automatically at the top floor. The light was on. Her heart skipped a beat—two beats. Her knees shook. Son of a bitch. To do that to me and come back like this, no call, just return, materialize, as if nothing had ever happened.

She picked up the groceries, the Cokes, her handbag, the *New York Times,* and made her way across the street. Everything down to open the mail box. Nothing interesting. Goddamn ads. I don't want to go up. I don't want to see the son of a bitch.

Slowly up the stairs. Goddamn packages. Weigh half as much as I do. What would he say to her when she came in? I love you, Ruth, I couldn't stay away. I tried to do without you; it just didn't work. I've decided to resign; will you marry me? There is a place for you in my life—in every part of my life.

She paused on the last landing and caught her breath. Who would speak first? Son of a bitch. Hard up for a woman, Jim? I'll tell him what I think of him. Like all the rest. Leaving me like that. When I get finished he'll know what hell this last week has been for me.

He must have heard her coming because as she reached the top stair, the door opened. He saw the packages, came forward to take them, and put them on the table. She walked in, stretched her aching arms, pulled off her boots, unwound the scarf, took off the long dark-blue coat and hung it up. He was putting the eggs and butter into the refrigerator. She looked around the apartment. The bed had been slept on. He had been waiting all afternoon.

She stood watching him. He closed the refrigerator, turned around, looked at the plants.

Would he say nothing? Would they spend the evening like two prisoners in solitary confinement, able to see each other but unable to communicate? The hell with him. He had had the whole afternoon to prepare an opening statement; she had had only five minutes. She would damn well take a shower and go to bed before she would say hello. She sat down at the table and pulled the *Times* over. When he spoke, she knew for the first time that coming up the stairs she had been right.

"I'm hungry," he said behind her softly.

"You're what?"

"I'm hungry. I thought maybe I could get some sandwiches and we could have supper."

Son of a bitch. You goddamn son of a bitch. She put her elbows on the table, clasped her hands behind her head, stared at the front page of the *Times,* and bit her lip, which was trembling now so badly she couldn't have said hello if she'd wanted to.

"Don't," he said. "Please, please don't."

She had a crazy feeling that if she cried, he would too and she couldn't cope with that, not now, not yet.

When she had herself under control again, she said, directing her words to the *New York Times,* "I have a steak in the freezer. Can you eat it purple in the middle?"

He put his hand on her back. "I can eat it purple. Maybe you could let it thaw fifteen or twenty minutes."

She nodded, got up without looking at him, went to the refrigerator and took out the steak. Tony had not failed her. It was damn near two and a half inches. She placed it on the range where it would be warmed by the pilot light. When she turned around, she walked into him.

How could she have forgotten how big he was? He

encompassed her. It was the feeling of all feelings in
the world that she craved right now, the feeling of
being totally enveloped, engulfed by this man. He took
her to bed and made love to her, swiftly, passionately,
quietly, not saying anything until the end, the very end,
when he made a sound, the sound of a man discovering
something beautiful, and he said, "Ruth, Ruth," over
and over, "Ruth," because, oh, God, he knew and he
remembered and he was inside her and he surrounded
her and he was part of her, finally, finally part of her.
For the first time he failed to satisfy her, failed even to
arouse her, but later she couldn't remember a time that
she had ever felt happier.

While they were eating, he said, "You were there
yesterday, weren't you?"

"Yes."

"Why did you go?"

"I was going to stop."

"When?"

"Last Thursday. I wasn't going to go again after
Thursday."

"Why did you go back?"

She shook her head. "They're such nice kids," she
said.

Before he left, he said, "Tomorrow is Ash Wednesday. There's a mass in the evening if you want to drop
in."

"No. I mean, I'm busy. I teach tomorrow night."

After he was gone, she remembered what she had
thought as she came up the stairs earlier in the evening.

Every word. He had said every word of it.

The following week she was off. Her mother had
asked her to visit but she said, no, she would take off

the first day of Passover, the day before Good Friday, and come home for the second Seder. This week she would stay in Boston. He dropped by on Monday morning at eight-thirty, dressed in uniform, woke her up, stayed till nine, sat eating nothing while she drank coffee.

"I wish you'd eat something," she said.

"It's Lent and I've eaten already."

"Sometimes I forget that you're a Catholic."

"I know you do. I try not to forget it myself."

On Tuesday he let himself in early while she slept and they had breakfast together (no eggs, no bacon). After breakfast he told her to do something for an hour and he sat down at the table with his black book. She ignored the absurdity of it, sitting in her apartment reading whatever it was. She made the bed, dressed, cleaned up the kitchen, ran the dishwasher. She went out for the *Times* and when she came back, he was done. They played some records, read the *Times* lying on the floor on their stomachs, talked about nothing; once he danced with her and they both laughed, suddenly, spontaneously, simultaneously, remembering the first time.

After lunch, he said, "Let's take a ride."

"Outside? In the world?"

"Out in the world. Wear your boots."

He drove them to a Jewish cemetery and they got out, walked around in the snow, arms crossed behind them.

After a long walk, he said, "I've been wondering what I would do—on the outside—if I were out in the world."

She trod gingerly. "Does it matter so much?" (I

wouldn't care. You could pump gas and I wouldn't care.)

"That's exactly what does matter."

"Couldn't you decide afterwards?"

"No."

"Why not?"

"If you don't understand, I don't think I can explain it."

"How can you feel you owe them so much? If they hadn't wanted you, they wouldn't have taken you."

"When I came to them, I needed them a lot more than they needed me. They did me the biggest favor of my life."

"You won't tell me about it, will you?"

"No."

They walked in silence, through new snow, crunching it, leaving footprints. Makes you feel real, leaving footprints.

"I wouldn't care what you did," she said softly, speaking out of turn, aware that she had not been asked.

"I know you wouldn't," he said.

"Tell me what's on your mind, then."

"There's only one thing really. I tried for it two years ago but I pulled out. I suppose I could try again but it would mean going back to school."

"So?"

"At my age? Do you know how old I am?"

"You've never told me. Maybe if you tell me it'll stop bothering you."

"Hey, are you cold?"

"No," she lied, wondering if Dr. Fischer made house

calls for pneumonia and if he would take her off the pill if she got it.

"I'll be thirty-nine in May."

"You're like a twenty-year-old in bed," she offered.

"How would you know?" he said, hugging her closer.

She made some more footprints. I should come back here in the spring and see if they're still here, she thought, our footprints.

"You could go to school, Jim. You're crazy to think that you couldn't."

"What would you do," he asked, "if I went back to school?"

It had been phrased in the conditional but she reacted inside as though it had been a direct question. "Do you mean, would I carry your books for you?"

"Yes, that's what I mean, would you carry my books?"

"I would carry your books. I'll carry your books."

"You're responsible, you know."

"For what?"

"For what I'm thinking about, for the fact that I'm thinking about it, for what I'm going to do."

"That's not true, Jim. What you're doing now, you would have done eventually anyway, without me. You have to accept that. You said something about two years ago. This is you, darling, not me. I'm the accident in all of this."

They had stopped under some trees. "No," he said, leaning against the trunk of one, holding her, shielding her from the wind.

"Yes," she said, leaning against the heavy black coat

turned up at the collar, "yes. Don't kid yourself. You don't like to hear it because down deep you're more of a goddamn romantic than I am, but you know it's true, and you especially don't like to hear it from me because I'm a kid, a baby, because you were already raising hell when I was in kindergarten and that kills you every time you think of it, but you know, I've lived a little too in the last couple of years and—"

"Let's go home," he interrupted. "I want to take you home."

"That's right, turn me off. God, you get me mad sometimes." She made a fist with her free mittened hand and struck a light blow on his chest.

"Come on," he said. "You can do better than that. Do it like you mean it."

"No," she said, wanting to go home now too. "I couldn't."

"Why not?" Softly, gently.

"Because—" her eyes filling with tears—"because I'd be afraid of hurting you."

He put his arm around her shoulder. "Let's go home," he said. "Let's find the car before you catch cold."

"Pneumonia," she told him as they left the tree. "I get pneumonia in election years. Just when I start to think nothing else can happen, I get pneumonia."

"Ah," he said, as the car came into view. "You had a lousy affair once, didn't you? When you were twenty-two."

"Son of a bitch," she said, swinging her hip into his side suddenly, almost knocking him off balance. "You goddamn son of a bitch."

In the car, driving home with the heater on high, she leaned back and closed her eyes. How could I ever have thought I came of age in January?

4

At the end of March, she was going home to visit her parents. It was not a visit she looked forward to. In fact, she began, late in February, to anticipate it with a kind of dread. The thought of it began to haunt her, intruding on her private moments, unannounced and unwelcome.

At brighter moments, she thought about buying him a present—not for a reason or for an occasion, just to satisfy some internal craving. But nothing seemed right, nothing stood out as the perfect gift.

She asked him when his birthday was.

"Don't buy me any presents," he said, reading her mind.

"Don't give me orders. Just give me a date."

"May twenty-fourth."

"Is it a Tuesday?"

"The odds are against it."

"The odds are against a lot of things."

"I know," he said.

It was late and he would leave soon. Sometimes in the hour before his departure, their tempers flared briefly.

"I wish you could spend the night," she said, looking at the keys on the table, which he would put in his pocket in a minute or two and then it would be over for tonight, maybe for a week.

"I can't. It's impossible."

"I know."

"I would if I could."

Then the feeling of guilt that she had provoked him.

"There'll be plenty of nights when I'm out of this," he said. "It won't be long now, another few months."

"Are you resigning, then?" He had never come out with it directly.

"Yes, but it'll take time. There's a formality, a kind of procedure. I'll have to explain my position to a bishop. He's not likely to let me go for a while."

"Isn't there a faster way?" (Dear Board of Education, Effective the last day of June . . .)

"I suppose there is but I can't do it that way."

"I didn't know it would be so long."

"You know—" he put his hands in his pockets and turned slightly away from her—"you know, this may not work out the way I want it to. I may be left with nothing. I could be pumping gas next September while I look around for something."

"Then pump gas."

"Even if it does work out, you may not want to go through it with me."

"Try me."

"What I mean is, you don't have to if you don't want to. You're not bound to anything."

"Are you trying to say you'd rather go it alone?"

He looked startled for a moment, then smiled. "I wish we could lop off the last hour of Tuesday," he said, coming back to the table. "Nothing makes sense after eleven o'clock. I don't want to go it alone, quite the opposite, in fact. I'm just trying to be fair to you."

"Why don't you tell me what your plans are?"

He picked up his keys and played with them for a minute. Then he put them in his pocket. "Half of me is afraid you'll be enthusiastic about it and you'll encourage me. The other half of me is afraid you'll think the whole idea is unworkable. In the long run, we'll both be better off if I do this my own way."

It was the closest he came to mentioning marriage and the absence of the word was a relief to her. The only men who had suggested marriage in the past were those she had already rejected or never even considered.

It was one less problem to worry about. Her big worry was Teresa. He asked one night if she still saw Teresa.

"I go on Fridays," she told him. "I was there last Friday."

"How does she seem?"

"She gets tired now. She's lost more weight."

"Andy said the same thing."

"Who's Andy?"

"My friend. I told you about him once. He's a priest in that parish. I'd like you to meet him some time."

"Not now," she said.

"Maybe in the summer."

"Maybe."

Besides Teresa, there was the trip to worry about, the Passover trip at the end of March. It would be her last visit home. That the relationships in Boston and Brooklyn excluded each other had been obvious from the start. By summer, she would no longer be able to visit her parents. The Passover trip would be a farewell to her family.

By the first Tuesday in March she had had plenty of time to think and worry about it. It was on her mind as she drove home, the inevitability of the trip, its finality.

The apartment was empty when she arrived and there was no sign that he had been there. Her mind was playing out a disturbing, interminable scene with her parents. To pass the time, she decided to bake a pie. She hadn't baked since that first night in January two months ago today. It was sort of an anniversary. She sifted some flour, measured it, sifted it into a bowl and went for the shortening, her mind gradually involving itself with the real and the present. Damn. It was Lent. He wouldn't eat it anyway. Disappointed, she poured the flour back and sat down with the paper and the ever present fantasy.

He came in at five, using his key. The last couple of weeks he had even stopped knocking.

He pulled a chair away from the table and sat down without saying anything, still wearing his coat. Something was wrong, his lateness, his preoccupation.

"Got any Scotch?" he asked after a minute in a kind of listless way, as if he didn't care, really, it was just something to do while you gathered up the strength to take your coat off.

There was a new bottle in the cabinet. "It's Lent, Jim," she said hesitantly.

He looked at her—or through her—stood up and went to the cabinet where she kept her liquor. Still wearing his coat, he took the unopened bottle out and put it on the counter. He started to open it, realized his coat was on, and went to the closet. She took a glass out and some ice and fixed the drink.

"They're tearing down the church," he said, taking the drink and walking.

Confused, she had an image of the whole hierarchy,

from the Pope on down, floating in a kind of free fall. "I don't understand. What church?"

"*My* church. They're razing it, clearing the site, putting up a monstrosity in its place. They're tearing down my church."

"I don't understand."

"He's getting old," Jim said. "He talks about retiring. He wants to go away but he's afraid of being forgotten. Maybe that's what happens when you get old and you're alone. He wants to leave a memorial behind, a legacy of sorts, a monument to his monumental efforts."

"I don't even know who you're talking about."

"Costello," he said, naming the pastor of the church ("the Admiral," he had once called him). "He was beaming when he told us about it. It's been approved by the bishop, the architect has drawn up the plans and they'll get started in about a year. Long, low, and yellow brick. I want a refill."

He went to the kitchen and helped himself to more Scotch. "And next door to his memorial will be that firetrap of a school. Do you know I make the kids meet in the church basement because the school is so unsafe? Someone'll flick an ash in there one day and it'll all be over in five minutes. But there's money for a new church."

"What did Father Reilly say?"

"Reilly? A sentence or two. He liked the church and thought we needed a new school."

"And the other one? What's-his-name?" she asked, disappointed in Father Reilly.

"Romero. He said 'Oh' or 'Yes' or something like that. Monosyllabic."

"But why? What's wrong with them?"

"They're part of a system," he said, sitting down. "They're the wrong age. Romero's too young to take up a fight—and maybe this isn't important enough to him. Reilly's too old. He'll have his own parish in a couple of years. He's starting to see himself that way. Why should he rock the boat? Besides, the whole thing is academic. The decision was made before we were told."

"What are you going to do about it?" she asked.

He looked up from the glass. "What do you mean?"

"What are you going to do? You're not going to sit back and let him tear down that church, are you?"

"You talk as though this were a political scandal. It isn't the sort of thing you write nasty letters to the *New York Times* about."

"Then what *do* you do?" she persisted. "Father Costello's not the last word, is he?"

"Let me explain something to you," he said. "The Catholic church is something like the navy. There's a chain of command. You're just not expected to use it."

"The bishop?"

He nodded. The bishop was his road to freedom.

She started to prepare dinner, thinking about the church—the old church—with its pews and stained-glass windows.

"Is this your first disagreement with Father Costello?" she asked from the counter.

"We've never agreed."

"Then how have you managed?"

"I've accommodated," he said.

"Why?"

"I don't think you'd understand."

"Is it because you were grateful?"

"Haven't you ever been grateful for anything?"

"I've always been grateful," she said. "I live here because I got sick of being grateful."

"Well, I'm not sick of it yet." He put his empty glass on the counter and started walking again.

"You said something about Father Reilly and Father Romero and how you accommodate. What exactly is the difference between you?"

"I accommodate for a reason," he said. "If I argued about everything, I wouldn't have lasted a year. Sometimes when you accommodate on some things, you get other things done."

"You make it sound like politics after all. Then it wasn't just gratitude."

"I didn't say it was."

"Did you know it would be like this when you went into it?"

"I grew up in it. I knew and I didn't care."

"What did you think you would accomplish all the years you were waiting to have a church of your own?"

"You win a lot of little battles," he said.

"You must lose some big wars though."

"That's what you don't understand. You lose the big wars whether you try to win them or not. I'm nobody in the system. That's what it means to be a curate."

She went back to her cooking. Why, then, had he wanted to be a curate, to face a life of little battles and big disappointments? And why wouldn't he talk to her about it?

Music came from the phonograph, plainsong.

"There are plenty of organizations that work the way the church does," he said from across the room, assuming a reasonable tone, explaining what had not been questioned. "The navy's just one of them. You win your little battles in the navy too."

Little battles. Wearing black, staying away from women, and winning little battles. Ten years of it.

"Jim, you didn't just get some girl pregnant, did you? That isn't what happened, is it?"

He looked disoriented for a moment, the jump in time catching him unprepared. "No," he said. "I didn't get some girl pregnant. I didn't get any girl pregnant. I'm not sure how I avoided it but I managed somehow." He walked around aimlessly; the apartment had grown small, confining. They really had to get out somewhere, anywhere. "You have a very limited imagination," he added.

They sat down to dinner, her feelings somewhat scorched by his comment. "You'll have to explain something to me," she said finally. "Slowly, word by word, so I get it. If the old church is adequate and the school isn't, why is he building a new church?"

"Schools are out," he said. "New churches are in. Churches make better memorials."

She felt suddenly sorry for the old man with the tiresome voice and the tiresome old ideas. That's what he was really, just an old man without a family. "You'll leave a better legacy," she said. "Yours won't be fragile."

He brooded through dinner and paced afterwards, asking her on occasional seemingly unrelated question —when she was going to New York, how long she would be away. He took out his little book, flipped a few pages and made some notes. Finally he asked if she had signed up for camp.

A letter had come the previous day offering her a job with a nice increase. "Did you get a letter from them too?" she asked.

"No. They told me they were sending them out."

"I thought—before I made up my mind—I wanted to know what you were planning."

"I'll be there," he said.

"For how long?"

"Two months."

"How will you manage it?"

"I'll be out," he said. "One way or another, I'll be out by July."

He left before eleven and she got ready for bed. The bed was still freshly made. He had come and gone without making love to her. It was the first time and she wondered if it indicated a change in their relationship—a kind of relaxing.

She had begun wondering lately about relationships, about people she knew. Did they or didn't they? Had they or hadn't they? She had become particularly curious about her brother's relationship with Joanna, the tall, slender, quiet girl he had brought from Washington to be his wife. She and Joanna had never gotten to know each other beyond pleasantries—as she had never, as an adult, gotten to know her own brother. What had there been to recommend Joanna besides a college degree and an attractive face? She never said anything. She had worked briefly at the start of their marriage three years ago at some job in Manhattan about which she never spoke and which she left the day the rabbit test was positive. She had a small child now, a little boy, and since his birth she had changed; she had become somebody.

Mother had responded predictably to the Washington-Brooklyn liaison. No girl was good enough for her son, no clean-shaven boy so objectionable that Ruth shouldn't go out with him just one more time is all I ask; maybe you'll find something there you never saw before.

What, Mother, valentines on his shorts?

What had gone on those weekends in Washington that had produced this unexpectedly, apparently dully successful match? Had they ever gone to bed together, there in the shadow of the Capitol where Joanna's father worked for some government agency? Unlikely. Joanna had lived at home. What assurance, then, had Joanna had that Dave Gold would not be a Sandy? Christ, Dave had even *liked* Sandy. What had given them the impetus to go through with it?

The phone rang.

"Hey," he said, sounding more like himself, "we didn't make love today."

She started to laugh. "What made you realize it?"

"You'll never believe it," he said. "It was when I took my keys out of my pocket."

The apartment began to get on her nerves. It had never been big but it had been adequate. Now it was small. She longed for a change of scenery, a chance at the out-of-doors.

For Jim, the apartment was a haven. His records sounded better there, he could stretch out, he relaxed. But he sensed her increasing agitation.

It was St. Patrick's Day—Friday—and he had worn a green tie. She had made a lime pie for the occasion—there was a special dispensation for St. Patrick's Day.

Crazy Catholics. Imagine giving a dispensation for
Yom Kippur because it came out on someone's birthday!

"You want to get away somewhere, don't you?" he
asked.

"I guess it shows."

"I wish I knew of a place. I've been trying to think."

But she knew of a place. Cassie's parents went away
every year the week after Easter. Their Cape Cod
house lay empty all winter, unheated but usable. During the week the judge and his wife were away, there
was no chance of an unexpected visit. Cassie had used
the house once that same week, two years ago. The arrangement was made for the Tuesday after Easter.

Another arrangement was made too, somewhat to
her surprise. The following Tuesday Frank Giraldi
dropped off some new "innovative" material at the end
of the day for her to look at. The message came
through loud and clear: Approve it. She accepted it
without promising anything and started to excuse herself.

"Oh, by the way, Ruth," Frank Giraldi said (Where
would he be, she wondered, without those three
words?) "Ellen Pascal's mother will call you today. I
thought you might want to set up an appointment."

She worried it over driving home. Was he admitting
defeat? Setting her up? She had thought he was pre-
dictable; seeing him do something unpredictable was
disturbing.

Ten minutes after she walked into the apartment,
Mrs. Pascal called. Could they get together about
Ellen?

"Any afternoon this week would be fine, Mrs. Pascal."

"Oh, I'm so busy this week, Miss Gold."

"How about next Monday?"

"I can't possibly make it Monday," the woman droned. "Can we say Tuesday?"

"Tuesday," she said, wondering if Frank Giraldi had had a hand in the arrangement after all, "Tuesday is very hard for me. Do you—"

She felt Jim's hand on her shoulder. He had his little notebook open and he was telling her Tuesday was OK. The appointment was made.

"I'll be late next Tuesday," he said when she was off the phone. "I have an appointment in the afternoon. By the way, I called my brother on your phone a little while ago. Remind me when you get the bill."

"I forgot you had a brother." It was stupid, of course, but she had never visualized him in a family.

"Three of them, then two sisters, then me."

"God. How do you keep track of them?"

"My next older sister keeps track of me and I stay close to the oldest brother. He has a daughter," he said offhandedly. "She must be about as old as you."

She felt herself staring.

"That surprises you, doesn't it? I officiated when she got married. Talk about feeling old." He shook his head and put the little notebook back in his pocket.

She awoke on the last Tuesday of the month with a sense of foreboding. She was going home the next day, leaving Jim and leaving Teresa. It was leaving Teresa, curiously, that caused the greater anguish. A change had taken place between her last two visits, a big

change, too big to have happened in seven days. She
had written her parents' telephone number down and
left it with Teresa last Friday. Did she know how to
call collect? You only needed a dime.

This afternoon was the meeting with Mrs. Pascal, a
meeting she felt was bound to go badly. Then later,
after his appointment, she would have to tell Jim of her
change in plans, that she was leaving Wednesday after
school rather than Thursday. She could arrive home
around eight and enter like Elijah. It would give her
extra time on her last trip home.

She dreaded the meeting with Mrs. Pascal. The
woman would be late and, for Ellen's sake, would force
her to accept an unworkable schedule. By afternoon,
she hated Ellen's mother. When she saw the woman
walk into her classroom exactly on time, she turned her
anger back on herself. Give her a chance, Ruthie.
Maybe she's human.

Mrs. Pascal was not only prompt, she was also
pleasant and very conciliatory. In less than fifteen minutes they agreed on the compromise Ruth had offered
Giraldi a month before, an offer that had somehow
never come across clearly to Mrs. Pascal. Having
agreed on Monday mornings and Wednesday afternoons, they left the room and started downstairs only
to meet Frank Giraldi, the great mediator, on his way
up. They left him there, directionless, and went home.

In the evening, she told Jim she was leaving the following day.

He took out a pen and the little book. "Give me
your phone number in New York," he said. "I'll call
you later in the week."

The request came as something of a shock. It

brought the ultimate confrontation of two worlds. You could keep them two hundred miles apart until you gave a telephone number; then the link was established.

"I don't think you should call," she said uneasily. "There really wouldn't be a good time."

He had to know she was lying. "I thought maybe Saturday night," he suggested.

"Don't call," she said. "There'll be a scene if you call. I'm not sure I can face it this week."

"OK." He put the book away. "I'll talk to you Sunday night then."

She felt an instant pang of regret and failure. She was weak; she was a disappointment to both of them. "I'll give you the number," she said.

He shook his head. "Not under pressure. I'll call you Sunday."

The following afternoon she started for home. "Home" had become an ambiguous word during the month of March. Just recently, she had started to confuse its referents. Where it had been clear to her in 1968 that the apartment in Brooklyn was "my mother's" and the little apartment in Cambridge was "home," the distinction had become less clear in the last weeks. Today she was going home to Brooklyn; Sunday night she was returning home.

The trip itself was a familiar experience. As the earth and the moon exerted a pull on the capsule traveling between them, so these two cities exerted their pull on her. Leaving Boston was dragging herself away from a strong magnetic field that diminished as the distance between her and the city increased. Somewhere along the New England Thruway, Boston dissolved, Jim became a memory, the four-poster turned into an

ancient dream and she started to feel an old tug—
Brooklyn, home, Mom and Dad, sleep, good food.

What would they talk about? she wondered as she
drove south and night fell. What could she possibly tell
them that they had not already heard a hundred times
before? Only about Jim . . .

At Christmas of her junior year, a guy she knew
from Cornell had come to New York to visit friends.
He had traveled out to Brooklyn twice to take her out
and her parents had met him. He was tall and good-
looking and his name was Clark Whitney. Her parents
had been taken aback. They had been coolly cordial
and the next morning they had asked questions.

"Did you say you worked on some committee with
him?" her father asked.

"Committee? I don't know what you mean."

"We're trying to find out what he was doing here,"
her mother said, never one to maneuver around a
point.

"I went out with him," she said. "I go out with people all the time."

"But Ruthie, he's not Jewish."

"So?"

"What your father is trying to say is this: he's not
acceptable," said her mother. Her mother, the great
explicator.

Then, in 1967, after Europe and before the pneumonia, someone with the unfortunate name of Mc-
Guire had taken her to a party. (He had taught in her
school.) The next morning, over bagels and lox, her
father had laid down the law.

"How many times do we have to tell you," he said,

referring most probably to the incident of Clark Whitney almost two years before, "that we are not interested in having you make a fool of yourself with a non-Jewish boy?"

After the second date of the Christmas vacation, she had stopped seeing Clark Whitney. Bill McGuire had taken the hint directly from her parents. She had been returned early and permanently to Ocean Parkway.

A year later, visiting her parents for the first time since leaving their home, she had cautiously mentioned Pete, cautiously because she cared so much and he responded so little.

"Pete?" her mother had said. "Peter? What kind of a name is Peter?"

They had been pleasantly surprised to find out.

When she arrived, she was more welcome than Elijah. The Seder was almost over but she ate everything in order and played the part they expected, saying all the right things, admiring new clothes and new jewelry, answering questions, telling stories. She was home where she was adored, home from God's country, home where someone would introduce her to such a nice boy on Saturday night, she would break her lease and come home in June, home to Mommy and Daddy, home to Brooklyn where she really belonged.

It was what they believed. They knew that if only they could find her a nice boy to love, she would rush back to them, be their baby again, and leave them one evening in a long white dress, trading the bed in their home for the bed in his home. Even her virginity would be restored—if they were capable of doubting it no longer existed—by the patient care of her devoted mother. Mother love could mend anything—at close range.

She filled herself with wine, kissed them all at midnight, and went to bed. It was the bed she had begun sleeping in after Mommy finally convinced her it was more fun to be dry at night, the bed in which Sandy had prepared her for life, the bed she would never sleep in with Jim.

The next morning, she went to her brother's apartment. Dave was out in the park with the baby. The baby—Robby was past two already but his name was never mentioned in the family. He was referred to by status—the baby.

Joanna was delighted to see her. She made some coffee and they sat in the dinette with a plate of almond macaroons. It was the first time they had ever been alone together.

"Mother said you did most of the cooking for last night, Joanna. It was very good, very professional."

Joanna seemed pleased. "Thank you. I never tried it before but Dave wants me to have one Seder here next year. This was just a practice."

"My mother's lucky to have you."

"I'm lucky to have her too. She's very good to me. She takes the baby once a week so I can shop and she's always around if I need her. She misses you, you know."

"I know."

Joanna's voice was smooth and poised like her bearing. She spoke the way she moved, with a kind of grace. "Why did you leave home, Ruth?" It was the first time Joanna had asked a personal question.

"A lot of reasons. I had to get away. You reach a

point when you can't live with your parents any more. You start to feel you're living in someone else's home. You have to be by yourself, away from them."

"Then you think you'll stay in Boston?"

"I'm sure of it."

"Your mother's big worry is that you'll marry someone who isn't Jewish."

"It's always been her big worry. It has a certain validity now, Joanna."

"Oh."

They sipped their coffee. Had Joanna been probing or transmitting a message?

"Dave said you went out with someone very nice four years ago, the year we were dating. He seemed surprised that you didn't marry him."

"I couldn't. He left me cold." It was the first time she had stated it accurately.

"I guess I can't quite understand your living all by yourself in a strange city."

"Didn't you ever have an apartment?"

"No."

"Did you ever want to?"

"No. When we were engaged, Dave wanted me to come up and live here, in this apartment, until we were married, but I couldn't. It seemed a shame to leave my parents for an empty apartment and besides, I would have had to use some of our new furniture and then it wouldn't have been new when we were married."

"You're too much, Joanna. You should have been my mother's daughter. She would have been so happy."

Joanna smiled. "Then whose daughter would you be?"

"I don't know. Whose daughter would I be if I told

them I was marrying someone who wasn't Jewish?"
(Or sleeping with him, Joanna, or living with him.)

It was an unfortunate question and she regretted
asking it. Joanna was too kind, too polite to give an
answer. Instead, she stood up and went for the perco-
lator.

"Are you seriously planning to marry someone who
isn't Jewish then?" she asked when she came back.

"Yes." (It was easier to speak of marriage than of
less well-defined relationships.)

"It must have been a terribly hard decision to
make."

"What decision?"

"To break with your parents and marry him."

"I never made a decision. It just happened."

Joanna smiled. "We are different, aren't we?" she
said.

"Does that matter to you?"

"No, it doesn't. We're family. We're related. And
when you have a baby, I'll be related to your husband
too."

"I don't get the connection."

Joanna colored. It made her look young and very
pretty. "It's something I thought up once. People aren't
really related until there's a baby between them. You
and I are related because of Robby. When you have
one, the blood line will run from your husband to me."

"You should have sat next to me on the shuttle,
Joanna."

"Am I supposed to understand that?"

"Not really." She looked around. The apartment had
been furnished with taste and great care. "Tell me

something. Why do you and Dave live in Brooklyn? Is this really where you want to live?"

Joanna shook her head. "No. I wanted to stay in the Washington area. I had hoped Dave would get a job with the Justice Department for a couple of years, but he was happy with his firm here. I'm not a city girl, you know. My parents have a small house with a garden in Virginia. I even went to college away from the city."

"Where did you go?"

"Brandeis."

"Oh." (It was where Mother had wanted her to go. She could have met a nice Jewish boy there and married him the weekend after graduation. Mother had planned that since her junior year in high school.)

"Dave wanted to live here. This is between us, Ruth, isn't it?"

"Everything we've said this morning is between us."

"Of course. Well, you were already in Boston by then and Dave felt someone should be close to the folks."

She felt devastated. It had never occurred to her that her decision to leave New York would have repercussions on her brother's family, on this lovely girl with whom she now had a direct blood line. "Do you mean that you'll stay as long as they're alive?"

"I don't know that we'll do that. We hope they'll live a long time. But we're comfortable here as long as we have only one child. I'd like a house some day. Where will you live?"

"I don't know."

"Haven't you talked about it?"

"No."

"Will you continue working?"

"I assume so. Why would I stop?"

Joanna started to laugh. "I just realized who you remind me of. Sitting here and talking to you all this time and thinking I was talking to someone else. My roommate at Brandeis, the dearest girl in the world, Ruth, and we never agreed on a thing except where to go for dinner on Sunday night."

"What became of her?"

"She married an archeologist and they go on digs together. She sends me postcards from the Middle East every few months. Once she asked me if I would raise a baby for her if she sent me the test tube."

"Did you?"

"Oh, Ruth." They were both laughing now. "Please don't send me your test tube."

"I won't, Joanna. I was just thinking, I wish my mother were more like you."

Her sister-in-law stood up and started to clear the cups and saucers. In two minutes, the room would look like the day the furniture had arrived. "She's your mother, Ruth. She'll never change. Even the blood line won't make things better."

The blood line. She started to think of herself and Jim united by a blood line. She felt a pull, something from the north and east, a kind of antigravity.

"You really love him, don't you?" It was her sister-in-law, in Brooklyn.

"Yes, I really do. I didn't know it showed."

She went home for lunch, hung around a respectable length of time, and then went to the Brooklyn Museum. It was empty of people this afternoon and haunted by ghosts. Where had he lingered? What had been his favorite part?

She went down to the shop and bought some mobiles. She would give one to Joanna tonight for Robby and take the others back to Boston. Maybe what her apartment needed was a mobile.

The second Seder had additional guests. Mother's sister, Aunt Sylvia, was there with Uncle Ben. Her father, Dave, and Uncle Ben alternated the reading. Little Robby, whose English was not yet comprehensible, mumbled the four questions—to everyone's delight—and was immediately put to bed in Dave's old room.

Passover had always been her favorite holiday. Until four years ago, Grandpa had presided as the great patriarch, all his progeny arranged around him. He had had a beautiful voice and she had listened to him chant with a kind of awe. She could remember way back to when she and Dave had argued over who would ask the four questions—(She's just a girl. I want to say them.) —but Grandpa had always settled it: all the grandchildren would ask the questions. We're not in a hurry tonight, are we?

Grandpa. The Passover after he died, his children had split up into their several nuclear families, as if they had waited twenty-five years for this. The fun was gone, the deep, beautiful voice was gone, the overcrowded, over-noisy Seders where everybody loved each other because Grandpa loved them all were all gone now. It was still the best holiday of the year but it had lost something. It had lost Abraham Gold.

She stayed around the house on Friday morning and for a while after lunch. Her mother was pleasant, talk-

ative, but unexpectedly not prying. Her father had also
been selective in the questions he had asked his daughter. It was as if they had made an agreement, turned
over a new leaf. After twenty-six years we have decided not to make you incriminate yourself. As with
Frank Giraldi's turnabout, it left her disturbed.

She had developed a certain sympathy for her
parents that she had not had years ago. They were sincere. They had wanted a daughter like Joanna and instead they had been given a Ruth. "Whither thou goest
. . ." Where was her Bible anyway? She got up and
went to her room. It was easy to find things there now.
Almost everything had been carried off to the promised land over the past three and a half years. The
Bible wasn't there. She would have to look more carefully in her apartment. At home.

Standing in the bedroom that had failed to grow up
with her, she felt a longing to be back in Cambridge,
among the things she loved—the old bed, the plants,
the books and records.

She went back to the kitchen and nibbled some matzoh. She always ate too much when she was home.
There was nothing else to do except talk and shop.

It was a good visit, really. She had discovered a
blood line and made friends with Joanna. It was a
friendship that would last, one that she could rely on,
she thought, crumbling a piece of matzoh on the table.

"You're making a mess."

"Sorry, Mom."

Her father got up from his nap and she sat and
talked to him, talked about nothing for hours until it
was time to eat again. There was nothing to talk about

any more. All they wanted to hear about now was the grandchildren—her missing offspring.

The really amazing thing about the weekend was the absence of the offer for the inevitable Saturday night blind date. Had Mother's bottomless well finally run dry? Had every eligible male in Brooklyn and Long Island really found a mate since Christmas? Or had her parents finally decided to accept her as she was? Unlikely, she thought. More probably Dave had had a word with them. Get off her back, Mom. When she's ready, she'll get married. Stop pushing so hard.

On Saturday morning her father walked to temple and she and her mother went into New York to shop. And the weekend was over.

Early on Sunday she started packing. She had assembled various items from her room that she wanted to keep—several books, a few mementos, some clothes. The suitcase was far too small.

"Mother," she called from her room, "do you have a carton I could use? I want to take some books back with me but they won't fit in my bag."

"I have something better," her mother said, coming to her door holding a dish towel. "I've been trying to get rid of it for years but your father wouldn't let me throw it out." She went to the closet in the master bedroom and came back with an old—no, an ancient—suitcase. The Czar himself must have packed his clothes in one like it.

"Grandpa's!" she said, delighted with her new acquisition. "He used to take that to Florida with him."

"How can you remember such a long time ago?"

How could anyone forget?

She repacked, ate with them, said goodbye, and left them forever. It was a moment she would never forget, seeing her parents for the last time. They would never forgive her for what she was going to do—never speak to her again and never forgive her. It was a fact of her life. Her parents were living proof that there was no objective world out there. It was all in how you saw it.

She drove away sadly, touched by the farewell. It was a long trip from Brooklyn. You had to go through most of New York to get to New England. The city hung on to you tenaciously. Even the car strained, as if it were driving uphill.

Two hours away from New York the magnetic field began to weaken. She was glad she had left them that way. She would be able to remember them with fondness, with affection.

Up ahead was a toll plaza. She pulled a bill out of her bag and drove up to the booth. The toll collector looked a little like her father. What was he doing there on this nice Easter Sunday? she asked.

Waiting for the first grandchild, he told her. He would have a week off as soon as it came and he and the wife would drive out to Minneapolis.

"Good luck to you," she said. "And have a happy Easter."

She must have been past the midpoint because after that she drove faster.

He called at nine. "I missed you," he said. "I was an idiot not to take your number."

"I was stubborn not to give it to you."

"Did you go to the Brooklyn Museum?"

"How did you know?"

"Did you see my favorite totem pole?" he asked, not bothering to answer the obvious.

"I saw them all. When will I see you tomorrow?"

"As close to eight-thirty as I can make it. Hey, how many toll booth receipts did you pick up?"

"God, I missed you," she said.

5

At lunch on Monday Jeff asked her to a movie, not for this night or that night, just how about a movie. She shook her head—avoiding the pipe which swung jerkily through the air in rhythm with his speech—and said she had too much to do.

She had almost forgotten about Jeff in the last two months. He and his pipe had been less visible lately, or perhaps she had become more myopic in her perception of him. In any case, he had stopped bothering her.

She had also almost forgotten about movies. It was months since she had seen one and the thought of a movie was appealing. It would be nice to sit in the dark, to lose yourself for an hour and a half in someone else's life and misery, maybe even to laugh. Hey, that was an idea—laugh at something funny. Why didn't anything strike her funny any more?

Mainly because of Teresa. After school she drove over to see Teresa, to make up for the visit she had missed last Friday. The church program was suspended for Easter week and Jim wasn't picking her up till eight-thirty.

Teresa was sitting in the living room watching television. Anthony was out playing and the door had been left unlocked.

"I missed you," Teresa said. "It wasn't like Friday without you. Turn off the TV and sit down."

"Why don't I take the laundry while I'm here? Then

we can talk." She said it casually, still afraid of hurt feelings. She had started taking the laundry last month.

"Gee, that's nice. I didn't get to it last week. You know, with Easter and all." Teresa started to get up, using both her hands against the sofa.

"Stay there, Teresa. I know where to find it."

On the way she stripped the beds—she had never found them unmade before—and took the bedding with her. She left the laundry with the attendant and went back. She had brought a mobile from the Brooklyn Museum with her and she gave it to Teresa, tiny Danish Viking ships sailing forever in a circle, seeking a new world, and Teresa told her to put it over Anthony's bed to surprise him. The boats changed the room. She had never noticed before that there were no curtains at the window. She had been coming here since September and she had never been aware of the windows, the bareness, in fact, of the whole room. The boats were the only thing besides the furniture and the cross over Anthony's bed that were not part of the structure of the building.

After the laundry was done, she made the beds and went home. When she left, Teresa was still in the corner of the sofa, still facing the screen. It had been an afternoon without a smile, without a light remark, as if the time for that had passed now.

She put it out of her mind. They were leaving it all behind tonight—Teresa, the church, Giraldi, her parents. They were getting away.

She was ready early, food packed in a carton and clothes in an overnight bag. At eight she called the school secretary at home and said she was feeling ill

and would stay home tomorrow. It would be her first
absence all year.

The weather forecast was disappointing. Rain was
on the way. At eight o'clock there were droplets on the
window. It would be damp and raw tonight. The house
was really not equipped for winter. The blankets were
light, woven more to enable the air to get in than to
keep the cold out. She went to her bottom dresser
drawer and hauled out a prize possession, a Hudson's
Bay blanket, the famous white one with the thick
stripes of black, yellow, green, and red at either end.
Between that and the fire, they would manage to keep
warm. She folded it with the stripes showing and laid it
on top of the carton, tucking in the edges. It made a
neat, colorful package.

At eight-thirty she heard footsteps. She started down
the stairs and met him halfway. When they touched,
she knew where home was and why she had come
back. He put his arm around her as they went up the
stairs and she noticed his raincoat. It was new and tan.
She had become so used to seeing him cloaked in
black, the black covering everything that only she saw
—the color, the warmth, even the fire inside—that the
absence of blackness startled her. Even his complexion
and hair seemed lighter. The coat felt new and hard to
her cheek and it smelled new in a chemical way that
she liked. He had been late on Tuesday. Jim on a
shopping spree?

He was more anxious to leave than she, more openly
excited. The day was Monday, the third of April. Three
months ago today she and Pete had gone to the church
to visit Pete's old buddy. That had been a Monday too.

Funny the way the calendar worked, sorting things out with a neat chronological symmetry.

He put the carton on the back seat behind him and started the car. He patted the seat next to him and for a moment she thought he wanted her to move closer but he frowned and looked down at the seat.

"I forgot something," he said. "Do you mind if we stop by the church? It'll only take a minute."

She didn't care. They could stop by a hundred churches tonight.

It was a short drive and it was raining gently by the time he parked near the church.

"I'll be right back, darling," he said. He walked along the side of the church to the entrance she used in the afternoon. As she watched him disappear into the building, she caught sight of a sign near the front entrance. She rolled the window down to try to make out what it said—something about "On this site." Ah, yes, the forthcoming monument of yellow brick. A light went on in the back of the church and suddenly someone was next to her open window, bending down, looking in at her, his face uncomfortably close to hers.

"Hi," he said and she jumped reflexively.

The face was familiar; she had seen it before and she didn't like it. She had never liked it. It was Angelo, Angelo of the car-stealing gang last fall, Angelo from the playground in January, Angelo who managed every now and then to get into just enough trouble so that Jim could get him out of it.

"Angelo," she said, making an effort at control, trying to be Miss Gold waiting for a ride home from the church on a rainy night. "What are you doing out here in the rain?"

"Just walkin'," he said, his jaws moving as he chewed his eternal piece of gum.

"Well, it's raining now. Why don't you go home and get out of the rain?"

"Nice car," he said, ignoring the suggestion. "I didn't know you had such a nice car."

"Angelo—"

"You gonna gimme a ride home in this nice car?"

"No, I'm not, Angelo."

"Too bad," he said. "That's really too bad. I'm gonna get all wet if I don't get a ride home." He grinned at her and drummed his fingers on the roof of the car. "Say," he said, as if the thought had just occurred to him, "are you the one that's screwin' with Father Kendall?"

She blanched. May you burn in hell for that, you son of a bitch, she thought, wishing for the first time in her life that she believed in a hell for him to burn in.

"Angelo," she said, turning to look at him squarely, the dark eyes, the ugly nose, the mouth with a permanent leer as it moved up and down in its endless task, "you're going to push it too far one day and nobody's going to bail you out. Nobody."

The leer remained and she felt her hands involuntarily forming fists. She began to understand the urge to kill, the desire to hurt beyond hurting. The footsteps were almost upon them when she became aware of them. Jim must have known even before he reached the car who it was because he said, "Angelo!" before he grabbed the boy's arm and turned him around, dragged him in the rain over to the steps at the front of the doomed church.

They stood almost eye to eye. Angelo, tall and very

thin, topped Jim's height by an inch. It was raining in the car now and she rolled the window back up and watched through the front. They were walking toward the car, Jim's hand still holding a thin arm in a firm grip. Angeleo would have a bruise in the morning, something to remember them by.

The back door opened. "Get in." She could feel the eyes piercing her hair, the leer that probably never left the skinny, ugly face. He was getting his ride home after all.

Jim sat down behind the wheel and dropped something on the seat between them. She looked down at it. It was the black book he had read at her apartment on a few Tuesdays. It was the reason they had returned to the church. It was why the three of them were together in the car now.

It was a short ride to Angelo's house, through a part of town she had never seen before, but it looked like the rest of the town—small houses, big families, sameness. The only sound between the church and the house was the rhythmic chewing of gum behind her, the occasional crackling to remind her that he had won this round, baby, and he would be back for more.

The car stopped so abruptly that she reached out a hand to keep from falling forward. It was the only sign so far that he was not quite in control. He got out, walked around to the street side, and opened the back door.

"Get out," he said and she had a sudden clear image of the carton covered with the blanket with the four famous stripes on it resting eighteen inches to the left of Angelo.

They walked to the nearest house, up the steps to

what once must have been called a veranda. A light over the door went on, the door opened, a woman with a tired face and hair pulled tightly behind her ears appeared, and all three of them went inside.

She was sitting like a statue. You can relax now, she told herself, but she had forgotten how. What did Angelo know? How far would it go?

The door opened and Jim appeared with the woman. They stood there for a minute, under the light, the woman's hair dull gray, Jim's slightly gold on top. It must bleach in the sun, she thought, the way hers used to when she was in high school. She hadn't noticed it last summer; she hadn't noticed anything last summer.

He got into the car and reached into his pants pocket. Under the raincoat, he was dressed for the beach, khaki pants, work boots. He took his hand out of his pocket and shook his head. He rubbed a cheek with the flat of one hand.

"What's wrong?"

"My keys."

"They're in the ignition."

He let his breath out in a rush. The incident had shaken him. He had seemed so cool, had put up such a good front, but Angelo had gotten to him this time. He must have seen the carton with the blanket on top because he muttered something that sounded like a familiar four-letter word. He started the car and pulled away from the curb.

"What did he say to you?"

"Nothing. It doesn't matter."

"Tell me what he said."

"How do you know he said anything at all?"

He concentrated on his driving. The windshield wipers were going, rhythmically, like Angelo's gum.

"I'll kill that son of a bitch one of these days," he said.

"You say it but you'll never do it."

"What does that mean?"

"He uses you and you let him get away with it." She had surprised herself. She had thought it for a long time but the opportunity to articulate it had never presented itself.

"Will you tell me exactly what you mean?" he said angrily. She wondered who his anger was directed against—her? Himself? Angelo? Or perhaps against all three of them in unequal parts.

"Does he ever get into trouble on a Tuesday?"

"I don't know," he said more quietly. "What if he doesn't? It's a coincidence. He doesn't get into trouble every day or even every week. It's happened once in a while. You're looking for things that aren't there."

"Maybe."

"He's just a kid. He needs help. He needs someone to straighten him out."

"He needs to be flattened by someone an inch shorter than he is."

They had crossed the river into Boston. Behind them, Cambridge was disappearing into the mist.

"Do you want the radio on?" she asked, just to say something neutral.

"No, I don't want the radio and I don't want to talk about Angelo. I want you to sit next to me, close, so I can touch you."

She felt herself relax, all the muscles loosening, as

she slid across the seat. He gave her his hand. Angelo
had at least failed to ruin their evening.

She had visited the house to which they were now
going almost every summer since 1964, when Cassie
had first invited her after their freshman year. The
house had been built by Judge Ballard's grandfather at
the turn of the century and, like most of the other
houses in the waterfront colony, had remained in the
family. All the original families had been New England
Protestant and that much at least had not changed. The
judge had been apologetic about the fact, had brought
it up himself during her first visit. One had neighbors,
he pointed out, and one had friends. As in the case of
Ruth's and Cassie's friends, the two sets rarely inter-
sected.

The judge and his wife had always shared their
daughter's affection for the girl from Brooklyn, so
much so that the judge had made a phone call in 1968
to get her her teaching job—a favor she had neither
requested nor anticipated. It had helped to shape her
destiny and it was fitting, somehow, that they would
spend this night at the Ballards' cottage.

She had known instinctively that he would never
take her to a hotel, as he had seemed to sense that she
would prefer not to go to one. They thought the same
way. It was something that pleased her. .

When they arrived, he took her watch and placed it
on top of the refrigerator, took off his own, compared
it with hers—"Keeps running down"—and put it next
to hers. Time had been dispatched until tomorrow.

After he had a fire going and they had brought down
a mattress from the cold upstairs and made it up on the

floor in front of the fireplace, they sat in two rattan chairs in a corner of the dark end of the living room and drank brandy. There was something incongruous about ski sweaters and summer furniture, about being alone with him and sitting in separate chairs.

They talked quietly, touching fingers. At the other end of the living room the fire was still blazing, crackling, lending light and background noise.

"I feel better now," he said. "I've even forgotten Angelo." He was smiling and relaxed.

"You forgive him too easily, Jim. You forgive everyone too easily. What do you do when someone does something unforgivable?"

"People don't tell me about unforgivable sins. That's part of what makes them unforgivable."

"I did something unforgivable once," she said, balking at the word "sin."

"I don't think you did."

"But I did. It was four years ago and even if it were forty years ago I could never forgive myself and no one could ever forgive me. It was that kind of thing."

He waited just long enough for her to learn something about him. "Do you want to tell me about it?" he asked, and she realized that he was making the offer to satisfy her, not himself. He was without curiosity; for him it was a burden to know; for her it was an agony not to.

It wasn't the way she had imagined the evening—a confession at the dark end of the living room—but she was on the brink of it now. She put her brandy down on the little round rattan table that stood in the corner between them.

"I was living at home then—with my parents, I mean, in Brooklyn. In May my aunt died. She lived in a little house in New Jersey." She looked up at him. "Do you know Jersey?"

"No, I've never been there."

"You lived all those years in New York and you never went to New Jersey?"

"We didn't go anywhere," he said. "We only went to Manhattan once a year."

"Well, she taught me to grow things. You know how those plants you get from a florist always die on you? My aunt's didn't. If she gave you something, it lived forever. She was that kind of a person."

He took his hand and moved his chair a little closer as if she might need him soon and he wanted to be there, close by, to answer her call.

"I knew she was dying. I knew it all winter and I intended to go out and see her, just one last time, just to say goodbye, maybe so she would give me something that would live forever." The tears were starting. There was no way of keeping them back now. She had waited four years to cry over this. "I never went. That's the whole story, really. In May, of course, when she died, I was in Oregon. I'm always away when they die. When I came back it was over; it was too late. I had missed the boat, missed my chance, missed everything. I think for the first time in my life I understood what irretrievable meant."

His hand had begun to sweat, suddenly, hotly, as if he had drawn all the heat from the fire at the other end of the room. She looked up and saw the glisten on his forehead. She had begun to shiver with cold.

She started to cry and he stood up and moved in

front of her, shielding her face from the sight of some chance passerby who had not earned the right to see her in tears, shielding her from his own sight because he could never earn that right—no one could ever earn the right. Tears were the ultimate privacy.

She cried and he sweated. It was almost funny. You could evolve a whole theory of grief based on the excretion of salt water.

"There wasn't even anyone to say I was sorry to," she said. "All the times I said I was sorry because it was the polite thing to do and this one time when I really felt it, there was no one to say it to. How can you ever be forgiven for that kind of thing? How many Hail Marys would you have to say? How many Our Fathers? How many days would you have to fast to be able to go back to New Jersey in 1968 and say goodbye to my aunt?"

He waited until it had passed, quietly, as though there were no limit to his patience. Then he sat down again and took her hand.

"Listen to me," he said softly. "Forgiving isn't retrieving. I would forgive you, not just because I love you, but because of what you are right now. There's no point system in my book; I don't give them and I don't take them away. I don't think your aunt did either. I think she forgave you before she died the way you would forgive someone else. I'm sure she gave you something that will live forever."

She shook her head very slightly, involuntarily. She had gone inside herself again, back four years.

"If only I could have told her I was sorry," she said, lingering. She was empty inside now. The tears had taken everything out of her. She wanted to lie down and go to sleep, sleep for fifteen hours, become whole again. It was only at that moment, wishing she could sleep, that she realized—hearing the echo of his words —that he had told her he loved her, told her as she might have expected to hear it, enmeshed in something else, so she could not respond to it.

She looked at him and smiled. He would misread the smile, think she had accepted forgiveness, but it didn't matter. At least he would know something had made her happy. He smiled back.

"Do you think," he asked tentatively, "that we'll be able to make it? I mean, together?"

"I don't know," she said. She had never thought about it before, as she had never thought about it in relation to anyone else. "I never asked myself that question."

His mood changed. He had been so sure of her reply that her honesty had come as a disappointment. "Well, what did you ask yourself?" he said with annoyance. "You must have asked yourself something."

"Yes," she said. "I asked myself if I could make it without you."

He turned to her—reached into his pocket and pulled out his keys. Her body became expectant as it always did when she anticipated lovemaking, but instead he opened the key chain and came toward her, skirting the made-up mattress that lay at the warm end of the room.

"Here," he said, removing the little gold cross. "I want you to have this. My sister gave it to me—" as if that explained its value, its meaning, the reason that he was giving it to her.

She took it in her hand without looking at it and made a fist around it. He started to close the chain.

"Wait," she said, touching his hands. She took her class ring off—C '67—and slipped it on the key chain. Her finger felt bare but she started to feel whole again inside, as if she had not cried, as if she had accepted forgiveness.

In the morning he told her that before that night he had never spent a night with a woman without making love to her. It gave her a little start. There was so much irony in their lives. He had never lived with anyone, never shared anything more than a bed.

After breakfast they went for a walk on the beach.

"Leave the bed," he said. "We're on vacation. Besides, you're going to tell me when you want to make love."

It was a statement this time, not a question. She had never told anyone she wanted to make love. It was her own curious inconsistency: Want it, do it, but don't ask for it.

They walked for hours, or what seemed like hours. Their watches lay in the judge's house, running down, making seconds into minutes and minutes into hours as their time together ran in reverse.

"Let's go back," she said finally, weary of the weather and the walking, wanting a glass of something hot, the warmth of the fire, wanting him.

"Why?"

"You know."

"Tell me."

"You son of a bitch," she said, raising her voice above the wind and the rain and the waves. "I want to get laid."

He laughed, laughed as if it were the first joke he had heard in years, and they turned around and headed back toward the house.

"I was afraid," he said, "that your speech had lost its picturesqueness permanently."

It came as a revelation. She hadn't listened to herself, had been unaware of any change at all. She started to think about it, to wonder if there had been a change, if it was merely superficial, how deep it went, whether it meant anything, whether other people saw it. Her parents had been different last week. Had she been the cause or the effect? Or neither. . . .

They made love on the bed on the living-room floor, keeping most of their clothes on against the cold dampness, her hands searching in vain for the smooth soft skin that she alone knew existed under the sweater and the shirts and the usual calm exterior that the rest of the world saw.

"You," he said afterwards, "are the best thing I've ever had in bed with me. Do you know that?"

"You are too. For me."

"Come here. I want to talk to you. Did I tell you last night that I love you? I meant to—I've been meaning to tell you for a long time—but I think I got carried away by something you said. I want to tell you something else too." He was incredibly relaxed, as if he lived here, as if it were their own home.

It was the time to say it, to exchange the pledge, but the moment slipped by.

"I saw the bishop," he said, and she drew in her breath. He was waiting for a reaction, for her to say something.

"When you got the raincoat?"

"I can't keep anything from you, can I?"

"It's a beautiful raincoat, Jim." Had he bought it before or after? Had it been a gesture to blind optimism or a reaction to a favorable interview?

"It was just a first meeting," he said.

"What is he like?"

"I'm not sure. I can tell you what he isn't, though. He isn't stupid, he's nobody's fool, he's not naïve, and he doesn't live in an ivory tower. And," he said with peculiar emphasis, "he's a very deeply religious Catholic."

"You aren't, are you?"

He shook his head on the pillow. "No, I'm afraid I'm not."

"But you're a good priest, Jim."

"I've wanted to be. I wanted to be for a long time."

"What did you talk about? What did he say?"

"Not much this time. I'll be seeing him again soon; this isn't over. But I think I've worked it out in my own mind now and what I have to do is get him to see what I've finally come to understand myself, that I've lost my value to the church in my present capacity, that I can do more if he lets me go and gives me a little help."

"More for the church?"

"Just more, period."

"Being a fireman?"

"I'd almost forgotten about being a fireman."

She waited for him to go on but he had finished. It was between him and the bishop. She would have to wait it out.

"There's something else I have to work out too," he said after a minute, "something I left unfinished almost eleven years ago. I thought it was over, I thought it was all behind me, but now I'm not so sure. Maybe it can't be done, putting things behind you."

"What was her name, Jim?"

He turned over on his back and looked up at the low cottage ceiling. "I hope I understand some day what it is that makes people want to know. You don't realize it, but there's no answer to your question. Her name is Carol. I suppose that's the answer you want."

She was disappointed. She had thought he would tell her about it, here in the privacy and intimacy of the cottage. "Let's eat," she said, getting up.

"I want to take you somewhere tonight. Maybe we can find a place to have coffee."

"Take me to a bar."

"You mean where you sit on a stool?"

"Yes, I'd like to sit on a barstool tonight."

"I'll take you to my favorite bar in Boston."

"When did you ever go to a bar in Boston?"

"I used to go on Tuesday afternoons sometimes, but I haven't gone since before Christmas. We'll go there tonight."

When they got into the car later, she saw the black book lying on the back seat.

"You never opened it," she said. "All that trouble and it stayed in the car."

"I'll do it tonight."

"Why do you read it?"

"Because it's part of the job."

"Is that the only reason?"

"It is now."

"I would think you could find better uses for an hour a day than reading a book for the thousandth time."

"You mean like seeing you?"

"No, I don't mean like seeing me. I mean like doing the parts of your job that you think are more important than that."

When they reached Boston, he took her to his bar. They parked around the corner in front of a jewelry store and walked in the rain.

"The bartender," he said as they approached the heavy, dark-stained oak door, "will know you got laid this afternoon."

"How will he know?"

"It's his job to know. He's a good bartender."

He opened the door and she walked in, taking in the wood paneling, the long bar, the dim lighting, the dark wood.

"Your church away from church," she said, thinking of the pews that would be firewood next year. He smiled and led her to the bar.

"Hey, Jim," the bartender said. "Haven't seen you in a month of Tuesdays."

"I've been busy," Jim said, shaking hands across the bar.

"So I see." The bartender nodded to her graciously, reached for a bottle of Scotch and poured a generous amount over ice. "What will the lady have?"

"A Bloody Mary," Jim said, "heavy on the tomato juice. She's been losing weight."

She hadn't known it showed. She opened her jacket to call their attention to one of the places where the bones didn't protrude.

"Well, how are the boys?" Jim asked.

"Pretty good, pretty good, except—Did you hear about Charlie?"

Jim shook his head.

"Lost his wife in February. Terrible shock, terrible blow. Heart attack. Very sudden." He snapped his fingers. "Here one minute, gone the next. Forty-three," he said. "Only forty-three years old."

"I'll look him up."

"Terrible month, February," the bartender went on. "Worst month of the year."

"You're right about February," she said to the bartender. "Who's Charlie?"

"One of the Tuesday people," Jim said.

"Nah," the bartender said. "Charlie's almost every day. He's a jeweler, makes jewelry, beautiful stuff." He held out a hammered gold tie clip for her to see. He was right. It was beautiful. "Has a place around the corner. I see him almost every day. Now Eddy—remember Eddy? He's Tuesday. Jerry, he's Tuesday and Thursday."

"How do you keep them straight?" she asked.

"It's like children's birthdays. Other people's children, you never get them straight. But your own, they come one at a time and they're individuals. You never forget them."

When they left, she offered the bartender her hand and when he shook it, he winked at her. "Come back again," he said, "when you have a free Tuesday."

At home, she told him she had a present for him.

"Don't buy me things," he said.

She handed him the bag from the Brooklyn Museum. In it was the same mobile she had given Anthony. He was delighted.

"I'll hang it in my room."

"Are you allowed?"

"Hey, I don't live in a prison."

the car, with some hesitation, that he had asked her out for the coming weekend.

"That's great, Judy. You'll have a good time."

"You used to go out with him, didn't you?"

"Quite a while ago."

"No hard feelings? I mean that he's asked me out."

She smiled, feeling suddenly old, almost maternal. "No hard feelings. Pete and I are friends. It was never any more than that. Have fun."

Judy dropped her off in Boston and she took the train downtown. The shopping part of the trip was to buy a gold chain for the cross Jim had given her. Cassie had told her the name and address of a jeweler and promised to meet her there after work to get back the key to the beach house.

Ruth took the train to Park, walked leisurely to Washington Street and turned north. It was a part of Boston she liked, old, crowded, narrow. The jeweler was on a side street and his name was Fleming, Henry Fleming and Son. As she turned the corner, she recognized where she was. Daylight had momentarily obscured her vision. Jim had parked outside of Henry Fleming and Son on Tuesday night. "Son" would be Charlie who had lost his wife in February.

She went inside the shop. Father and son were both there and the son was indeed Charlie. He was a black-haired, sad-looking, long-faced, hollow-eyed version of the white-haired old man. The father nodded to her and told Charlie he was going out. The sad, dark eyes met hers.

"Miss Ballard sent me," she said.

The whole face smiled in response. "How is she? I haven't seen her since before Christmas."

"She's fine. She'll be here soon, in fact. She's meeting me here."

"May I show you something?"

"Yes. I'd like a gold chain, down to here." She pointed to a button on her blouse.

He brought a tray of chains, from the finest she had ever seen to the most exquisite. When she had made her selection, he asked if she had the ornament with her. "I can put it on for you," he offered.

She took the cross out of her bag. Idiotically, she had wrapped it in tissue paper to protect it, idiotically because it had spent almost five years being scratched on both sides by his keys. She unwrapped it and gave it to the jeweler. One side was perfectly plain; the other had a list of initials and a date marking an occasion almost five years before.

"It'll take a little while," the jeweler said. "Why don't you have a seat?"

"Thank you. I'll look around."

She looked at the jewelry. Jim had a birthday next month and she wanted to get him something, something good and beautiful, but above all, the right thing. What would be the right thing to give Jim?

The cross and chain were ready a few minutes before Cassie arrived. She put it on and slipped the cross inside her blouse.

Cassie came in and began selecting gifts, thinking ahead (Cassie always thought ahead) to birthdays and anniversaries halfway around the calendar. The elder Fleming returned and passed his greetings on to her parents.

When they were outside, she told Cassie Charlie's wife had died.

"How do you know?"

"It's a complicated story but someone told me. She died in February."

"Wait for me." Cassie went back in and spent a few minutes with the jeweler. "It was a heart attack," she said when she returned.

They started to walk back up Washington Street.

"You look terrible, Ruth. Do you know that?"

"That's absurd." She spoke curtly, dismissing the comment.

"It's not absurd. You've lost weight; you look run-down."

They walked on for a while in silence. It would be unlike Cassie to pry. In her family, people volunteered exactly as much information as they chose and the rest accepted it. Ruth had originally mistaken the Ballards' attitude toward each other as a lack of closeness but a later reassessment had changed her mind. They were exceedingly close and their respect for each other had engendered a mutual trust. In fact, they tended to confide in each other more than she had ever been able to confide in her own parents.

"Teresa's dying," she said as they reached the corner. "I was there yesterday. She's just fading away. I've never seen anyone die before."

They were facing each other on the curb. Cassie reached out a hand, touched her, and dropped her hand. It was a rare gesture, one that had been made only once before.

"Let's have a drink and dinner somewhere," Cassie said. "It's after five and I've suddenly lost my desire to spend money."

Cassie took up a brisk lead and Ruth began to follow. They went back up Washington Street, all the history gone now. After the mention of Teresa she had lost the will, even the ability to do anything but follow. All day she kept the thought pushed away, below the surface, hidden from herself, so that she would be able to function, but the mention of the name broke the delicate façade. She quickened her pace to keep up with Cassie, who suddenly seemed to be in a hurry.

They turned right at Temple, leaving Washington Street, walked to the end of the block, and stopped. They had reached Tremont Street. Across from them lay the Common, the great gold dome in the right-hand corner shining like the sun it reflected.

"Let's get a cab," Cassie said.

"It's a bad time to get a cab." It was worse than bad. Even if they got one, it was the wrong time to be on wheels in downtown Boston.

The light changed. "Let's cross the street. We can sit down for a minute and think where to go."

She stepped off the curb, still following. As they reached the other side, she heard her name called. It was Jim, moving through the crowd, his hand raised in a greeting, a salute, his face aglow above the Roman collar. Without warning, she began to feel outrageously, explosively happy, light inside, giddy on her feet. It struck her that this was the happiest moment of her life, meeting him like this in a crowd, meeting him unexpectedly.

"Keep your cool, Cassie," she said to the last person in the world who would ever lose it.

He joined them and there was one moment of absolute joy.

"Hi, darling," he said, and she started to breathe again, saw the crowds again, remembered that Cassie was there, keeping her cool.

"Cassie," she said, trying desperately to remember whose name you mentioned first in an introduction, "this is Jim," and she added, "Kendall. This is Cassie."

Cassie's face changed. She had inadvertently stumbled on a secret; all sorts of little details were clicking into place. She kept her lips closed around a smile, held out the same white, long-fingered, well-manicured hand that had touched her friend and shook his hand.

"Let me take you both to dinner," he said. "At least a hamburger. A cheeseburger for you, little one; you need the calories."

Cassie shook her head and declined. "Go yourselves," she said, the point of the threesome eluding her.

"Impossible," he said. "All or nothing."

"Then come to my place. I have frozen hamburgers and plenty of cheese."

"Cassie, they'll never thaw." Ruth was on the brink of laughter, still feeling the giddiness.

"Yes, they will. I have a microwave oven. Let's go."

He looked at his watch. "Give me a dime, darling. I have to make a call."

A dime. The man carried more change in one pocket than came into her possession in a month. She dug in her bag, found two nickels, and handed them to him. He took them with both hands, caressing hers. "Start walking," he said. "I'll meet you up the block and we'll get my car." He headed for a phone booth.

"He's beautiful," Cassie said.

"I think he's lost his mind." She still felt giddy. "He must have ten dimes in his pocket for every one I have."

"He wanted to touch you."

"You're insane."

"Am I?"

"What possessed you to get a microwave oven?"

"Daddy gave it to me for Christmas."

"Cassie, what will he have left to give you when you get married?"

Cassie smiled, the smugness coming through. "My freedom," she said.

Cassie's apartment was on Beacon Street in a new co-op that overlooked the Charles. The judge had made the down payment and she paid the monthly maintenance. Every September, on her birthday, her parents gave her a large sum of money with no strings. It was enough to maintain the apartment or go to Europe or buy a fur coat—or just squander recklessly, a little here and a lot there. The money was not replenished until the next birthday. Recently she had begun saving, being careful, putting some away. The only time in her life that she had ever needed money, she had had none and her birthday had been two months off. It had taken a friend to see her through.

They had microwave cheeseburgers and lemonade. Jim refused a drink; he had several hours of work ahead of him. At the table, she showed him the cross on the new chain.

"I didn't realize you were going to wear it," he said. "I could have gotten the chain for you." He reached for the ketchup.

"Did you burn your hand?" Cassie asked, looking at the scar.

"A long time ago," he said lightly, as if the pain had long since gone. "Ruth and I were at your cottage the other day. It's a beautiful place and we thank you."

"Maybe you'll come again in swimming weather."

"I hope we can," he said. "I understand your father is a judge."

"Yes, but not in the city. His domain is Middlesex County."

"We may need a judge in a couple of months. Would it matter if it were Middlesex County?" He turned to his silent partner.

"It wouldn't matter."

He left her there after supper and went home by himself. Cassie made coffee and they sat in the carpeted living room, watching the sky over Cambridge grow dark.

"You look better now," Cassie said. "You look as though your health has improved."

"He does that to me."

"Will everything work out?"

"After a fashion. Yes, I think it'll work out." She stood up and walked to the huge window, which formed most of one wall of the living room. Across the Charles, nocturnal Cambridge was dominated by the blue Electronics Corporation of America sign. "You know, Cassie, I feel old. I see him once or twice a week and when he leaves me I feel old and lonesome and even though I believe it'll work out I stop feeling it when he's gone. I just feel sorry for myself. That doesn't sound like me, does it?"

"You'll feel better again after it works out. You know you will."

She shook her head. "There's Teresa. That's not going to work out. I'm having a problem at school; I'm thinking of transferring because of it. My parents. Then there's Teresa," she said, forgetting she had mentioned her first. "And there's something to do with Jim too, something he won't tell me, as if he didn't love me enough or trust me enough or as if it were something he felt I couldn't understand."

"He loves you and he trusts you. You can't really believe he doesn't."

"Then maybe he's right about me. Maybe I'm just governed by an overpowering curiosity, like my mother. Why am I so desperate to know this one thing?"

"Because you're unsure of your feelings?"

"No. No, that's not it at all. Maybe because I'm unsure of his, because I can't understand why he won't share one little fact of his existence with me."

"Obviously it isn't just a little fact."

She turned away from the window. It had become totally dark outside while they were talking and Cassie had turned on the lamps.

"Whatever it was, it happened ten or eleven years ago. He was in his late twenties and there was a woman involved. That's all I know about it. After it was over, he went into a seminary."

"Maybe it was the obvious thing," Cassie said.

"No. I asked him that. He said I had a limited imagination." The wound still stung slightly.

"Well, figure it out now. Think of the worst thing he might have done, accept it as a fact, and reckon with it.

Maybe you'll feel better. Maybe you'll even understand why he's never told you."

"But what could he have done if he didn't get some girl pregnant and run out on her?"

"You're too hung up on the girl. Stop thinking of her as a victim and assume that she was more of an accomplice."

"Accomplice? What are you talking about? You think he robbed a bank? That's kind of silly. Anyway, what became of all the profits?"

"He doesn't strike me as the bank-robbing type," Cassie said, putting down her coffee cup with a frown of concentration. "He'd be involved in something much more human, something unplanned, I think, accidental. Maybe he killed someone. He accidentally killed a man, her husband or something."

"That's absurd." She said it angrily.

"If it's absurd enough to get you angry, then maybe we've hit on the right thing. He killed a man, he entered a seminary, he became a priest. It all fits."

"You're insane, Cassie. I know him. He couldn't kill anyone, not intentionally and not by accident. He couldn't even hurt anyone." Her hands were trembling in a mixture of anger and fear. The truth never made you free; it made you angry and afraid.

"Don't reject it. You'll be right back where you started. Accept it. He killed a man." It was the voice of anthority, the voice of sanity.

"No." It came out hoarsely.

Listen to me. Forgiving isn't retrieving.

"It's not possible."

I would forgive you, not just because I love you . . .

"Oh, he couldn't have."

. . . but because of what you are right now.

She walked to the nearest chair and sat down.

"Do you want a drink, Ruth?"

"Brandy, please."

She heard the cork come out of the bottle, heard the gurgle as it was poured. The bottle had been nearly full. She sipped it and felt it burn its way down. She would never really get used to it but it was theirs; it was something they shared.

"If that were true," she said, "I could never let him tell me about it. I would rather go through the rest of my life not knowing than have to sit and watch him tell me that."

Cassie poured herself a drink. "Does it make a difference to you? Does knowing change anything?"

She shook her head and touched the little cross under her blouse with taut knuckles. "I've been sitting here and asking myself that. It doesn't. It doesn't change a thing. I didn't know him then. He's somebody else now."

"Then whatever happened is really irrelevant, isn't it?" Cassie said, putting the whole thing in final perspective.

"Irrelevant. Funny you should pick that word. But tell me something. What's the matter with me that I can't put things in perspective for myself? Why do I always need someone else to do it for me?"

"Why do you always think you're so different from everyone else in the world?"

After a while, Cassie drove her home. They made a detour and drove by the church, the sign telling of its impending demise reflecting the light from the street lamps.

As they reached her apartment Ruth said, "I didn't even ask you. How are you and—" what was his name, the one Cassie had been seeing since New Year's?— "you and Hal doing?"

"We're getting married in August," Cassie said, watching for the reaction.

"Oh, God, what a bitch I am. I've spent four hours with you and I've done nothing but talk about myself. Congratulations."

"Thank you. You'll have to be my maid of honor. Maybe you'll be the matron of honor."

"It's a nice thought." She paused. "Did you tell him?"

Cassie nodded.

"And it didn't make any difference, did it?"

"No. It was just the way you said it would be. You put everything in perspective very neatly, bitch."

When she undressed that night, she was still wearing the cross. She had never worn jewelry to bed, not her ring—which was now gone—or her watch. But this, she decided, she would wear. In a way, she had just earned it. She had accepted him on his own terms.

7 ~~~~~~

She went to see Teresa the next day after school to do some chores and bring some noise into the apartment. Lately, even when Anthony was there, it had become very quiet, Teresa waiting in her home with a kind of patience and resignation, an incomprehensible acceptance.

She parked the car, looked around for Anthony, and went upstairs. In front of Teresa's door, she stopped dead. From inside came the sound of a man's voice.

Joe. Oh, God, Teresa's husband had returned. She felt panicky, completely unprepared for this. Somehow, she would have to get Anthony out before that madman hurt him. But how?

She heard the man laugh. Then she heard Teresa laugh. It struck her as she listened that it was almost the first time she had ever heard Teresa laugh. It was a warm, beautiful sound.

She tapped gingerly at the door, as if not to anger the man inside, and called, "Teresa?" very softly and again, "Teresa?"

"It's Ruth!" Anthony shouted, and the door opened.

She walked in and looked around. Teresa was standing in the living room looking flushed and healthy, and next to her stood a priest. She swallowed and took a deep breath.

"This is Ruth Gold," Teresa said. "She comes to see me and help me out."

The priest walked toward her and held out his hand.

"How do you do?" he said formally, a trace of Scotland in his speech. "I'm Thomas McAndrew. Father Kendall has told me about you."

She shook his hand, avoiding his eyes. She had never imagined she might run into him here, on a day like this when she was toatlly unprepared, dressed in jeans —the same jeans she had worn Tuesday at the cottage.

Jim had told him about her. Hearing it from a stranger gave a kind of physical substance to their relationship, as when Jim had told Cassie yesterday that it was he who had shared the cottage with her. She took her coat off and touched the little cross under her sweater.

Now that she had arrived, the priest showed no sign of wanting to leave. He sat down in a heavy chair and leaned forward, talking to Teresa, entertaining her. Teresa sat back and laughed, her face flushed. She was enjoying herself.

So this was Andy, a jokester, a tale-teller. She had imagined a serious man, more like Jim, more concerned. She got up quietly and walked to the back of the apartment. The laundry was ready in two laundry bags. She took them and walked as unobtrusively as possible through the living room, stopping for her coat and bag.

"Are you leaving now?" the priest asked.

"No. I just have an errand."

"Let me walk down with you. It's time I was on my way."

But Anthony wanted him to see the boats, the little Viking boats from the Brooklyn Museum. The priest went back into the bedroom with him.

"Ruth gave them to me," she heard Anthony say.

"What a fine gift," the priest said. "When you can't fall asleep, you can climb into a ship and sail away. I was in the navy once, you know, and I sailed halfway round the world in a boat like those."

"You never told me you were in the navy, Father," Teresa said.

"Teresa, my dear, I'm saving those stories for when you grow up."

He carried the laundry bags downstairs and they stood in front of the house.

"So you're Jimmy's friend," he said.

"I beg your pardon?"

"You're Jimmy's friend—ah, you call him 'Jim,' do you?"

"Yes, I do."

"Where are you taking these?"

"Around the corner."

He started in that direction. She walked next to him, saying nothing, having nothing to say, and being afraid of saying the wrong thing.

"You're trying to decide whether you like me, aren't you?" he asked.

She felt herself becoming flustered. "No, of course not."

"Well, I like you." He was smiling at her. There was something of an imp in him.

"Tell me something, please," she said. "Teresa's husband, Joe. What is he like?"

"He's a boor," the priest said, the smile gone. "And beyond that, he's a brute. He is unfit to be a husband, a father, a citizen, or a man. He'll probably turn up here one day when we've all but forgotten him. If you happen to be the first to see him, I'd like you to call Jim from the nearest phone. I hope I've made my point."

"I understand." They had reached the laundromat.

The priest offered his hand. "I do like you," he said. "Tell Jimmy I said hello."

All the way home she listened to the echo of Teresa laughing. Why in all these months had it never occurred to her to make Teresa laugh?

She decided that the best thing for Ellen Pascal would be a month at camp. Over the weekend, she wrote to the camp office and wrote a letter to Mrs. Pascal. The idea pleased her the more she thought about it. Away from school—from Giraldi in particular—Ellen might blossom.

On Monday she visited Teresa after church. Without Father McAndrew there, Teresa seemed to have wilted, to have returned to her previous condition. Teresa herself seemed to be aware of it. She had stopped protesting when Ruth did little things for her, made coffee, cleaned up, took the laundry. The lack of protestation bothered Ruth; it was as if Teresa had given up a fight, had settled down to accept her fate without an argument, without even an angry word.

"Do me a favor," Teresa said. "Make yourself a key to my door. Then if it's locked, you can always get in."

She took the key down to the hardware store, found Anthony on the way back and brought him up.

"He's a good boy, isn't he?" Teresa said. "I wish he would stay home more but he's a good boy."

The next day was Tuesday. Except for the meeting on the Common, she hadn't seen Jim since their trip to the cottage, but when she came home, he was asleep. She banged around for fifteen minutes but he slept through the noise. Finally, she sat down next to him.

"Hey," she said softly, rubbing his warm back, "get up. I want you to talk to me."

He opened his eyes and touched her. "Give me another hour, darling, OK?"

Disappointed, she went to the kitchen and looked for something to do. In the refrigerator was a bag of apples. She pulled out half a dozen and started to peel and core them. She would make a pie. Doing it would be a kind of therapy, using her hands while she turned her mind loose. When the pie was in the oven, she set the timer and sat down with the paper.

When the smell of apples and cinnamon reached the four-poster, he woke up.

"Are you OK?" she asked.

"Come here," he said. "I want to tell you something." She crawled in under the canopy. "I decided to take your advice."

"I never gave you any advice. I know better than that."

"About what you call my little black book."

"You mean you've given it up for an hour's sleep?"

"I'm doing some volunteer work on Tuesdays. I started this morning."

"What are you talking about?"

"I'm working in a hospital for seven hours on Tuesday. I started in the kitchen today. It's a good thing for me." He was enthusiastic. "You come into something new and you feel like an idiot, like a total incompetent. It puts you in your place."

"I think you're insane." It came out angrily. "It's a stupid, irrational thing to do."

He stopped and looked at her for a moment. "I thought about it all last week," he said evenly, "and I —what's that?" The timer had started to ring.

"My pie is ready." She got up.

"Wait a minute. Stay here, don't go yet."

"It'll burn. It'll drip on my oven." She went to the kitchen and took the pie out. The aroma swam around her like a rich perfume. Why did women wear musk when they could wear apples and cinnamon?

"What are you so touchy about?" he said from the bed.

Touchy? What am I so touchy about? Because I'm watching someone die, that's why. Because I'm watching her slip away without a fight, without a show of anger. Shouldn't she be out making a deal, making a bargain with the devil? I would be. I'd be selling my soul now for a couple of years more on earth.

"What are you trying to prove," she said aloud, "that you can kill yourself before your thirty-ninth birthday? Isn't it enough that you work fifteen hours a day six days a week? Do you have to spend your one miserable day off in a rotten hospital kitchen?" She sat down on the bed, worn out by her outburst, by the cause of the outburst.

"Come here," he said. "I want to see where you keep my cross."

It was the only thing now that kept her going, the knowledge that once a week, or maybe twice a week, she could lie with him on their bed, love him without thought, without care, without reservation, believe for half an hour that spring was somewhere, that it would come to her, that it would envelop them.

Because after he left, she lay awake and she thought about Teresa and she thought about Jim and she was filled with an inarticulate anger. He said nothing about Teresa, he asked nothing. If only he would, she would have someone to share it with, someone who would say, Take it easy. I love you. Everything'll turn out.

But she had no one. Nothing would turn out.

Her anger touched almost everything she saw. She made her butcher grumble once—poor Tony, he had done nothing to deserve it. And time and again, it settled blackly on herself. It was a stupid thing. She had never told him about Abraham and she had never told him she loved him. The moment—at the cottage—had come and gone.

April and the beginning of May were a horror, a nightmare from which it became almost impossible to wake up. She told Mrs. McConnell she would have to leave early on Mondays. Mrs. McConnell told her to take the day off; spring was coming; they would be outside soon. Everything would be easier.

Easier. Everything would be easier. But when? When Teresa died? Did she have to wait for Teresa to die for everything to be easier?

Everything around her began to change, to become unreliable. The car failed to start one morning and she was late for school. No one had ever told her that batteries died. She called Cassie once and the line was out of order. Because of an error, the teachers' checks were delayed.

Jim changed—something she had found impossible to conceive. He had seemed like a rock, incapable of altering, and yet April made him change too, not toward her but toward himself.

He went through a constant introspection, a finding fault with himself, with everything he had ever done.

"Do you know how many things I've started in my life," he said one night, his keys and the old frayed black wallet lying on the coffee table, "that I've never finished? There are only beginnings, no ends. I was going to be a navy man twenty years ago."

"You were going to be a cowboy when you were six. Do you want me to weep over that?" Everything came out harsher than she intended. She took out her anger about Teresa at everyone. Even the children in school jumped now and then when she sopke.

The camp wrote back with an application blank for Ellen. Mrs. Pascal was delighted. Ellen had never been to camp. Would Miss Gold keep an eye on her there? Ellen was doing so much better now. She was a different child.

Sometimes at night the phone would ring and when she answered no one was there. Once or twice she heard a television set in the background, once the voice of a child, but when it rang late, after midnight, there was no sound at all.

She accepted it as she accepted the headaches on Wednesdays. By three o'clock on Wednesday afternoon, her head was splitting. She still had a session with Ellen to get through, then a quick trip to Teresa's— dear God, let her be all right—then her Wednesday night dinner with a teacher she had met last fall. It was something she didn't want to give up, that dinner. It represented an hour of sanity in a week of delirium. Then there was the class.

"Your health is not the best, Miss Gold," Mr. Gerstenwald said.

"Does your mother worry about you, dear?" Mrs. O'Hara, the youngest member of the class, asked.

"All the time. She never stops worrying."

"Mr. Gerstenwald," Miss O'Hara said, "I'm sure her mother worries enough for all of us. Leave the poor thing alone."

By the time she got home on Wednesdays, she was too tired to think, too tired even to make love if Jim was there. She sat with him, curled up like an unborn child, and listened to music until it was time for him to go.

Saturdays she slept till noon, trying to replenish her body, as if she could drain it all week and get it back in shape over one night or two. But she awoke on Saturday as if drugged, dragging herself out only because it was the last day of the week to buy some food, get her clothes washed, remind herself that she had to keep herself alive for some reason she couldn't quite remember.

Everyone who entered her field of vision in April and most of May seemed worried, everyone except Judy Greene. Judy was falling in love with Pete. She was wide-eyed and ecstatic; she bought new clothes, changed her hair style, danced as she walked.

Did I look like that in January? she wondered. Did I exude happiness? Was I a ray of sunshine?

But if Judy loved Pete, Pete seemed to be less than reciprocating. The three A.M. calls abated somewhat, but continued. It was just one of the hazards of being alive.

Once, in the morning, she thought she saw Angelo

up the street as she left for school but she didn't care any more. He was an annoyance but he was no more than that. She would live with it.

It became impossible, while she was awake, to keep her mind off Teresa. Even with Jim, sitting and eating a steak on a Tuesday night, she would worry. What would happen to Anthony if he came home to find his mother dead? What if the father returned? How long could she drag herself through the nightmare?

And across from her, lost in his own thoughts, Jim sat, newly uncommunicative. She had expected progress reports; she had thought he would eventually tell her his plans, but he had said no, when she asked him, this was one decision he would take sole responsibility for, and if it didn't work out, she would be spared the anguish of disappointment.

But there was something else, something new bothering him, something that lay neither in the present nor in the future.

Once he looked up at her and smiled, the old smile, the January smile when they were young and happy.

"You got your papers in for camp, didn't you?" he asked.

"Yes. They sent me an acknowledgment. They're even raising my salary." She had told them she would return as a show of faith, faith in Jim, faith that the earth would still be intact in July, faith that she herself would still exist, whole and sane, when summer came.

"You want to know if I've talked to the bishop about the building of the new church, don't you?"

She shook her head. "I don't care any more. Let them tear down anything they want to. I've stopped caring."

"I'm sure you haven't," he said. He got up and walked to where she was sitting. "Ruth, if there were something I could say or do, I would."

"I know you would." It should have made her a little less angry at someone, but it didn't. It was the anger that kept her going now, that saved her. Without it, she might have been lost. "What I really want to know is what's going on in your therapy sessions with the bishop."

He started to laugh. "I guess that's really what they are," he said. "I've been doing a lot of soul-searching lately, a lot of digging." He was touching her now, her shoulder, rubbing it gently, standing behind her chair. "There's a lot you don't know about me, do you know that?"

"There nothing I don't know about you."

"I'll have to tell you some day."

"Don't."

"You'll really have to know before we do anything serious."

"Do what serious, Jim? Do you think there's anything serious that we haven't done yet?"

"You know what I mean."

It was as if the ballet that had started in January had finally come to its ultimate conclusion, with the two dancers having exchanged places, and still at opposite sides of the stage.

She knew that when it came it would be an avalanche, but the first rumblings came from such a distant corner that she failed to recognize them. She got a phone call at home from Mrs. Pascal. She had decided against sending Ellen to camp and could she have the application back?

"Why, Mrs. Pascal? What happened?"

"I talked to Mr. Giraldi about it. He doesn't think it's a good idea."

"Why isn't it a good idea?"

"Well—" She paused. You could almost touch the reluctance. "He has some doubts about the people who run it, you know, the counselors. He mentioned something about their qualifications." Another pause. "And their politics."

"I see." Her voice had dropped in pitch and had become very soft. "I think you're right, Mrs. Pascal. I think it would be a mistake to send Ellen to camp. I'll drop them a note and ask them to return your application. I'm sure you wouldn't want any record of ever having applied."

When she got off the phone, she wrote the letter requesting a transfer to another school. She stamped the envelope and propped it up on the table where she would see it the next time she went out.

It remained there all weekend. She walked out of the house a dozen times between Mrs. Pascal's call on Friday night and the next Monday morning but she never remembered to mail it. She looked at it during six or seven meals, splattered some tomato juice on a corner of it, but left it on the table when she went to school on Monday.

As she got into her car, she saw Angelo. He stood his ground and smiled at her, the ugly, crooked smile. She got into her car and drove away. The incident left her slightly shaken. It was a bad omen; it would be a bad week.

She saw Teresa after school, thin, quiet Teresa. Teresa the girl, the mother, the deserted wife, the old woman.

"I'm inviting myself for dinner, Teresa. I brought something good."

Teresa nodded and smiled. "Come here a minute."

She walked over to where Teresa sat.

"Look at my hair. Can you see the gray?" Teresa bent her head forward so that you could see the whole beautiful expanse of black. The silver was there, showing through like the gentlest frosting.

"There are only a couple. It's hardly noticeable, your hair is so thick."

"Would you do me a favor?"

"Sure."

"Could you stop in a drugstore next time you come and bring me something to get rid of the gray?"

"Sure, Teresa. I'll bring it next time I come back."

She roasted a large chicken, putting away enough to hold the two of them for a couple of days. On her way home, she stopped at a drugstore for the dye for Teresa and then went on to her dark apartment. She turned on a lamp and her eye fell on the envelope on the table, the letter requesting a transfer. Why couldn't she remember to mail it?

The next day was Tuesday. Jim was awake when she came in. (She knew why. The previous week she had had no school and she had expected him to spend Tuesday with her. Instead, he had put in seven hours at the hospital. He was making up for it today.)

When they sat down to eat, she saw the envelope still propped up on the table. Annoyed that she had forgotten it for the fourth day in a row, she shoved it to the side. Tomorrow she would mail it if she had to do it at eleven at night after her class. She would not let this drag on forever.

Jim was easy and relaxed. "They let me ride an ambulance today," he said, like a little boy fulfilling his dream.

She smiled in spite of herself. This was his third Tuesday at the hospital. He had started going there to make up for the hours he no longer spent reading the black book. His sense of fairness had almost overwhelmed her: an hour for an hour. But it was more than honor that made him continue; he enjoyed it. He wanted to talk about it.

"You liked it, huh?"

"I was as excited as a kid. When I think of the afternoons I spent in a bar, I'm a little sick. I could have been doing so many other things."

"It was your day off, darling, remember? Even priests are entitled to a day off."

"You know," he said, ignoring her comment—he always ignored comments from her that reminded him that he was only human—"I'm starting to feel more sanguine about the things I've done over the past twenty years. I think I pity guys that get out of college and get a job with a big company and start waiting for retirement. I think they must begin to die on the first day of the job."

"Two weeks ago you said you'd never finished anything."

"I know. But you said something once that made me look at it in a new way. You kind of put things in perspective for me."

"I? For you?"

He shrugged. "I'll tell you about it some day."

"I guess I'm one of your people who took a job and started to die, aren't I?"

"You? Never. You left Brooklyn after a year, didn't you? You do a dozen things I would never have thought of doing at your age—teaching at night, camp, the church—and you do them at the same time. I've always been a sequential person. Give something your all for a while, get discouraged, give it up, and start something new. I think watching you made me realize it didn't have to be that way."

"I'm afraid I do everything for the wrong reasons."

"No, you don't. If you did, you would stop after a while. We practically had to twist your arm to give up Monday at the church."

"I don't know how she does it by herself."

"We're getting someone else in soon," he said, "for the early part of the week, someone's who interested in doing this next year."

When he was ready to leave, he walked over to the table. "Do you want me to mail your letter?"

"What letter?"

He picked up the four-day-old letter from the table.

Damn. She didn't really want it mailed. She wanted one more night to think about it, to convince herself that this was what she really wanted.

He looked at the address. "Are you transferring?"

She nodded.

"I'm sorry to hear that," he said.

"I can't get along with him, Jim," she said defensively. She told him about Ellen and camp. "The accusations, the inferences. No one can stand him." She said it as though she meant it. She knew who she was trying to convince.

"Then maybe he won't last."

She knew he was right. She hadn't met anyone who could get along with Giraldi. There were rumors now about why he had left his last school.

"I hate him," she said angrily, trying to convince herself.

"Then transfer."

"Damn it, if you think I shouldn't, why don't you tear the letter up?" She said it with a flood of relief. It was why the letter had remained on her table for four days. She wanted someone else to make the decision for her. She wanted the decision to be made by Jim.

He looked at her with a curious mixture of surprise and disappointment. "Don't ever confuse me with your mother," he said. "I don't tear up other people's letters."

She walked over to him, yanked the letter out of his hand, ripped it into tiny bits, and threw them on the floor. "Good night," she said, her voice quivering, regretting it as she said it, unable to keep from saying it, unable to control the anger within her.

He made a move for the door and stopped. "I love you," he said and the anger dissipated momentarily. She went to him, walking over the pieces of white paper she had strewn on the floor, and put her arms around him and listened to the echo of it, the one thing she had never told him.

"I'm sorry," she said. "I'm not angry at you, Jim. I'm just angry. Sometimes I think I'll never stop being angry."

By three o'clock on Wednesday, her head was splitting, and there was still a session with Ellen ahead of
her. She took two aspirins and sat down with the little
girl. They worked until four. There was still time to get
to Teresa's but she decided to take a nap instead. The
decision did more to alleviate the pain than the aspirins
had. It was easier sometimes to live with the guilt of
not going than with the reality of a visit.

After school on Friday, she took the stuff for Teresa's hair and drove over. Anthony was nowhere to be
seen in the street She went upstairs and knocked. No
answer. "Teresa?" Nothing.

Apprehensively, she took out the key—she had
never used it before—and went inside.

"Teresa?" Her voice had a hollow sound, as if she
had entered a cavern and the only way out was behind
her.

She walked past the kitchen and stopped. The sink
was piled with dirty dishes and silver. The table was a
mess. There were half-eaten sandwiches, chicken
bones, crumbs, garbage over all the surfaces in the
kitchen. Only the Pope, staring across the room,
seemed serene and untouched, immune from the ruin
around him.

She went back to Anthony's little room, her heart
beating faster now, and poked her head inside. The bed
was unmade; clothes lay on the floor. Above the bed,
the Viking boats started suddenly and unevenly to
move, provoked by the currents of air she had disturbed by walking in uninvited.

Turn around, she thought, her hands suddenly clam-
my. Get out. Run. Run like hell.

She walked the last few steps to Teresa's room. There was a smell, a strangely foul smell as she approached. She stopped at the doorway for one terrible second, wiped her palms on her coat, and went in.

"Teresa!"

Inside the room, the smell was worse, the disarray was worse, dresses lying on the floor near the open closet as if a small boy had pulled them down one by one, asking, "This one? This one?" each time and then, unable to reach high enough to replace them, had dropped them where he stood.

Teresa opened her eyes. "You came," she said, her voice thick with sleep or a drug or something infinitely worse. "Is it Thursday yet?"

"It's Friday," she said, fighting the choking feeling in her throat, the trembling in her damp hands. "I couldn't make it Wednesday—" and the guilt for having slept an hour Wednesday when she should have been here, when she was needed here.

"I don't feel too good," Teresa said, "and I'm tired. I'm so tired."

"Why didn't you call me?"

"I thought you would come."

"Why didn't you call a doctor?"

There was no answer.

"Don't you have a doctor, Teresa?" With horror, she heard her voice rising, heard the anger spilling out, finally, after all these months. "Why don't you see a doctor? Why don't you take your medicine? Why do you lie here and rot when someone could help you? Don't you want to get better?"

Teresa started to cry, for the first time in seven months losing her self-possession. "I thought you understood," she said, reaching out a thin hand for a Kleenex. "You got a college education, Ruth. You're a teacher. How come you don't understand? I'm not going to get better."

"I'm sorry, Teresa," she said softly, breathing hard from her outburst, unwittingly inhaling even more of the acrid air. "I'm not angry at you. I'm angry that you're sick. I'm angry—" She stopped. Shut up, she told herself. Stop philosophizing. Do something.

"I know," Teresa said, comforting her in her grief. "Sometimes it's easier to be the sick one. You're the only one who knows what's happening. Nobody else does, not even the doctors."

"Let me get you to a hospital. I can take care of Anthony for you."

"No!"

"They'll make you comfortable."

"No, they won't. They'll stick tubes in me like they did in July. They're not doing that to me again. I'm staying here. I have my kid and my apartment and the neighbors are nice to me."

The invisible neighbors. Where the hell was even one neighbor?

"OK." It had been a last attempt, really, to save herself, not Teresa. She had known from the start that Teresa would never leave.

"Could you help me take a bath?"

She nodded and turned to the bathroom. It took two and a half hours, hours during which she kept from crying, kept from throwing up, kept from screaming by an act of will. She cleaned, she washed, she bathed, she took laundry, she straightened up, she bought paper plates, she cooked, she served and finally, she got into her car, trembling, holding on to the steering wheel as if it would somehow save her, made a U turn and drove, not sure where or why or for how long.

Why go home? What was there at home besides emptiness, an empty room, an empty bed, even an empty refrigerator? She wanted fullness now, not emptiness, warmth, a crowd, laughter, a party. It was Friday night. She would go to a bar, some noisy, crummy bar where the working men came to use up their checks on beer so their wives would have something to get mad about, to scream about, the way she wanted to scream.

No. She smiled as it came to her. She would go to Jim's bar, the dark, paneled bar with the bartender who knew his patrons by first names and days of the week. Walk in and say, Hi, I'm Jimmy's girl. You remember Jimmy, he's Tuesday.

And all her friends would be there, everyone she'd ever flown with, everyone who had ever needed her, everyone she had ever listened to, touched, crawled inside for a hasty moment and never seen again. Only Jim would be absent, Jim, who had troubles enough of his own—the man he had killed and the woman he had wronged.

And when they were all together—

"Ow!"

The car hit hers with such suddenness, such impact, that it took her breath away for a moment and she leaned forward on the steering wheel she was clutching to get it back.

"You OK, Miss?"

"Didn't you know that was a red light?"

"Someone go look at the kid. I think he's hurt."

Oh my God, I've killed a child.

She turned the key in the ignition and removed it, her hand moving without orders from her brain. Strangely, the motor had stopped before she turned the key. If the motor was off, how could she have been driving? She got out, circled the rear of her car, and walked to the car whose nose had hit her right door. At the wheel was a young, scared boy.

"Are you all right?" she aksed.

He nodded.

"Is it your car?" It was new and large.

"My father's."

"Tell your father it was my fault, OK? I'll give you my telephone number and he can call me up and I'll tell him myself."

"Thanks."

When she got home, the phone was ringing.

"What happened?" he asked. "I was getting worried."

"Can you come over tonight, Jim?" Her voice sounded small and foreign.

There was a pause, the pause that meant he had an obligation at the church, he couldn't come. "For a little while, maybe. Is something wrong? You don't sound right."

"Just come. Please."

It was dark when he got there—but she always saw him in the dark—or by artificial light. It was part of the unrealness.

"Tell me what happened."

"I saw Teresa today. Could we sit down for a minute?"

They sat on the couch and she curled up next to him, letting her body relax for the first time all day.

There were footsteps on the stairs and she straightened up. A knock.

"Go ahead," he said.

She opened the door. A man with an attaché case stood in the hall. "I'm Johnny Gordon's father. You know, the accident."

She let him come in, not introducing him.

"Johnny told me about the accident," he said. "Were you hurt? The car looked pretty bad."

"I'm not hurt. It was my fault. I went through a red light."

"He just got his license last week," the man said, frowning. "I told him not to take the car, but you know how kids are. But he's a good boy and I've watched him drive. He drives well."

"Please don't blame him. It was my fault. It was all my fault."

He didn't want to go. He wanted to stay and take some of the blame for the accident. She got rid of him finally and walked to the kitchen and started watering the herbs. She hadn't meant for Jim to know; she hadn't called him for that.

"You want to tell me about it?"

"It happened after I left Teresa," she said, putting down the watering can. "I was sick when I left her. I couldn't think straight." She turned to face him, to hand him her ultimatum, to pass the buck. "It was terrible today. I screamed at her, Jim. I was so angry I screamed at her. I don't want to go there any more."

He came over and put an arm around her shoulder.

His face had not changed. "Then don't go," the voice of sanity said. "There's no reason to do this to yourself. We can get a visiting nurse to stop in."

She was off the hook, she was free. Relief poured into her, warming her, sustaining her. The feeling lasted almost sixty seconds.

"I didn't say I wouldn't go," she said carefully. "I said I didn't want to. I couldn't really stop now. I'll see it through."

After that, she started feeling a little less angry.

She handled the next seven days better, making her visits on the weekend days and Tuesday as well—Jim needed the sleep anyway; the hospital knocked him out—so that if she missed Wednesday, there would be no catastrophe. In addition, she exacted from Teresa the promise that a neighbor would be told to call if anything happened.

She got there Wednesday after all, walking in at four-fifteen. She could stay awhile and still miss the worst of the traffic on her way to the evening class.

She knocked, heard with relief the "Come in," and opened the door. In the living room, on the coffee table in front of the sofa, was a pitcher full of pink and white carnations. They rang a faint bell in her mind. Someone had sent her a bunch of carnations once but who? When?

"They're nice, aren't they?" Teresa said from the sofa.

"Beautiful. Who's your admirer?"

"Father Kendall brought them this morning. He came over, just like that. I haven't seen him since last year."

"That was nice of him."

"Yeah. I told you he was nice, remember? Take a flower for yourself."

When she left, she took with her a pink carnation. It was her first flower from Jim.

She brought it with her to dinner and up to the classroom. She walked in five minutes late, carrying her bag, her papers, and her pink carnation.

"Hi," she said, putting her things down and unbuttoning her coat.

There was an unusual silence from the class, a lack of response, a look of gloom on their collective face.

"What's wrong?" she said, automatically reaching for the roll book.

"Don't take roll tonight, Miss Gold," Mr. Gerstenwald said. "Everyone is here. You don't have to check."

She slid her finger down the list. Abrams, Dorgan, Gerstenwald, Halloran, Jenkins, Larkin, Mancuso, Muller, O'Hara. She looked up. "Mrs. O'Hara?"

They were silent. She looked around. No eyes were lifted to meet hers. She heard a sound from the side of the room, from behind Mr. Gerstenwald where Mrs. Rand sat, Mrs. Rand who was Mrs. O'Hara's friend. Mrs. Rand was crying quietly in a handkerchief.

"Oh my God," she said, sitting down heavily. Mrs. O'Hara had been the youngest member of the class. She turned her head away from them and started to cry, without reason and without restraint, for all of them together, Mrs. O'Hara, Teresa, Professor Hillman who had missed the azaleas, and Abraham Gold, that giant of a man whose voice had been loud enough to reach God and who had died so quietly that the sound of his death had not reached her for more than a thousand hours.

They gathered around her, grandmothers and grandfathers, touching her, talking to her, comforting her, as if she were the bereaved, as if the loss had been hers alone, as if they understood the meaning of her tears.

Finally, Mr. Gerstenwald took over. "Sit down," he said to them. "It's time we learned something tonight."

They sat down and she closed the roll book and found her notes. She felt curiously purged as the tears dried, and light, as if grief were a thing behind her now. She had shed her private tears for Teresa here in this public place while they all looked on, misreading her grief. The bell rang eventually—it was time—and the bar closed for the evening.

She sat at her desk and watched them go, with their smiles, their words of assurance. Then she picked up her things and started for the door.

"Miss Gold."

She turned around. Mr. Gerstenwald was standing at her desk, holding the pink carnation in his ancient fingers and smiling.

"Don't forget your flower," he said. "I'm sure a wonderful person gave it to you and he wouldn't want it left in a dark, lonely classroom."

"Thank you," she said, taking the carnation. He patted her shoulder and she went home.

At three o'clock on Thursday of the following week, Judy Greene stood at the door to Ruth's classroom. "Do you go somewhere today or are you free for coffee?"

"I'm free this time. Give me one minute." It was a

Catholic holiday and the program had been canceled for the afternoon.

They walked to a nearby place where the pastry was good and the coffee lousy. They had drunk coffee together there once before, on a Tuesday in February.

"Are you going to camp?" Judy asked when they were sitting down. She looked somewhat uncomfortable, as if she hadn't planned to begin this way but the words had just come out.

"Yes. Aren't you?"

"Pete's going," Judy said, avoiding the question. She sat waiting for a response. When it failed to come, she went on reluctantly. "Things aren't going well with us. The whole thing has got me down. I'm thinking of withdrawing from the camp. I wanted to talk to you about it."

Oh God, she thought helplessly, I've been taken. We aren't here for half an hour of bitter coffee and sweet pastry, we're here so I can solve this girl's stupid, insignificant problem.

She fought the urge to get up and run. Oh, Jimmy, Jimmy. Where was he now, when she needed him so much? It was a holy day today, the day of the Ascension. He was probably wearing one of those long black robes and sitting behind the door with the brass plate that said Rev. James M. Kendall, listening to someone confess some very unoriginal sin.

I yelled at my mother again, Father. I know I told you that last week and the week before but I'm sorry for it this time. You'll forgive me, Father, won't you?

I said a four-letter word yesterday, Father, a bad one. Do you want to hear it? I could tell it to you.

Judy looked as if she were on the verge of tears. Was

she really so concerned about Pete after going out with him for three or four weeks?

"What's wrong, Judy?" she asked gently, gathering her black robe around her.

"I've done something very foolish."

"Listen to me, Judy. You think there's something between Pete and me, don't you? Well, there isn't. There's nothing. There never was." She told the lie easily, as if lying had been a lifelong habit. "I've known him for three and a half years and we've been nothing more than friends. He's going through a trying time now. Don't ask me about it; just take my word for it. Give him a couple of weeks, maybe a month. It'll work out."

She felt suddenly very sorry for both of them, for Judy because she didn't understand, and for Pete because he was trying now and he couldn't quite make it by himself. He would have to be told; Jim would have to tell him about them. When Pete knew, the cord would be severed. He would be free.

She went home and changed her clothes. She might as well have something to eat with Teresa, she decided, looking at the clock. It would save cooking twice.

She was hanging up her dress when the phone rang.

"Hello?"

"This Mrs. Gold?" It was a woman's voice.

"Yes." Tentatively.

"I been trying to get you since yesterday afternoon. What do you do all day?"

She squelched the desire to say that she worked. "Who is this, please?"

"This is a friend of Teresa's. I live downstairs of her. She asked me to call you. She don't feel too good."

"She asked you yesterday?"

"Yeah. I tried to get you till almost eleven. Then you were gone again this morning. Don't you ever stay home?"

"Thank you for calling. I'll be right over."

There was a place to park in front of Teresa's house, behind an old Ford with a New York State license. She went upstairs with a feeling of dread, of finality. Halfway up, she heard a man's voice. Father McAndrew, she thought with a mixture of relief and discomfort. The thought of seeing him again made her feel very uneasy. In spite of what he had said, she was sure he disliked her.

There was something wrong with the sounds from the apartment, she thought as she reached the door. An old woman had yelled, "Leave him alone," as she came up the stairs. Was it possible that the voice had been Teresa's?

And the man's voice was strictly New England, no hint of Scotland, no hint, in fact, of humor. He was angry, he was bellowing. She stood at the door and listened. There was no single object of his wrath. Everything he saw was a four-lettered disappointment, the furniture, the apartment, his kid, the neighborhood. Why the hell had he bothered to come back?

She listened in the dark hallway while the old Ford and the new voice matched up with an image in her mind. She knocked softly. The tirade continued. She knocked so that the door shook.

The monologue within stopped. "Yeah?" the voice said.

"Is Teresa there?"

"She's in bed, resting. Who is it?"

"A neighbor. I came to see Teresa."

"Well, go home, neighbor. She don't want to see you."

"Anthony?" she called. "Are you all right?"

The door opened suddenly and Anthony ran out, almost knocking her over. "I want to go with you," he said. "Please?"

She took his hand and turned toward the stairs, but she was too slow. The man appeared, grabbed Anthony by the collar, and threw him violently into the apartment so that he slid across the bare living room floor on his back, coming to rest in a quiet little huddle against the opposite wall.

"Get lost," the man said to her and she retreated down the stairs.

Call Jim. It was the only clear thought in her possession. Find a telephone and call Jim. She knocked on the downstairs door. No answer. A minute wasted.

She got into the car. There had to be a phone booth around. She started driving, from corner to corner, looking for a phone booth. She went for blocks, going in circles and wasting time. Finally she saw a bar on the next corner. She pulled over to the curb, ran in, and found the telephone.

She sat down in the booth and closed the door. The light went on but the fan didn't. It was hot and she had started to sweat as she walked in from the street. She looked at her watch. It was a little after six. They would be eating now. She found the number in her wallet, where it had been waiting for this moment since January. She had never called it before, and just the thought of dialing it made her feel sick. What if the pastor answered? What if he asked who she was?

On the fourth ring, a woman answered. "Rectory," she said coldly.

"I'd like to speak to Father Kendall, please." Her voice sounded young and scared. The telephone booth was stifling. She had probably used up half of its oxygen. Under her hair, her neck was damp.

"He's busy now," the woman said. "What did you want?"

In the background, she heard a man's voice, an unfamiliar voice. From its cadence, she knew that he was telling a story.

"I have to talk to him. It's very important."

"Could you talk to someone else?"

Oh God, she knows. This bitch knows who I am and she knows about us. Angelo guessed and now everyone knows. We're the only two people in the world that we have fooled.

"No," she said, keeping her voice steady. "I must speak to Father Kendall."

"Just a minute."

The phone was laid down with a clatter that jarred her. There was a roar of male laughter as the tale in the distance ended. She had never thought of them as laughing, as having anything to laugh about. Somehow she had never thought of them as quite that human, none of them except Jim.

There was a click. "Father Reilly here," in a voice still ringing with laughter.

"I'm sorry. I wanted to speak to Father Kendall."

"Oh, of course. Just a minute." He put the phone down gently. "For you, Jim," she heard him say, and the sick feeling abated slightly.

She had waited to hear a second click but it had never come. The bitch was listening on an extension.

"Father Kendall."

"Hi," she said, shaking now with relief. "Can you hear me?"

"Not too well."

"I think someone may have forgotten to hang up the extension," she said pointedly.

"Hold on. I'll take care of it."

The click was immediate.

"It's OK now," he said. "She hung up. What happened?"

"Teresa's neighbor called. Teresa's been feeling sick since yesterday. When I got there, I heard all kinds of ranting and raving. Her husband must have just come back. He sounds like a madman."

"He is."

"Jim, get Anthony out of there. Give him to me."

There was no answer.

"Please, Jim. Teresa asked me once. Listen, I have a key to her apartment."

"Where are you?"

"In a bar."

"Where is the bar?" he asked impatiently.

"I don't know," she wailed. "I don't have any idea. I just drove until—"

"Ruth, listen to me. Go back to Teresa's. Wait downstairs. After I call Andy, I'll be right over."

Her car was parked in front of the bar, the smashed door facing her as she stepped outside.

She found her way back to Teresa's and sat at the wheel, waiting, the key in her hand. A car pulled up across the street a few minutes later and she saw Andy's strawberry blond head make its exit. He crossed the street and came toward her car.

"Jim said you had a key," he said, bypassing formalities.

She handed it to him. "Will you bring Anthony to me?" she asked. It was suddenly very important that he come to her and not to some stranger. She had promised Teresa.

"I'll bring Anthony to you. Go home now and wait."

After he went inside the house, she drove home. It was barely six-thirty.

She called the drugstore. Yes, they had folding beds and television sets to rent. Yes, they would send one of each over within the hour. Finally, she thought, I am going to see "Sesame Street."

They came up the stairs at a little after seven, Jim talking softly while Anthony said nothing. She had never seen him look so glum. She realized as the door closed that Anthony had come almost empty-handed. He carried a red rubber ball and wore an outfit she had gotten him in September (now neatly patched on both knees). She poured him a glass of milk and called Cassie. Please, if she could make it before the stores closed, some clothes for Anthony in the size after seven. Don't forget pajamas. And please, not Saks Fifth Avenue. Try Filene's.

"I'm getting you a television set, Anthony," she said when she was off the phone.

He bounced the ball once but said nothing.

"Where's your friend?" she asked Jim.

He handed her the key. "Waiting for the ambulance. I forgot she had no phone. I had to stop at the hospital before I came over and ask them to send one."

"She didn't want to go to the hospital." Her voice sounded slightly hysterical.

"There was no choice any more," he said.

She turned away from him and went to the refrigerator. There was a chunk of roast beef there that would feed them all. She took it out and kept herself busy with it for a few minutes while she pushed aside the feeling of having betrayed Teresa.

"Andy will look into a foster hor e. Does anyone— did you say your name over there?"

"No. I said I was a neighbor."

"Good." He looked at his watch. 'What time do you have?"

"Almost seven-thirty."

He set his watch and wound it. "I have to be on my way."

"You missed dinner."

"It's that kind of a day."

She went to the refrigerator and got him an apple. He smiled and took it, touching her fingers the way he had that day on the Common when he had asked her for a dime.

"The woman who answered the phone," she said.

"Don't worry about it. She's protective but she doesn't pry." He turned to Anthony. "I'll see you to-morrow, Anthony," he said but Anthony was sitting on the floor in a heap and crying.

"What's the matter, love?" she asked, getting down on her knees.

"My boats. I want my boats."

"What boats docs he mean?" Jim asked.

"The Brooklyn Museum. I gave him a mobile too."

"I'll get them for you, Anthony. I'll bring them over tomorrow before you go to sleep.

"Honest?" He rubbed the tears with the back of a dirty hand.

"Honest."

At eight, the bed and television set arrived. At eight-thirty, Father McAndrew dropped in, solemn and official. He had come to see Anthony; she kept out of his way. At ten to nine he looked at his watch. (They were always looking at their watches, these men, parceling their time into tiny, precious packages.)

"I'll be back tomorrow," he said, and left.

She had wanted to ask about Teresa but he made her feel uncomfortable, ill at ease. He didn't like her and the feeling was mutual. The one person this year she had wanted to impress favorably and she had botched it. She could feel the tension ease as his footsteps receded down the stairs.

Cassie appeared almost immediately afterwards. The sound of footsteps on the stairs was starting to beat a pattern on her brain.

"I charged everything," Cassie said. "You don't owe me a cent till I get the bill." She glanced briefly at Anthony. "How long?"

"I don't know. They're looking into a foster home. I wish I could keep him."

"Think about it," Cassie said. "You have a one-room apartment. You're getting married soon."

"Am I?"

"You know you are."

"Thanks for everything."

"Call me at work," Cassie said. "If there's anything else—My father knows people, you know."

She ran a bath for Anthony after Cassie left and called the school secretary to say she was ill. Anthony came out half an hour later looking slightly cleaner and wearing new pajamas.

"What kind of pills do you take?" he asked.

Her eyes widened. Pills? Half the people she knew took pills but the thought of an eight-year-old—

"I don't take pills," she said, her horror genuine. "What makes you think I do?"

"You got a sign on the mirror. I read it." He was proud of his accomplishment.

She walked into the bathroom. TAKE A PILL TODAY was pasted on the lower left-hand corner of the mirror, where she had placed it triumphantly at the end of January. She took the piece of paper off the mirror and threw it in the basket.

"I take vitamins," she said, sitting at her desk to write a new reminder. "Don't you?"

"No," he said. "But the sister said pills were bad for you."

"The sister was right. But vitamins are OK." She wrote VITAMINS on the piece of paper and taped it up on the mirror. Teach them to read, she thought. Just teach them to read.

In the morning, he woke her up. "It's seven o'clock, Ruth. I have to get to school."

"You're staying home with me today. Go back to sleep."

"I have to go," he said. "I have a Mother's Day present in school. I have to bring it home today."

Mother's Day. Jesus Christ, Sunday was Mother's Day and today was Friday.

"I'll tell Father McAndrew. He'll give it to your mom."

"Call him up."

"Later."

After breakfast she turned on "Sesame Street." That, Anthony informed her, was for kids. She left him fiddling with the dial and called Cassie.

"Did you know Sunday was Mother's Day?"

"Didn't you?"

"I didn't even have my kids at school make something. I'll have to send a message to the sub. Listen, is there a florist among your charge accounts?"

"Of course."

"Have them wire something to my mother. Sign it with love and kisses."

"Ruth or Ruthie?"

She took a deep breath. Every problem had become insurmountable. "My love is monosyllabic this year," she said.

When she got off the phone. Anthony reminded her to call Father McAndrew. She was unable to think of an excuse. Her call from the bar yesterday had drained her.

"What's the name of your church, Anthony?"

He thought a minute. "Our Lady."

"Just 'Our Lady'?"

"Yeah."

She went to the phone book. There would be ten churches starting with Our Lady and she would be off the hook. No luck. Exactly one in the whole city, Our

Lady of Sorrows. She dialed while her stomach tightened. A woman answered.

"Is Father McAndrew there?"

"I saw him just a minute ago. Can you hold?"

"Yes."

There was a short wait. "Hello?"

"Father McAndrew?"

"Yes, speaking."

"This is Ruth Gold."

"Good morning. How is everything today?"

"Just fine. Uh, Sunday is Mother's Day." Idiot, get to the point. "Anthony made something in school for his mother. He asked me to call you. . . ."

"I'll pick it right up and take it with me this afternoon. I appreciate your calling. I'm sure there's nothing that would please Teresa more."

"How is she?"

"She's conscious and they're making her comfortable."

Cassie had brought a Monopoly set and halfway through the morning they sat down on the floor and started a game. They broke for lunch. There was very little left to eat; ordinarily, Saturday was her shopping day. Jim had told her to stay off the street with Anthony, but what harm would there be in going out to shop? Teresa's husband was unlikely to be in this neighborhood and what difference did it make anyway? It wasn't as if he wanted the child.

She put the dishes in the dishwasher and cleaned up. "Let's go out," she said. "We'll do some shopping."

She locked the door and they started down the stairs. When they reached the landing, she heard her phone.

She listened to it ring twice, then turned and went back up.

"Where were you?" It was Jim.

"I thought I'd do some shopping. I'm running out of—"

"Stay where you are. Andy just called. Teresa's husband is going to court to get Anthony back."

"Why?" She was aghast.

"I don't know why. Look, do you know the name of Teresa's caseworker?"

"No. She mentioned him once or twice but never by name. I don't even know for sure that it's a man. Can't you ask her?"

"Yes, I guess we can ask her." He sounded incredibly tired. "I'll see you sometime later today. Tell Anthony I have his boats."

"Would you bring me some milk?"

"I'll bring you some milk."

He came at six with the mobile.

"Put it over my bed," Anthony ordered.

"I was in the navy once, Anthony," Jim said, taking a chair over to the folding bed.

"So was Father McAndrew. He told me."

"That's where I got to know him. I bet he didn't tell you that."

"I didn't know priests went in the navy."

"We weren't priests then. We were kids."

Anthony smiled, showing his dimples. "Kids can't go in the navy."

"Some of them make it," Jim said. "This one right here did." He turned to Ruth. "Cassie's father is a judge, isn't he?"

She nodded. "But not in this county."

"But he knows people, doesn't he?"

"He knows everyone."

"Can you get her on the phone?"

Cassie had been in the shower. Hal was coming to take her to dinner in half an hour. Yes, Daddy knew everyone everywhere. Why didn't Jim join them for dinner?

He wrote down the address and left. It was the first time she had felt a pang of jealousy since January. It was absurd and irrational but it was painfully real. Father McAndrew came and went. She got ready for bed and waited, but there was no call. At midnight, she went to sleep.

At ten in the morning, Cassie called. "Can I baby-sit while you shop?"

"I'd appreciate it. You must have a sixth sense."

"Jim suggested I call. He's afraid you're going stir-crazy."

"Where did you have dinner?"

"Nowhere special. By the time Jim left, we had missed our reservation."

"Didn't he eat with you?"

"No. He said he didn't have time. When do you want me?"

"As soon as you get here."

She hung up and sat for a quiet minute looking at the telephone. Bitch, she thought. I will never stop being a bitch.

She was finished by two, the laundry, the shopping, and a milkshake to go for Anthony.

"Did you talk to your father?" she asked before Cassie left.

"Jim was supposed to meet him this morning." She frowned. "I may see him. I don't know. How is—?" She nodded toward Anthony.

"The last description was 'conscious.' I feel like a traitor, Cassie. I didn't realize when I called Jim Thursday night that they would take her to a hospital. She wanted to stay home. I didn't mean to do that to her.".

Cassie stood up. "Play Monopoly," she said.

At three, the phone rang.

"It's me," Jim said, his voice strange, barely recognizable.

"What happened?"

"Andy just called. Teresa died about an hour ago."

The chill started at the back of her neck and crawled slowly down her arms. For a moment, she did nothing but breathe. Anthony was sitting on the floor, oblivious, counting hundred-dollar bills.

"Ruth?"

"Yes?"

"Will you tell Anthony?"

"What?"

"Andy will be over soon. Will you tell Anthony before he gets there?"

She sat looking at the clock. "Was anyone with her?" she said finally.

"Andy was."

"Oh."

"I can't come over," he said.

No, of course not. I never expected you would. I always knew that when this moment came, I would be utterly alone.

She replaced the receiver. It wasn't until later that

she remembered she had said nothing to let him know she had even heard him.

"Anthony?"

What had she ever experienced to prepare her for this? How does one go about telling a little child that his mother has died? She felt a tremondous wave of resentment against them, against Father McAndrew for not coming here and doing it himself, against Jim for calling and passing the buck. So he'd miss a few goddamn confessions. Let them stop sinning; there would be fewer confessions to hear.

Anthony looked up. "I got nine hundred dollars," he said.

"Anthony, you know your mom's been sick."

"Yeah. She was always laying in bed."

"That was Father Kendall on the phone. You remember you got an ambulance the other night?"

"Yeah, so she could go to the hospital where my father couldn't find her."

"Anthony, your mom was very sick. She died a little while ago."

He put the pile of hundred-dollar bills down in their place on the floor and picked up the pile of fifties.

"Are they going to bury her?" he asked.

She felt the urge to run again, the way she had felt it Thursday when Judy started talking about her troubles. Run away. Leave the door open. When Andy comes, he'll pick up the pieces.

"Yes," she said, "they will."

He put the fifties down and looked up at her. 'Won't she be cold?" he asked.

She got down on the floor and hugged him, the most purely selfish act of her life. She had never before felt quite so strongly the need to touch another human being. She was still holding him when the priest came.

He nodded to her at the door, walked over to Anthony and took him to the folding bed at the rear of the apartment and sat down next to him. She turned away, feeling lonesome and alone. It had come as a shock. She had seen it coming, watched its progress, raged against it impotently and futilely, but its coming had been as much of a shock as if she had known nothing.

She walked to the bookcase and ran her hand along the assembled bindings. Stupidly she began to wonder if the azaleas were in bloom. She looked out the window. Nothing but green shrubbery.

She felt a hand very lightly on her shoulder and she turned. The priest was standing behind her holding Anthony's hand. "Are you all right?" he asked gently.

They must take a course on how to talk gently. Some day she would make inquiries and sign up for the course herself.

She nodded.

"I was with her," he said.

"Thank you," she said, encompassing everything—telling her, being there, coming here. She was starting to hate herself. Even if he had done it a hundred times before, it could never be easy.

"Anthony and I have been talking. He's very happy to stay here until we find a more permanent home for him."

She nodded again.

"I think they'll hear the case on Monday. Perhaps we'll have a decision early in the week."

"Yes."

"Do you keep liquor in the house?" he asked.

"Yes." She got up, opened the liquor cabinet, and stood aside.

"Might I have a brandy? Neat. No ice. You might want one for yourself."

She poured two, her hand moving mechanically, filling the snifters she and Jim used when they had brandy after they made love. The priest drank his quickly. She sat and sipped hers.

"I see you have your boats back, Anthony," Father McAndrew said.

"Yeah. Father Kendall got them."

"Did he tell you we were in the navy together?"

"Yeah. He said you were kids in the navy."

The priest smiled. "Did he now? I thought he was pretty grown up when we were in the navy."

In the middle of the night, Anthony woke her up. She sat up in bed and turned on the lamp.

Why did they bury dead people? he wanted to know. Where had his mother gone?

"What did Father McAndrew tell you?"

"That she went to heaven."

"He's right, Anthony."

"Did she walk there?"

"No."

"Then how did she get there?"

It was the moment when she realized that she would be unable to keep him. She could tell him anything, but sooner or later he would know she had said it without conviction.

"God took her," she said.

"I want her back."

It's too late, Anthony. It's too late for all of us.

"I'm sorry," she said.

He started to cry. It was the first time all day that he had cried. She found she was almost relieved to see his tears. You could cope with tears; you could feel them. But the questions—how could you ever answer the questions?

She put her arms around him but he fought her, screamed at her, kicked her. He didn't want her; he wanted his mother. Get out of here, he screamed, and get me my mother.

She hung on to him as if he were hers, as if she had given birth to him, nursed him, bathed him, and sent him off to school, and finally he relaxed and lay next to her in the bed she had never shared with anyone except Jim. The telephone rang once but he didn't hear it and it never rang again. It was an echo from the tomb, an echo she would hear for the rest of her life.

He fell asleep after the sobbing ended and she lay there, holding him, not wanting to leave him because they belonged to each other and she knew now she would be unable to keep him.

Jim called at eleven in the morning. He had spoken to Judge Ballard yesterday and the judge had impressed him tremendously. There were no promises, no guarantees, just his word that he would do his best for Anthony.

The case would probably be heard tomorrow. The funeral was scheduled for Tuesday morning.

"How are you holding up, darling?" he asked, finishing his monologue.

"We're doing fine."

"Do you need anything."

"Just milk."

"Can it wait till tomorrow?"

"Sure." Another day alone.

Monday there was a delay at court. The caseworker couldn't be located until afternoon and Joe, the devoted father, had to make a hurried trip to New York. But at least now the judge had a name.

She called Cassie.

"Yes, Daddy knows him."

"Casually?"

"No. They've served on committees together. They've known each other for years."

"Then there's hope."

"There's hope even without Daddy. By the way, he was very impressed with Jim."

"It was mutual."

. That night Jeff called. She had missed two days of school and he wondered how she was. Just a cold, she said. The weather had been so changeable. She would be back soon.

How about this weekend? Was she free?

She got rid of him and sat down to the continuing game of Monopoly. Real Estate was starting to save her sanity.

Tuesday was the funeral. She opened a kitchen window in the morning and stood in front of it, as if by listening hard enough she could hear the bells tolling for Teresa. There were no bells, just an occasional car going down the street and the sounds of children too little to be in school. It was a Tuesday but this one had begun differently and would end differently. After the funeral, they would go to the courthouse where justice would be done.

The day dragged, the Monopoly game grew sour. No one had brought her a newspaper or a paperback book. Daytime television was for imbeciles, but she watched it to keep her mind off what was going on in the church and the cemetery and the courthouse. The afternoon passed but the telephone remained quiet. She set the table for dinner and they sat down. Who had attended Teresa's funeral, she wondered, besides a priest and the husband who had deserted her?

No one called. How bad could it be that no one would call? A Tuesday had come and almost gone and she hadn't seen Jim. It was the first time since February.

Father McAndrew had visited daily since Thursday. On the days they had both visited, they had happened or maneuvered not to come at the same time. She had been grateful for that. She could manage a kind of charade as long as Jim was not present. What did Father McAndrew know? He must know that they shared the four-poster. He was the first person to have come into the apartment and not commented on it.

At seven-thirty, she ran a bath for Anthony. As he came out of the bathroom, smelling of soap and toothpaste, someone came up the stairs.

It was Father McAndrew, dressed in sports clothes and looking tired.

"What happened?" she asked.

"Why don't we talk about it later?" he said with a small smile. "How long is it since you've been out?"

"I don't remember. Two days, three." She shrugged.

"Go for a walk," he said. "Anthony and I will start a

new Monopoly game. The wealth seems to have been pretty well distributed in this one."

"Are you sure?"

"Go," he said tiredly. "Put a coat on. It's cool out."

She put a key in her pocket, took a jacket from the closet, and went downstairs. Outside, she stood in front of the door and drew a deep breath. It was starting to smell like spring.

"Ruth?"

She turned to her right. He was leaning against his car, which was parked next to the street lamp. He looked terrible—tired, old, worn, lined. He put his arms around her in the street and some of the tension relaxed.

"I thought I wouldn't see you," she said.

"It's Tuesday, remember?"

"Tell me what happened."

"Let's go for a ride."

"I can't. I said I'd be right back."

"It's OK," he said. "Andy knows."

They got in the car and he started to drive.

"I know the judge," he said finally.

"Personally?"

"Legally. Remember that night in January?" He stopped. "Our first night," he said, with a change of expression.

"I remember."

"I had been in court that day. It was a custody case."

"You lost it."

"It was the same judge."

She could feel everything inside her drop.

"He remembered me. I can't say there was any warmth in the memory."

"What are we going to do if we lose this one?"

"I don't know. Andy and I have been batting it around for three hours."

"Did you testify?"

"I testified, Andy testified. I never saw anything, you know. I heard and I saw the results. She came to me a few times last year before he left her and told me what was going on. But I never really saw anything. It's like the case in January."

Her stomach had started to tighten. "It's not over yet, is it?"

"No. They'll probably finish it up tomorrow." He stopped for a light. There were trees and small houses along the road. They had driven north. It was growing dark and all the cars had turned a dull gray-blue. He switched his lights on. "The most incredible part of the hearing was Joe. Suddenly he's the bereaved husband, the father desperate for his son. He had a haircut, a shirt and tie, and a script out of a soap opera. They treated him with deference." He swallowed. "It made me sick."

"He was that believable?"

"He had a stack of canceled checks that Teresa had endorsed since he left her. He went back to New York yesterday to get them. His story is that he went there to find work when he was laid off here. But he was never laid off."

"How do you know?"

"I checked. He's shacking up in New York. I don't know what motivated him to send money and I don't know what motivates him to get this child back. The money didn't even help her. They cut off her welfare payments when she told them he sent checks."

"I know."

"Well, why didn't you tell me?"

"Because I didn't know you. Leave me alone."

He pulled the car off the road and turned off the motor and the lights. "I don't know how she ever made ends meet," he said. "The checks couldn't have covered much more than the rent." He sat quietly for a minute. "Were you helping her?"

"Just groceries."

"For how long?"

"I don't know."

"I wish you had said something," he said gently.

"What difference does it make?" she said, feeling close to tears. "I didn't do any of the things that were really important to her. She wanted to stay home. She wanted to die at home, not in a goddamn hospital, and I ended up sending her to one."

"You weren't responsible for that," he said. "It was my decision."

"Then why did you do it?"

He took a moment to answer. "Because she was hemorrhaging."

She closed her eyes. "I'm sorry. I didn't mean to yell."

"It's been a rough day."

"Were you there this morning?"

"Yes." He got out of the car and walked around to her side, his feet making crackling sounds in the dirt, the sound of camp, the country, the out-of-doors. He opened her door. "Let's take a walk."

She got out and he reached into the back of the car, pulled out a blanket, and shut the door.

"No," she said.

"No what?"

"Not tonight. Not here."

"Why?"

"Please. I can't."

"Why can't you? Isn't it nice enough here for you? Does your sex have to be nice and clean in an antique bed with a shower afterwards?"

"It isn't that."

He opened the car door. "Get in. I'll take you home. I'll see you next week. By appointment."

It stung as if he had slapped her face. "He's not a bartender," she said into the darkness in front of her where he was standing. "He's a priest."

"Yeah," he said. "My friend Andy is a priest. It almost slipped my mind. We have to protect him from the things that go on between people, don't we? Thanks for being so solicitous of my friend. Where the hell are you when I need you?"

She shut the car door. It had been a worse day than she had imagined. At home, she had only imagined. He had been there, had seen it, heard it, even smelled it firsthand. The day had touched him, wounded him perhaps, made him afraid. She had never seen him afraid, never imagined him afraid, had never thought to look for the signs, the little things that would give his fear away. She slipped an arm around his waist and he touched her face with his palm in the darkness, running his hand through her hair harshly, gripping her hair as if it were something to hold onto after a day in which nothing had been tangible except a pile of checks.

"I'm sorry," he said, his face against hers. "You know I didn't mean that. I'm sorry."

"Shh."

He started walking, leading her away from the car, away from the road, to a place on the ground where she would lie next to him and lose herself in him, bring him to her, with her, inside her, make time stop for both of them—there would be no time in the forest tonight—hold him, hold him without letting him move until the ticking started, until the wind, holding its breath at the edge of the wood began to whisper again, hush, hush, I love you.

She lay on his arm and listened to his breathing subside, listened to his heart beating strongly through his shirt.

"You're the first woman I've ever said I was sorry to," he said. "I keep thinking if I had told her—"

"Don't, Jim. It's so long ago, it can't make any difference any more."

"I haven't been able to stop thinking about it. Something you said last month started me off. It's gotten all wrapped up in what's going on now. I'm not sure I even see my way out of it."

"Was she—what was she to you?"

He breathed deeply. It was almost a sigh. "She was a good lay," he said. "That was the beginning and the end of it."

She had expected half a dozen other answers. This one took her by surprise. She had expected to hate Carol, to blame her for everything that had happened, but she found herself feeling sorry for her, felt her body stiffen with cold anger as Carol's might have if she had heard herself described that way.

"Hey," he said, trying to relax the stiffness in the shoulders, "you're a better one. You know that, don't you? And it wasn't the beginning and it isn't the end."

"Did she know? Did she know that was all she was to you?"

She waited for the answer, but it never came.

"You never found your Bible, did you?" he said instead.

"No. I put it away last fall. I wish I could remember where."

"I'll give you one of mine," he said.

They walked back to the car, staying very close to each other, feeling renewed. On the way home, he apologized. "I'll go up with you," he said. "I won't make you face Andy alone."

"Don't, Jim. I'm not ready to face the two of you together." She had left without a comb and without a Kleenex. He had brushed her off but bits of leaves clung to her jacket and hair. She looked down at her jeans. Going up the stairs she would start to feel it.

"Can I take you out for my birthday?" he asked. God, it was next Wednesday.

"Out?"

"To a restaurant. Where someone else does the cooking and cleaning up."

"You can take me out."

"We'll make it Tuesday. I'll pick you up at six."

She took a last look in the car mirror.

"You look very pretty," he said. "I don't tell you that much, do I?"

He didn't and it bothered her that it bothered her.

"I figure you know it every time you look in the mirror."

"Go to hell," she said.

Anthony was asleep at the back of the apartment, which was dark. The priest had been sitting on the sofa and reading.

"I'm sorry about the time," she said, closing the door, feeling awkward in her own home.

"I enjoyed the game. I haven't had that much money in my hand since I was in the navy."

She had hoped he would leave as she walked in but he missed his cue.

"Would you like some coffee?" she asked.

He shook his head. "Perhaps a brandy."

She poured two and sat in the chair next to the sofa. He took his to the kitchen counter and surveyed the windows.

"My mother grew flowers," he said to the darkness outside.

"I enjoy it. It's relaxing and rewarding."

"Relaxing and rewarding." He turned around, a slight smile on his face.

Damn. He had misunderstood her. She had made a comment about a pastime and he had taken it as a philosophy of life.

"You don't like me very much, do you?" she asked.

The smile left his face. His face, like his body, was spare, bony, like a flexible wire. He had looked much the same fifteen years ago and would look almost like this fifteen years from now. Without Jim as a guidepost, she would have been unable to guess his age.

"I'm sorry I've given you that impression," he said without denying her charge.

"I love him." It was the first time she had ever said it aloud. She had the unusual feeling that she was sitting in the aisle seat for a change.

"I have no doubt that you do."

"But you're not happy about what he's doing now."

He moved his hands in a a small gesture of despair. "Happy is as out of context here as hungry is. What Jim is doing makes me neither happy nor hungry—nor the opposite of either. I hope it makes him happy. I confess I had some doubts when we first talked about it. I have fewer doubts now."

"You've known him a long time, haven't you?"

"Twenty years. We met in boot camp and went across the Pacific together."

"And back?"

He shook his head. "I was hurt. I came back alone."

"Are you better now?" she asked with concern, as if the wound had been inflicted this morning.

He smiled. "All better," he said reassuringly. "I recovered."

"Were you both hurt at the same time?"

He looked puzzled. "No," he said uncertainly. "Jim wasn't hurt that I know of, surely not at the time I was. If he had been, there might be one less of us today."

"Oh." She looked at him quickly and then away, picked up her brandy and took a sip. "I was just wondering when he hurt his hands."

"His hands?"

She ran one hand over the back of the other and up the arm. "The scars," she said.

He frowned, "I don't remember. Perhaps—Oh, of course, the scars." He looked at her, still frowning. "I believe that happened after I left."

He looked troubled. It was foolish to pursue it. "What was he like then?" she asked.

His face smoothed back to its usual blandness.

"That's an odd question, one I think Jim would never ask."

"Jim has no curiosity. He takes everything as he sees it."

"You're quite wrong. He has a tremendous curiosity, but his curiosity is scientific, not frivolous."

"I'm sorry I asked," she said. She was sorry he had stayed, sorry she had offered hospitality, sorry she had begun to talk.

She had made him uncomfortable. They seemed to be unable to prevent doing it to each other. "He hasn't changed," he said. "A man doesn't change much in the years between twenty and forty. He does some things a little differently—we all do—but he thinks the same. His loves are the same."

She had listened to him attentively but had failed to distinguish where he had spoken of Jim and where he had spoken of people in general.

"I've changed since twenty," she said. "Not enough, I suppose, but I've changed. I thought in January I'd come all the way but I guess that was foolish of me."

"All the way is rather far."

"Too far to do it alone. Did you encourage him to become a priest?"

"I?" He smiled. "I spent the better part of two months trying to talk him out of it. I had much the better reasons, too," he said with a certain amount of pride, as if the argument had in fact been based on reason. "I don't regret that I lost and I don't regret that I was right."

"I like you," she said without thinking.

"Women always do. The younger they are, the greater the passion."

He had made her smile. "I knew Teresa for eight months and the only time I ever heard her laugh was the day you were there. It never even occurred to me to make her laugh."

"And despite what you think of as a terrible failure on your part, she entrusted you with her child."

It had a mildly comforting effect. He was uniquely adapted to his profession. "Did you always intend to be a priest?" she asked.

"Ever since I became rational."

"I never knew what I would do—or be. I've just fallen into things. I wonder sometimes if I would have done better or worse if I had planned."

"You can't plan everything."

"No." She turned and looked at Anthony, asleep under the slowly moving boats. "In January, when I met Jim—"

"In January?" he said, interrupting. "Excuse me, I was under the impression you had known each other longer than that."

'No, it was January. Well, yes, we were at the same camp for a while last summer but nothing—that is—well, he was a—" She broke off, feeling suddenly embarrassed. She hadn't meant it to sound that way, that Jim had existed and she had been unaware of him, but it was, after all, the way it had happened.

"I understand," he said. "Forgive me for interrupting you, but I understand now."

She had lost her train of thought. January. Coming of age. "I was thinking about Anthony."

"How do you come to know a judge so well that you can consult him on a case of this sort?"

"I don't. His daugher is my friend. She did the asking."

"I never think of women as having strong friendships." He smiled. "I see I must alter my thinking."

"What are we going to do if it doesn't work?" she said. "What if he decides the other way?"

"We talked about it earlier this evening. It occurs to me now that you ought to have been included in the discussion. I can't say we came to any conclusion. For my part, I intend to rely on a higher Judge."

"Oh."

"Have I surprised you or disappointed you?"

She smiled at him. "Neither. You brought something back." She went to the bookcase and hunted through the lower shelves. It was there, worn by her own fingers, annotated with her own well-sharpened pencil. She turned the pages until she found it, heavily underlined and checked in the margin: "Where there is no judge on earth," she read, "the appeal lies to God in heaven."

"You're very like him," Father McAndrew said.

"Like whom?"

"Like Jimmy Kendall. All right, tell me what obscure American wrote it."

She laughed. "It was Locke, the Second Treatise on Government. It's the only thing I remember from a fifteen-thousand-dollar education."

"An Englishman," he said, shaking his head. He picked up his jacket and held out his hand. "I asked Jimmy to get you out of here for two hours. He brought you back at least a quarter of an hour early and it's taken this long for you to laugh." He shook her hand and went to the door. "By the way, my mother used the same words you did. She always said gardening was relaxing and rewarding. And I liked my mother."

The next day dragged. They were sick of Monopoly and sick of television. Cassie called. Her voice was strangely depressed but her words were cheering. Don't worry. Daddy would take care of everything.

"Listen, Cassie, Jim told me something about this judge. If it doesn't work out, it's no one's fault. I want you to know that I understand that."

"I took care of it," Cassie said, her voice low. "I promise you it'll work out."

She found a book and read with Anthony. They did some arithmetic. Sometimes she asked him a question and drifted away before he answered.

"You aren't listening to me," he said.

It was true. Her mind was running wild—Teresa dead, the judge condemning the accused, a priest wounded in a war, a blanket on the ground and a distant voice saying, Jimmy, Jimmy, I love you, Jimmy.

At three-thirty she made some coffee. Anthony lay down on his bed and turned on the television set. She sat down at the table and sipped the coffee, missing the newspaper as if it were a meal, as if it were her daily sustenance.

Two people were coming up the stairs. She looked at her watch. A quarter to four. It was an odd hour for them to come. If they had news, they would call. Unless the news were bad . . .

"Up there," she heard a voice say, an unfamiliar voice and she put down the coffee cup and stood up as someone knocked.

She opened the door. Two policemen stood in front of her.

"Yes?" she said, holding on to the doorknob.

"Miss Gold?" one of them asked.

"Yes."

"May we come in?"

She looked at them, sizing them up, a taller one, a not-so-tall one; one about her age, one a little older; a slim one, a heavier one. One of you, she thought, one of you has to do me a favor. She appraised them, her colleagues in civil service. The taller one. He had fewer hang-ups, had more fun. He thought she was pretty.

She looked at him directly. "Please," she said, "do I have to let you in?"

The other one stared past her shoulder in the kitchen, to last night's Monopoly game still open on the floor, to the herbs growing in the lengthening daylight. At the other end of the apartment, the television set, invisible to the visitors, played a children's program.

"No ma'am," the taller one said, "not if you don't want to."

She shook her head and started to breathe again. "Not this time," she told him.

"Let's go," he said to his partner and they went down the stairs.

She went to the kitchen windows and looked. Double-parked in front of the door stood a squad car. The two uniforms emerged from the obscured doorway and got into the car. Two or three minutes passed. Then the street-side door opened, the taller policeman got out, and the car pulled away from the curb. The one left behind leaned against the lamppost, his face toward the door.

It was ten to four.

The telephone number. What had she done with the

telephone number? She ran the length of the apartment. The folding bed was in the way. The television set was in the way. She pulled open her top dresser drawer and pulled wildly at the neat piles of clothes. She could feel herself panicking. She ran to the night table and opened the drawer. A telephone book, some bank-books, clippings from newspapers, a booklet on how to take the pill.

"What are you looking for?" Anthony asked.

"Nothing. Watch your program."

"Who was at the door?"

"Nobody."

She ran around the enormous bed to the other night table, which she never used, never put anything in, and yanked the drawer open. A white box lay alone inside. She frowned, her curiosity momentarily overcoming her panic. Inside was her Bible. On the verge of laughter, she threw the top of the box back in the drawer and slammed it shut. Where had she put Jim's number.

She sat down on the bed, ready to scream or laugh. She had just had that number last Thursday.

"Idiot," she said aloud, reaching for her bag. The slip of paper was in her wallet. It had been there since January.

The phone was answered on the first ring by Father Reilly. He would find Father Kendall. It was four o'clock. Jim came to the phone. She said it all quickly, breathlessly.

"I'll be right over," he said.

She hung up. It was all over now. They had lost. They would take Anthony away now. In an hour or two, he would be with his father.

She looked at him lying on his stomach, watching the

screen. She, more than any of them, had lost. Wherever he was going, he was going away. "Are you hungry?" she asked.

"Yeah. Could I have something?"

"Sure. Anything you want."

"Peanut butter and jelly."

She went to the kitchen and made the sandwich, spreading the peanut butter thickly. On the street, the taller policeman was still watching the door. She poured a glass of milk and stood watching him while he ate.

"More?" she asked.

"Could I have another sandwich?"

She nodded and touched his head. He needed a haircut. She wondered if he would ever get one. She made a second sandwich and found some cookies. She would have to get his clothes together. It was all over. He was going away.

She looked out the window and saw Jim's car pull up in front of the house and double-park where the squad car had been. He got out, buttoning his jacket. He was in uniform, as he had been almost every time since last Thursday. He walked toward the policeman, smiled, said something, and held out his hand. He had stopped being a priest; he was a politician now. A second car pulled up and double-parked behind Jim's car. It was Father McAndrew. He greeted the policeman like an old friend. She watched the three of them in their crazy pantomime on the sidewalk next to the lamppost. It lasted about a minute. Then Jim detached himself from the triangle and disappeared inside the house. She exchanged the silent visual image through the window for the sound of footsteps mounting the stairs rapidly, as if a second might make a difference now, could change a decision, could alter a destiny.

She opened the door and saw him turn the corner at the landing, fusing the two images.

"It's OK," he said, grinning up the stairs at her. "Andy got a call just before I talked to him. We won. It's OK. Take it easy."

She closed her eyes and she was trembling slightly. He put an arm around her—purely a clerical gesture.

"Just before you talked to him?" she asked.

"He had just hung up when I called."

In God we trust. She knew exactly when the judge had announced his decision. It had been at the moment she opened the drawer and found the Bible.

Anthony was eating his cookies. Jim sat down with him and started to explain what was happening. She listened for a minute.

"Don't take him now," she said. "Let me keep him another day."

"Darling—"

"Couldn't it wait till tomorrow? Just until morning?"

"They're on their way over for him now."

She got his clothes together, putting the dirty ones in a plastic bag. She packed up the Monopoly set and took his clean, unworn clothes out of her drawer. He would still have something fresh to wear tomorrow. She went for a shopping bag but stopped midway across the room. Not a shopping bag. Anthony shouldn't walk into someone's home with all his belongings in a crummy shopping bag.

In the rear closet was Abraham Gold's ancient suitcase. She hauled it out and opened it on the bed. There was something elegantly fitting in giving the suitcase of

Abraham Gold, b. 1885, d. 1967 to a little boy born in Boston in 1963.

She packed the suitcase and called him over. He got up from the table and came to her while Jim went to the window and looked away from them.

"Come here, Anthony," she said. "I love you. You know that, don't you?"

"Then why do I have to go?"

"Because your mom would want you to live in a family. I'm not a family. I'm just me."

"I don't care about a family. I want to stay here."

Jim turned from the window and cleared his throat. "You'll see Ruth again. She'll be at camp this summer." He looked back outside. "The troops are here," he said.

She gave a banana to Anthony and put some cookies in a plastic bag. Jim picked up the suitcase.

"Don't forget my boats," Anthony said.

Jim smiled, put down the suitcase, stood on the bed with one foot and pulled the tape off the ceiling. He laid the mobile gently in the suitcase and took Anthony downstairs.

The apartment was suddenly frighteningly quiet, as if she had already grown accustomed to the almost inaudible sound of a little boy breathing, of his heart beating, of his smile. She walked to the window and looked downstairs. There were two squad cars, two priests, several policemen both in and out of uniform.

She looked at her watch. Not yet five. She might still reach Cassie at her office.

Cassie answered.

"We made it, Cassie. Anthony's going to a foster home."

It was incredible, but Cassie started to cry. "I'm so glad," she said. "Daddy didn't think there was a chance at first."

"For God's sake, take it easy. It's over. It worked out." There was a knock at the door. "Thank him for me."

It was Jim. "Andy knew the cop downstairs," he said, shutting the door. "We were lucky all around. I was afraid they'd take you down to ask you questions."

"It's so empty without him."

"You couldn't keep him, darling."

"I know."

"Let me ask you something. Who could have called the police?"

She shrugged. It was so irrelevant now. She hadn't even thought about it. It was just another part of the nightmare. If something else could happen, it would. Somewhere along the way, she had accepted it. The police had simply come.

"Who knew Anthony was here?" he persisted.

"You, me, Andy, Cassie. Maybe Cassie's father."

"There had to be someone else. Did you take him out?"

"No."

"Well, think. Did anyone come here?"

She shook her head. "I had the men who brought the bed leave it at the door. They never saw him."

He walked around the apartment deep in thought. "Could someone have seen me bring him here?"

"You mean a neighbor? The neighbors don't even know me. They wouldn't—" She stopped. "My God," she said, "I know who it was. I just realized who did it."

He looked at her without asking.

"It was Angelo," she said.

"Oh, come on."

"Of course it was," she said, the circumstantial evidence of the last month and a half amassing in her mind. "I've seen him downstairs sometimes when I went to school. Once he was coming down the street. Another time he was watching the house from across the street. There were other times too. Maybe there were times he was there and I missed him. Maybe he was there the night you brought Anthony." She was almost breathless with the excitement of knowing, with the certainty of Angelo's guilt.

"You're imagining things," he said. "You don't like the kid so it seems like an obvious answer. This wouldn't be his idea of fun."

"Imagining things? Why don't you confront him and find out? He's been in trouble with the cops, hasn't he? What could be more fun than getting someone else in trouble? When are you going to stop protecting him?"

He gave her a sharp look and turned toward the door.

"Go," she said. "When you don't want to hear any more, get up and go. You're like me that way, except I've learned to sit through it. I don't run any more."

She had touched an open wound. He came back and sat down at the table. "I'll talk to him about it," he said but she knew it was only to satisfy her. He would phrase his questions negatively to give Angelo a grammatically easy out. You didn't by any chance? Nah. Me?

"What day is today?" she asked, looking at her watch.

"Wednesday."

"I have a class tonight. I forgot to cancel it." She started to undress. "I have to meet someone for dinner at six-thirty and I'll never make it."

"Who are you meeting for dinner?" he asked with a slight edge to his voice.

"The girl who teaches next door to me." She dropped her blouse on the bed, unsnapped the jeans, stepped out of them as they fell to the floor and bent to pick them up. As she straightened up, she felt him touch her shoulder.

"Don't," she said. "I have to go."

"I just wanted to touch you. Why don't you call in sick and take the rest of the week off? You need a rest."

She turned to face him. He was wearing clerical black and involuntarily she shrank from it. She could never have put her arms around him if he wore those clothes.

"Would you stay with me tonight?" she asked, her voice sounding like a child's.

"You know I can't. You know it's impossible. Give me another month and I'll stay with you every night."

"No you won't. That's not the way this year is going. Teresa's dead and Anthony's gone and it'll never work out for us. It'll go on and on and nothing will ever work out."

"Darling, don't go in tonight. Stay home and rest."

"No!" It was almost a scream. "Don't you understand? They took Anthony away and I'm alone now. I don't want to be alone tonight. I want to be with people. I want to be with people who love me."

He put his arm around her and kissed her.

"Don't," she said. "I don't want you to make love to me for ten minutes and then go away and leave me to sleep alone for six nights. I want to wake up next to you. I don't even care if you don't make love to me. I just want to wake up next to you."

But it was only half a truth. Later tonight she would hate herself for having said it, for the ache, for having given him one more insoluble problem.

She started to dress. "You'd better go," she said, her voice lower now, "so we don't have to walk out together. It's still very light out."

"I'll wait for you. I'll walk out with you."

He put her in the car and stood outside the open window. "Are you helping Mrs. McConnell tomorrow?"

"Yes."

"I don't think I'll be around."

"Sure."

"Will I see you Tuesday?"

"You don't have to ask."

"Look," he said. "I'll talk to Angelo."

"It's OK, Jim. I was probably wrong anyway."

She drove to class. A whole week had elapsed since Teresa had tried to reach her.

On Thursday, she went to the church. Mrs. McConnell had news for her. "I think we've found someone for next year," she said. "They're still haggling over the price but I think they'll come to an agreement. She's a lovely woman."

She stayed late, not wanting to go home. Eventually Mrs. McConnell sent her away.

She went to sleep early and when the phone rang she expected her anonymous caller. But it was Jim.

"Anthony's father cleared out," he said. "Picked up and left. No forwarding address."

"I hope it's the last of him."

"Were you asleep?"

"It's OK, darling. I'm glad you called. I'll run over tomorrow and return my key to the landlord."

She went back to sleep. Tonight was even worse than the night before. The folding bed and the television set were gone. The apartment was pre-Anthony again, lonely, empty, incomplete.

And then there were the dreams—Teresa in a coffin, Teresa crying in her bed, priests around a grave, all black and indistinguishable from one another. A priest is a priest. Once a priest, always a priest. And a voice —an unrecognizable voice attached to no one—saying over and over, I'm sorry, I'm sorry, I'm sorry.

After school on Friday she drove to Teresa's apartment. It was a farewell visit, or at least she hoped it would be. She had decided to call the Salvation Army and have them pick up the furniture. She would take the religious articles and Anthony's clothes and send them to him when Father McAndrew found out the address.

She parked across the street and went upstairs, saturated with the knowledge that it was a final visit, that this moment of going up these stairs would never be repeated. She put the key in the lock, opened the door, and gasped. The living room was empty, bare, clean, shiny. The wooden floor had been polished, the windows scrubbed. The furniture was gone along with the worn rug, the television set, the pitcher of carnations. No one had ever lived here. It was a room without warmth and without character.

She pivoted slowly, looking for evidence of life, a life that was or a life that had been—the scuffmark of a small sneaker or a piece of dust lodged in a corner. There was none.

A pair of heavy feet were making their way up the stairs. She turned and stood facing the open door. A short, heavy woman in a housedress appeared, panting slightly from the climb. Her hair was dyed yellow and pulled back and up into a knot behind her chubby face. The gold band on her left hand was immersed in flesh, recalling, with every drop of blood that failed to get through, a leaner time.

"He got a U-Haul yesterday and took it all, everything, lock, stock and barrel."

"Oh."

"So I come up this morning and cleaned it good. It needed it, I can tell you."

"Yes."

"Was he her husband?"

"Of course he was her husband."

"Just asking," the woman said, miffed at her tone. "You don't always know with these people."

She looked at the woman, turned away, and walked to the window. Across the street was her car, the good side facing out.

"Did she die?" the woman asked.

"Yes."

"Poor thing."

Go away, she thought. Why don't you just go away? Why can I never be alone?

"I didn't know nobody else had the key," the woman said.

"Nobody else does. I'll give you this one when I come downstairs."

"Were you her friend?"

She turned from the window and looked at the little round woman topped in artificial gold. "Of course I was her friend," she said.

The woman looked disturbed, as if she had missed something in the converstaion. "I'll see you downstairs," she said and walked out, closing the door.

She waited for the sound of the door closing downstairs. Then she went into the kitchen, bare except for the stove and refrigerator. The Pope was gone, and the saints, and Anthony too. It had been a shock to see them all there but they had been a kind of company; maybe they had kept Teresa from being lonely when Joe left her, or at the end as she was leaving, they were people to say goodbye to.

She walked to the end of the hall and looked into Teresa's room. It was as bare as the rest of the rooms. The closet was empty, the satin wedding dress gone with the television set and the Pope.

She turned to go. There was no reason to linger. There was nothing in the apartment except air and wax on the floors, no ghosts, no spirits. She stopped at the door to Anthony's room. Just for a moment she would go in and look around. Maybe she would hear an echo there, something that another tenant might hear to remind him that once a family lived here, a woman and her child, and that they had loved each other.

The room was an empty box. She tried to imagine where the chest had stood, and the bed. She raised her

eyes over the invisible bed and held her breath. Bob-
bing in the sea of air were the boats, Anthony's Viking
boats from the Brooklyn Museum. She walked over
and blew them.

The boats in Abraham Gold's suitcase had been
Jim's. She reached up to take these down, to give them
back to him, but she stopped. She would have to break
the fine thread that held them. Besides, it wasn't part of
the great plan. Joe had left them there and the landlord's wife had missed them. Perhaps they were the
echo she had been looking for, the sign that people had
lived here, that something of them had been left.

She tapped one of the boats, watched them start another journey, and went out.

8

His birthday was less than a week away and she had neither a gift nor an idea. Somewhere in the time they had spent together there must be a clue to the one thing that would mean something to both of them. She searched the scenes that moved through her mind, going from month to month and week to week, Tuesday after Tuesday, season after season, and found nothing.

He had given her a book; she had given him a key. Those had been perhaps the two most perfect presents they would ever exchange. There was something depressing in that, that the best was behind them, that their love had peaked somewhere—at the cottage perhaps—and was on the decline.

At night, the dreams continued. Only in the daylight world had Teresa ceased to exist; at night, her life and death had become a nightmare.

On Sunday she bought him a wallet, choosing one in brown pigskin only because it was not black, and had it stamped in gold with his initials. She also bought herself a dress. It was the first thing she had bought herself in a long time. It made her aware, looking in the front and back mirrors in the glare of the dressing-room lights, that she had lost weight where she could least afford to.

On her way home, she ordered a birthday cake to be ready after school on Tuesday. Happy Birthday Jimmy.

The inscription would surprise him. She would watch his face as he read it.

When he called her on Sunday evening, he told her he wouldn't be able to see her after class on Wednesday. He showed up only irregularly on Wednesdays and rarely by appointment. This Wednesday was his birthday.

"My sister's coming in from Connecticut," he said. "I'll be going out to dinner with her."

"Is she the one who gave you the cross?"

"Yes. She always remembers birthdays. I'd rather— if you don't mind—I think it would be better if you didn't meet her."

"Whatever you say." She could have phrased it better, made it sound more affirmative, but she had lost the touch.

She picked up the cake on Tuesday and hid it in one of the cabinets where she kept the dishes. After a nap, she showered and started to dress. The wallet, wrapped and ribboned, lay on the kitchen table.

When he knocked at five to six, she was sitting at her desk in a bra and half-slip, filing her nails. He came in with his key and walked back to where she was sitting. He was wearing a sport coat and his tie had red in it. Seeing him was being renewed, being reassured.

"Get dressed," he said, kissing her. "I have a reservation and it's a long ride."

"Your birthday present is on the table."

He shook his head and went to the table. She loved watching him walk, watching him move, watching him be himself.

She finished dressing while he opened the package. Over the weekend, she had had her period. The days right after were always like this, a yearning for fulfillment, and edginess, a nearness to excitement, as if nature had planned it this way. Now that you can conceive again, lean toward it, reach for it. Except, of course, that she could not conceive.

"It's very nice," he said, holding it between his palms. "It even smells good."

She walked over to him, turned around, and stood waiting. He touched her back, zipped the dress, and put his arms around her.

"You're not playing fair tonight," he said. "Cover yourself up or we'll never get out of here."

He took his old black wallet out, emptied it, filled the new one, and threw the old one away. "I know," he said, looking at her as she watched him, "you would have put it away as a memento. We sequential people—"

"You sequential people have all the answers. Take me to dinner."

They drove for three-quarters of an hour while the sun went down. The restaurant was on a country road in a wooded area. The earth fell away behind it and a brook or a stream or perhaps the start of a great river flowed below in the gully.

She watched him as if she were a person apart from them as he guided her in, talked to the headwaiter, refused a small table for two by a window overlooking the brook and chose instead a round table in a dark corner where they could sit next to each other on the semicircular seat built into the corner.

He took her hand under the table and, impulsively, she pulled the chain under her dress and let the cross lie on the outside. She had a feeling of contentment and well-being that she had forgotten—or never had known—existed.

"What do we do if we see someone you know?" she asked, voicing her only conern.

"We won't."

"You checked everyone out?"

"You're a worrier. I never figured you for a worrier. I'll introduce you as Ruth Kendall and let them guess."

"Do I look like your sister?"

"Are you kidding?"

The waiter had a French accent and she spoke to him in French. He bowed slightly and smiled, complimenting her on her French, and telling her about his wife and baby who would join him in July. Jim watched them with interest and amusement, still holding her hand.

"You never told me you spoke French," he said.

"You never asked. Do you?"

"I read it. You sounded very good."

Across the large room was a party, about half a dozen couples, celebrating something. The men were tinged with gray and the women were frosted. They were popping champagne corks and enjoying themselves. Otherwise, the restaurant was half empty.

The drinks came.

"I want to tell you something," he said. "I talked to Angelo last week. He denied everything, but I wanted you to know that I talked to him."

"It doesn't matter, darling. I was very upset that night. I didn't mean to say any of those things to you." She sipped her drink. "I still dream about her every night."

"We'll go away for a while," he said. "When this is over, we'll go somewhere."

"Sometimes I think it'll go on this way forever."

"It won't. I've given myself a deadline. But if it's at all possible, I don't want to leave without permission. It would mean giving up any chance of remaining a Catholic."

"Oh. I didn't know you cared."

"I want the right to make my own decision. Would you give up that right?"

"No." The word came out without hesitation and without thought. She was Abraham Gold's granddaughter for all that she was sitting with a priest and wearing a cross.

It was something she had always known, always taken for granted, but it loomed now as something profoundly important in her life, something deeply relevant to their relationship. She had never talked to him about it, and actually avoided it once or twice, so that it now stood between them hard and cold like a block of ice, a block, the thing that held her back, that kept her from saying the only thing she had ever wanted to tell him.

"You're far away," he said.

"No, I'm right here. I just remembered I have something to show you when we go home tonight." The Bible. She had forgotten to tell him she had found her Bible.

The meal was beautiful. They had wine and she felt herself relax more completely than she had in months. She told him not to order dessert. The cake was a surprise; she told him she had something for him at home but she wouldn't say what. The waiter brought them cookies with their coffee just because she had spoken French to him.

"When did you tell Andy about me?" she asked.

"I never told him about you."

She looked at him. "You did."

"I told him about myself, not about you. I first said something last September."

"But nothing happened last summer."

"Do you think that the only things that happen are things you can see?"

"Let's go home." She yawned. She would sleep all the way home, curled up against him in the car, dreaming of springtime.

"I'll get the waiter."

The party across the room was starting to break up. Women were kissing each other and men shaking hands. The French waiter was nowhere around. There was a sound of a dish or a glass breaking and then a groan from the direction of the party. She looked toward them. One of the men was leaning crazily on a chair, as if he had been struck as he arose, and as she watched he fell clumsily to the floor.

"We need a doctor here," one of the men called and she felt Jim's body lurch forward slightly, become tense, like a cat ready to spring.

"Maybe I can—"

Waiters put down trays and started to run. A woman screamed, a pure, clear sound like a bell. The head-waiter rushed toward the man on the floor next to the long table. People everywhere were standing up, talking softly.

And then she heard it, felt it rather, like a dart in the middle of her body. "A priest," someone said, not very loud, but the sound of the word carried. "Somebody get a priest."

Jim exhaled. His shoulders relaxed. His eyes closed and opened again.

"Go," she said.

He put his hand in his pocket and dumped his keys on the table. "Call an ambulance," he said in a low controlled voice. "Don't leave until it comes. Then go home." He was sliding away from her on the seat. "I'll pick up my keys later."

"How will you get back?"

"I'll get a ride."

"Call me if you need me." But he was already halfway across the room.

She went to the headwaiter's station. He was on the phone, calling an ambulance. When he hung up, he turned around.

"Where do I find a priest?" he asked in despair. He reached for the telephone book and started flipping crazily through the yellow pages.

"There's a priest with him now," she said, checking her watch to time the ambulance.

"There is?" The headwaiter was incredulous. He knew everyone who had entered the restaurant tonight.

He took a few steps into the dining room to look. She followed him. Jim was kneeling on the floor next to the man whose eyes were flickering with life in a pasty face. Jim's jacket was open and incongruously the new tie had fallen away from his body and was touching the shirt of the man on the floor. Jim was talking to him, touching him. Nearby, one of the expensively dressed women was crying, her fresh hairdo still unscathed, her cheeks black with mascara.

From the distance there came the sound of a siren. The headwaiter turned around. She took a last look at the man on the floor, the red-flecked tie touching the other man's shirt, and turned away. She felt torn apart, as if there was not enough love to go around—for the man on the floor and the woman standing up and crying.

The ambulance attendants hurried in with a stretcher. She moved out of the way of the exiting procession, where they would not see her as they passed, the men with the stretcher between them, the priest and the woman, the members of the party now the members of the funeral.

"I'd like to pay the bill," she said to the headwaiter when they had left.

"No, no. Please." He was embarrassed. "I couldn't let you."

"He'll be back here tomorrow to pay it if you don't let me take care of it now. Spare him that, OK?"

He relented. The bill was enormous. She would have to cash another check tomorrow to get through the week.

In the car, she took out his keys and tried them, one by one, in the ignition. After the third try, she came to the ring, C '67, that she had given him in April. She had forgotten about their second exchange of gifts, the ring for the cross. How curiously symbolic their gifts had been, from him one straight line cut by another, from her a circle.

It was well past eleven when she got home. She lay

in bed with the lights on, and tried to read. Around midnight, she fell asleep, the book still open in her hand.

The knocking was so soft that it was more a feeling than a sound that woke her up. It was three o'clock. She opened the door, still half asleep, and looked at his face as he walked in. There was no need to ask about the man; the answer was apparent.

His shirt was open, his tie put away. He put his arm around her and led her to the sofa.

"How did you get back?"

"Andy picked me up."

"I could have come."

"I wanted to talk to him."

He took his jacket off, dropped it on a chair, and they sat on the sofa, his arm around her, both of hers around him.

They sat for an eternity. She fell asleep, she woke up. She listened for a sound but she heard only their breathing, only the sounds that showed they were alive.

Finally, there was a long sigh. He looked at his watch. "I forgot to pay them," he said. "It's too late to go back now."

"I took care of it."

Only the sound of his breathing. She closed her eyes and listened for another sound, the sound of time passing, but there was nothing.

"I want to ask you," he said, startling her out of a doze. "If I went back, what would you do?"

"Went back where? Where would you go?"

"If I—if we broke this up, if I went back again, the way it was before I met you."

She was stunned. It was a question she had stopped

anticipating months ago. But she knew why he had asked it. He was afflicted by the same magnetism that held her in Boston, drew her to New York, had made a slave of her once and kept her free now. He must be nearer the end, nearer the break, than she had thought. The old love was exerting its last frantic pull, dragging him back, jealously, not wanting to let him go.

A man doesn't change much, Father McAndrew had said. His loves are the same.

The love for the man on the floor, for the statues in Teresa's kitchen, for the children in the basement.

She had to answer his question. It had taken him an hour to ask it and he was waiting for an answer. A month ago she could not have answered it because she would not have known what she would do or how she would do it.

I don't know. I can't make it without you.

But something had happened to her since then, even though the folding bed and the television set were gone, and she loved him too much to lie to him.

"I would never forget you," she said, letting the tears do what they chose. "I would never feel this way about anyone else," she said, carefully using the conditional because he had asked a conditional question, "but I want to give birth. I want to have children. I would marry someone some day."

He looked at her. "You would?" It was a tone of disbelief.

"Did you think I would go into a convent?"

He leaned against the back of the sofa as if exhausted by the exchange. Minutes passed.

"I'll never go back," he said finally. "Wait for me, Ruth. I'll never go back."

"I'll wait for you. You know I could never leave you."

He was quiet again for a long time. It occurred to her that it was his birthday, that they had missed the celebration, that the cake was still hidden in a cabinet.

"How many days does May have?" he asked.

"Thirty-one."

"Another week."

"Yes."

"Listen, I can't—" He stopped. "I want to tell you . . ." But he left it unfinished. "I'll wrap everything up this week. I'll leave on the last of May."

"You can't, Jim." He had been spending this night fighting to put some continuity in his life, to do one thing in a different way, to be the same man at thirty-nine that he had been at thirty-eight. "You can't give up your right to make that decision for yourself. I'm not going anywhere and I'm not in a hurry."

He turned his wrist so that she could see the face of his watch. It had stopped at four. She showed him hers. It was after five. The sky had lightened slightly, even in the west in front of them.

"I have to be there at six."

"How will you manage without sleep?"

"I'll sleep after supper. Oh," he said, as if in pain. "Margaret's coming."

"Call her."

"I can't. She lives for these days."

He stood up, dragged himself up, really, and held out a hand. She got up and leaned against him tiredly.

"You stayed all night," she said.

"I guess I did. It wasn't what you had in mind."

"I told you you didn't have to make love to me."

He smiled, very, very slightly. "I guess you did."

After he left, she took the birthday cake out of the cabinet and opened the box. With a spoon, she carefully scraped off the word Jimmy and repaired the icing underneath. She had never baked a cake when Mr. Gerstenwald turned eighty. Tonight she would bring a cake for all of them.

After that night, she stopped dreaming about Teresa.

9

Physically he seemed indestructible. She got through Wednesday on three hours of sleep and woke up Thursday morning feeling numb. He was outside the church when she got there and he came over to talk to her.

"We've got someone to run the program next year," he said. He stood with his hands behind his back, looking well rested and rather triumphant.

She knew he was pleased but she was unable to respond adequately. As time went on, the numbness got worse. One evening she took a straight pin and punctured the skin on her upper arm; there was no feeling.

People spoke to her and she failed to hear them. When she did hear them, what they said made little sense. They talked of irrelevancies. The sentence that came through most often was "Are you all right?"

Of course she was all right. Why did they bother asking?

On Saturday Father McAndrew called. He had Anthony's address.

She called and wangled an invitation for Monday, Memorial Day.

It was the best thing she could have done. She returned feeling human, feeling warm. Her blood had begun to circulate again.

Anthony was happy. There were other children in the house, a dog, a cat, gerbils and a parrot. The weather was good. They asked her to come back again.

When she got home, she opened some windows, watered the plants, turned on the record player and cooked herself a meal.

Tuesday she hurried home after school, found a large parking space at the beginning of her block, and pulled in forward. As she gathered up her things, a car parked behind her. She glanced in the mirror; it was Jim. She walked back to his car and got in next to him.

"You're late," she said.

"You're early."

"I hurried."

"I stopped at the rectory to pick up my mail."

"Something important?"

"Not yet. Maybe soon."

"About what?"

"My hypothetical future."

"In the mail?"

"Part of it in the mail. Don't worry. I'm still on speaking terms with the bishop. He even offered me a cigar the other day."

"Did you take it?"

He shook his head. "It's not my religion. Hey, you look better today."

"I saw Anthony yesterday."

"Did you call Andy?"

"He called me."

"Anthony must have the gift. You're starting to look human again. Come on. Give me your packages and we'll go upstairs."

"Oh." Her heart fell. She realized why she had gotten home so early. "I forgot to stop at the butcher's."

"Well, don't worry, we'll—"

"I can't remember anything any more, Jim." She

had starting shaking. "How could I have forgotten after all these months?"

"It's not a crisis, darling. We'll go somewhere for dinner."

"No."

"Because of last week?"

She nodded.

"I'll go out for sandwiches."

They sat for a minute. Then he said, "Are you still taking the pill?"

"Of course."

"Have you been back for a checkup?"

"No."

"Look, maybe you should see him, have him look you over. Maybe you should stop the pill for a couple of months, till you feel better."

"Don't do that to me, Jim," she said, as if he had made a pronouncement, given an order. "It's the only thing that works for me any more, Tuesday, when you make love to me. Don't take that away from me."

"It was just a suggestion."

He reached back, took a black book off the back seat, put it under his left arm, and got out of the car.

Damn. The black book, a reaffirmation of faith. There was no end, no end to anything.

They started down the street. Next to her car, he stopped. He had not seen the car since the accident. His hand tightened very slightly on her shoulder.

"You should have it fixed," he said, very calmly, very matter-of-factly, as if it were the spark plugs that needed changing, or the oil. "I could take it in for you in the morning. Maybe you could call Pete or someone to drive you for the next week."

Pete. Pete and Judy. She had forgotten to talk to him about Pete.

"I don't want to be without it. Maybe when school is over."

"You shouldn't drive if you're not feeling well."

They started walking.

"I should have moved in with you in January," he said. "I shouldn't have let you go through this by yourself."

"I would have leaned on you. Like I did with the letter."

"Isn't that better than almost getting yourself killed?"

"You would have given up everything you care about, Jim. You would have done things because you were pressured to instead of thinking them out. You wouldn't be a Catholic any more."

"Maybe not, but maybe my priorities have been all wrong."

Pete. I have to talk to him about Pete.

"Jim?"

He stopped, looking across the street. "Are they painting your house?"

"No."

"Are you sure?"

"Positive."

They were facing the driveway on the left side of her house, the neighbor's driveway. A long ladder leaned against a top-floor window, the only window on that floor on that side of the house. Hanging from the top of the ladder was a paint can. There was no one in sight.

"Is that your bathroom window?"

"Yes."

"Did you leave it open?"

"Yes." In a moment of happiness, when she had returned from seeing Anthony.

"Stay here."

"No!"

He took her hand and led her across the street, running. "Try the landlord."

No one was home.

"Let me take a look up there," he said.

"Call the police."

"Maybe it's a painter."

"Maybe it isn't."

"Come with me. You can come up to the landing."

"Please be careful."

They went up to the last landing and stopped. Whoever was in the apartment was having a drunken party, laughing, jumping, cheering at the attainment of some unknown goal.

He had his keys out and she watched from the landing as he went softly up the remaining stairs, turned the key in the lock, opened the door and walked out of her line of vision.

As he disappeared, the noise stopped abruptly, as if someone had lifted the arm off a record.

"You son of a bitch," she heard Jim say.

There was no response.

"Get your feet on the floor."

A scramble.

"What's your name, son?" Jim.

She inched up two steps.

"Joe. Joseph."

"Joseph what?"

"Joseph DiAngelis." A pause. "Sir."

"Pick that up, Joe. Put it back where you got it. And don't step on anything."

There was a sound of movement. She went up another two steps.

"Do you go to school?" Jim.

"Yes, sir."

"Were you in school today?"

"This morning. I left after lunch."

Two more steps.

"Where did you get the ladder?"

"From a garage."

"You took it out of someone's garage?" Calmly, quietly.

"Yes, sir."

She walked up the last step and stood at the threshold to her apartment. In her line of sight were the kitchen, the windows, the bookcase, the hi-fi, all intact, all sanely, beautifully serene.

There were a few footsteps and Jim appeared in the doorway, almost running into her, the black book still held under his left arm.

"You can come in now," he said, standing back from the door.

She walked in, turned right, and saw a boy standing almost next to her, tall, heavyish, his belt a notch too tight, his neck thick, his eyes scared. She looked to her left. Standing next to the bed—the bed, her beautiful bed with the ruffle at the edge of the canopy falling now in strips like sad streamers after a riotously sad party, the spread filthy and disarrayed—was Angelo, stooped and silent, even the jaws stopped for once.

At the back of the apartment her dresser drawers were pulled out, their contents thrown recklessly

around, on the floor, the bed, the canopy, the dresser—
the white of the underclothes forming a background for
the flesh of the stockings, the color of the sweaters.

She turned and looked at Jim. He was staring at the
bed. "Which one of you called the police two weeks
ago," he asked, "about the boy?"

The boys exchanged looks.

"I asked you a question," Jim said. "I want an answer."

Angelo seemed to have been struck dumb. He
opened his mouth and closed it again.

"He dialed," the other boy said, "and I talked to the
cop."

Jim nodded, his eyes half closed. "Between you you
have one rotten set of guts." He turned to her. "I'm
calling the police," he said and started for the phone.

"Don't," she said, putting a hand out to stop him.
"It's my apartment; I'll call the police."

He let her go and she sat down gingerly on the
spoiled bed and called the number in the book, wondering idiotically if this constituted an emergency.
Something glistening on the bathroom floor caught her
eye. When she hung up, she went to look. Pieces of the
mirror were scattered on the floor, in the sink and
around the tub. How many years of bad luck did it
amount to? Five? Seven? The rest of her life? She
turned and walked out of the bathroom. The two boys,
their backs to her, were still standing at attention. Jim
had been looking out the window. Now he turned
around and faced Angelo.

"Listen to me," he said. "If you volunteer any information to the police that you're not asked for, you'll
answer to me for it. Do you understand?"

"Yes, sir." It was the first time Angelo has spoken.

His voice was still echoing in the room when the police came.

They took her down to the police station on Western Avenue and she made an official complaint. Jim gave them his name and the camp office as a business address and stayed behind. They drove her back in a police car, reassuring her that the area was a good one, that it was one of those freaky things, that the kids weren't even from Cambridge. But keep the bathroom window locked just to be on the safe side.

He met her inside the front door.

"I'm sorry," she said.

"No. I'm the one—"

"No."

They went up the stairs.

She stopped at the door. "It was the bed, wasn't it?"

"Partly."

He had stacked the clothes on the bed, cleaned up the bathroom, and bought sandwiches. She stood looking at the bed.

"The spread just needs a cleaning," he said.

She nodded. Maybe a needle and thread would salvage the canopy.

"Hey," he said, "I brought you something." He walked over to the table where the black book lay open, closed it, and handed it to her. On the cover in gold were the words, "The Holy Bible."

She smiled and went to the night table, opened the drawer, and took out the white box. "I forgot to tell you," she said, handing it to him.

"You found it." He was pleased. "You weren't holding out on me." He took both of them, the worn black and the virgin white, and put them together on a shelf. "Let's eat," he said. "It's early but I feel hungry —and purged."

It was almost a month before she realized that after that day the telephone stopped ringing in the middle of the night.

10 〰〰〰〰〰〰〰〰〰〰

She began sleeping through the night. Even unaware of the reason, she noticed the difference. It meant waking up in the morning feeling rested. It was a pleasurably surprising feeling. She mistakenly attributed the new feeling to the return of health. In fact, her health was a result, not a cause.

Even Pete had finally stopped calling. The conversations had disintegrated and with them the need. He had never mentioned Judy, never alluded to her even slightly. It was as if she did not exist.

The bed had been a problem.

After supper that Tuesday, she had sorted the clothes and put some of them away. But the bed stood there, desecrated, a quiet reminder that she had pushed him too hard, that it was too late for regrets, that there had been no triumph in seeing the proof that she had been right.

"Want to go out somewhere?" he asked.

"No."

"You going to stand and look at it all night?"

She shook her head.

"Shall we strip it?"

She took a deep breath. "Yes, maybe we should strip it."

They stripped it and remade it with fresh sheets, working together without a word until he hit her with a pillow. Startled, she looked across the bed to where he stood watching her.

"You forget how to laugh?"

It evoked a smile.

"Let's leave the spread off."

"OK."

Absentmindedly, she started to undress. She was still wearing her school clothes. She stepped out of her shoes, feeling the flatness of the floor gratefully, enjoying the gentle tug of the back leg muscles for the first time all day. She looked around. He was watching her with a quiet enjoyment.

"It's almost June," he said.

"Maybe June will be good."

"Maybe we'll get married."

"Girls still get married in June?"

"We're booked solid."

"No kidding. Gee." She thought about it, letting the dress slide down to the floor the way her mother hated, picking it up and walking to the closet. "I read nobody gets married any more."

"I guess the Catholics haven't heard about it."

She leaned against the closet door to close it. It was the opening she needed.

Look, Jim, there's something you ought to know about me. I inherited something from my grandfather.

I'm a descendant of Abraham Gold.

Once, a long time ago, my grandfather and I . . .

Listen, do you know I'm not a goddamned atheist?

"I have to talk to you," she said, her back against the closet door.

"Next year. We'll have plenty of time to talk next year."

"No, now. Right now." She went to the dresser and took out a clean pair of jeans and a fresh shirt, the little gold cross swinging as she bent over.

"Don't get dressed," he said. He was unbuttoning his shirt.

"But I have to talk to you."

"Later."

She dropped the clothes on the dresser. It was hopeless. She looked at the bed with apprehension. He probably thought she was stalling. Maybe she was. Maybe it was all very unimportant.

"I never felt that way about an inanimate object," he said.

"I know. It kind of grows on you."

"I remember the first time I saw it."

"I remember what you said." She touched one of the posts at the foot of the bed.

"It was the most neutral thing I could think of." He had taken off his belt and stopped.

"Did you think the bed was an invitation?" They were on opposite sides of it. She watched him thinking, remembering.

"No. You weren't what I would call cordial." He looked across the bed at her, a stranger with blue eyes and a calm voice half a mile away, the clean sheets crisp between them. "Would you like to sit down for a while? Over there?" He turned his head toward the sofa.

She was still standing with a hand around the post. "You have a nice bedside manner," she said. "You must be good in your work. You'll miss it, won't you?"

"I'll take part of it with me."

"That would be nice. It would give some continuity. . . ." She started walking in front of the bed.

"You're lecturing me."

"No. I'm just coming around to your side."

And afterwards, when they talked, it was about something else.

"I may have to miss a Tuesday," he said.

So what else is new? she thought. When the world starts disintegrating, it goes from all four corners at once. "Where are you going?" she asked evenly.

"The bishop wants me to go to a retreat for a week or so. He'll tell me when."

"What for?"

"To make a final decision."

"I thought you'd made it."

"I have, but he feels I should have some time away —by myself—no outside pressures. I can use the time," he admitted. "There are some things I want to work out."

"Will you come back?" she asked, ashamed of herself for even thinking of it.

"You know I'll come back."

So she began to feel better. On Wednesday, when she came home, Pete dropped over. It was his first visit in months. He wanted to borrow a couple of books for a paper he was doing. She noted the casualness of the way he had come by, his tacit assumption that she would be alone, that there was no one else in her life. She found the books and gave them to him.

"Your place looks different," he said.

"How?" She was intrigued by his question, by his perceptiveness. The apartment was different. Something of Jim was there. She had thought she was the only one able to see it.

"I can't put my finger on it Maybe it's just a feeling. You're different too."

"Oh?"

"You've aged, Ruthie."

"It was a rough winter."

"You look like you need a rest. You set for camp this summer?"

She let a second go by. "Yes."

"Good. I'll see you there." Not a word about Judy. Nothing.

"OK."

"I'll bring these back over the weekend."

"Don't bother. Monday's soon enough."

She looked in the mirror in her bag when he was gone. No wonder Jim had never told her she was pretty. She looked ready to collect Social Security. She put the mirror away and drove into Boston for a good hot meal before her last evening class of the year.

By Saturday morning the hollowness was starting to fade. She took the bedspread to the cleaner, dropped off her laundry, and went back to tackle the canopy. It was an awkward job, standing on a chair and pinning, but the frame was too hard to manipulate singlehandedly.

When the phone rang at noon, she swore. Which she regretted. It was Jim. He had an hour and a half. Could he come over?

She put coffee on, took out bread, cheese and tomato juice. It was a first, the first Saturday in June, the first time he had ever come for lunch. She heard him on the stairs, taking them by twos. There was just a chance, just the vaguest possibility, that her luck was turning.

"You got a letter," she said when he came in and hugged her.

"I got a letter."

"Well?"

"I'll tell you about it next week."

"Ah, you're a son of a bitch." It was more than a flicker of diappointment.

"Next week, I promise. The end of the week." He was unbuttoning her shirt.

"What are you doing?"

"I want to make love to you."

"You're mad."

"Not mad enough. How do you set your kitchen timer?"

"Why?" She was starting to feel just a little giddy, slightly off balance.

"Because I want to see if you can come in five minutes."

"You've lost your mind." She would giggle in a minute, giggle like an eight-year-old.

"Set the timer."

"Ten minutes."

"Five."

She set it for five. It was a matter of pride. It would be his achievement. "Come here," he said. "I'll make you come in five."

The bell rang. There were always bells ringing, in school, at mass, in bars, on kitchen timers, marking the great accomplishments of one's life.

The bell made her laugh. It also made her miss her

mark. But he was happy. She had never felt him so warm or so happy.

He got up, turned off the timer, and drank one of the glasses of tomato juice on the table. Then he came back and sat on the bed facing her. He looked at his watch. "What time do you have?"

"Twelve-thirty. Did it stop?"

"Yes." He shook it and listened. "Well, I'll need one with a second hand now anyway."

"Why?"

He grinned at her. "So I can clock how long it takes you to come."

"You're a—"

"I know. You told me. Do you know you make love better now than you did in January?"

Her eyes widened and she pulled herself up to a sitting position.

He was laughing. "You're speechless," he said, touching her. "It's a first. You're really speechless." He kissed her, stood up, stretched, and began to dress.

Second hand. Son of a bitch. God, she felt good. She watched him for a minute, then got lazily out of bed and started to dress.

He went to the bookcase and took the white box off the shelf, removing the book and looking at it, the white leather cover with her name in the corner, the white Bible which had waited all these years for someone to marry her so she could carry it down the aisle covered with stephanotis and white orchids.

"Have you looked at it?" he asked.

"Not yet."

He opened it to the page marked by the ribbon and read for a moment. "Did you mark this page?"

"Is it Isaiah?"

"Yes."

"I marked it." She sat down to tie her sneakers.

He stood holding the open Bible, reading to himself. "I like the passage," he said looking up. "I've always liked it."

"I used to read it sometimes on Saturday morning in temple. My grandfather used to be there listening." Her voice was an echo, another time, another place.

He put the open Bible on the table. "What's troubling you?"

"Nothing—just a silly thing. I just wanted to tell you—"

"Wait a minute." He put up a hand and turned toward the door. Someone was coming up the stairs. Past the landing. Knocking twice.

She stood up frowning, moved toward the door, stopped and gave him a quick look. "Who is it?" she called, her voice brittle.

"It's me," Pete's voice came back cheerily. "I've got your books."

She winced and a hand moved of its own accord to cover her eyes. She felt him touch her back. "Go ahead," he said.

She opened the door, standing carefully in the open space. "Gee, thanks, Pete. You really didn't have to—"

"Aren't you going to invite me in?" he said, pushing the door.

Defeated, she stepped back. "Someone you know just dropped over," she said, her feet freezing where she stood, watching him move in as if the action were on a piece of film racing through an unstoppable projector.

"Jim! How the hell are you, buddy?"

"Fine, Pete," the voice steady and controlled. "I was just on my way out. Can I walk you downstairs?"

"Sure." He put the books on the table next to the open Bible.

He was so thick, so unbelievably thick. The table was set for two. How could he not see it?

Jim was walking toward the door. Pete turned to her. "Thanks for the books, Ruthie. I'll see you—" He stopped abruptly as his eye fell, for the first time, on the unmade bed behind her, moved to her face, and finally back to the table.

"Let's go down," Jim said. "I'd like to talk to you."

"About what?" Pete said, using a borrowed voice, harder and harsher than his own. "You want to teach me something you forgot last summer?"

"Pete—"

"Forget it," he snapped. "Thanks a lot, Ruthie. So long—" he turned to Jim—"Father." The door shut and the footsteps marched heavily and evenly down the stairs.

"Shit." The word reverberated through the room.

Her vocal cords failed; her vocabulary failed. How many times had she thought of talking to him about Pete and had let the opportunity slip by? Of all people in the world to have hurt. Of all ways to have done it.

"I just have to be the prize bungler of the year," he said. "I've thought of him fifty times. I never picked up a phone once."

There was an ache in her chest. She tried to think which one of them it was for. She looked at her watch. "It's after one," she said.

"It doesn't matter. I'm not going back."

"What the hell is the matter with you?"

"I have to find Pete."

"You can see him tomorrow. You can see him Tuesday."

"I'll see him this afternoon."

"Please go to your church."

"Shit."

"I heard you the first time."

"Let me tell you, if I were doing this over, I would do everything differently. What have I gained playing two parts?"

"You spent weeks deciding what you would do. You're so close. Don't pull out now."

He reached into his inside coat pocket, drew out a thick envelope, and dropped it on the table. "Go ahead and read it."

She glanced at it. It was addressed to Rev. James M. Kendall. "Put it away," she said. "Show it to your bishop. It's getting late. Will you please go?"

"Don't you see anything inconsistent in my going to that church when Pete is walking around feeling the way he feels?"

"Listen, the list of casualties of this year is so long—"

"Has it occurred to you that you're one of them?"

"Everybody is one of them. Don't add all the people that are waiting for you at that church."

"What makes you so anxious to save my soul?"

"I'm not." She looked at him and pursed her lips. "I don't even think you have one to be saved." She watched as the hard line of his mouth softened and the eyes became human again.

"Thanks," he said, stopping short of a smile. He

picked up the envelope and pushed it back in his inside coat pocket.

She felt her shoulders drop as the tension broke. "Eat something?"

He shook his head. "What time is it?" he asked wearily.

"Twenty after."

He nodded absently and walked toward the door. In the hall, he turned around.

"Why does he call you 'Ruthie'?"

"Because he doesn't know me."

He nodded and went down the stairs.

On Sunday morning she bought the paper and propped herself up with pillows on the sofa so she could enjoy it physically as well as mentally. The weather was nice for a change. Maybe later she would go out. Maybe she would call someone. Maybe she would spend a pleasant afternoon.

She didn't. Sometime after noon the telephone rang. It was her Aunt Sylvia, her mother's older sister, calling from Brooklyn to tell her her father had died that morning, suddenly, unexpectedly, a heart attack while he sat reading the paper, all that terrible news in the Sunday paper.

There was a pause. "Honey?" Aunt Sylvia said.

"Yes. Yes. I'll take the first plane."

"We'll meet you."

"I want to take a cab," she heard herself say angrily. "Tell Mother—I don't know—tell Mother I'm sorry." She hung up.

Sorry. Had she really said sorry?

She stood up and looked around. Jimmy. What do I do first?

Jimmy, Jimmy, walk in the door and tell me what to do first.

The kitchen counter was covered with dishes, last night's dishes, this morning's. She walked slowly to the kitchen and stood looking at the clutter. How can I leave a kitchen looking like this?

Jimmy. Just this once, I'll never ask you again. Now, when I need you.

There were flowers on the coriander. The parsley was a deep, rich, aromatic green. The plants, the plants would all die. She filled the watering can and watered them. Then she watered them again until they dripped on the counter and on the dirty dishes, making little round brown puddles.

She started putting clothes in a suitcase. Halfway through, she slid her jeans down and stepped out of them, took her shirt off and dropped it on the bed, got dressed again in the first dark dress she found and finished her packing. She went into the bathroom to look at her image in the mirror but there was no mirror; Angelo had seen to that.

She sat at the desk and took a piece of paper. "Sunday," she wrote.

Jim—
   My father died this morning. Call me. Please call me. Person to person. And water the plants.
   I miss you already.

                                        R

She added her mother's phone number and read the

note over. Something was wrong with the last sentence. She drew a circle around "already" and an arrow placing it between "I" and "miss." That was better. It was more grammatical now, more coherent.

She propped the note up on the kitchen table. Her Bible was still lying there, open to Isaiah. "They that wait for the Lord shall renew their strength." She thought about it as she went to the telephone and dialed a number.

"Pete," she said in a voice she herself failed to recognize, "this is Ruth."

"Yes?" He hated her. She could hear it in his voice. It was over a year since there had been anything between them, he was sleeping with Judy, and still he hated her for loving someone else.

"My father died this morning," the strange voice said. "I wonder—"

"Oh, God, Ruthie, I'm sorry. Look, I'll be right over."

"Don't, Pete. I'm on my way to the airport. I just wanted—"

"Wait for me," he said and hung up.

She went to the sink and took a glass of water. She drank it slowly, looking at the plants. There was a little water left in the glass. She poured it in the nearest flowerpot and watched it drip.

She turned on the water to rinse the glass. It hit the faucet and broke in her hand. She let go of the piece she was holding and turned off the faucet.

They drove most of the way in silence. It was a nice day. After all that rotten spring weather, Daddy had picked a nice day to die.

She was surprised when the car entered the tunnel.

There was almost no traffic today. She would just make the two o'clock flight.

In the semidarkness of the tunnel, Pete reached over to touch her. It was the touch of a brother or perhaps of a friend. They had never been lovers, had they? They had managed to spare each other that.

"Is there anything I can do?" he asked.

"No, nothing. Just school."

"I mean—" He turned his head slightly and looked at her in the dim light of the tunnel. "Would you like me to call Jim?"

She felt her eyes fill and she swallowed. It would be absurd to cry now simply because she was touched by his kindness. "Thanks," she said thickly. "I left a note for him."

"I could drive you to New York, Ruthie. It's early; I'd be back by midnight. Why don't I drive you?"

She shook her head. "I want to fly, Pete. I just want to sit by myself for an hour in a plane."

They were coming to the end of the tunnel. "Would you tell me one thing?" he asked.

"Sure."

"When we went there in January—to the church— was it going on then, between you and Jim?"

Ah, the male ego, that tenuous, tissuey film that quivered, even as her voice quivered, threatening to break at the slightest insensitive touch. Reassure me, he was saying. Now, in the depths of your sorrow, reassure me that I gave you up before you abandoned me.

"No," she comforted him soothingly. "It wasn't going on then. I didn't know him at all that day."

They came out into the June sunshine and she saw the airport.

"Will you be getting married?" he asked.

It was such a beautiful day. Even New York would be beautiful on a day like this.

"Yes," she said, feeling for the first time the confidence of her words. "I think we'll probably get married at the end of June."

"So soon? I mean, with your father and everything."

"Oh, Pete," she said, her patience snapping like an overextended rubber band, "we're already married. What difference does standing in front of a judge make?"

"I'll park the car," he mumbled.

"Don't. Just drop me off, OK? I can still make the two o'clock flight."

"Do you need money?"

"Thanks," she said. "I have my checkbook."

It was almost two. She walked up the aisle, took a window seat over the left wing, and buckled the belt. A man came in her direction and stopped briefly. He was young, attractive, the crease, the coat, the tie all impeccable, the colors and patterns carefully selected, meticulously harmonized, the hair styled, arranged and sprayed so that no one—well, almost no one—would know that it wasn't the June breeze across the windshield of the Jag that had arranged it. His left hand held an expensive attaché case, the right a copy of *Playboy*. Their eyes met and there was a flicker of something in his that she was unable to read. Then he continued up the aisle.

Outside, the stairs were being taken away. The engines started and the plane moved slowly out to the runway. There would be no one today, no one in the aisle seat, no stranger who would share an intimacy with her and then vanish forever.

Tired, she closed her eyes. When she opened them, they were coming in low over Flushing Bay.

The apartment was misty with tears. She had hoped to be able to retire to her room in semiquiet, but her presence was expected in the living room. Joanna looked a wreck. She and Dave had rushed over when Mother had called this morning, and they had seen him, dead, in his favorite chair. The chair, in fact, had disappeared. Its absence made the living room much larger, less crowded.

The day wore on. She found herself nodding rather than speaking. Her mother, under the influence of pills from a generous G.P. in the building, sat immovably in one chair for hours, occasionally reaching out to hold the hand of one of her children.

The aunts came and the uncles, from both sides of the family. He was the first of his family to die and he was one of the youngest. Their sadness was mixed with shock—and with fear of mortality.

They drifted away in the evening to prepare themselves for the next morning. All but Aunt Sylvia. She would stay the night.

Thank God. Thank God for Aunt Sylvia, that brick, that foundation of strength. It was the Aunt Sylvias of the world that kept it turning, that remembered to wind it up every night and adjust it every few weeks when it went askew.

But Mother, weeping as the pills wore off, said no. Ruthie was here and Sylvia had things to do at home.

Her place was with her family. Ruthie could take care of everything.

The thought, just the naked thought of spending the night alone with her mother, made her tremble. Surely Aunt Sylvia would insist. But Aunt Sylvia allowed herself to be persuaded and mother and daughter were left alone.

Her mother bathed, took pills, and went to her room dressed in a nightgown. The sound of crying continued, an echo of grief in an echoless room, a plea, a call.

She undressed, hearing without listening, the little gold cross swinging out as she bent to take off her stockings. She had only a robe to put on. After Anthony had left, she had stopped wearing anything to bed. All the pajamas, the pretty shirts and gowns, had been put away and she had neglected to pack anything but a light summer robe. She put it on now and knocked softly on the door to her parents' room. Her mother said something and she walked in.

"Would you like me to sit here awhile, Mom?"

"Yes. Bring a chair over."

The lamp on the night table was on and her mother was lying carefully on one side of the double bed. How many years had they slept together on that bed? Dave was thirty now. They must be married at least thirty-one years.

In thirty-one years, Jim would be seventy—she sat down and took her mother's hand—and she herself would be fifty-seven. Her father had died today at the age of fifty-seven.

"You're a good girl, Ruthie," her mother told her. "I always said you were a good girl."

"Let me turn off the light. I'll stay until you sleep."

"I miss you when you're not here, honey."

"I know, Mom."

"Maybe this summer you'll come home. We'll spend the summer together. You can rest the whole summer."

She sat very quietly in the darkness.

"Ruth?"

"I'll think about it, Mom."

"Promise me you'll come."

"I promise I'll think about it."

She was sitting on an old bentwood rocking chair that her mother had sat in to nurse her babies. She rocked for a long time after the breathing became even. Then she got up and opened the door. The light from the hall lit up the bedroom, silhouetting the single figure on the double bed.

The funeral was at eleven o'clock Monday morning. Somehow they all got there and were led to seats in the front row. Dave sat on one side and she on the other side of their mother. Strangely, Joanna sat next to her sister-in-law instead of beside her husband.

Ruth looked up. There was a—what did you call it? a casket? a coffin?—a handsome open box in front of her. Inside was a man. She reached out her free hand and took Joanna's.

"Joanna, I think I'm going to throw up." She felt a firm pressure on her hand.

"No you won't. Look away. Look down. I have lemon drops."

"Give me one." It came quickly and she sucked it fiercely like a pacifier. "Thank you. Give me another one." She put it on her lap and leaned back, her eyes on the floor.

A man began to talk. It was a voice she knew and she turned her head carefully and looked up. Rabbi Goldberg who had confirmed her thirteen years ago this month, who had handed her the little white Bible. How gray he had become. ". . . A man devoted to his family," he was saying. ". . . Remembered for his many contributions . . . his wife . . . a son and a daughter whom he loved."

It was all over very quickly and Dave stood up and tenderly turned to his mother, who sat weeping between her children.

"Come," Joanna whispered, tucking a handkerchief in her bag.

They both stood up and there was a sharp sound, a clatter that echoed and resounded in the quiet room. She looked down. The second lemon drop had fallen on the only uncarpeted section of floor in the whole room.

"It's OK," Joanna murmured. "No one heard it except you and me."

It was a long ride out to the cemetery. Why were Jews always buried on Long Island? With all the Jews buried there, was there any room left for people to live?

How remarkably efficient everything was. She wondered who had made the arrangements, how all the little details had been synchronized so neatly, everything and everyone at the right place at the right time without a rehearsal.

The car stopped and her mother, whose tears had not subsided since eight in the morning in spite of the pills, got out unsteadily. It was a pretty place, good-smelling like the country. She stood with her family and thought about Teresa. How many people had been there the day Teresa was buried? God, the unfairness of it. It occurred to her as she stood and listened to the murmur of the rabbi's voice that she had never sent flowers when Teresa died. People did that for Catholics. Why hadn't she thought of it?

There was a wail next to her which brought her back and she turned. Her mother seemed ready to collapse.

"It's OK," Dave said and led their mother to the waiting limousine. The crowd began to disperse, walking slowly to the assorted cars parked not far from the gravesite.

She stood and watched them go. The rabbi came by, patted her shoulder, and walked toward the cars. Except for the workmen, she was the only one left there now. One or two cars were starting to move. She turned slowly and started to walk. There were gravestones near the open grave. She went to the first one, looked at the inscription with mild curiosity, heard herself say "Oh God" and felt herself—what? trip? catch her shoe? turn her ankle?—fall in a tearful heap on the ground where she stayed, almost forever, until her brother—poor Dave, that he should be put through all this—came and helped her up, her stockings ruined, her dress filthy, and led her away from the one plot of earth she had wanted to see for five years but had never before set foot on, the resting place of Abraham Gold, 1885–1967.

In the evening, the crowds came, not just the relatives, friends and business acquaintances of the deceased, but the high school friends of his daughter. She stood with amazement as one after the other they came in, wearing their fashionably correct dark clothes, their hair glittering, their left hands glittering. ("Oh, Ruthie, I'm so sorry. He was such a wonderful person.")

Almost to her surprise, she was touched. She had been away almost four years; she rarely called any of them on visits to Brooklyn. How had they even heard? What had moved them to come?

When they left, she thanked each one for coming, meaning it, touched by their having taken the time. How kind of their husbands to have stayed home with the children on behalf of a stranger.

Her mother, in a semistupor, went to bed unwashed, her eyes half glazed "Sit with me," she said heavily and her daughter drew the rocker next to the bed and sat holding the hand and thinking that perhaps they had achieved something finally, the two of them, that they could not have achieved without this awful catalyst.

She went to bed feeling slightly lifted.

She knew he would call on Tuesday. He would reach her apartment by three, possibly even earlier, and read her note. From three o'clock on, she was on edge. Why didn't he call? Why hadn't she written that he should call immediately? What had she said in that stupid, incoherent, ungrammatical note?

The phone rang and she jumped. It was not for her. It rang again and she sat there and let Joanna answer it or one of the cousins who seemed to be stationed permanently in the kitchen eternally preparing sustenance.

Joanna went home to care for Robby and still no call. Joanna returned. They had all nibbled at some turkey, eaten a slice of bread, sipped some stale coffee.

At eight o'clock Joanna answered the phone, said something, and walked into the living room. "Long distance, Ruth. Person to person."

How absurd to tremble over a phone call. She went into the kitchen and stood facing the wall, blocking out the cousins, the turkeys, the enormous coffeemaker. The operator put her through.

"Hello?"

"Are you OK?"

"I'm fine, darling. Where've you been?"

"I thought you'd be out," he said.

"Out?"

"When is the funeral?"

"It was yesterday morning."

There was a pause. "Oh. Oh, of course. I didn't think. Are you sure you're all right?"

"Yes. Just keep talking."

"When do you want to come home?"

Home. When do I want to go home? She smiled at the wall. "Sunday."

"I'll come and get you. What's your address there?"

She shook her head at the wall. "I'm taking the shuttle," she said. "I'll take the six o'clock flight."

"I could drive down. . . ."

"No. You know you can't. Just talk to me."

"I'll be at the airport then, at seven."

"How can—?"

"Let me arrange that."

"Listen, if you're hungry, there are eggs in the refrigerator."

"I found them. Don't worry about anything. I'll see you Sunday night."

They said goodbye and she hung up and leaned her forehead against the wall. When you break the connection, you know Brooklyn is an island. She closed her eyes. She was going home on Sunday.

It struck her that it was very quiet in the kitchen. She glanced part way around. The cousins stood frozen as in a movie that has been stopped on a single frame, their hands holding kitchen utensils awkwardly aloft, their eyes—where? not on her. She turned slightly. Her mother, eyes alert, body rigid, stood in the doorway, blocking her path, her exit, her only escape.

"Who was that?" her mother asked crisply.

"A friend, Mom," she said gently.

"A friend? From God's country up there?"

"Yes, Mom, someone I know in Boston."

"A boy?"

She was midway between laughter and despair. It would never occur to her mother that some of her male friends had grown to be men. "Yes," she said comfortingly, "a boy."

"He has a key to your apartment, this boy?" The cousins were now working busily preparing food that would never be eaten in a hundred weeks of mourning.

What had she said to give away the key? She bit her lower lip—eggs in the refrigerator. Damn. "Let's go out and sit down, Mom."

"Is he Jewish?"

"Come on, let's sit down. We'll talk later."

"What's his name?"

"Jim," she said, wilting, starting to taste defeat, wishing there were one other way out of the kitchen besides the window.

"Jim? James? A nice Jewish name, James."

She swallowed.

"So that's what goes on up there in God's country."

"Please, Mom," she pleaded, hating herself for pleading.

"You going to marry him, this James?"

"Anna," Aunt Sylvia said, sliding her bosom deftly by her sister into the kitchen, "it was just a phone call. Don't upset yourself over a phone call. Leave her alone."

"I shouldn't worry about it, what this girl does up there where she lives? That she does it with goyem? Her father—may he rest in peace—buried only twenty-four hours and already they're calling her on the phone? Did she cry for her father? Did you see her shed one tear for her father, Sylvia?"

She put a hand to the front of her dress and touched the little gold cross that hung inside down to the point where cleavage would have started if there had been anything to cleave.

Her mother had turned to face her again. "Fifty-seven years old. A man shouldn't die at fifty-seven of a heart attack. He should have lived another twenty-five years like his father."

Abraham Gold. My friend, Abraham.

"You know why he died?" the widow went on, recovered now from the effects of her grief, bent on her maternal mission.

"Stop it, Anna," one of the cousins warned sharply. "You'll make yourself sick."

"He died from worry, that's what he died of, worrying that you were going out with goyem in God's country there."

She leaned against the wall, her hand still touching the cross. She would hear her mother out, pack her suitcase, and leave. Jim might still be at the apartment. She would call and ask him to meet her at the airport. She had had it. She was through. This was the end.

"That's what killed him," her mother said trium-phantly, her face almost joyous at the discovery at last of a purpose to the tragedy. "Think of that when you're getting married." She closed her eyes momentarily, put a hand to her forehead, and left the kitchen.

Her daughter followed her out, then turned toward her bedroom.

"Ruth?"

She stopped. It was her brother.

"Where are you going?" he asked.

"Home. I've worn out my welcome."

"Don't do it," he said. "Stick it out till Sunday."

"What for?"

He took his time. "Do it for Joanna. If you go, one of us will have to—"

"I'm sorry," she said, relenting. "I didn't think." She started toward the light and noise at the front of the apartment. When she reached Dave, he put a hand on her shoulder to stop her.

"Is he important? Joanna said something to me after Passover."

"He's important."

"Well, bring him around next time you're in New York."

She looked at him in disbelief. It was her mother's son. "Thanks," she said gratefully, "I will."

She hung around casually after they had all gone, keeping herself available for another bedside vigil. The request never came and she made no offer. They un-derstood each other now. For better or for worse.

It took a long time for Sunday to come but she con-cealed her anticipation and then, later, her excitement. One of the relatives handed her several foil-wrapped packages of turkey and roast beef—lest she starve between the two cities. She had prepared herself to say goodbye warmly to her mother, but she was thwarted at the door.

"When you send the invitations," her mother said, "you can cross my name off the list. I'm not coming."

When the plane took off from LaGuardia the seat beside her was still vacant. She sat back, appreciating the aloneness. She had wept at the grave of Abraham Gold this week, finally, after five years. What had been on his mind all those years ago when he had written his will? What did he expect of her?

She tried to remember him as she had last seen him, at the airport the night she had left for Europe, her parents throwing cautions at her—"Don't lose your traveler's checks." "Don't drink the water." "Don't trust anybody." "Don't forget to write"—on and on until the flight was called and her mother started to cry. Grandpa had spent the time reading a Yiddish newspaper through his gold-rimmed glasses, occasionally looking up and shaking his head in bewilderment at his son and daughter-in-law. "Leave her alone, leave her alone," he would mutter. "I came to this country when I was sixteen, I didn't have half the brains she has now."

He had walked down the long hall with them to the last door and had folded her free hand around a bill. "Don't listen to them," he had said. "Have a wonderful time, darling. Have the time of your life. Buy everything you want and what you can't buy, steal. If they give you trouble bringing it back, smuggle it in."

"Poppa!" his son had admonished.

"It's a family tradition," Abraham Gold had retorted. "Who are you to break with tradition?" He had turned back to his granddaughter—"If you need help, don't go to the American Embassy. They're only there for the rich and the goyem. Just stop someone in the street and tell him you're a friend of Abraham Gold."

The bill in her hand had turned out to be a fifty. She had never seen Abraham Gold again.

The plane landed and she hurried into the terminal where Jim was waiting. They held each other as passengers-turned-spectators meandered by.

They walked slowly to the waiting room. She stopped when they got there and looked around. How pretty it was in contrast to the barrackslike construction in New York, the comfortable seats she had never had time to sit in, the green plants, the large windows. Farewell to the shuttle.

"Forget something?" he asked. It was the first thing he had said to her.

"No, just saying goodbye."

"Let me take you home." They started to walk.

"Jim?"

"What, darling?"

"I want to get married." She looked up at him. He was pleased. His whole face reflected his pleasure.

"Could we wait a few days?" he asked, smiling slightly. "It's a little late to leave for Maryland tonight."

"We can wait."

She walked to the parking lot with him, letting her hair get wet in the rain, and they drove back. She sat next to him, feeling the contentment of being home. For a few minutes she dozed; when she opened her eyes, they were on her block.

She walked through the apartment dimly registering small changes: the empty sink, the clean kitchen counter, the absence of last Sunday's jeans and shirt on the bed. In the bathroom, she saw her reflection in a new mirror, the manufacturer's label still adhering to one corner.

"You missed dinner, didn't you?" she said, returning.

"I drank some tomato juice."

She took the foil-wrapped packages out of the tote and put them on the table. "Eat."

He took a few slices of meat with his fingers and ate them. She sat on the sofa and watched him wash his hands at the kitchen sink and dry them on a paper towel.

"Why don't you go to sleep?" he suggested.

"Do I look that bad?"

"You don't look bad. You look tired. You fell asleep in the car."

"I know," she said, not moving.

He joined her on the sofa. "Who sat next to you on the shuttle?"

What a long time ago it was that she had mentioned the shuttle to him. "Nobody," she said, and stopped. "My grandfather. My grandfather sat next to me. We talked all the way home. Did I ever tell you about my grandfather?"

He reached out a hand and touched her. "No."

"He was a beautiful person," she said. "He spoke Hebrew and Yiddish and Russian and his English was perfect even though it wasn't his first language. I think all he ever cared about was learning. When I went away to school he asked me to save my books so he

could get an American college education. He was in his
late seventies then and I think he read every book I
gave him.

"I remember once he got angry about something and
he wrote a letter to the *New York Times* and they
printed it. He was very surprised. He said he thought
the *Times* threw your letter away if your name was
Abraham Gold. Afterwards, he said they made an
American out of him." She was starting to feel vaguely
drunk although she had not had a drink for weeks.

"He was nothing like you," she went on. "He had no
universal love. He wasn't that kind of person at all. If
he felt anything universal, I think it was disdain, disdain
for people who tried to tell other people what to do
and what to think and what to love. I suppose in a way
he made a misfit out of me because he taught me to do
what I wanted to and I always did—well, most of the
time I did.

"I wasn't the only one he talked to or the only one
who listened to him. He talked to God all his life and
during one period, when he was very lonely, God talked
to him." She was breathing rapidly now and her hands
were sweating. "It's not a family legend," she said. "In
fact, I'm the only one in the family who believes it
happened. I know it happened. I was there once and I
heard the voice." She closed her eyes for a second and
all the images merged, the glass of tea next to the open
books on the flowered tablecloth, the glass of lemonade
on the round white umbrellaed table in the sunshine,
the gravestone in the cemetery, the empty seat on the
aisle. "Would you get me some brandy, please?" she
asked, feeling faint.

He brought two glasses of brandy and sat down

again. "I think," he said, very casually, "I'll stay here tonight."

"Why? Do you think there's something wrong with me?"

"No, I don't think there's anything wrong with you. I just want to stay with you tonight."

"You don't believe me, do you?"

"I believe you. I believed you the first time I heard you talk about it."

The faintness had dissipated with the sip of brandy. "The first time?"

"Last summer."

"I told you last summer?" She was confused now, confused and very tired.

"You talked about it one night in the lodge. Pete was there and one or two of the others."

She shrugged. The memory had gone. Ironically, he remembered and she had forgotten.

"It was the first time I looked at you," he said. "I mean looked."

"Because of what I said?"

He nodded.

She leaned back. "Grandpa would get a laugh out of that." She finished her brandy and felt relief flood her body with warmth like a fireplace on a night in winter, like a cup of hot tea. To think she had worried about it since January. "Don't stay tonight," she said. "I'm OK. You don't have to worry."

"I want to stay," he told her, "for very personal, selfish reasons."

"Come here. I want to tell you something." That she was free. That she loved him. That she would wait forever. That—

The telephone rang. She got up with a groan, sat down on the far side of the bed, and answered. It was the long arm of Brooklyn. She closed her eyes.

"Hi, Mom," she said in a monotone.

"You're back there already?" the voice asked cheerfully.

"Yes, Mom."

"It was a good flight?"

"Yes."

"I'm going to sleep without the pills tonight."

"That's great."

"You don't sound so good, Ruthie."

"I'm fine."

"You'll come home after school is over?" her mother asked hopefully, divulging the reason for the call.

"I told you I'd think about it."

"But you'll come." The voice was insistent. It had been insistent all her life.

She shook her head. "I'll think about it, Mom."

"Don't forget to write."

She opened her eyes and hung up. He was standing next to the bed.

"They never let you go," she said.

He sat down next to her.

"Where was she when they cut the cord?"

"Probably asleep," he said reasonably.

"The biggest moment of her life and she slept through it."

"Did something happen between you at home?"

"I guess something happened. Something usually does."

"Do you want to go back and fix it up?"

"I'll never go back," she said, hearing her voice like an echo.

He stood up. "Why don't we go to sleep? You're tired and—"

"Go home, Jim. Please go home."

His reluctance to leave was almost tangible. He fidgeted, walked around, finally went to the door. "I'll see you tomorrow," he said.

"Tomorrow's Monday," she reminded him gently.

"I know. I'll be over about—maybe nine."

She showered, set the alarm, and got into bed. He had known about Grandpa, right from the start. It made the whole world look different, their relationship, their love, their understanding of each other. She would say it tomorrow night. It was the right time.

In the middle of the night, the phone rang. She picked up the receiver with her eyes half closed and said, "Oh, Pete."

"It's not Pete. It's me."

She shook herself awake. "What's wrong? Where are you?"

"Out for a walk."

She looked at the luminous dial. "It's one-thirty."

"I didn't feel like sleeping. How are you?"

"I'm OK. Go home, will you? I get nervous thinking about you walking around at this hour."

There was a pause. Then he said, "I'll see you at nine."

She lay back on the pillow. What was bothering him? What was he so concerned about? It occurred to her for the first time that he had really wanted to stay with her tonight.

Frank Giraldi was the first to offer condolences. He sounded warm and sincere and she found herself forgiving him for half the things he had done all year. Jeff was practically on Frank's heels. He was very sweet. She started to feel a little sorry for him.

She played records when she got home and cooked herself a good meal. Then she showered, put on her robe, and folded down the bed. She kept moving around nervously, doing unnecessary chores, doing them again, the feeling of expectancy making her jittery. He was late and she had worked off most of dinner by the time she heard his knock.

He was wet from the rain and she shivered when she touched him.

"I'm sorry about last night," she apologized. "You really wanted to stay here, didn't you?"

"I told you I did." There was something strange in his response, something distant.

"Sometimes we go around in circles."

"Most of the time lately."

"Make love to me."

He moved away from her. "Do you mind if I turn off the record player?"

"No."

She watched him walk, his shoulders sloped. He yawned as he pressed the button. "Did you sleep last night?" she asked.

He shook his head.

"Well, sleep with me now."

He turned some of the lights off. She started to feel chilly. He came to her and touched her, a hesitant, fumbling touch, the touch of a boy unsure of where to put his hand, where it would do the most good, a boy not quite ready to go through with it.

She was cold now and the light summer robe was only a covering, not a comfort. She had put it all together in the last ten seconds, the hesitancy, the fatigue, the need for quiet. She wasn't ready for it but she would never be ready.

She took his hand away and said, "Let's sit down."

"You're cold." But not as cold as he was.

"I don't want to know," she said. "I don't have to know."

"But I have to tell you. I've been trying for months and now my time's run out."

"Time doesn't run out."

"It does for me."

"I'll listen."

"It was in California," he began, "eleven years ago. I had stopped there after the navy and never left. I was working on a masters and teaching freshman English. I lived alone. I think she sat down at my table one day in the spring when I was having lunch. She was a good-looking blonde and she was interested. I was always interested. She had some kind of part-time job with the administration and her husband was a salesman. He left almost every Monday morning and came back on Friday night. The whole situation was just made for me.

"She had three kids, two boys and a little girl about two years old. I ran into them one Sunday morning by accident in a park she had taken them to. Nice kids. I played ball with the boys for a while." He stopped as if remembering the day, the woman, the children, the sunshine.

"I used to call her in the afternoon a couple of times

a week and tell her what time I'd pick her up. We used to go to my room or once in a while to a motel. I suppose it was crazy but I couldn't go to bed with her in that house, not with those kids there.

"It went on that way for a few months. I wish I could tell you something about her. When it was all over, I sat down and I tried to think what I knew about her, and all I could come up with was her name, her address, and what she looked like. I think if you'd asked me her name when I was in bed with her, I wouldn't have been able to tell you. She was the mother of those kids; she must have talked about them. She was someone's wife, someone's neighbor, she had an identity, and all she was to me was a phone call, a drink, getting into bed, driving home."

He stopped and moved his body uncomfortably and she knew that the story had changed in his mind over the years; the facts had remained the same but the story had undergone a metamorphosis. It had begun with a shattering incident; it had ended as a condemnation of a way of life.

"The last time I saw her," he said, picking up the story, "I had just gotten a check and a job offer. I called her and said I'd pick her up at eight. She used to meet me on the corner. I took her to a motel that night and we must have been later than usual—I don't know why—and on the way home she asked me to hurry. She said she had left the kids without a sitter."

She was so cold now that she had lost the battle to control the trembling. For an instant, she hated the woman. I would have killed her, she thought. I would have stopped the car and killed her.

"I wanted to kill her," he said. "I reacted like a lunatic. I stepped on the gas and I shouted at her, telling her what a great mother she was. I don't think you can begin to imagine what I said. I just pushed the pedal down to the floor and ranted. Talk about casting the first stone."

"Don't tell me the rest," she said, seeing the crash, the dead woman with blond hair, the orphaned children alone in the empty house.

"I turned down her street," he went on, ignoring her or perhaps too far away now to have heard, "and there was a kind of pretty glow. It didn't sink in until I was on top of it. One upper corner of the house was burning."

She was still holding his hand, the hesitant, fumbling hand that had touched her before his time had run out. He took a deep breath.

"We got the little boys out," he said, and stopped.

"Oh God," she said.

"Yeah. Oh God."

It was the beginning of June and outside there was rain and inside an Arctic ice mass had crept in, chilling the air and the blood and the skin.

"I got in my car," he said, very calmly, after a short pause, "and I drove home, as if that were the end of the whole thing. I left her there to cope with everything by herself, with the loss of that little baby, with her husband, her home." He was enumerating them now, his shortcomings, his failings, his sins.

"I threw up when I got home. It's stupid but that's all I remember about those days, staying in my room and throwing up. I know I saw a doctor—" he stretched out his one free hand—"but I don't remember where or which day. The night before the funeral, I made up my mind to go over there and talk to her husband. I got dressed." He stopped. "I never got there. I never even got out of my room."

His shirt was wet and his face and the hand she had refused to let go.

"I went to the funeral," he said. "It was the first time I'd been in a church since the navy. I think it was the first time in my life I really prayed. In the afternoon, I went back to the same church and confessed. The priest spent hours with me. We walked, he took me somewhere for dinner. When I got home, I wrote a letter turning down the job. The next day I came back east."

He relaxed and closed his eyes and for a minute she thought he had fallen asleep, but he roused himself, looked at her and brushed the back of one hand along her cheeks, and she could feel the wetness streaking. "Don't do that," he said gently. "It was a long time ago." He reached inside her robe and found the little cross and held it, rubbing his knuckles over her breast. "I didn't expect you to wear it, you know that? Margaret's family gave it to me when I was ordained. I wish," he said, and the word sounded strangely out of place, out of character, "I wish we had met a dozen years ago. It would have spared a lot of people a lot of misery."

"A dozen years ago," she said. "Sure. When I was fourteen."

He looked at her, the impact of the simple subtraction reflected in his eyes. "How old are you?" he asked.

"Twenty-six."

"Twenty-six. What am I now?" His face shone with moisture.

"I don't remember," she lied.

"There was no way it could have worked, was there?"

"No way."

He stood up unsteadily, rubbed one hand over a cheek and looked at the damp palm. Then he turned and walked back to the bathroom. She heard the water running and went back and stood in the open doorway. He was dousing his face with cold water. He glanced up and saw her in the mirror.

"Thank you for the mirror," she said.

"You're such a pretty girl," he said, "and I never tell you. I thought you ought to at least be able to look at yourself."

She turned and walked out of the bathroom, heavy with the grief of a decade.

"Was your grandfather a rabbi?" His voice came from behind her.

"No. Nothing even vaguely resembling a rabbi."

"What did he do for a living?"

"He was an international smuggler."

"A what?"

"He was an importer but he smuggled things into the country—presents for me, for the rest of the family. It was a way of life with him. He was nothing like you, Jim. He was as fierce in what he hated as in what he loved. He was an Old Testament patriarch, and if he hated you he forgave you nothing and if he loved you you could do no wrong. Somewhere along the way he decided he loved me."

"How old were you when you heard the conversation?"

"Six."

"Six." He thrust his hands in his pockets. "Do you remember any of it?"

She shook her head. "It was in Hebrew. I've never known any Hebrew."

He walked to the kitchen and took a glass of water, standing and looking toward the windows. "Would you like a greenhouse to work in?" he asked.

"Very much."

"Maybe we'll get one for you some day."

She sat down on the bed.

"You didn't say anything before," he said, still looking out the windows. "Was there anything you wanted to say? Anything you want to know? Anything I left out?"

She took her time answering. For some people, time ran out. For others it never began and never ended; it just went on and on. But for all of them there was a right time.

"You gave Anthony your mobile, didn't you?" she said.

"Yes. I couldn't get back in the apartment. Were you angry?"

"No. I thought it was nice. It kind of linked the three of us."

"That day—the day before the judge made the decision—I was going to take you and Anthony and leave the state, leave the country if I had to."

"That doesn't sound like you. I always think of you as being so well thought out. Why didn't you?"

"Andy said he'd have me locked up. I think he meant it."

"So he sent us out and he stayed home with Anthony."

He nodded and went slowly for his jacket. "I'm going away tomorrow," he said.

"Away?" Her voice was tinged with hysteria. "Where are you going?"

"Did I forget to tell you? The bishop asked me—"

"Hang the bishop. I don't want you to go away. I need you."

"I have to."

"You don't have to. Please. I've never asked you before. Please don't go." He was leaving her, leaving her as he had left Carol, as he had left a hundred women before Carol. "You'll never come back," she said. "If you go, you'll never come back."

He put his arms around her. "I'll be back next week."

"When?"

"I don't know. Tuesday, Wednesday, maybe Thursday, I'm not sure. I'm sorry, darling. I'm sorry it's worked out this way. I know this is a bad time for you. I haven't made it any easier."

"Where will you be?" she asked a little more calmly.

"It's a place in western Massachusetts. I'll drive there in the morning."

She held his hand, not wanting to let him go, and just to make him stay another minute she asked, "The job you turned down, where was it?"

"The University of Oregon. It's in Eugene. Beautiful country up there."

"Yes," she said, "I remember."

The door closed, the footsteps receded, the car started downstairs in the rain. When the sounds stop, you are alone. She went to the bookcase, pulled out the white box and flipped through the pages till she found it. Page 973. She turned on a lamp beside the bed and lay down on his pillow.

And it came to pass in the days when the judges judged, that there was a famine in the land. And a certain man of Bethlehem in Judah went to sojourn in the field of Moab, he, and his wife, and his two sons. And the name of the man was Elimelech, and the name of his wife Naomi, and the name of his two sons Mahlon and Chilion, Ephrathites of Bethlehem in Judah. And they came into the field of Moab, and continued there. And Elimelech Naomi's husband died; and she was left, and her two sons. And they took them wives of the women of Moab: the name of one was Orpah, and the name of the other Ruth. . . .

11

She took the Bible to school with her on Tuesday and read the Book of Ruth a second time in a vacant classroom during lunch. It was as if this were the last link between them; if she read this Book enough times, he would come back to her.

She went home holding the Bible and thinking about Carol.

These are the things we do to each other, she thought, Jim to Carol and Carol to someone else.

Her period was due on Friday and the symptoms began to claw at her, expanding her body beneath her skin so that by late evening she was sure her skin would burst.

Sometime after nine the telephone rang.

"Ruth?"

"Yes?"

"Hi, this is Al."

It was no use. The voice was that of a stranger. "Who?"

"Al Rifkin."

Al Rifkin. Jesus Christ, New Year's Eve. "Hello, Al. How are you?"

"Fine, just fine. Look. I know we haven't seen much of each other lately but I thought maybe we could do something this weekend."

Ah, yes, the spring affair has come to an end and it's

315

back to the little black book. No one available from A
to F, Al? Well forget it. Ruthie's going to have her
period this weekend. "I'm sorry," she told him. "I'm all
tied up. Thanks for calling."

"Nice talking to you."

Yeah. Try the H's.

She went to the bathroom and took a hot shower. It
was an old wives' tale that a hot bath would bring on
your period. At school the girls who were afraid they
were pregnant were forever soaking in tubs of steaming
water—to no avail. It came when it wanted to—if it
would come at all.

Cassie had soaked in hot tubs two years ago—all in
vain. She had adored him and then she had become
pregnant and he had decided that the place for him was
far away without her. He had dropped her a short note,
which she received the day after his departure. Her
parental endowment had been depleted for the year
and it was only through the generosity of Abraham
Gold, deceased, and his granddaughter that an abortion
had been arranged, all nice and legal in Brooklyn, New
York, two weeks after the state legalized them.

We are all the same, she thought, all of us—Cassie's
boyfriend, Al, Jimmy, me. What had Jimmy done that
was different from all the rest?

And who else? Maybe everybody she knew. She
dried herself, walked out of the bathroom nude, and
dialed a familiar number.

"Yes?" Pete answered curtly.

"This is Ruth."

"I can't talk now."

"I want to ask you something. It'll just take a minute."

"I *can't talk* now," he said with emphasis. "Do you understand?"

"I understand perfectly. She can wait a minute and a half."

"What do you want to know?" he asked wearily.

"When I first met you three and a half years ago, were you involved with someone?"

"I don't remember."

"Yes you do."

"Well, maybe I was."

"Were you living with her?"

"No."

"But you were sleeping with her."

"What difference does it make? Look, I can't talk now."

"You were sleeping with her. Yes or no."

She could hear him breathing heavily into the receiver. She felt a little sorry for Judy. "Yes," he said, "I was."

"Thank you, Pete. Good night. I'm sorry I bothered you."

She lay down in bed and thought about them—Sandy, Pete, Al, Frank Giraldi.

It was a good story—retreat, the bishop, decisions. She knew now where he had gone. He was on his way to California.

The headache began at two o'clock Wednesday as she was writing on the board. She put the chalk down and turned around, brushing her right hip against the chalk tray and leaving the inevitable mark of her trade on her dress.

She got by till the end of the schoolday, took an aspirin at the water fountain, and drove home.

He needed time. She could see it now, now as she put the Bible back in the bookcase, the Bible with the story she was starting to know by heart. Without meaning to, she had pressured him into making decisions, feeling guilty about her, turning against Angelo. The night of his birthday dinner he had mentioned going back. He had been thinking about it. He just needed time. Give him all the time he needs. Time doesn't run out.

It does for me.

She put her raincoat on and took the train into Boston.

She told Henry Fleming she wanted a man's gold watch with a second hand, that it had to be beautiful, and it had to last the rest of his life; it couldn't run out.

"You'll have to have a very fine watch," he told her, rubbing the tips of his fingers on a sheet of black velvet.

"That's exactly what I want."

"A fine watch may be very expensive."

"I would expect it to be." It didn't matter. She wasn't really paying for it anyway.

It was the first time in her life that she bought something without first checking the price tag. That and the headache made her feel light, exhilarated, somewhat heady. When Mr. Fleming told her the price, she was actually slightly disappointed.

She ordered the engraving and asked to have it by

Monday. Before leaving, she admired Charlie Fleming's hammered gold jewelry in the glass case. Some other time.

The headache came back as the train went north and west into Cambridge.

"Kendall next. Kendall is next." What an irony that she had passed through this station on a hundred trains in her years in Boston and the name had meant nothing to her.

She walked up the stairs of the Harvard station into the remnants of daylight at Harvard Square. Most of the students were gone now, the semester over, June almost half over. Three girls walked by, their hair long, their jeans beltless. She looked for a distinguishing mark among them; there was none. She thought, I will stand here in the rain until one girl comes by wearing a belt in her jeans.

She waited. They were all beltless.

She thought, I will wait until one girl comes by who does not have long hair arranged one quarter left front, one quarter right front, one half back.

The rain penetrated the shoulders of her raincoat. Their hair was all long and all uniformly arranged—a quarter, a quarter, a half.

She walked to the curb and took a taxi home.

By the time she reached her apartment her head was throbbing. She took another aspirin and lay down under the shelter of the canopy to wait for it to take effect.

Let him think things out. Don't make the same mistakes you've made before.

If I could only talk to someone sane, she thought.

How did you go about finding a sane person? Were they listed in the yellow pages, she wondered, Sane People, $40 an hour?

She was sweating now—disgustingly—at the back of her neck, under her arms and at every point where her back rested on the bed. The aspirin had failed. Her head was worse and her stomach had become sick.

What pressure she had exerted on him—spend the night with me (when she knew he couldn't), tell me Teresa will live (when she knew she wouldn't), why do you read that damned book every day? Wouldn't you be better off breaking your back at a hospital on your day off? The bishop, hang the bishop, don't go away, Jimmy, I need you.

And the things she had said to him. With a groan she turned on her side, vainly seeking a momentary relief from the pain, the nausea, the sweat, but there was none, there would never be any. Surely this was the worst night of her life.

She rolled on her back again and looked up at the canopy, which was swimming slightly. She would go away. Pick up the watch on Monday, leave it for him, and go away.

At a sudden internal signal, she leaped out of bed, flew into the bathroom and vomited for the first time in two decades. The event left her weak and feverish. She drank water, took aspirins, drank more water, and lay down again, falling into a dream that lasted until the phone rang.

"Is this Miss Ruth Gold?" It was the voice of an old man, an unnervingly familiar voice, slightly accented but almost hypercorrect in enunciation and grammar, the voice of a man who knew all the rules and whose difficulty was simply in getting them to work. It was a voice she knew.

She was overcome with a sudden case of chills, shaking her shoulders, her knees, and everything in between. She controlled her voice. "Yes, this is Ruth Gold."

"Oh, Miss Gold, I'm so glad I didn't miss you. I was afraid you might have gone away. This is Leo Gerstenwald—from the Wednesday night class. Do you remember me? I sat in the corner."

"Of course I remember you, Mr. Gerstenwald," she breathed. "It's very kind of you to call."

"I was a little afraid—I thought you might not remember me. We liked your course so much. Will you teach something in the fall? Even my wife wants to come to your classes. She says, 'Who is this Miss Gold Leo always talks about?' You aren't going away, are you? Something made me think you might be going away. My wife tells me I'm psychic. Is that the right word?"

"Yes, it's the right word. They have my name for the fall semester, Mr. Gerstenwald. If enough people register, I'll teach a class."

"Oh, you'll have enough. We'll all be there. You weren't planning to go away then, were you?"

She was almost unbearably cold. "No, I guess not."

"I'm glad to hear it, I really am. You would disappoint so many people. I wonder—I know you're very busy—do you think, maybe, in the fall you could find the time to have dinner with us?"

"Of course I will. I'd love to."

"And—" There was a pause and she heard the muffled voice of a woman. "If there's someone you want to bring along, it would make us very happy. You cook for three you cook for four. It's no trouble. I was thinking—I was thinking of the carnation."

"I'll bring him," she said. "I promise I'll bring him with me."

When she hung up, she got under the covers, still dressed, to stop the shaking. The man had said he was Leo Gerstenwald but the voice had been that of Abraham Gold.

It was a Thursday in April in 1952 and it was raining. Ruthie's mommy had let her wear her good shiny black party shoes to school this afternoon even though there was no party and it was raining because Ruthie was going to visit Grandpa after school while Mommy took Davey to the dentist.

"Can I get you something, Poppa?" Mommy asked, standing on the mat inside the door and dripping. "I go right by the delicatessen on my way back."

"Not a thing, darling. Sarah was here today. I should only have as much room as it would take to put away what she buys for me."

"Then I'll go now. Be a good girl, Ruthie. Don't bother Grandpa too much."

After Mommy left, Ruthie and Grandpa played the game called "finding things." Grandpa said Aunt Sarah was a nice girl—it was funny the way he called her a girl; she was really a big lady like Mommy—but whenever she cleaned the apartment she put everything away in the wrong place and poor Grandpa had to spend the rest of the day finding them.

Grandpa lived all by himself. Last year, when Ruthie was only five, Grandma had gone away and died and left Grandpa all alone. Ruthie's grandma had been very, very old with gray hair and her face all wrinkled, not like Gloria's grandma who had blond hair and used pretty nail polish. Ruthie's grandma didn't even like nail polish, not even for mommies.

After they played the game of finding things, Grandpa asked Ruthie if she wanted a glass of milk and some cookies. She really did but she knew Grandpa would put the milk in a pot and warm it up and she hated warm milk so she said she just wanted the cookies.

"Maybe someone thinks she's too big for me to warm up her milk."

"I am too big, Grandpa. I'm six."

"What grade are you in now?"

"First and I can read."

Grandpa sighed. "If you can read, you can drink cold milk." He poured the milk and put a box of cookies on the table. "Aunt Sarah would tell me I should put them on a plate but to me they taste better out of the box. What do you think, little one?"

"I like them better out of the box too."

"You know, I'm thinking, if you're this big already, maybe we should stop calling you 'Ruthie.' "

"Mommy calls me Ruthie."

"Your mother is a wonderful woman but she's so close to you maybe she doesn't see how big you've gotten. Do you know who you were named after?"

Ruthie shook her head.

"After my mother, *alovo ha-sholom*."

Ruthie giggled. "You don't have a mother, Grandpa. You're too old."

"But I had one once and she was a beautiful, wonderful woman, the way you will be when you grow up. So, no more Ruthie. Agreed?"

"What's 'agreed'?"

"It means 'OK.' "

"OK." She yawned.

"A little sleepy, darling?"

She nodded.

"Come. You'll lie down a little while and I'll have a glass of tea."

She lay down on the bed in Grandma's sewing room. In the corner was the old machine with the treadle that said Singer on it. She was big enough to read that now. Grandma used to sit there and sew all afternoon.

Grandpa covered her with the patchwork quilt Grandma had made by piecing together everybody's leftover scraps—Mommy's, Aunt Sarah's, everybody's. It was a nice, warm quilt and she fell asleep right away.

When she woke up, Grandpa had company. From the bedroom she could hear them talking. The company was a man with a big voice and he was talking Hebrew.

She opened the door and listened for a moment. Grandpa was talking and his voice was different in Hebrew, louder and not so old. She tiptoed down the hall to the dinette. Grandpa was sitting in the middle of the long side of the table. On the flowered tablecloth was half a glass of tea, a bowl of sugar cubes, and an open book. The company was talking. She looked around. There was no one in the room beside Grandpa.

She waited until the company finished talking. Then she said, "Where is he hiding, Grandpa?"

Grandpa turned and smiled. "Right here," he said.

"But who is it?"

"It's God."

"I didn't know you could talk to God."

"You never know until you try."

"Could I talk to him?"

Grandpa put a lump of sugar in his mouth. "Go on," he said, sipping the tea through the sugar, "try."

She looked around the room, feeling shy all of a sudden and not so big as she had felt before. Finally she said softly, "Hi, God."

There was no answer. In the quiet, Grandpa finished his tea.

"How do you like secrets?" Grandpa asked.

"They're fun."

"Then let's keep this our secret."

"And not even tell Mommy?"

"Not even Mommy."

"OK. I can keep a secret."

But she couldn't. She kept it on the way home and through dinner but when she was getting ready for bed, she told Mommy.

Mommy frowned and asked her some silly questions. Then she called Daddy and made Ruth tell the story over again, just as if she hadn't told it before. Then she put Ruth to bed.

It wasn't the end of it. Later, she woke up hearing Mommy and Daddy talking about Grandpa.

"I would be afraid to leave her there alone with him," Mommy said.

"It was a fantasy. You're taking it too seriously."

"I think you should call Sarah. Your father should give up the apartment and move in with Sarah."

"That shows how little you know my father. Before he would move in with—"

"Well, something has to be done. He can't stay alone with his hallucinations."

In the morning, she asked Mommy what hallucinations were and Mommy gave her a funny look and said they were dreams.

She didn't see Grandpa for a couple of weeks and when she did, most of the family was there and she was afraid Grandpa would be angry about the secret. But he wasn't. He was never angry with her. But it was a long, long time before Mommy would let her stay with him again.

It took her thirteen years to broach the subject with him. He was eighty by then and she had come to think of him as Abraham but she never called him that.

"I really loused you up with the family that time, didn't I?" she said, visiting him after the spring semester and bringing him her books.

"Well, I learned something from it. Never make a deal with a six-year-old—unless you're the six-year-old's mother."

"They thought you were crazy, didn't they?"

"Maybe I was, maybe I was. You were the only one who didn't think so. Imagine, all the evidence on my side coming from the faith of a six-year-old."

"It wasn't faith in you, Grandpa. It was faith in my own faculties. I heard the voice, you know. It woke me up."

Abraham Gold lifted the kettle on the stove, replaced it, and turned on the fire. "Tea?" he asked.

"Sure. Was that the only time you talked to him?"

"No, it was one of five, maybe six times. You say you heard the voice too?"

"Loud and clear."

"So maybe I wasn't so crazy."

At the end of August in 1967, she and Cassie flew back from Europe. They had left Amsterdam at one o'clock and the plane touched down on time at four P.M. It was one of those times in her life that she was excited about seeing her mother and father.

It took forever to get through customs and it was after five when the girls reached their parents (who had located each other in the crowd and had spent God knew how long making polite, uncommunicative conversation). The Ballards whisked Cassie away a little too quickly and the Golds dragged their luggage out to a distant parking lot. She started talking as they pulled out of the lot and she went on and on. She told them about Amsterdam, about the Anne Frank house with the staircase almost vertical and the secret door to the hidden house behind.

"And you know we flew to Berlin," she said, screwing up the itinerary. "God, you should hear Cassie speak German. She's incredible. I thought my French was good but her German is unbelievable. She gives them this cold look when she talks and they fall all over themselves trying to make her happy. The French just ignore me, but I guess the French—Where's Grandpa?"

They were on the Belt now, headed for home. Her parents looked at each other grimly. They had argued about it on the way to the airport and had reached no decision.

"Honey," her father said, but he didn't go on.

"Grandpa died," Mother said quietly.

She was sitting alone in the back seat, holding on to the few breakable items she had carried back with her. She sat back and just concentrated on breathing for half a minute. It wasn't possible, not Grandpa. She bit her lip and the tears started coming.

"When did it happen?" she asked.

"At the beginning of July, honey," her father said.

"July! July!" she screamed. "It happened in July and you never told me?"

"We were afraid it would spoil your summer," Mother said.

"Spoil my *summer*. Don't you think I had a right to know?"

"I know how you felt about him, honey," Daddy said. "But we had a decision to make. You couldn't even have gotten home for the funeral. Mother talked to him in the morning and he was fine. Aunt Sarah went over in the afternoon and he was gone."

"Take me to the cemetery," she ordered.

"It's on the Island. It's too far."

"Take me to the cemetery," she screamed. "I want to see where he's buried."

Her father looked at his watch. "It's almost six and they close at six. We'll make it another day."

She looked at her own new watch that she had bought with Abraham's fifty-dollar bill. It was a quarter to eleven in Amsterdam. Was it possible she had awakened in Amsterdam that morning?

She looked out the window in defeat and watched Brooklyn go by. After awhile, the car left the Belt and she recognized Ocean Parkway. In a few minutes, they would be home.

"Mr. Feinberg, the lawyer, wants to see you," her mother said irrelevantly. "I made an appointment for next Wednesday."

She went to the lawyer alone, although her mother had intended to go along. The office was in Manhattan, on lower Broadway, and she got mixed up on the subway and was fifteen minutes late. The lawyer didn't care; he seemed happy to see her.

"I'm Joshua Feinberg," he said, holding out his hand. "I suppose your family has told you the news."

"They told me my grandfather had died."

"That's all?"

"That was enough."

"Abraham Gold left all his money to you."

"His money? To me? Why would he leave me money?"

"I'm sure he had his reasons. He and my father were closest friends, you know. My father always thought he was the wisest man he knew."

"What did he leave to the others?"

"The dishes, the silver, a little jewelry."

"I can't believe it." She walked around the little booklined office feeling like an idiot.

"There'll be about eight thousand dollars. You'll get it next spring, I should think."

"What will I do with it?" It was a stupid question but she felt totally lost. Why would Abraham have left her money?

"Whatever you want, Ruth. It's yours without

strings, without obligations. When a person leaves you money this way, he's telling you you're not responsible to anyone but yourself, not even to him. Buy yourself an expensive present or invest it or go away somewhere or just have the time of your life."

"That's what he said to me in June when I left for Europe."

"Then that's probably why he gave you the money."

"Thank you, Mr. Feinberg." She picked up her bag.

"I asked you to come down here because there's something I thought you might want to see. Have a look." He went to his cluttered desk and opened a folder in the center. "Abraham drafted the will himself and sent it to my father, who was his attorney at the time."

The top sheets in the folder were written in Hebrew in Abraham Gold's fine hand.

"My father wrote a translation—" he lifted two sheets in English for her to see— "and then the will was typed in English by the secretary. So you see, everything in the will was his own idea."

"It was kind of you to show me."

"Do you have any questions?"

"When did my grandfather write the draft?"

The lawyer pursed his lips. "That's a tough one. The date is from the Jewish calendar. I suppose I could check it if it's really important to you, but my father's translation is dated May 15, 1952. I would assume Abraham wrote the draft a day or two before that."

"You're probably right."

"You must have been very young in 1952."

"I was six."

"You must have made a big impression on him."

"Not as big as the one he made on me."

It had taken five years, but she was convinced now that Mr. Feinberg had been right. Abraham had wanted her to have the time of her life in her own way.

It was her money. Today she had used part of it to buy a gold watch for Jimmy Kendall.

She awoke on Thursday feeling weak, but after school she went to the church. It was another farewell; this was the last week of the program, her last day with the children.

It was a strange afternoon. She felt her body on edge, on the verge of responding to some absent stimulus, as if the nerve endings were awaiting a touch that never came. She had grown so used to the sudden awareness of his presence that her skin responded to the sight of him.

No one said goodbye. She promised Mrs. McConnell she would return a week later to help clean up the room. Then she left, her tenure expired.

As she walked out, she noticed some hi-fi equipment on the floor near the door, not yet hooked up. It gave her an idea.

She walked up the stairs and went into the sanctuary through the back door. There would be no goodbyes today, not from Father Reilly who had shown her these pews that day in January and not from Father Costello whose memorial would rise on this site next spring.

She closed the door behind her and left the church by the back way, the way she knew best. This was what it was like to be sequential, to live a portion of your life

with a clear beginning and a clear end. It was the ends
that bothered her most. They were too depressing, too
permanent.

Across the driveway and playground was the rectory,
a large old frame house that needed more than a coat
of paint. She raised her eyes to the upstairs windows
and wondered for the thousandth time what his room
looked like, what kind of furniture he had, whether
there was a crucifix over his bed, if he would remain a
Catholic when he came back, if he was coming back at
all.

She crossed the street and walked toward the corner
where her car was parked. Standing and looking at the
bashed-in door was Angelo. He looked up as she approached, recognition reflecting pain, a desire to run,
but he stepped back from the car and stood his ground,
a first step toward courage.

"Hello, Angelo," she greeted him pleasantly.

"Hi," he said sullenly, turned, and hurried around
the corner.

At home there was a post card in the mailbox from
Jim. It showed two cartoon figures—a man in an open
shirt and a girl wearing a large six-pointed star on her
chest. Inside the star was a tiny cross. The figures were
holding hands.

She went upstairs and found the map of Brooklyn he
had drawn for her in January. The man on the map
was wearing a clerical collar and had a cross on his
chest. The two drawings of the girl were almost identi-
cal. Strange that he had thought that he was the one
who had changed.

Seeing the children at the church again had left her

thinking longingly of Anthony. On Saturday she went
visiting. His foster mother told her Anthony would be
at camp in July.

She returned to Cambridge happy; she would see
Anthony in a couple of weeks.

After school on Monday, she made the trip to Henry
Fleming and Son and picked up the watch. It was more
beautiful than she remembered. It was worth having
been half out of her mind to have selected it. She left
the store, package in hand, and started back. At the
corner of Washington Street she ran into Jeff.

Flustered, he greeted her profusely, reached into a
pocket for his pipe and began to walk with her up
Washington Street. There was no way to shake him;
they were headed for the same train.

By the time they reached Harvard Square, he had
invited himself for coffee.

It struck her for the first time as she entered her
apartment with this young man, who was really little
more than a stranger, that her home, like her life, was
continuous, that one could move from one functional
part of another without being aware of a transition.
And the functional areas themselves were only loosely
defined; one could hear music anywhere, smell food
anywhere, read anywhere, make love anywhere. The
realization gave her an uncomfortable feeling of expo-
sure.

She began to make coffee while Jeff walked around
awkwardly, as if looking for the nonexistent transition
points that would help him stay in place. Finally he
asked for an ashtray.

She gave him a large one from a cabinet and watched as he went through the ritual of tapping and cleaning his pipe, using all the paraphernalia that pipe smokers use to impress themselves. She heard a match strike and a moment later the aroma drifted to the kitchen and hung tantalizingly over the sink. She inhaled it skeptically.

"That's delicious," she said, half in surprise.

"Nice blend, isn't it? My brother-in-law gave it to me for my birthday."

That was when she started to feel sorry for him. It had never occurred to her that creeps had brothers-in-law. Being a creep was half of a relationship. Now that she was irrevocably out of it, she saw him differently. He was just a grown-up little kid who had never mastered the rudiments of coordination or the elements of heterosexual conversation.

He inspected her books and she set the table. The aroma became less intense and she saw that he was no longer holding his pipe. For some reason, he had relaxed.

As she turned away from the table, she felt his hand on the back of her neck, awkwardly touching her through her hair.

"Don't," she said, moving away.

He put a hand in his pocket but apparently the pipe wasn't there and he sat down, dejected, his hand unsteady.

"I'm getting married soon," she told him, as if she were describing the weather. "I don't know when— maybe next week, maybe after the summer."

"I suppose I'm the last one to hear about it."

"No. In fact, you're almost the first. We haven't discussed it with many people."

He put his cup down and sat looking around for a moment. "I think I'll go," he said.

"Don't go. Have your coffee."

He put his forehead in his palms, his elbows on the table, his face bent toward the sweetened coffee, as if it were tea and he was reading his fortune, but there was no fortune in the coffee, no future, surely no future in this apartment. For one terrible moment she was afraid he would burst into tears, and she had had enough of tears in this calendar year. She kept her eyes on the head, on the exact center where the hair was already thinning, and after the moment he looked up, composed.

"OK," he said. "Is Pete Gruber the guy you're marrying?"

"No."

"Because I heard something."

"It isn't Pete. It isn't anyone at school." She took a cookie, broke it in half, and ran her fingers over the crumbs. "Will you be around next fall?"

"I suppose so. I'll probably look around for something again this summer but I suppose I won't find anything. That guy Giraldi drives me up the wall."

"He does that to everyone."

"I thought it was only me." He looked very earnest, very young, and quite suddenly, at ease. He started to talk and she let him go on and on until he ran down, until he was utterly done, and then he went home.

In the morning she awoke into a foul smell. The

pleasant aroma of Jeff's tobacco had changed overnight and the apartment smelled acrid. She opened a window over the sink—with some trepidation, remembering Angelo—and hoped the air would freshen by evening.

After school, she bought several children's records for the kids in the basement. She had decided to give them to Mrs. McConnell as a parting gift. She took them with her Thursday afternoon when she went to the church to help clean up.

"The children will love these, Ruth," Mrs. McConnell said, looking at each jacket. "It's a wonderful coincidence that you thought to bring records. Father Kendall gave us his phonograph when he moved out of the rectory."

"When he what?" She wondered if the panic showed, if it would be interpreted merely as surprise.

"He's left our church, dear. Didn't you know?"

Ruth shook her head slowly. Moved out of the rectory. Left our church. The finality of the phrases. "I didn't know."

"He had dinner with us last week—no, it must have been the week before, the week you were away. We hadn't seen much of him lately—he's been so preoccupied these last months." Mrs. McConnell put the records in a cupboard and started taking the cartoons off the wall. "That's when he told us he was leaving. It was a terrible shock to us. We had come to think of him as—I don't know—permanent, I suppose. Perhaps nothing is permanent any more." She scratched unsuccessfully at the mark the tape had left on the wall. "Well, almost nothing," she said with an attempt at cheerfulness. And then, more somberly, "I hope—I hope we haven't lost him."

Leaving the referent of "we" forever a mystery: We the McConnells, we the Catholic Church, we the people of the United States, in order to form a more perfect union . . .

We've all lost him, she thought, listening to the echo of the voice and the noise of the boys on the playground outside.

She started to feel lonely again, the loneliness of losing Anthony, of seeing a gravestone on Long Island.

Where was she when they cut the cord?

Probably asleep.

Cord after cord after cord.

When the job was done, she took her loneliness and went home.

12

By car one can travel in about three hours from the beautiful, less populous portions of western Massachusetts to Boston at the eastern end of the state. At Logan Airport there are direct flights to Los Angeles several times each day. One can board a plane, set one's ailing watch back, and land in Los Angeles hardly more than a few hours after the flight began. At the airport it is a simple matter to acquire a rental car on a Wednesday afternoon, to drive to a motel one has never seen before, or to a church one has. With the difference in time, one might even manage to secure an unusually long night's sleep—if one were very tired and had little on his mind to keep him awake.

The clock on the dashboard of the rented car showed three minutes to nine. The house, set tastefully back from the curb, was one story high, every room affording an easy egress to the outside. In the driveway at the left end of the long house a car stood empty, waiting for the occupant of the house to emerge on this warm Thursday morning.

At exactly nine, he left the car, walked to the front door and rang the bell.

Ten, fifteen, twenty—

He rang again.

"Coming." A musical voice from a far room.

The door opened and the woman looked at his face,

frowning and leaning forward myopically. She took a pair of glasses from a pocket and put them on.

"I'm Jim Kendall," he said and the woman moved back a step and froze.

"May I come in?"

Her head moved slightly but she said nothing.

"Just for a few minutes," he said.

She took her glasses off and put them in the jacket pocket. "I was going to—" She cleared her throat. "I'm not—Yes, all right. Come in."

She closed the door behind him and pointed voicelessly toward the living room a few steps from the door. She took the first chair, sat down and closed her eyes, as if trying to calm herself. Then she put her glasses back on and focused on him, looking him up and down with an appraising eye.

"How are you, Carol?" he asked, standing uncomfortably across the room from her.

"Don't," she said, her voice indicating the return of control. "Don't pretend you came in off the street to ask about my health. How did you find me?" The number was unlisted, the house in a different town."

"Jack Hines found you for me."

"I don't know any Jack Hines."

"Father Hines."

"From our old church?"

"Yes."

She sat back, sagging. "So you've come to remind me of Father Hines." She coughed for no apparent reason. "When you look up and see a priest, you know you've really lost someone."

"I found that out."

Carol stood up. She had aged since opening the door. "Let me get you an ashtray." The perfect hostess, even now, even after eleven years.

"Thank you, I don't smoke any more. I gave it up one year for Lent and I never took it up again."

"I didn't know you knew Father Hines," she said, as if there were some connection between the priest and the missing ashtray.

"Carol, I came here to—"

"Are you married?" It was almost an accusation.

"Yes I am."

"Do you have children?"

"No. We've only been married a short time. Since April."

"We had another child." She stated it flatly.

"I'm glad to hear that."

"A boy," she said quickly, failing to hide the disappointment.

"Carol, I came here to—what I want to say is that I'm sorry. I know it's taken—"

"You're sorry," she said shrilly. "You're *sorry*. When I called your room you weren't sorry. You were gone."

"I left town after the funeral. I never came back."

"And when I wrote to you at that—where was it?— that University of Oregon, you didn't even answer me. You sent the letter back."

"I didn't go there, Carol. I changed my plans."

"I wish I could have changed mine."

"I know."

"So you've come back now to say you're sorry."

He cleared his throat. "Well—"

"Well I accept your apology," Carol said briskly.

"Thank you for coming." She stood up again. "Let me show you to the door."

He stood without moving, his eyes on the woman waiting to show him out. Then he looked at his watch, a brief, unthinking movement of the left hand, made a face of disgust, took the watch from his wrist and dropped it in a pocket.

"Did it stop?" Her voice had returned to normal, had assumed a note of mild concern.

"For the last time, I'm afraid. I've been nursing it along for weeks." His face relaxed. "I suppose twenty years is long enough to expect a one-sided partnership to last."

"That's how long I'm married."

"Does your husband still travel?"

"Not still, again. He got an office job for a while after—" She shrugged wordlessly. "That lasted a few years. He's been back on the road for a long time now."

"When will he be home?"

"Why?" The word shot out like a challenge.

"I'd like to talk to him."

"I don't understand. What could you have to say to my husband?"

"I want to explain what happened, that I was the one, that I share—"

"You *can't*." It was almost a whisper. "He doesn't know about you. He doesn't know about *any* of them. He would kill me if he found out. He would—" She paused. "He would leave me if he knew."

"What did you tell him, Carol? What did you say when he came home?"

"Nothing," she said in a high, little-girl's voice

tinged with an underlying hysteria. "I didn't say anything. He never asked." She sat down heavily, her
shoulders shaking, the hysterics surfacing, tears over-
flowing. "In eleven years he's never asked me anything."

The carpet and draperies absorbed the sound of her
crying, reducing the magnitude of her misery to a mere
trickle.

"Now will you go?" she said. "There's nothing you
can do here except make things worse."

She kept her head in her hands. He walked toward
her, glanced briefly at the door and put a hand on her
shoulder. Under his hand, her body relaxed.

"Even if I had been home that night," she said, "it
wouldn't have done any good. I used to sleep through
anything in those days, even the alarm. It was the only
way to keep from being lonely when Paul was away.
That and going out with other men."

"You don't have to explain to me."

"They all thought they were using me," she went on,
"because I slept with them, but the truth was I was the
one who was using them. They kept me from being
lonely." She drew a deep breath. "It took me months—
years—to accept the fact that I meant no more to you
than they did to me."

It was the moment for the polite denial, the socially
acceptable phrase to reassure her that she had truly
been loved, but it never came. He had been brought up
to choose honesty over tact as Paul had been raised to
answer questions but not to ask them.

"I used to wonder sometimes what he did all the
nights he was away."

"It only hurts to wonder."

"Maybe it's why he never asked. Maybe he was afraid of what I would ask him."

"Maybe he just didn't want to know. Maybe he drove home that night and he worked it all out, that he wanted you and the boys more than he wanted to know what happened."

"I remember one time he was late coming home," she said, as if, like Paul, he had never spoken, "very late, hours late, and he didn't call and I was in a panic. One minute I hated him for being out and having a good time and the next minute I was frantic, thinking he was lying dead on the freeway and in the morning I would have to make funeral arrangements. Finally I ran upstairs—it was in the old house, a long time ago—and I found where Paul kept his papers and I added up his insurance policies. Even figuring double for an accident, it wasn't enough to live on for long. So I prayed that he was alive and drunk instead of dead and sober." She turned slightly and looked at Jim. "I still believed in God then."

He walked away from her, across the room, plunging his hands in his pockets as he went.

"It was after that that I started working part time," she said, "to prove to myself I could do it if I had to. It was also a way to meet other men."

Jim took his left hand out of his pocket, looked at the empty wrist, and shoved it back in his pocket.

"You want to leave now, don't you?" Carol said, her voice sounding like someone else's, calm, controlled, and very distant. "It hasn't turned out the way you planned, has it? You thought I would do the listening and you would leave forgiven."

"I didn't write a script, Carol."

"No, but you must have planned it. What were you going to tell Paul—that his daughter died because you wouldn't go to bed with me with children in the house?"

"Yes," he said dully. "I suppose that's what I was going to tell him."

"That's why she's dead, you know."

"I know why she's dead." He looked at his left wrist again.

"Goodbye, Jim."

"Goodbye."

She turned away from him.

"I'll find the door."

"Yes."

The visit was over. He went to the door and opened it. The air on the other side was warm and moist.

"Wait a minute," Carol called.

He stepped back across the threshold.

"I never told anyone," she said breathlessly.

He closed the door.

"I haven't even been to church since the funeral."

"Take it easy." The voice was very gentle, a doctor at a bedside. "It's OK."

"I never told anybody, not my mother, not Paul, not my closest friend."

"What is it?"

"Were you really going to talk to Paul?"

"That's what I came for."

"Listen to me—Jim—oh, God, I killed her, Jim. It wasn't your fault. I did it, I killed her."

"Nobody killed her. It was an accident."

"It looked like an accident but I used to dream

about something like that happening, as if I wanted it to happen. I wanted Paul to find out and make me stop and stay home so I wouldn't be alone. I left a cigarette on her dresser that night, Jim. Paul always screamed at me about that. It was the only thing I did that got to him, that and leaving them without a sitter when I went to the store at night. I could see it on the edge of the dresser where I left it. It was like a dream come true. My cigarette. And he never said a word. He came home and he never said a word."

"He forgave you, Carol. He loved you."

"He punished me. He knew me. He knew there was no one I could ever tell. He knew I would have to live with it alone for the rest of my life, the way I've always lived alone."

"He wouldn't do that to you."

"If not for you, even my boys . . ."

"That's not true. You would have done it yourself. Anyone would have—"

"I gave up smoking."

"Talk to him, Carol."

"I stopped going out with other men."

"He'll understand. Don't you think this has been killing him too?"

"I had another baby."

"Carol, for God's sake—"

"Do you believe in God?"

He looked suddenly ill, as if a meal had begun to disagree with him. He gripped his bare wrist with his right hand. "I don't know," he said. "I can't answer that any more. I just don't know."

"Nobody knows," Carol said. "They just hope. I used to think they were in there praying but they're not. They're hoping there's something around to save them. Do you remember that night?"

He nodded, painfully, as if the movement caused him anguish.

"I mean before, before we came home, when we were in that motel."

Still looking ill, he went back to the door and closed his fingers on the handle.

"It was the first time for me," she said. "It was the first time I—the first time anyone ever satisfied me. All those years and all those men and that night was the first time it ever happened."

His hand turned the doorknob and he moved from the cool interior to the heat of the morning sun. He stood on the step only long enough to hear the whisper of the woman's voice, talking more to herself than to him.

"Don't come back," she said softly. "Don't ever come back."

And the sound of the door closing behind him.

13 〰〰〰〰〰〰〰〰〰〰〰〰〰〰

The little girls all dressed up for the last day of school, and two of them brought Miss Gold small, carefully wrapped presents. Then it was over. They were in the third grade now, and, like little conspirators, they whispered the names of next year's teachers as they left the classroom to begin summer.

Summer had not yet begun for their teacher. She stayed after they were gone, taking down pictures, cleaning up her desk, finishing paper work. The staff was expected back for a brief session on Monday morning. Then it would all be over for them too.

"Lunch, Ruth?"

She looked up. Judy Greene stood at the door holding raincoat and umbrella. "Sure."

She gathered up her things and they went down the hall, collecting people as they went. There were ten of them, eventually, and they left their fatigue behind as they left the building.

She sat at the lunch table listening, feeling detached even from them, from the certainty of their plans, the orderliness of their arrangements, the sanity of their concerns. Their phones did not ring late at night with remembered voices from a dismembered past. They struggled with the tangible, reasonable present and the foreseeable future; they were not plagued by ghosts.

It had been ten days now. Halfway through her coffee, she stood up, dropped some money on the table, and excused herself. One of her lunch companions seemed surprised to see her leave, as if perhaps she had never been there. She wondered if she was beginning to cease to exist.

There was a place to park across the street from the house. She picked up the Bible, which had lain unread on the front seat since morning, and a large brown envelope with the gifts and some papers she wanted to salvage from the year's teaching and locked the car. She glanced perfunctorily in both directions to check for nonexistent traffic and saw him halfway down the block, taking a suitcase out of the trunk of his car.

Sometimes the body reacts before the mind has sent its signal. She walked to his car, staying in the street, watching him as he put the suitcase down, closed the trunk, and brushed his palms together as if wiping away the soil of the journey. It wasn't until he turned around and saw her that she realized he was dressed in the priestly black of the Roman clergy. It was the last thing she had expected, a kind of dark omen. She stopped next to the car.

"You came back."

"I told you I would."

His voice was low and tired. Ordinarily he wore clothes as though they were a natural appendage. Today they looked like someone else's, a suit borrowed or handed down or newly outgrown.

"You look exhausted, Jim."

"I am."

"Let's go up."

"Wait a minute." He seemed undecided about something, unready to cross the street. "I'm here to stay this time, Ruth. It's over."

"I expected an earthquake when I heard that, or at least lightning."

"There was both. He gave me hell."

"Your bishop?"

"My bishop. Three hours of polite, eloquent hell."

"But it's over now, right?"

"Except for Rome. But it's over as far as I'm concerned, hell or no hell."

"Then let's go up."

It was almost a reflex movement, shrugging free of his hand to avoid the appearance of public intimacy, to protect a façade that had only this moment ceased to exist.

"Can't I touch you?"

"Upstairs."

He dropped his hand.

"I'm sorry," she said nervously. "It's—"

"Forget it."

They went upstairs without speaking. She tried to think of something to say to explain, something about the surprise and the awkwardness. She unlocked the door and they went in.

"Hey, it's OK," he said. "Relax."

"I'm glad you're back."

He touched her. "So am I."

He put his suitcase on the bed and opened it. "I need a shower," he said, "and a couple of hours of sleep."

"Some coffee first?"

"I could use some. Maybe a piece of toast, too."

"Did you miss breakfast?" She hung her coat up and started to fill the kettle.

"I think so. I'm a little foggy right now. I may have missed dinner last night too."

"I'll have something ready when you get out of the shower."

He unbuttoned his jacket and emptied his pockets, dropping his keys and the brown wallet on the table.

"Do we have a date to get married," he asked, "or do you want a request in writing?"

She turned around. "I'm glad you're back," she said again. "I'd forgotten what it was like talking to you."

"You didn't answer me."

"You said something about Rome."

"Rome is a formality. I went through my last formality this morning."

"Getting married isn't?"

"No."

"I'll call Cassie when I'm finished with the coffee."

She turned back to the kitchen, feeling the delayed excitement start to work, and turned on the stove. Butter, she told herself. Get the butter out. Coffee, bread. She moved on instruction, too excited now to do anything automatically.

"Was Pete here?"

"Huh-uh, I haven't seen him for a while."

"Then who was?"

"No one, darling. It was a long, lonely—"

"Then who left this?"

She turned around. He was pointing to an ashtray on the night table on his side of the bed. In the ashtray, on a bed of ash, was Jeff's pipe.

"The pipe!" she said jubilantly. "That's what's been smelling this place up. Give me the ashtray and I'll empty it."

He didn't move. "Whose is it?"

"A guy I teach with. He came up for coffee on Monday and—"

"You invited him up here?"

"No, darling, he invited himself. It was all I—"

"Did he touch you?"

"Hey, come on."

"I asked if he touched you," he said, his voice rising. "Answer me. Did he touch you? Did he go to bed with you?"

She could feel the edge of the counter pressing against her back. "What's come over you?" she said softly. "I love you."

"You should have thought of that when you asked him up here."

"Jim, he's just a lonely guy who wanted to talk to someone."

"Don't give me that shit. How naïve do you think I am?"

"Do you want me to stop talking to toll collectors too?"

"Who you talk to is your decision."

He sat down on the edge of the bed, tied a shoelace, stood up and buttoned his jacket. With two loudly perceptible clicks, the suitcase was snapped shut.

"What are you doing?"

"I'm leaving."

He walked to the table and picked up the brown wallet, the wallet that matched nothing he was wearing, the wallet she had given him for the birthday they had been unable to celebrate, the gift that had been supposed to mark the start of a new era. He put it in his pocket and then, very deliberately, opened the key

chain, dropped one key on the table, closed the chain
and put it in his pocket.

She reacted instinctively, as if a switch had been
thrown, walking around the table to where he stood
and reaching her hands to his shoulders, touching the
fabric of his uniform for the first time.

"Jim—"

"Don't touch me," he said, stepping backward and at
the same time pushing her, lightly but firmly, with both
hands.

She moved backward, her feet doing an awkward
dance, a violent overreaction to the small force which
had set them in motion. How does a ballet end?

The way the world ends, a key dropping on a table.

"You have to do it, don't you?" she said. "Hack everything to pieces. Your friend Andy was right. He said
a man didn't change much in the years from twenty to
forty."

"Leave Andy out of this."

"I had hoped he didn't mean you. I had hoped you
would leave one link unsevered. What will you put on
the chopping block next?"

"Leave me alone."

"I spent the time you were away putting my own life
in order. Somehow I thought you were doing the same
thing with yours."

"Spare me the lecture."

"Then go." She sat down at the opposite end of the
table. "Nothing's holding you."

"I'll go when I'm ready."

Entreat me not to leave thee. . . .

"I read the Bible while you were gone, the part you

wanted me to read, the part I was too stubborn to read while you were around." She lifted the brown envelope on the table in front of her and uncovered the white book. "You were right about it. It has lots of good lines besides the one I misquoted last January. 'The Lord do so to me, and more also, if aught but death part thee and me.' For a while there, I thought we were kinsmen, you and I."

"Kinsmen don't screw around." He walked to the bed, took the suitcase off it, and carried it to the door.

"You know damned well—"

"You haven't even denied it. You're sitting there talking about a lot of irrelevant crap and you haven't answered me."

"I can't answer you," she said quietly. "What good will it do either one of us if I deny it? You don't want the truth, Jimmy, you're looking for a fight. You want me to shout at you so you'll feel better when you walk out of here. Well, you're a year too late. I can't do it any more. You'll have to walk out the way you walked in, on your own initiative."

She had stopped looking at him. Instead, she kept her eyes on the white Bible on the table. He had given her a Bible not too long ago, a Catholic Bible. It would have to be sent back now.

"I'm sorry," she said. "I'm sorry about the guy and I'm sorry about the pipe. I didn't think. I do so many things without thinking first. It didn't go well in California, did it? That's what's getting to you now, isn't it? First California and then the bishop."

"Who said anything about California?" The bravado was slipping.

"You know, I learned something from you, Jimmy,

back in April, something about forgiving and retrieving. How can you forgive everyone else so easily when you aren't able to forgive yourself?"

"I asked you about California," he said, the fatigue slipping back into his voice, "not about forgiving."

"I knew," she said simply, "the way I knew this would happen, the way I knew they would take Anthony away from me. That's what tragedy is all about, I suppose, knowing and not being able to prevent it. God, I love that kid."

There was a silence, a sound and a word. "Listen—"

"It's too late, Jimmy. I listened all winter and I changed because I listened, and this is where we've ended. You got me through the winter, do you know that? I couldn't have made it without you, not the way I was at New Year's." She pressed the bit of metal at her breast, the little gold cross he had given her in April. She would have to send it back, that and the books and the records.

"Something happened to me after I met you." She closed her eyes and it was all there—the garden in sunlight, the dog barking, the old man carrying a book and walking among his flowers. "I've become someone because of you."

She stopped and let her eyes move along the table, the envelope, the Bible, and at the other end, the key.

"You can go now," she said, still looking at the table. "I'm finished. I have nothing else to say."

There was a sudden eruption of sound behind her and her shoulders moved reflexively. As she turned toward it, the sound stabilized into a high-pitched squeal, a whistle, a steady, unending scream.

A river of steam was pouring out of the kettle on the

stove. She stood up wearily, turned off the stove, and emptied the kettle. Outside it was afternoon, sunless, misty, the end of a season that had never begun. She touched the leaves of a plant, stalling for time, listening for the sound of a closing door so that she could start adjusting to the new life, start packing, begin preparing for the inevitable exodus.

"Please turn around," he said.

There was no bed, no canopy, no rewarding climax after fulfillment of an old ritual; only the touch of fabric, a baptism in salt water after the end of a ballet, an echo of a whistle, an unexpected explosion.

When he went into the shower, she put the key back on the chain. Then she went out and returned the pipe to Jeff.

He was asleep when she returned, and he slept without moving through the sounds of telephone calls, water running, and once a book dropping. He had left a note for her on the table, propped up where it caught her eyes as she walked in, written with the black felt tip he had used to inscribe the Keats on the Eve of St. Agnes.

> *Judge Ballard available any* A.M. *next week except Thursday. Something about a blood test. Can you make an appointment? Wake me if you get one today. Also a license. Not to worry about elapsed time. Court will give us a waver (waiver?). How about Monday?*
>
> *Jim*

Dr. Fischer agreed to see them as his last appointment of the day. Jim was exhausted and she drove both ways. When they got back, he said something incoherent and went back to bed.

She herself slept soundly, peacefully, uninterruptedly, and finally without the dreams that had recurred after her return to Boston almost two weeks ago. She awoke on Saturday—early—to the sane, calm sounds of morning, symphonic music playing softly on the radio and water running in the bathroom.

She was reluctant to initiate conversation, her wounds lasting almost as long as her memory, but he was not, and they talked easily, on and on through dressing, coffee-making, and breakfasting. He had thought the trip to the doctor was a dream until he saw the circle of flesh-colored plaster on his arm. When had she stopped wearing pajamas to bed? The judge wanted them to have the cottage the remainder of next week. Did she mind if his brother came, the oldest one, his favorite? How was Monday? And, by the way, what time was it?

The watch was in her dresser drawer where she had placed it on Monday. Without fanfare she gave it to him now, slightly shaken by the silence that greeted the presentation and the opening. She was momentarily pained by unexpected misgivings: she had overspent, he would think she had saved months to afford it, he would be afraid to wear it.

"I'll keep it," he said finally, putting it on.

"Where's your old one?" she asked, relaxing.

"In a wastebasket in the L.A. airport." It was his first admission that he had been there. "I won't do that to this one, not even if I outlive it."

He went off by himself to gather his belongings and say some farewells. She met Cassie for shopping (a dress, new, white, and linen, at Cassie's insistence) and eventually a late lunch.

"Your father's too generous, Cassie, I mean about the beach house. Why should he give up a week of his own vacation?"

"He likes you and he admires Jim. It really gave him a lift to have a hand in the decision on Anthony."

"Still, he seems to be going overboard."

"You'll be doing him a kindness, both of you. Your staying in that house will establish his liberal credentials—at least for this decade. Think of it as doing

Daddy a service rather than accepting a favor. By the way," Cassie went on smoothly, "Mother wants a guest list."

"For the house?"

"For your wedding, for the ceremony marking the end of your affair."

"Tell her a very small handful. Jim's asking his brother down."

"Mother wants to come too."

"Bring Mother."

"I wondered—" Cassie inspected five well-manicured nails. "Have you talked to your mother?"

"No."

"Do you intend to?"

"No. When I'm ready, I'll write a letter."

There were assorted boxes and cartons against the one empty wall of the apartment when she returned. At Jim's invitation, she indulged her curiosity while he watched, answering half her questions before she asked them.

In one carton there was a small television set, still in its original plastic cover.

"From Margaret," he said, referring with some embarrassment to the sister from Connecticut.

"You've never used it."

He shrugged. "She thought I needed it."

A smaller box had an unused electric shaver.

"I'm her pet project," he said. "I give most of the stuff away."

"What's that?"

It was a square black leather case with a handle on the top. He put it on the table, opened it, and walked away. The case was lined in black velvet. In it was the gold cup he had drunk from during the mass in February.

"It's called a chalice," he said, anticipating one question. "It was a gift from my family."

"It's very beautiful." Decisively, she set aside the memory of February. "It must have given you pleasure just to handle it."

"Touch it," he said.

Her hands were behind her back. "Jim, are you leaving the church?"

"I've given up the choice. I made other choices instead. Each one opened one door and closed another."

"But if you had the choice . . ."

"Why does it make such a difference to you?"

"I look to you for a kind of stability."

"After yesterday?"

She traced the rim of the chalice with her index finger. "I always thought your middle name was equanimity."

"What's he the saint of?"

She let it pass and closed the case. He put it back against the wall.

"You had a phone call while you were out," he said. "I'm sorry, you're not going to like it."

"My mother?" she asked apprehensively.

"A Mrs. Levinson."

Levinson, Levinson.

"Am I supposed to know her?"

"She said she was your friend."

"Does she have a first name?"

"She may have said Marilyn."

"Marilyn!" She was pleased. It had been a long time since she had heard from Marilyn. "No kidding, Marilyn Klein. I never could remember David's name. How's Marilyn? She pregnant?"

He ran a hand through his hair. "We didn't get to that. She called about the bed. It's a long, complicated story but she has to have it back."

"That bed?" She pointed with the index finger that had touched the chalice.

He nodded.

"Well, she can't have it."

"There was an error in communication somewhere along the way," he explained patiently. "Something about her aunt giving it to her but it turns out now it was only meant to be a loan. The aunt thought she was storing it, not giving it away. It's very old, there's a lot of sentiment attached to it. She said it was a family heirloom."

"Well it's our heirloom now. If I hadn't taken it off Marilyn's hands she would have called the Salvation Army. She has no claim to it any more."

"You're right," he said reasonably. "You're perfectly right. She should have gotten the story straight in the beginning and this whole mix-up wouldn't have happened. But she didn't, and now she's in the middle with her aunt on one side and you—you and me on the other. It isn't her aunt's fault that Marilyn gave the bed away."

"Jim, our lives are wrapped up in that bed."

"I know, and I feel it just as deeply as you do."

"Then how can you—?"

"Look, we've had it, we've enjoyed it, it's given us pleasure, but we don't need it. We can sleep anywhere, on anything."

"I'm not giving it back."

"I thought I might try building one like it for us. I've never tried anything harder than bookcases but—"

"Forget it. I'm not giving it back."

Strangely, it affected her more strongly than the events of the previous week. Getting rid of ghosts was one thing; dismembering a home was another. The bed was part of her present, not her past. It had been given care and love and it had given in return. She hated Marilyn; it was just like her to do this. How could one expect a girl who had to be reassured that her medication worked to get a simple story straight? She was even more annoyed at Jim for being so damned reasonable. She didn't want a mediator; she wanted to keep the bed.

For the rest of the day she refused to call Marilyn back. Put it off (the way she was putting off the letter to her mother) and eventually the whole thing would resolve itself.

He woke her early on Sunday morning and took her for a drive while she was still too sleepy to argue the unreasonableness of it. There was no rain but the air was close, and she slept until the car stopped at the side of a road she had never seen before.

"Walk with me," he said, and she got out of the car, still groggy, still half asleep, and she looked around at this place she had never seen and, eerily, she knew it somehow; she had passed this way once, she was making a return visit.

"I'm hungry," she said irrelevantly, responding to an almost forgotten instinct.

"Coming from you, that's quite a statement."

"I've been eating better this week," she said, yawning, "Don't you see a difference? I've been concentrating on cleavage."

"I'll keep my eyes open," he said drily. "Let me be the first to know if there's any improvement."

"Is your brother coming Tuesday?" she asked, switching to a higher level of certainty. (The day had been changed to Tuesday to accommodate a final morning at school.)

"Yes, he is. By the way, Pete's coming too." He sounded wide awake, as though the day had begun hours ago. "I talked to him while you were out yesterday. Say, did you know he was getting married?"

"Not officially. But I thought, after the day he walked in on us, that something would happen soon. Pete couldn't—I think he needed some encouragement."

"Another mortal among us."

They were in a wooded place now, soggy with the effects of the long rain.

"Is Andy coming?" She asked the question tentatively.

"I haven't asked him. I don't want to put him in an awkward position."

"Maybe he'd like the chance to make his own decision."

He picked up a small rock with his free left hand and threw it in the air a few times, catching it with some difficulty. "I think he'd rather not," he said, referring ambiguously to the chance and the decision both. "Do you know that you haven't asked me what I'm going to do now? I thought you'd be bubbling over with curiosity."

"I thought I would too, once. I'm still curious but I don't seem able to bubble any more. Besides, I never cared what you decided to do."

"I'm starting medical school in the fall."

"You?" She caught her breath. "But you were—I thought you were an English major," she said insanely.

"Chemistry. I told you that once. It goes way back. It's the only thing I ever wanted to do."

"Andy knew then, didn't he? That was the other thing he said that night—'his loves are the same.' "

"I suppose he was right. He encouraged me two years ago when I applied for the first time. I pulled out after I was accepted and I think I disappointed him."

"Why did you do that?"

He rolled a rock out of the way with his boot. Underneath, the weeds were brown and sickly. In a week there would be green shoots pushing out of the straw. "I thought I was too old. I didn't think I could make it."

"But you will this time."

"I have to. They're paying my tuition."

"He must be a nice guy, your bishop."

"He is. I'm sure he twisted some arms for the tuition."

"You'll be a parish doctor, won't you?"

"If you think you can stand it. That's sort of a nice way of putting it."

Some half-thought flitted through her mind about a volunteer fireman.

"More years of being a curate," she said, thinking out loud.

"That's what appeals to me, that it's a lateral move. You're looking at the world's worst administrator and lousiest fund raiser. I'm a hammer-and-nails man, not a foreman. Can you picture me running the show?"

"I picture you a mixed metaphor."

"Touché," he said lightly. "Now tell me how you knew I went to California."

Ah, Jimmy, Jimmy, she thought, will you always believe that questions have answers, that answers have beginnings and ends like a semester of school? You ask me for a perception and you wait to hear it in words, pure words of Germanic origin, following each other in grammatical sequence. . . .

"I would have to start with the day I was born."

"You mean it was just a guess?"

"Call it a guess, call it an intuition. I went back over a lot of things after you left."

"Ghosts," he said. "Ghosts and more ghosts. Bury them once and for all, will you?"

"I did. It was easier than I thought it would be, but you find ghosts of yourself, too, and they're harder to shake off. I thought about all the people I knew and I thought about myself too. There've been times—I've been an awful bitch, Jim."

He began to laugh. "Bitch," he said. "So you discovered you were a bitch."

"I was trying to explain," she put in defensively, "that we see things the same way. I knew what you would do because I understood what you were thinking."

"Ruth Gold looks in the mirror and sees James Kendall."

"You are distorting—"

"Do you remember what happened that night in

April when we stayed at the judge's house, when I asked you if you thought we could make it together?"

"Vaguely, yes. You seemed angry with me when I answered. I didn't know why. We had been very close for a while."

"I was angry at myself, not at you." His voice changed and they stopped walking altogether. Unaccountably, she began to shiver. "It's something you've done to me several times, turn things around when I think I've looked at every angle, put it in a new perspective. It really got to me that night. I lay awake half the night thinking about California, trying to turn it around for myself."

"That was the beginning."

"That was the beginning. In the end, I botched it. I made a mess of the whole thing."

"Don't tell me about it."

"After I left," he went on, "I stopped the car a few blocks away from her house and I got out and threw up."

"Please, Jim."

"Listen to me, bitch. I can't make it without you either."

Such a long time coming.

"I flew the shuttle Friday morning," he said.

"But you came from California."

"I switched planes and airports in New York. I was intrigued. I wanted to know what it was all about."

She felt touched. It had been months since she had told him about the shuttle. It must have been a complicated and costly business—transferring from one airport to another in the earliest morning, paying the extra fare.

"Who sat next to you?" she asked, playing out her part.

"Now how did I know you were going to ask me that? No one sat next to me. I sat in an aisle seat and I chose my companion."

Briefly, very briefly, she felt something akin to jealousy or anger or a little of each—he had done it all wrong, he had flouted the rules—and then it all fell in place.

"A woman, I suppose."

"A girl," he corrected her, "a very pretty girl. She interrogated hell out of me." His eyes were twinkling. It had been a long time since she had seen the twinkle.

"What did you tell her?" she asked soberly.

"I told her that I was making it with my wife."

They had been standing next to a newly fallen tree, a casualty of the long rain. They sat down on it, switching places as if by some prior design. She always walked to his right; unexplainably, she slept on his left.

"I have something for you," he said, reaching into his pocket and taking out something small and wrapped in layers of white tissue paper. He unwrapped it and held it on his upturned palm, a sacred offering. It was a continuous band of reddish gold, thick and wide, shaped and hammered by the hand of Charlie Fleming. Inside were two sets of initials.

She swallowed. "May I wear it?"

"It's yours. You can do what you want with it."

She held out her left hand. It went on easily, smoothly, all the way.

Where were you married?

In the woods, Mother, on a fallen log.

Mazel tov.

"You have a middle name now," he said.

"My mother always wanted me to marry a doctor."

She stretched out her fingers. "How did you get it to fit so well?"

He reached into his pocket again and brought out his keys, the supply almost depleted now, only some car keys and the key to her apartment left. He held up the Cornell ring. "It was easy. You gave me a large hint." He put his keys away. "After the summer, we can take the ring to Charlie and have him put a date on it."

"No date," she said firmly.

"What do you mean? You always put a date in a wedding ring."

"Not in this one."

"Why not?"

"What date would you put in it? Tuesday—today—April?" She paused, reluctant to confess. "January?" It came out softly. "How would you know what date to choose?"

"OK," he said, relenting. "OK, no date."

"Jim?" The question was hesitant.

"What, darling?"

"Will you take me somewhere this afternoon?"

"Anywhere," he said, "anywhere. I love you."

"Where Teresa's buried. I never even sent her flowers." She waited apprehensively. He would tell her that the flowers were unnecessary, that they were superfluous, that she had taken Anthony and that had been more than enough. . . .

"Let's get something to eat first," he said. "We can pick up the flowers on the way to the cemetery."

He stood up and gave her his hand. They started

walking, back towards the road, toward morning in the civilized world.

She felt heady from the denseness of the air, high on an empty stomach, caught midway between tears and something else.

"I have to tell you about the school," he said.

School, second grade, medical school? The school next to the doomed church. "Don't tell me. If it had been good, you would have told me before."

"I suppose so."

"You tried. It was all decided before you knew about it. Tell me about the shuttle instead. Tell me if it was worth it."

"More than worth it. It was everything you said it was. Hey, are you scared about Tuesday?"

"I've never been scared of a Tuesday."

"I just thought—"

"Hey, Jim."

"What, darling?"

"What does it look like when you're not circumcised?"

He started to laugh. "At breakfast," he said, "I'll draw you a picture on a paper napkin."

The rumor made its way from classroom to classroom on Monday morning.

"Have you heard about Frank?" It was Rose Granite, standing in the doorway.

"What's he done now?"

"He's leaving. 'Industry' has made him an offer too tempting to turn down." Her quotes were audible; so was her sarcasm.

"Who leaked the rumor?"

"Who else? Frank Giraldi. Now that he's made his mark in public education, he's moving to the private sector. He's taking over the training department of some company he's not free to name."

She laughed. "I wish them all luck."

"I almost took early retirement because of him," Rose Grantie said, "but I couldn't persuade them to give it at thirty-four."

"Relax, Rose. You're not the only one."

In the afternoon they got their license and at dinnertime Jim drove into Boston to spend the night with his brother at a hotel.

She was annoyed at being left alone. In some peculiarly sentimental way, she had looked forward to spending this night with him. Besides, there were too many things she wanted an excuse not to do. For a while she packed, gathered the plants together, and cleaned up, playing records while she worked, sad songs, the saddest she could find, but summer had begun and she was unable to feel sad. She packed the brandy and two snifters and answered the phone once when Cassie called. Was there anything else they could do? Mother was so anxious that everything be perfect.

Generosity, she thought, putting down the phone. What is it that makes some people so generous?

She pushed away all thoughts of calling Marilyn, and instead sat down at the desk to write to her mother. It was an exercise in conspicuous consumption. After each unsuccessful attempt, she balled up the paper and threw it over her left shoulder. She began to get panicky and giggly. "Dear Mother." No good. Over the shoulder. "Dear Mom, By the time you read this . . ."

Suicide. Over the shoulder. "Dear Mom, After much thought . . ." Over the shoulder. "Dear Mom, You'll remember when I was home a couple of weeks ago we talked about . . ." Oh, God. Over the shoulder.

Eventually it was three telegraphic lines, folded, sealed, and stamped. She picked up the wads, threw them away, and looked up an address in the phone book.

She had to go by cab because Jim had taken her car in to have the smashed-in door repaired. It gave her an oddly dependent feeling, requiring someone else to drive her, being at the mercy of a stranger.

The driver went through Harvard Square and stopped for a light. Out the window, a young couple strolled by, the girl wearing a summer dress, the boy with a shirt and tie. Another girl walked by, her jeans belted, her hair cut short and unparted. Then another girl in jeans with a bright red belt.

The light changed and the taxi started with a jolt. She leaned forward and changed her original instructions slightly, routing him down a seldom-used street. She touched his shoulder and he slowed down. The lights were on in the second-floor living room, the windows covered with sheer white curtains. Probably the television set was on; perhaps children slept in the little bedroom down the hall; maybe a new picture of the Pope hung on one of the newly painted walls.

"Go on," she said, feeling the discomfort of one unused to issuing orders, and the driver took her to her destination.

It was an old house, shingled, with numerous windows, lighted and unlighted, on all three stories. The grass was infested with weeds and needed work, but halfway between the street and the house was a statue, lighted, in the center of a small, cared-for rose garden mulched with large, unweathered wood chips. The sign in front of the statue said "Our Lady of Sorrows Rectory."

She went up the steps and rang the bell.

The priest who opened the door had scrubbed pink cheeks, rimless glasses, and no hairline. "Yes? Can I help you?"

"Is Father McAndrew home?"

"Yes, of course. Come in, won't you?"

He smiled a practiced smile and went upstairs, leaving her in the hall with only the sound of a television set from the next room. She counted black umbrellas in a gilt umbrella stand until Andy came.

"Jim and I are being married tomorrow morning," she told him.

"I see," he said noncommittally.

"I want to invite you to the ceremony. Jim won't do it because he doesn't want to put you in the position of having to say no. I wanted to let you make your own decision."

"That's very kind of you."

She reached into her bag. "This is the address. Judge Ballard is marrying us in the courthouse. He'd really like you to come, you know—Jim, I mean. He's very keen on having friends and family and I think he considers you both."

"May I reserve my decision?"

"Of course."

"Let me walk you to your car."

"Thanks, I came by cab. I'll just walk over to—"

"Then I'll drive you home. Wait here a moment." He walked into the living room before she had a chance to protest.

"I didn't mean to inconvenience you," she apologized when he returned.

"Not at all," he said, holding the door for her. "I can use a breath of air after all that rain. Do you know, I've been reading John Locke lately."

"Locke?" The reference evaded her.

"His Second Treatise on Government. Don't you remember? You mentioned it that evening."

"Yes, of course, the appeal to heaven. I think perhaps it worked."

They got in the car and started for home, bypassing the street Teresa had lived on.

"I saw Anthony last week," she said as they drove.

"He's doing well, isn't he?"

"Yes. She's a lovely woman, his foster mother. I didn't think I'd ever admit that." She swallowed. "I wanted to keep him myself."

"It was very generous of you to give him up."

Generous. That word again. "No, not generous. It was realistic. He asked me a question one night I couldn't answer. I knew if I kept him there would be other questions and I wouldn't be able to answer them either. It didn't make it any easier; it just made it necessary—and inevitable."

"Those decisions are never easy to make. Perhaps it's their inevitability, as you put it, that makes them easier to live with afterwards." He stopped to allow the car ahead to pull into a parking space. The driver was working frantically to get into a tight space. "Take your time," Andy called genially. "We're in no hurry."

The driver waved an acknowledgment, made another attempt, and eased the car in.

"I was sorry to hear about your father," Andy said, putting the car in drive.

"Thank you."

"You've had a hellish spring, I'd say. I was surprised, when I first saw you tonight, at how well you look, a good deal better than the last time."

"I feel better. I feel relieved—and very happy."

"Solved all your problems, have you?"

"None of them, not a single one. But I've come to terms; I've made my peace."

"It sounds enviable."

He stopped the car without warning and turned to look at her, rather like a small boy with an embarrassing problem.

"I'm ashamed to admit it," he said, "but I've forgotten where you live."

She smiled. He seemed very concerned by the lapse. "Two blocks down and turn left. Let me write down the address for you, and the phone number. We'll be living there for a while, maybe a long while, and you should know how to reach Jim."

"Thank you."

He doubled-parked in front of the house and put the second piece of paper together with the first. "I have a full schedule," he said, looking at the first piece.

"I understand."

"I wonder," he said.

When she went for her shower, she saw the letter to

her mother, sealed and stamped, lying on the desk where she had left it.

In the morning, she put the letter next to her bag so she would not forget it. Somewhere along the way they would pass a mailbox. Cassie and Hal were to pick her up at nine. By eight-thirty she was ready, nervous in spite of herself. Cassie called that they were on the way.

"Cassie, my mother isn't going to be there, is she?"

"I wouldn't do that to you."

"I'm sorry. I just had to know."

Links. She kept thinking of links, people linked together, irrevocably, for better or worse. She and Abraham. She and her mother. She and Jim. Finally, in the last minutes before they would come for her, she called her sister-in-law, Joanna, who was linked to her through a blood line, and she told Joanna she was being married.

When Hal knocked at the door five minutes later, she was calm.

He left them at the back door to the little courthouse and went ahead.

"Is there an empty courtroom?" she asked Cassie as they walked up to the second floor.

"They're all empty today."

"I'd like to see one."

Cassie opened a door and they walked inside. The seats reminded her vaguely of the pews in the doomed church, except that the wood was lighter here and there were no benches for kneeling and no curtained cubicles for confessing. All confessions were public in this room and recorded meticulously. She moved her eye to the judge's bench and behind it to the cream-colored wall. There it was, in raised capital letters, "IN GOD WE TRUST."

"Do you believe in God, Cassie?"

There was only the slightest pause. "I don't know. I haven't thought about it much since we graduated. It's one of the things I left behind in Ithaca, that and a few thousand other unanswered questions. There have been times—" She glanced around the courtroom. "Sometimes I wondered if God believed in me."

Between the long windows was a clock with Roman numerals. It was two minutes to ten.

"Hold my bag for me," she said, and they left the courtroom and went down the hall to take part in the marriage ceremony.

Afterwards, she remembered very little except that Cassie—of all people—was crying, ridiculously streaking her mascara, and Jim was hugging everybody.

"Darling, this is Bobby. Take a good look; that's me in twelve years."

Bobby, she thought, trying to get used to the sound of it. It was probably true, what he had said, twenty more pounds, gray hair. The manner was the same, and the voice. He gave her an envelope and invited them to Maine for Christmas.

Pete had brought Judy, and Mrs. Ballard had ordered champagne and pretty little things to eat. Father McAndrew had not come.

They were ready to leave when Mrs. Ballard took her aside. "We're so grateful to you, dear," she said.

"To me? I'm the one—"

"No, for all you did for Cassie."

"I don't understand."

"Two years ago, when you took her to New York."

On the shuttle in July to see a doctor, the D and C in the hospital in Brooklyn, paying cash for Cassie, whose funds had expired until September.

"She told you?"

"Yes. We were so ashamed that she wasn't able to turn to us."

"But why—?" Oh, God, the pieces fitting together. "When did she tell you?"

"Last month, I think, about the time the little boy's case was in court."

The inflexible judge, Cassie crying over the telephone, an attempt that failed. She must have put it to her father then that he had to do this now because her friend had done that for her two years ago. In friends we trust, Daddy. Buy him, sell him, destroy him but get Anthony into a foster home.

"It was nothing," she heard herself say. "We're friends."

"Let's go, darling."

She let herself be led away, down the stairs, out the door, into his car. She opened her bag to put Bobby's envelope away and saw the letter to her mother.

"I need a mailbox," she said.

"There's one on the corner." He held out his hand. "I'll take it over."

"No." She was still sensitive about letters.

"Is it to your mother?"

"Yes."

"Can I make you an offer?"

"Go on."

"We have until Sunday. What do you say we get up

one morning and decide to go to New York. I can't afford the shuttle but we can drive down and we'll talk to your mother together."

"She'll scream, Jim. You don't know my mother. It would be terrible. You don't know what she would say to you."

"Then we'll walk out." The simple, obvious solution.

"I couldn't face it. I start feeling sick just thinking about facing her."

"Because you think about doing it alone. Do you think I could have gone to California alone?"

She let half a minute pass. Then she handed him the letter. He put it in his inside pocket, started the motor, and looked at his watch.

"I still get a start when I look at it," he said.

"Will you take me somewhere when we're in New York?"

"Anywhere."

"It's on Long Island, a cemetery."

"Where your father's buried?"

"My grandfather too. He died while I was in Europe and they never told me till I came back."

"And you hate them for it."

"I suppose I do."

"What a summer they must have had. They must have known every day of it what would happen the day you came back."

"Why are Jews always buried on Long Island?"

He put his hand momentarily on the hem of her white linen dress. "Everyone is buried on Long Island. My mother is buried on Long Island."

"I didn't know that, I mean about everybody. Would you take me to the Brooklyn Museum too?"

"I'll take you."

"I want to get you another mobile. If we don't have a canopy, at least there'll be something."

"Have you decided to give the bed back?"

"I haven't decided anything." She patted her bag. "I think your brother gave us a check."

"My brother is too good," he said affectionately.

"Do you see him often?"

"No. I saw him after camp for a few days." He took a breath. "And briefly in February. You probably remember the date. It was a Tuesday."

"Yes."

"Maybe we could use Bobby's check to buy a dog."

"In our apartment?" She looked to see if he was serious. He was.

"Well, maybe later then. It's something I've always wanted, that and a gold watch." He smiled. "Say, would you mind if I grew a beard? Just for camp. I'll get rid of it in September."

"I wouldn't mind. Grow two beards."

"No kidding, would it be OK?"

"It would be OK. Anything is OK. What's your assignment at camp this summer?"

"I'm associate director."

"Wow. Then you'll earn piles more than last summer."

"I didn't earn anything last summer."

"You built that lodge just for the fun of it?"

"They gave me three meals and a place to sleep," he said, making it sound very simple. "My vacation was paid."

The day was beautiful. Elsewhere, rivers were cresting and people were forced from their homes but here it was dry and the sun was shining.

"I called Andy this morning," Jim said. "He said you invited him."

"You invited Pete; I invited Andy."

"His schedule was full. He said to tell you he couldn't get there short of making an appeal to heaven. He said you would understand that."

"I do."

"I didn't know you and Andy had secrets."

"One secret. You left us alone one night. It was long enough for one secret."

"Do you mind if we stop somewhere on the way?"

"I'm not in a hurry."

He turned off the road at New Bedford. She had been there once with Cassie on one of her summer visits. Jim had apparently been there too. He drove through the streets as if he knew them, as if he had a destination. Eventually he pulled up to the curb in front of a large church, stopping the car just past the entrance.

"Will you come in with me?"

"Yes."

He walked around the car, opened the door, and held out his hand. Her bag and the white Bible were on her lap. She took them with her and they walked up the steps together.

Inside, the church was massive, dark and cool. Nothing new here, Father Reilly, nothing fragile. Jim touched the holy water and crossed himself. She felt her hand start to sweat as they walked down the aisle, almost to the front row. The church was utterly empty.

He stopped at the second row and stood, holding her hand, looking ahead at the altar. Then he motioned her to move into a pew.

The seats were hard and she straightened her back. They sat together for several minutes, saying nothing.

Where were you married?

In a church in New Bedford, Mother.

Better a forest.

He took the Bible off her lap and opened it to the page marked by the ribbon.

Even the youths shall faint and be weary,
And the young men shall utterly fall;
But they that wait for the Lord shall renew their strength;
They shall mount up with wings as eagles;
They shall run, and not be weary;
They shall walk, and not faint.

"Let's go," he said, closing the Bible, and they went back up the aisle.

They had almost reached the door when he stopped, bent down, and picked up a gum wrapper, saying something softly under his breath. Under the wrapper was a small safety pin. He picked it up too and they went outside.

The brightness of the day made her blink. You could almost believe it was summer.

"Here," he said, holding the pin on his palm. "A little luck."

"I don't need any, Jim."

"Then let's give it to someone else." He slid it onto a fingertip and flicked it off with his thumb. The gum wrapper went into a pocket. "I'm for a swim," he said.

"The water'll be freezing, "she hedged.

"Then we'll build a fire."

"I'm for a fire."

"Then let's go."

He put his arm around her and they walked down the steps of the church.

MODERN CLASSICS

Isaac Bashevis Singer